1st September 2009

(41) Forty-one

'Thought-provoking and surprising, *What if...?* is a gripping, roller coaster of a story with a stunning ending, and complex and very human characters - both heroes and villains made me cringe as I recognized bits of myself.'

'Of humanity and the state of the world, *What if...?* says a lot, says it well, and manages to achieve that remarkable balance between a really good story well told and saying something of vital importance without preaching! The ending is remarkable and not to be read first!'

'*What if...?* is a fast-paced tale brimming with surprises and twists. Well-developed characters and a gripping plot will excite even fans of James Patterson and James Rollins. Devotees of television shows such as 'Heroes' will find it especially appealing. *What if...?* is a very good read indeed.'

'Have you ever dreamed of changing the world? Of getting rid of poverty, of diseases? Read *What if...?* and see what may happen if such a vision would come true. It's a wonderful piece of escapism with a great story full of intriguing twists.'

What if...?

What if...?

Steve N. Lee

Blue Zoo, Huddersfield, England

Published by
Blue Zoo
Huddersfield, West Yorkshire
England

ISBN 978-0-9556525-1-6

Steve N. Lee and Blue Zoo thank the following for kindly giving
permission to reprint previously copyrighted work:

'Wish You Were Here' - Pink Floyd
Lyrics by Roger Waters,
copyright reproduced courtesy of Warner Chappell.

'The Exposed Nest' - Robert Frost
From The Poetry of Robert Frost edited by Edward Connery Lathem,
published by Jonathan Cape.
Reprinted by permission of The Random House Group Ltd.

Typeset by Blue Zoo in Goudy Old Style 11.5/14

A catalogue record may be obtained from the British Library

First printed and bound in the USA by Thomson-Shore, Inc. using recycled paper
and vegetable-based ink.
10 9 8 7 6 5 4 3 2 1

For those who never stopped believing.

1

Consequences...

With the shimmer of a Christmas bauble caught in a crackling log fire's glow, the crisp winter sunlight glistened on the pooling blood.

On her back on the sidewalk, the concrete giants of Manhattan rearing over her, Mary gazed up at Old Glory rippling against a peaceful blue sky. She shivered. In broken pants, her breathing shuddered like a beat-up Oldsmobile fighting to start on an icy morning. She tried to push up, to move muscles Pilates had sculpted taut and lean.

Oh, God help her, she couldn't move.

She cried out. But the only scream screamed in her head. She wasn't even sure she'd even moved her mouth.

No. No, this couldn't be happening. Not now. Not like this. Not after seeing all she'd seen. Not knowing all she knew. Not after they'd all sacrificed so much. Rashid. Ben. Even Vincent. Sacrificed everything. All for him. No!

Her lungs hack-hack-hacked at the air again.

If only he was here. Why wasn't he? He'd promised never to leave her. To always love her. To save her. So why had he abandoned her?

And all those people. So many people. Why was no one helping? The screams had died. The blur of panic calmed. The terror was over — everything was so still, so silent. Or ... was this how it ended? The world simply spun on as if nothing had changed, while you faded away like a misplaced pencil mark being erased. A lifetime vanished in a blink, with barely a word, a tear, a memory to show for it.

She strained to scramble up, to run to him, but she couldn't feel her arms, couldn't feel her legs. Couldn't feel anything.

Devoured by shadows, the sky – the world – disappeared.

This was really happening. Oh, please, no. But ... even if she could, would she change one single moment of the life that had brought her here?

But where– where was he? He– he'd pro– promised.

Her breath hack-hack-ha–

...

Her mouth flickered the tiniest of smiles.

There... Him.

2

Unhappy the Land that has no Heroes

What felt like an age ago, even though it was only weeks...

***

What if this was as good as it was ever going to get?

"Jeez." Slumped against the doorjamb of O'Leary's Bar, Mary snorted. Her breath billowed into the falling snow. The giant shadows of Manhattan clawed it away into the night, as if it had never existed.

The wind cried, biting through her leather jacket, coaxing a shiver. Time to go back in? She flicked her chestnut hair out of her green eyes and, like a failed party crasher, peered through the window. Faces glowed; arms hugged; laughter splashed. It all looked so easy. She turned back, jamming her hands deep into her pockets.

The inner door behind her squealed open. The sounds of partying momentarily gushed out.

"Hey!"

She cringed. He'd found her.

"You're missing everything," he said.

She shrugged. That was her — always the bridesmaid.

An arm snaked around her waist. Larry hugged her. "Come on, babe, you didn't even miss *me* a little bit? *I* missed you."

Yeah, well, this 'babe' knew exactly what he'd missed and it wasn't Mary Shelley, journalist; lover of literature; documenter of life. Oh, no.

The bulge pressing into the small of her back proved exactly what good old Larry had missed: Mary Shelley, arm candy; flatterer; sex toy. Boy, was she living the dream or what?

Larry nuzzled her ear. "So, another beer, or wanna steam up my car windows?"

If only his mind was as chiseled as his jaw. She squirmed free. "One for the road?" She smiled. "Just give me a minute, yeah?"

"Just one." He sidled back in.

She slumped again. Talk about making your bed and lying in it.

She toyed with the crucifix hanging at her throat. If she stepped off the curb and was splattered by a speeding bus, could she die happy with what she'd made of her life? Okay, not everyone could be a Fleming and discover penicillin, or walk on the moon like Armstrong. But shouldn't there be more than just struggling to keep your head above water? Or was it really all just about another Prada purse, the tears and joys of PTAs and Little League, or that endless cycle of résumés, brown-nosing, and corporate handshakes? If life was such a wondrous gift, why was doing something worthwhile, even something minuscule, such a damn trial? She hung her head. So many dreams. So few achievements.

A flickering of the shadows caught her eye.

A mangy mutt skulked through the darkness. Left foreleg held off the ground, it lurched through the sidewalk slush as if each step was its last. It saw her. Froze. Stared, shivering, as if judging her. Its brown fur was as matted as a carpet buried at the bottom of a dumpster, though even the extra layers of filth couldn't hide its ribs.

Mary tutted. "Awww." She rummaged in her pockets. A handful of breath mints wasn't exactly a juicy 10-ounce steak, but if you were starving, it might literally make the difference between seeing another day or not. "Where the... " Finally finding her mints, she looked up.

But the dog had turned tail and was now lurching along the road, oblivious to the danger.

"Oh, no." And she'd thought her Christmas Eve couldn't get any worse. There was little traffic, but it only took one inattentive driver — she'd never relax now for worrying whether the dog was okay. She marched into the road, moving at an angle to force the dog back onto the sidewalk and not into greater danger. She shouted, "Hey!"

Frightened, it lurched more quickly along the road.

Hell. How could she drive it to safety?

A horn blared.

She jumped.

A taxi shot past, so close it splattered slush up her legs.

She scurried back to the sidewalk. "And Merry Christmas to you, too!" Some people. Okay, the dog wouldn't let her get close enough to shoo it, so now what? An idea. Grabbing a handful of snow from the curb, she stepped back into the road. The snow was dirty, icy, grainy, as if it was past its sell-by and was decaying fast. She balled it. Hurled it. Missed. "Damn!"

As a kid in Philly she'd played baseball with her friends. They'd even let her pitch occasionally because she didn't throw like a girl. But that was over 20 years ago. She grabbed more snow. Packed it harder for greater accuracy. Hurled again.

Hit, the dog yelped.

Mary cringed. But at least she'd saved it — the mutt lumbered toward an alley.

She sighed. Yeah, right, like she had it so bad. Though an image of starvation, poverty, and abandonment was as representative as any, that was a Christmas scene Hallmark wasn't eager to depict. Season of goodwill, her ass. Peace, love, and charity? The only Christmas message these days was '*Spend, spend, spend!*'. Or the one spread by weak-willed morons concerning the Word. The Word? Like unquestioningly believing some outlandish, out-dated fairy tale wasn't the root of all the world's ills. She was with James Madison, the fourth U.S. president, on this one: '*What are the fruits of Christianity? Bigotry, superstition and persecution.*'. Enough said.

Her hands burning with cold, she blew on them, scurrying back to O'Leary's. She glanced in at the partying. Well, she had to face it sooner or later. And it was warm in there.

She yanked the bar's door open. Slurred merriment burst forth, accompanying Bing's dream for a white Christmas.

"Oh, Jeez." Why was she putting herself through this?

***

"No!" The party nightmare over, Mary peered through the car passenger window at the pelting snow.

Larry knocked the wipers up a notch. "Babe!"

"I said no."

As he hung a right, the bottles of beer behind his seat clinked. "Come on, pass me one!"

"Don't be an asshole. You wanted to drive."

"Fine. You don't wanna celebrate Christmas, we won't celebrate Christmas."

"Fine."

"Fine... No turkey ... no party hats ... no gifts." He shot her a smile, his gaze drifting to her cleavage.

She drew a labored breath. She wouldn't mind, but she knew he was an asshole. Her best friend Greta knew he was an asshole. Even her mom, who swore everyone had a little of the saints in them, knew he was an asshole. So why date him? Because she was weak. If you were thirty-two, childless, and single, Christmas was a mighty lonely time.

He still grinned at her. She shoved him. "Watch the road!"

"What? You wanna live forever?"

"Yeah, I wanna live forever." She pushed his face to make him look at the road.

"Only losers wanna live forever. Me? I'm gonna change the world, die young, go out in a blaze of glory."

"And only a moron thinks he can change the world instead of just survive it."

"Hell, who died and made you Aristotle?" He grinned at her again. *Thuddum!*

His attention shot to the road.

Mary glanced anxiously around. "What was that?"

Larry checked his mirrors. "What was what?"

Mary twisted to look out of the rear windshield. There'd been a definite impact. She'd felt it. Heard it. "We hit something."

Larry scoured his rearview mirror. "No, we didn't."

"We did." She unfastened her belt and knelt in her seat for a better view, but couldn't see anything behind them for the darkness and driving snow. "You better stop."

"You see anything? No. 'Cause we didn't hit anything."

What was wrong with him? Didn't he care if someone was face down on the asphalt, dying? She cuffed the back of his head. "Just stop. Okay?"

14

He recoiled. "Hey." He didn't stop the car, but glued his gaze to his mirror again.

Why wouldn't he stop? Oh, no. He'd been guzzling vodka shots again while chatting with Mel and knew he was over the limit. Damn him! She smacked him again. "Stop the damn car!"

He spun around to her and shouted, "You crazy? Quit hitting!"

Apart from checking what they'd hit, she wanted a cab home and this loser out of her life. She glared at him. "So stop!"

"Okay." He turned back to the road. "Just quit the— Shit!"

From the corner of her eye, Mary glimpsed a red stoplight. And a black Mazda — dead ahead.

Larry hammered the brakes.

Mary hurtled into the windshield.

***

Lounging in the back of his limo, cruising through Manhattan, Tom Stevens eased off his other black loafer. "Ahhh." He pulled off his cummerbund and exhaled with relief. "Don't get me wrong, I love Jürgen's parties, but don't you wish we could attend just one and it'd be fish sticks, beans, and a cold beer, instead of black tie, five courses, and speeches?"

"Get a portable karaoke," said Beth. "Keep it in the trunk for emergencies."

He chuckled. Beth swore the only sound in the world worse than his snoring was his jazz guitar playing, but some beered-up Bavarian behemoth crucifying 'I Will Always Love You'? Oh, she'd soon change her tune. He looked at her. Smiled. All these years, and still she could make him laugh without even trying. And she was still as beautiful as the day they'd met. More so — now she oozed confidence. He hoped he was wearing as well. But it could be worse. Yes, the cummerbund was tighter than last time and, though people said it gave him a distinguished air, yes, he was graying. But he could be bald as a cue ball and just as round.

He ran his fingers through her brown locks.

She turned. "Hmm?"

He smiled and shook his head. He sensed the car decelerating quickly. Ahead, the lights at the intersection were green. "Robert?"

The chauffeur glanced in his mirror. "A crash, sir."

Tom saw no emergency vehicle, just two smashed cars. "Pull over."

"Sir, it's against protocol to—"

"Robert, even before our itinerary changed, only a handful of people knew where we'd be tonight. We've all year to be paranoid — I'll be damned if someone's going to die at Christmas, of all times, just 'cause I sat scratching my ass instead of helping. Now, pull over. That's an order."

The headlights illuminated two figures: one lay on the road; one crouched, back to them, presumably administering first aid.

From an SUV in front of Tom's limo, two men raced over to a black Mazda, its driver's side as crumpled as if slammed by a wrecking ball. Someone was slumped at the wheel, unmoving.

Tom dashed for the figures in the road, joined by a stocky man and a tall woman from the car behind who were so conservatively dressed they looked like accountants.

Tom shouted, "You called 911?"

Beside the car with the smashed-in front, the crouched figure said nothing.

"Has anyone called 911?" Reaching him, Tom grabbed the crouching man by the shoulder where the padding had burst through his overcoat. The man turned. Wet hair streaked around a face so ingrained with grime Tom couldn't tell where it ended and the beard began. The bluest eyes nailed Tom.

He wasn't the driver, but a vagrant. Was he helping?

A halo of blood in the snow around her head, a woman lay in the road, her eyelids fluttering as she drifted in and out of consciousness. The vagrant's hands were inside her blood-drenched blouse, groping her breasts.

"What the... ?" Tom recoiled. The sick bastard was feeling her up! An accident victim, for crying out loud. "Get the hell off her!" Tom kicked him in the ribs.

The vagrant sprawled in the slush.

The stocky man pounced, immobilizing him.

Tom jabbed at the tall woman. "Robert's calling 911 — get a response time. Then get the blanket from my car." She scurried away.

He peered into the mangled wreckage. Where was the driver? Blood plastered the windshield and dashboard in front of the passenger seat,

16

but the driver's airbag had deployed. Had he staggered away for help? Dragging off his jacket, Tom looked to the accountant. "Find the driver. He might need help."

The stocky man gestured toward the vagrant. "What about him?"

"Forget him. The injured are the priority." The sicko deserved as many years as the law could throw at him, but not at the expense of someone's life.

The stocky man dashed away.

Tom placed his jacket over the woman. She lay twisted like a rag doll that had been flung away by a kid in a tantrum. And there was blood oozing from her ears. "Oh, hell." That was never good. "Don't worry, ma'am, you're going to be just fine."

He grimaced at all the blood. Of all things, to die a violent death, feeling alone and abandoned, must be the worst. He took her bloody hand and squeezed so that, even unconscious, some part of her might sense she wasn't alone.

Her lips moved.

Hearing nothing over the engine noise and howling wind, Tom leaned down. "Sorry?" He couldn't tell if she was delirious or trying to speak. "I can't hear. Sorry. But don't worry, paramedics will be here in no time."

Tom raised back up. The vagrant was fleeing down the center of the road. He stopped momentarily, crouched to a mound on the asphalt — something one of the cars had hit? — then was off again. The mound clambered up and trotted after him — a dog.

Tom scowled. Hell, had this sorry excuse for a man picked the wrong place, wrong time, tonight? Tom had sworn to uphold what was right, to protect the innocent from the scum that stalked the streets. He'd be damned if this piece of filth wasn't going to be caught and made to pay. "Run, you sick mother, run. There's nowhere we won't find you."

3

The Darkness Within

B lackness...

***

Whining... Screeching, piercing, whining. Deafening. On and on...
A siren?

And freckles.

Mary saw so many freckles. Like a blotchy suntan.

Blinding light in her left eye. Then her right.

"Emergency bracelet," said Freckles. "We've got a diabetic."

Something hard, restricting — a collar — wedged around her neck.

Lifted.

Sharp. Stabbing into her arm.

Tube under her nose.

Blackness...

***

Doors crashing open.

Nurses, doctors peering down at her. Voices. Urgent. Fluorescent
bars flying by overhead.

Freckles again, "... 17 and regular. Pulse 75. BP 111 over 72. Sats
96. Unresponsive..."

Bifocals on a nose big enough for two people. "Automobile accident
and sexually assaulted? Jeez. And I thought I was having a bad day."

Sexually assaulted?!

Christmas lights. Plastic Santas.

Big nose again, "Okay, type and cross for four. CBC, electrolyte panel, tox screen, and blood alcohol—"

Crashed through another door...

"— Let's get her endoscoped. See where all this blood's coming from. Then I want a CT. Unconscious with vitals this good, we're talking serious head trauma."

Her head?

Lifted.

"Call X-ray. Get a portable head, chest, and neck."

A tube forced down her throat. Horrible. HORRIBLE!

Clothes cut away.

"We got a next of kin?"

Next of kin? Why— dying?!

Blackness...

4

Mysteries Deep, Mysteries Old

An orderly pushed Mary in a wheelchair; the big-nosed man, Dr. Turco, strolled alongside. Wearing green scrubs, she shoved herself out of the chair.

"Please, Mary." Turco tried to guide her back down. "Until we get the other results back, you need to stay off your feet."

She'd regained consciousness not long after the paramedics had dashed her into the ER, and now, after four hours of it, the endless babying was driving her absolutely crazy. She shrugged Turco off. "Thanks, but I feel a doofus. And anyway, you said there's nothing wrong with me."

"Nothing we can find. And there's the problem."

"Ain't a problem to me."

"Miss Shelley? Mary Shelley?" A middle-aged man lurched up from one of the red plastic seats beside a battered vending machine.

"Yes?"

Frowning, he eyed her up and down. Normally, anyone she caught staring she'd floor with an icy putdown. Only this guy wasn't ogling, but gawking as if she had two heads.

He studied her face. "Mary Shelley, car crash victim from..." He referred to his notes.

"Look, I'm Mary Shelley. Now, who's asking?"

"Sorry." He flashed a badge. "Detective Cale. Arresting officer."

Police. She should've guessed from the clichéd doughnut-ravaged gut.

"Just a moment, Detective." Turco took her arm. "Mary, I'd really rather you let us call someone to sit with you for a few hours. A friend or relative maybe?"

"And drag someone away from their family Christmas morning?" Not that there was anyone to drag away within a 100-mile radius. These days, her friends were more interested in pension plans than tequila slammers, carpet stain remover than skiing in Vermont, child car seats than gratifying sex. Friendships could stand the test of time, but not the test of conflicting interests. Well, no ... there was Greta. But she had Amy, so that was out of the question.

"There's no one?" asked Turco.

"Really, I'll be fine." She folded her arms — Cale still staring — feeling like the bearded lady at some freak show. "What?!"

Cale looked to Turco. "So what's Miss Shelley's condition, Doc? Any reason I can't take a statement?"

"Hey!" Mary scowled. "I'm standing right here."

"Please." The doctor gestured for him to proceed.

"I'm sorry, ma'am, it's just..." Cale shrugged. "I'm surprised to see you on your feet so soon."

Backing away, Turco said, "Any problems in the next few days, *anything*, phone us, immediately."

"No worries." She smiled. "Thanks, Dr. Turco."

Turco turned to leave, but glanced back to Cale, "Did you say 'arresting officer'?"

"Uh-huh."

"So you have the attacker in custody?"

Cale nodded. "Soup kitchen's gonna be one short for Christmas dinner."

"When you processed him, did you notice any injuries, bleeding?"

"No. But I can check."

Turco waved. "No need. The size of wound needed for so much blood, it would've been obvious."

Puzzled, Cale looked Mary up and down again. "There something I should know about here, Doc?"

To draw his curiosity from her, Mary held up a cellophane bag stuffed with her blood-drenched clothes. "The blood's mine, but it's not mine."

Cale rubbed his chin. "You're gonna have to help me out here."

Turco said, "Miss Shelley has no lacerations or hemorrhaging, which suggests that this," he pointed to her clothes, "isn't her blood. Yet according to the lab, it is her blood. Plus she's diabetic, but the tests say she isn't."

"Been injecting myself since I was 11," said Mary.

Turco shook his head. "Our protocols are very reliable, but, what with Christmas staffing, it seems someone's messed up. Twice."

Cale scratched his head. "But all the blood. And I mean blood. Not just a drop. It was everywhere."

"Frankly, we're stumped," said Turco. "But we'll have conclusive results later today." He patted her arm. "Until then, please, take it easy. And any problems, call."

She nodded. "Thanks."

He left.

"Oh..." Cale lumbered back to his seat. On returning, he handed her a brown paper evidence bag. "Retrieved from the wreckage. I figured you'd be missing it."

She opened it — her purse. "Hey, thanks." She dug out her cell phone.

"Calling a cab?"

"Some Christmas, huh?"

"Could be worse. You could be working." Cale gestured to the seats. "If you can spare a few minutes first to tell me what happened, I'll personally see you get home safely." He smiled.

It was 4:53 a.m., Christmas Day. Today was the calendar event of the year for her mom, and Mary was supposed to be in Philadelphia by 10 o'clock to help cook the celebratory dinner. She needed sleep. Even more, she ached to be home, showered, in her own clothes and surrounded by her own things. But Cale's smiling eyes crinkled just like her dad's had when she used to sit on his knee for stories of castles and princesses, ogres and heroes. Funny how you make snap decisions about liking someone over the most trivial of details. She shrugged. "Nothing much to tell."

"You don't recall anything?"

She shook her head. "Last thing I remember is O'Leary's."

"But you can confirm Larry Goodman as the driver of the vehicle you were in?"

Could *she* confirm it? Couldn't Larry? "Why? He's not..."

"No, his airbag saved him. But we're holding him on a DUI and for abandoning the scene of an accident because we thought you were ... well ... seriously injured."

He'd abandoned her? Crashed the car and abandoned her? Left her to die? Son of a bitch. A charge of driving under the influence was way too light — it was a crime he wasn't dead. She drew a steadying breath.

"So you don't remember anything else? Not the journey? The crash? The assault?"

She snickered.

"What?"

"All the nurses have been horrified by this 'assault' and..." She shrugged.

"You don't recall anything?"

"No, I—" Pain. She remembered excruciating pain. Then ... peace. Not just relief from the pain, but peace — the kind you feel lying in a meadow, on a beautiful day, beside someone you love. And ... blue eyes. It was dark. The entire crash was a blank. Why did she remember blue eyes?

"Yeah?" said Cale, pen poised.

"No. Sorry... So who is he?"

Cale didn't need to refer to his notes. "John Connolly. 36. Vagrant." It was his turn to shrug. "First time he's shown up on radar for almost 20 years."

Vagrant? That explained all the drugs they'd pumped into her for God only knew what, in case it was his blood.

"But hey, what am I thinking? The night you've had, this can wait." Cale put his notebook away. "Have to say, when I saw you at the scene, I'd have given anyone a hundred to one it'd be the meat wagon taking you to the morgue tonight, not me driving you home."

She flicked him a glance. Why did everyone think she should be dead? She felt fine. And if one more person was horrified by this 'assault', she'd scream. But what if she had been attacked? What if he'd discovered her name? What if he tracked her down? Wanted payback? "You will notify me when you release him?"

Cale sniggered. "Release him? Miss Shelley, I'm first to admit the system ain't perfect, but second-degree sexual assault's a felony, so even if he could afford bail, d'you really think we're gonna let such a high-flight-risk loser back on the streets? Believe me, he'll be in a borough lockup 'til his trial." He rooted in his pocket and handed her his card. "But you got any worries, call me. Day or night."

It was a kind gesture, but she'd still jam a chair against her bedroom door. And stash a knife under her pillow. "Thanks." She stared into space. "John Connolly." She shrugged. The name meant nothing.

5

Home Sweet Home

The lock clicked, a kick thumped into the bottom of the door where it always stuck, and Mary finally trudged into her apartment.

No one dashed to her, teary-eyed at almost losing her; no furry companion jumped for the joy of reunion; no tiny, paint-daubed fingers tugged her for appreciation of a picture displayed on the refrigerator. No one. Just cold ... dark ... emptiness.

She flicked on a lamp.

A sense of normality more important than food, rest, anything, she lumbered over to the TV and clicked it on. She collapsed onto the heap of clean laundry awaiting sorting on the couch while a chirpy blonde blathered on about the projected outcome of the impending presidential primaries. Mary didn't hear, didn't see.

A shower, then bed had been her dream combination at the hospital. But on the way home, she'd seen Larry's car, now at the roadside, awaiting towing. It looked like it'd been in a demolition derby with a tank. Not that that had bothered her: cars were designed to crumple, to absorb an impact and protect you. But then she'd spotted all the blood on the dashboard and windshield in front of the passenger seat. Her seat.

Everyone thought she should be dead. And, looking at the car, the blood, everyone was right.

She toyed with her crucifix. She'd been devastated at the hospital when she'd thought it lost. Luckily, it'd been removed for the CT scan and was safe with her clothes.

Devastated? Strange, considering how she'd slung it back at her dad all those years ago, cast him and it aside as symbols of all she hated. Oh, she still loathed religion for what it had done to her, but now her crucifix was a symbol of something very different — of love, out of which it had been given. If only she'd realized that at the time. And that was why she wore it — as a reminder not to take things on face value, but to delve deeper, ask questions, seek answers. Because love is not expecting others never to wrong you, but accepting they will and forgiving them when they do. She'd lost having a relationship with her dad for the best part of a decade because of acting on snap judgments instead of looking for answers. She wouldn't be making a mistake like that again any time soon. Maybe that was why she'd been drawn to journalism — an on-going search for answers. But, at times, that could be as much of a curse as it was a blessing.

She gazed around her apartment: her desk with its state-of-the-art laptop, a bookcase straining beneath literary classics, a Swiss cheese plant — the only living thing to celebrate an anniversary with her for ... how long? Didn't matter. She wasn't going down the same road as her mom. The pain of solitude was far easier to handle than the pain of abandonment. But in the cold, the gloom ... was it? After the night's trauma, wouldn't it be comforting to feel the warmth of someone's hug, the concern in its tightness? Long ago, she'd sworn if she couldn't have Mr. Right, she wouldn't have anyone. It was forever or not at all. But would settling for second best be so bad? Even third best? Forget that spark with someone who could make you tingle with just a phone call. How long could that last? But someone who could still smile at you on waking, even after five, six, 10 years? Someone who could be relied upon to pay the bills and not blow the money on beer? Someone who could teach your son how to ride a bike, instead of hide a beating? Wasn't that worth something? More than some fairy-tale emotion? Would having someone, *anyone*, to hold be such a bad thing?

Bringing her knees up, Mary slowly keeled over onto the laundry. And sobbed.

***

A jarring noise blared.

Mary groaned and hit out at her alarm clock. Not there. She groped. Nothing. And that noise wasn't her clock. But it was equally grating. What was it? Her weary eyes struggled open.

She rolled over.

A TV weatherman predicted storms. The floor was strewn with laundry. As was she. She was on the couch. Why? Had she dozed off during a late movie? What day was it?

The weatherman grinned. "So have a very Merry Christmas..."

Mary gawked. She spun to her living-room clock: 9:28.

"Oh, no!" She was supposed to be almost in Philadelphia by now.

She leapt up, laundry falling to the floor. She was still wearing green scrubs. "Nooo!"

That awful noise blared again.

Doorbell. "Who the hell...?" Pulling on a black sweater, Mary dashed to the intercom. "Yeah?"

Two female voices came in unison, one very young. "Merry Christmas!"

Greta and Amy. What were they doing here?

"Hey ... er ... yeah."

"We come at a bad time?" Greta added in a whisper, "The asshole still there?"

"No ... er—"

"So let us in; it's freezing."

"Give me a minute. I'm coming down."

A shower and breakfast would have to wait for her mom's. Kicking off the scrub pants, Mary grabbed a pair of jeans from the couch and, hopping for the kitchen, yanked them on. She grabbed a pre-prepped shot of insulin from the refrigerator. The smell of rotting vegetables wafted up from the bottom shelf — so much for another healthy eating kick. She jabbed her butt. Winced. Her diabetes was a hassle, but luckily her blood sugar was predictable enough that, barring a daily injection, it barely interfered with her life. She snagged the insulin supply for tomorrow, darted for the door, dragged on her boots, grabbed her coat, the bag she'd pre-packed, and scrabbled at the marble ashtray in which she kept her car keys...

Where the hell were her keys?

She glanced around. Where had she had them last? She dashed to her immaculately tidy desk. No. Rooted through the papers piled on top of the refrigerator. No. The kitchen counter — amongst last night's Chinese takeout cartons. "Oh, come on!" Her gaze whirled.

Greta buzzed again.

"I'm coming. I'm coming. Just — Ah!" On top of the TV! Who the hell put them there?

***

Emerging from her apartment building onto a quiet street of Greenwich Village, Mary smiled. "Sorry. Running late." She hugged Greta. "Merry Christmas."

"Merry Christmas."

The odd car crawled slowly along; a few people sauntered by with bags, presumably crammed with gifts — possibly the quietest few hours of a New York year.

"Mary! Mary! Look at my bike! Look at my bike!" shouted a tiny girl with pigtails splaying from under a pink pompom hat. Complete with training wheels, her bike made waves in the light covering of snow on the sidewalk.

"Hey, kiddo." Mary ambled down the stoop's steps. "What a great bike."

Ringing her bell, Amy cycled over. "What did Santa bring you, Mary?"

"Oh, he brought me the best present ever."

"Really?"

"Yeah." Mary scooped snow off a Ford's trunk and lunged at Amy. "He brought me you, kiddo."

Amy screamed and turned. Feet pedaling like crazy, she giggled away down the street.

Mary grinned. If Bloomingdale's sold Amys, she'd take a dozen. But Amys didn't come pre-assembled, guaranteed to last a lifetime. 3:00 a.m. feedings, diapers, bad report cards, puberty, teenage pregnancies... Mary wasn't ready to put her life on hold for a decade or more. Maybe she never would be.

Pulling her woolen coat around her, Greta ambled over, chubby cheeks ruddy. "Figured you'd be at your mom's by now, but Amy wouldn't stop nagging 'til I said we'd check."

"Long story."

"In that case, I'll chill two bottles of wine for tomorrow."

Mary smiled. "And have me drinking alone?"

"That bad, huh?"

"Like you won't believe. I mean—" She didn't have time to get into this. "Look, I don't want to cut and run but..."

"I know — if you don't get to Philly, who's gonna burn your mom's turkey?" Greta pushed Mary's arm. "Go. Be festive."

"Amy?" Mary pointed at her when she turned. "Second Christmas tomorrow. Be excited. Be very excited." Mary waved, then dashed for her little, red Chevy.

As the wipers cleared the windshield, Mary cranked up the heater. She waved as Greta and Amy passed, then checked back to pull out, but hesitated. She was an hour and a half late. What story could she concoct that wouldn't make her look like a selfish, uncaring bitch, but also wouldn't alarm everyone, today of all days? Well, she'd going on two hours to figure out that one.

She texted her mom, '*Late. Sorry. See you soon. Merry Xmas!*' Pulling away from the curb, she smiled. At least all that self-pity had vanished. Must have been delayed shock and tiredness. Having a guy around would solve all her troubles? Yeah, right. Like all those guys she'd dumped over the years had gone on to be Nobel Laureates or pioneers of industry. Well ... they hadn't all been losers— "Holy crap." What was wrong with her? Sooner or later, they'd all have cheated on her, or abandoned her, or conned or abused her. She had to get a grip. She was doing just *fine* alone.

Recalling the weather forecast she'd awoken to, she gazed up at the crisp, blue heavens. Storms? What storms?

6

Into the Unknown

"A rghhh!"

Correctional Officer Schwartz glanced at Duncan and Garcia, then bolted for the shower block. A mass of orange jumpsuit-clad Hispanics jostled out. Pot-bellied as a pig and with a face to match, Schwartz barged into them. "Out of the way, or you'll be in the hole 'til next Christmas."

The inmates grudgingly parted.

"Garcia, hold these clowns," shouted Schwartz.

"Hey, whoa there, boss," said Pinto, a tattoo of a coiled cobra on his arm. "Ain't my fault some moron slips on the soap."

"Out the way, smart-ass." Schwartz slammed him aside and burst into the communal shower area.

Naked. Silent. Still. So still.

Face down lay Rufus Lambert Junior, big as a felled tree. An ocean of pooling blood swirled across the beige tiles and away down the drain.

But someone else was present. Someone not in Pinto's gang.

Normally, any innocent con would've bolted the instant trouble flared. But this was one of the new fish. So it was understandable. Except this guy wasn't cowering in a corner, blubbering. Wasn't gawking, frozen with shock. Wasn't swearing on his mother's life he had nothing to do with it. No. This guy was standing at a washbasin rinsing blood off his hands as calmly as if he were doing the dishes after Sunday lunch. This guy wasn't trying to avoid trouble, he was looking for it!

Schwartz marched over. He swiped the backs of the prisoner's knees with his nightstick. The prisoner crashed to the tiles like a drunk on black ice.

Schwartz wedged his black size-11 boot across the prisoner's neck, the toe shining like polished onyx under the fluorescent bars. He admired the shine for a moment — well, if a job was worth doing, as his dear old dad used to say. "You got a death wish, boy?"

The prisoner croaked, "No."

Schwartz pressed harder. "No, 'sir'."

Unable to speak, the prisoner made choking noises.

Duncan clicked his radio. "This is Duncan, Shower Block Two. We need medics and backup, ASAP."

Schwartz stabbed at the drain. "Check for the shank." Five would get you 10 it was nowhere to be found. Prisoners weren't dumb. But they had off days like everyone. Maybe it had lodged on a concrete lip.

He looked at his captive. Oh, how he ached to administer justice. Eye for an eye, tooth for a tooth justice. He pressed harder. The prisoner tore at the boot, his face turning a bluish-red. But Schwartz relaxed. It'd be a mountain of paperwork. And the imprint of his boot on the guy's throat would be hard to explain. Hard, but not impossible. Jeez, criminals just had it made these days.

He glanced at Duncan, who was peering through the grate.

"Nothing. I'll check under the body." Crouching, Duncan hauled up a black arm with a bicep the size of his thigh. Nothing.

The arm flexed.

Duncan gasped and fell backward.

Rufus groaned, then clambered up.

"What the..." Schwartz stared, mouth agape. The prisoner slipped out from under his foot, spluttering.

Rufus stretched as though he'd just awoken from a nap after a particularly large meal. He nodded to the C.O.s, "Boss," then grabbed a towel and patted himself down.

***

"So you'll appreciate my predicament, Connolly, er, John." Warden Kramer looked up from a silver-framed photo of himself and his heavy-set wife of 31 years. "Now, Mr. Schwartz here has described today's incident. Says it's the darnedest thing he's ever seen. And anyone who knows Mr. Schwartz will vouch he's not prone to embellishment, let alone moved enough to call me in on Christmas Day. As for me? For the life of me, I can't figure out what happened."

Connolly stared back as if he hadn't realized a question had been asked.

Schwartz jabbed him with his nightstick. "This is when you tell your side of things." He didn't hold with all this new-age hocus pocus, but these days Kramer was so desperate he'd stoop to anything, be suckered by anything. So whatever helped his own career progression was to be welcomed. Still, something weird was going down here. People didn't get stabbed and then just up and get on with their day as if they'd simply stubbed a toe. He didn't like it. And what he didn't like, he broke.

While replacing the photo on the mahogany bureau under the marlin he'd landed four years ago in Cabo San Lucas, Kramer held up his free hand to Schwartz, a hand almost as gray as his hair. "I'm sure John's just mulling over the right turn of phrase. Isn't that right?"

Still Connolly remained silent.

Schwartz hated inmates acting up — it interfered with the smooth running of the jail, the smooth running of the system, and, most importantly, the smooth running of his life. As his Amazon account testified, he was something of an authority on correctional techniques across the ages — his favorite period being that which covered the Spanish Inquisition. How he wished he'd been born five centuries earlier. He leaned right into Connolly's ear. "I respect a man with spirit. After all, where's the fun in breaking some weak-willed pussy?"

Kramer sank into his leather chair. His buttoned navy jacket strained against his gut, so he unfastened it. His hands fell naturally to the armrests, perfectly aligned with the smoothly scuffed, light brown patches. "John, I've done my best to explain my situation. I do hope we're not going to have a problem here." Kramer brushed his graying bushy moustache between his right thumb and forefinger, studying Connolly, then leaned forward and rested his arms on his oak desk. "When I was maybe five or six, my grandpa had terrible gout. I don't know if you're familiar with the illness. It's not life-threatening, but it is debilitating, leaving you in constant pain. Anyway, he'd struggled for years, but as he grew older, he couldn't cope and he'd spend days, sometimes weeks, laid up, unable to work. Now, in Mississippi, in the '60s, it wasn't always easy for the self-employed to eke out a living, especially if they were struggling with illness." He toyed with his fountain pen. "One day, a preacher came to town. A black preacher. Black as pitch. Some said he'd been kissed by the devil; others by Jesus. But I saw him lay hands on my grandpa and blow me if my grandpa didn't up and dance a jig like a 20-year-old on his wedding day." He replaced his pen. "You ever hear of anything like that, John?" He waited, but received only Connolly's stare. He smiled. "Of course not. Except in old wives' tales... But I saw it."

Kramer looked away and drew a long breath. "A black preacher and an old man who'd lived all his life in Mississippi. See, son, sometimes you've got to go against every fiber of your being for the sake of those you love." He looked back at Connolly. "Elizabeth used to love musicals. *Cats, Phantom, Les Mis* — we've seen them all. Many a time I'd get home and find her in the kitchen, singing 'All I Ask of You' or something. Knew them all, she did. Remarkable memory. Remarkable. Now," he sighed, "some days, she barely recognizes *me*." He smiled. "Still, that's my problem."

He studied Connolly's file. "Second-degree sexual assault?" He nodded. "Now, while I'm no lawyer, I think it's pretty safe to say you'll be our guest for quite some time." He flung the file aside. "The way I see it, son, to have friends is one of life's greatest gifts. Particularly if those friends are in high places. On the other hand..." his stare drilled into Connolly's blue eyes, "enemies in high places... Well, let's just hope it never comes to that, huh?" He smiled.

Schwartz readied his nightstick.

Connolly showed no sign of doubt or fear. His voice was firm yet soft, smooth yet penetrating. It was honey off a spoon. "You'd like me to help your wife?"

Kramer grinned and slapped the green leather inlay in his desk. "That's my boy."

Schwartz smirked. So much for the hard-man act. Pussy. Or maybe he was just slow.

7

Where the Brave Fear to Tread

At a rest stop on I-95, 22 miles outside New York City, Mary's car mounted the curb and jolted to a stop. Her door flew open. With barely time to lean out, she vomited all over the frosty asphalt.

She slumped against the door. It was 7:33 a.m., December 26. Unable to sleep for the whirl of questions over what had truly happened on Christmas Eve, she'd seen no option but to go in search of answers. But this? This wasn't lack of sleep or overdoing the Christmas fare. No. The world was a jumbled blur, as if she'd downed a bottle of tequila. Pulling out, she'd almost clipped a truck five minutes ago, simply because she didn't see it. Didn't see an 18-wheeler! Something was seriously wrong.

She heaved her weary body back in the car and brushed the sweat from her face with her forearm. Apart from seeing her mom's tears of joy when Mary and her sisters gave her the tickets for a trip to Paris, France — fulfilling her mom's dream — this was the worst Christmas ever. She'd been so late, and in such a bedraggled state, she'd been forced to come clean about the consequences of dating a loser, then had to run the gauntlet of concern, single-life commiseration, and relationship advice. Oh, they were always supportive, but she couldn't help feeling the disappointment of the family, her the only one not climbing the career ladder, popping out kids, or laying claim to realty. Excellent. It's a harsh reality check the day you look in the mirror and see someone who'll never be applauded by their peers, never inspire others to reach for their dreams, never leave a legacy for future generations to cherish. It's a soul-destroying moment, the moment you admit you're not special, not gifted, barely even ordinary.

Her hands trembled on the wheel. During a weekend of partying in her first semester at Columbia, she'd missed an insulin shot or two and ended up in the campus infirmary with ketoacidosis — she could've died. That involved nausea, fatigue, hand tremors... No, no tremors. No, wait. Yes... Well, maybe. If she had her test kit now, she'd check her blood sugar, but she rarely used it daily and so hadn't brought it. But that didn't matter — she'd had her shot. Usual time. Usual dosage. Hadn't she? She had. She was sure. So what the hell was wrong? "What if Turco was right?" What if that sicko *had* bled all over her? Bled blood festering with tuberculosis? Hepatitis? "Oh, God." AIDS?

She swallowed hard. How could she tell her mom? And at Christmas, too. But how could she not tell her? Bury herself in her work and pretend the problem would disappear?

The wheels skidded as she hammered the gas. If she was going to die, she sure wasn't going out without answers. Then someone would pay. Big time. To hell with the law. She wanted justice. Real justice. Eye for an eye, tooth for a tooth justice. Boy, was someone going to pay for destroying her life.

***

At an oak table in a huge kitchen lavished with chocolate-colored marble counters and oak units, a little boy in a Superman T-shirt munched a spoonful of honey-coated breakfast cereal. "Grandpa, is it true you can do anything you want? Anything in the world?"

Tom Stevens looked up from pouring freshly ground coffee. He liked to think he could do anything, but the reality was never that easy. "Anything your Grandma lets me, Danny, yeah."

Heading for the refrigerator, Beth patted him on the butt. "You better believe it."

He smiled at her.

"No," said Danny. "I mean, is it true you can do anything you want when you're big?"

"Oh." Tom plonked his steaming coffee at the table and sat. "Why? What you fixing on being? An astronaut, pop star, a superhero?"

Without missing a beat and straight-faced, Danny said, "A taxi driver."

Tom smiled. There was a time when people dreamed of honest work, of sweat and sacrifice bringing them pride and respect. They aspired to helping others; moving others; bringing beauty, goodness, or functionality into the world. Nowadays? Nowadays, so many people dreamed only of reality TV transforming them into overnight celebrities, with their only commitments to breathe and talk inanities. How refreshing the voice of innocence could be. "A cab driver, huh?"

"I like listening to the radio in the car, so if I have a taxi, I can do it all day."

Tom chuckled. Oh, yes, the beauty of innocence: see a goal; see the straightest path to it; follow that path. If only life could always be so simple. "Well, Danny, you've got better reasoning there than the whole world's got for most of the things it does, so I'm sure you'll be the best darn taxi driver anyone's ever seen."

Danny grinned.

Martha, their gray-haired cook, placed Tom's breakfast before him — a bowl of cereal. Oh, no. Not bran and skim milk. Where were his eggs, hash browns, bacon...? "Twigs? In white-colored water?"

She shrugged. "Sorry, sir."

Beth said, "I said it was back to healthy eating after Christmas."

"No, after the holidays, you said. Not Christmas. And what's healthy about this, anyway?"

"High fiber, reduced fat — what's not healthy?"

Tom groaned. "You know, there's no point in physical well-being if you're suffering mentally."

Beth laughed. "Suffering? Eating a balanced diet is suffering?"

"Too right." Spooning twigs, he winked at Danny. "I bet even woodpeckers would turn their noses up at moldy old twigs." He knew he was onto a loser, so best to make light of it. Danny giggled.

Beth smirked. "Yes? Well, Woody better get used to it."

The phone rang. Beth answered it, then handed it to Tom. "Simon."

Smiling, Tom winked at Danny, again. "Hey, Simon, what d'you give an overweight woodpecker for breakfast?" His smile dropped. "Uh-huh."

36

Martha placed plates of scrambled egg and bacon on the table, one before Beth, who was watching Tom intently. Frowning, Beth nodded her thanks.

The conversation was short. Staccato. Dire.

Tom hung up. "Ah, hell!" He rubbed his face. "Dinner's off. Jean's had a bad night. Simon's at the hospital with her now."

"Oh, poor Jean. And at Christmas of all times."

Her blonde hair damp from showering, Courtney ambled in. She ruffled Danny's hair and clicked on the TV. "Can I borrow your straightener later, please, Mom?"

Beth merely nodded and gestured to one of the cooked breakfasts.

"Something wrong?" Courtney sat at the table.

On TV, a vagrant collected a bowl of steaming porridge. His filthy coat concealed so many layers for warmth against the cruel winter he looked as if he weighed 250 pounds, yet his sunken cheeks said he'd be closer to half that. Ladling the porridge beside a reporter with a mike, Senator Tanner spread an easy grin across a lined face made to look younger with spray tan. "I know Christmas is a time for families, Richie, but, as all the good people watching will know, it's also a time for Christian charity." He served the next filthy wretch and smiled, "You enjoy that now, you hear." He looked back at Richie. "See, it's not just a case of knowing the right thing to do, but a case of getting off your tush and actually doing it."

Beth tutted. "Doing it as long as a camera's rolling. The second that one's off, he'll be taking two showers and demanding a tetanus jab."

Drumming his fingers on the table, Tom sighed, then stood. "I'm going over."

"What?" said Beth. "Why? It's a nice gesture, but you won't be able to do anything."

Not for Jean. No one could. But Tom could sit with Simon and try to take his mind off the nightmare to come. "I don't have to do anything. I just have to be there." He snatched the phone. Hit speed dial number 5. "Andrew, we're going to Mercy General. Now." Marching out, he clicked off the TV. "And you might not live with us anymore, young lady, but the rules still apply — no TV during meals. Especially garbage like that." Disintegration of the family, of basic values, was at the core of many of society's problems and with the hectic pace of life these days, mealtimes were some of the few chances families had of connecting. Those brief moments should be embraced, not sabotaged.

Courtney groaned. "Dad, just 'cause someone disagrees with your politics doesn't mean he's a moron."

Hadn't he brought her up to be more discerning? "You wanna raise your son to be suckered by every sycophant and con man out there, fine. But not under my roof." He left.

***

"But—" Mary laughed. After three hours on a glucose IV to wash the insulin out of her system, she felt fine. But that was so wrong. With so much glucose in her bloodstream she should be comatose, if not dead. "That— that's impossible."

Turco shrugged. "The tests are conclusive: you are *not* diabetic."

She glanced around Turco's office. Everywhere was white. Everywhere electric light. Everywhere papers and files and books and journals. If she put in the hours he obviously did, such a cold, plastic hovel would see her stealing the patients' meds. "But I've been diabetic for 24 years. It's incurable."

Grinning like a child seeing his first firework, Turco leaned forward. "Exactly. Now, I've spoken to my colleague, Dr. Olembe, and he's eager for you to come in for a battery of tests. Oh, this is fascinating. If—"

"Whoa. Whoa. Whoa. A battery of tests? Like spending most of my Christmas here wasn't enough, you think I want to waste all the holidays being poked and prodded?"

Turco heaved a great sigh. "Well, that's your prerogative, of course. But if you'll—"

"Sorry, Doc. Never gonna happen."

Turco slumped back in his seat. "Okay... So in that case, think of it as a wonderful Christmas gift. A Christmas miracle."

"Yeah, right, 'cause the world's just bursting with miracles."

"Not big on religion?"

"Hey, I got diabetes, not dementia."

"Well, it works for a lot of people."

"So does Prozac, but that'll run you 75 bucks a month. So you're poor, weak, and troubled, which you gonna pick?"

Turco snorted a laugh. "Aren't you a little young to be so cynical?"

"I'm a reporter — cynical pays the rent."

Turco smiled. "Look, just stop your shots and you'll be fine. Believe me, you're not diabetic."

"But how?"

Turco just shrugged.

***

Mary strolled across the parking lot. She looked at her hands, which had trembled so uncontrollably earlier. Statue still. She laughed. This was incredible. She'd never again have to jab needles in her butt. Never again have to worry about what she ate, what she drank. And the savings on insulin — that was a week's skiing in Vermont every year in itself. This was fantastic. Unbelievable!

She skipped toward her Chevy, but then slumped against its roof. Yes, that was the word for it: unbelievable. She watched the *Discovery Channel*. Read *National Geographic*. She'd heard of faith healers, Lourdes, church statues that wept. Miracles happened. But here? To her?

She sniggered. "Yeah, right." Crying Madonnas and healing only happened in ancient cities that dated back to biblical times, or poverty-stricken villages where the local economy fluctuated with the number of hens you got for a pig. Miracles did *not* happen in 21st century New York, *the* most advanced city in *the* most advanced nation on the planet.

She yanked her car door open. Miracle, her ass. Someone was messing with her life. She would know who, why, and how. And she knew exactly where to start.

***

The green and blue splotches did complement the strawberry, lemon, and peach ones, but the painting would only ever brighten up Mary's bathroom, not take pride of place over her fireplace. Kandinsky might be one of the 20th century's great painters but ... splotches were just splotches. But then most of the Guggenheim Museum's exhibits wouldn't even see her bathroom, let alone anywhere else.

"Come here often?" she asked.

His mouth full of salami panini, Detective Cale nodded, then swallowed. "How I get around the 'No food in the gallery' rule."

She read the splotch picture's plaque: *Black Lines*. "There some deep meaning I'm missing?" She nodded to the picture.

He laughed. "You got me."

"So why come?"

39

He jabbed with his sandwich. "It's not a spectacular landscape or a stunning portrait, just blotches, but after all the crap I see out there," he gestured toward outside, "it's kinda soothing to just drift into something like that. Know what I'm saying?" He savaged his panini.

Mary nodded. In the same way she lost herself in books, to shut out the world, maybe Cale lost himself in fine art. A little odd, given his vocation. What would it be next? Inter-precinct ballet troupes?

"You said something weird yesterday," said Mary. Yesterday? Was it still only the early hours of yesterday when her life had been turned upside-down?

He ripped another chunk from his sandwich. "Hm?"

"How you thought I'd be going to the morgue, not home."

"Uh-huh."

"But..." She shrugged. "I'm fine."

"In this job you see a lot of injuries. And I mean a lot. People stabbed, shot," he gestured toward her, "smashed up in a car, caught in a fire. All kinds of crap. After a while, you get a feeling for whether someone's gonna make it or not."

"And you had my family picking out caskets."

He stared at her, as if he still couldn't believe she wasn't dead. "Thank God I was wrong, huh?"

She bit her lip, staring into the blankness of the concave, concrete walls of the circular building. Turco couldn't explain where all the blood, all *her* blood, had come from. Cale had been stunned to see her still breathing. And how could someone suffer a 30-mph collision, no seatbelt, no airbag, and just walk away without even a broken fingernail?

If she could find them, maybe other pieces of the jigsaw might reveal the picture. "Maybe the witnesses saw something you didn't."

"Nah-huh. Don't even go there."

"Sorry?"

"Unless all the physical evidence against Connolly goes down the pan and he refuses a plea, there are no witnesses."

"I don't get it."

"And you won't." He blew out a breath. "Look, all I know is, soon as I got to the scene, this Secret Service agent handed me his cell and who is it? Only the police commissioner himself — nearly 1:00 a.m. Christmas morning! Anyway, he tells me not to detain the witnesses but just let them get on their way. So..." He shrugged. "Someone high-profile obviously wanted to be kept out the limelight, and who was I to argue?"

High profile? Secret Service agents? As if surviving a crash and an incurable disease being cured weren't puzzling enough! This was straight out of *The X-Files*. What the hell was going on? And she was just supposed to grin and bear it? Oh, yeah, that was going to happen. "Something stinks here. I'm not going to just sit back and—"

Cale shook his head. "Trust me. Let it go." He stood. "Shall we?"

They meandered down the gently sloping spiral walkway for the ground level. They passed a Max Ernst canvas, a guy who obviously had trouble with relationships if the demonic woman was any indication, then a string of flaccid Salvador Dalis.

Someone was screwing with her mentally; screwing with her physically. If they'd messed with her metabolism to somehow cure her diabetes, who knew what else they might have done to her? If she couldn't get answers from the witnesses, police, or doctors, it only left one option. "What can you tell me about this Connolly?"

"Ha. He's a nobody. Literally. We got squat. The DMV got squat. IRS, too. It's like the guy just fell outta the sky." He rubbed his chin. "And there's the puzzle. Why's a guy fly so low on the radar for so long that he's invisible suddenly do the dumbest thing and get himself hauled into the system? I mean, to drop out, totally, so there's no file, *anywhere*, takes some doing. Why jeopardize all that for a cheap, sleazy thrill?" He smiled. "No insult intended."

She waved her hand, gesturing it was okay. She scanned the people celebrating the holidays with a little culture instead of simply slumping in front of the box with a mountain of candy. The 'average Joe' was such a conundrum because he was only average when it suited the system to pigeonhole him so. Take a guy 25–35; middle-class Caucasian; ordered pizza twice a week; card-carrying Democrat; hired the occasional flick from Blockbuster... You could imagine such a guy, because he was so ordinary he could be your neighbor. But did that mean you knew him? Each 'average Joe' was one enormous ball of passions: fears, fetishes, dreams, desires, needs, nightmares... Each totally different from the next. And that was what made the world such a wondrous place: people were all the same and yet all so incredibly different. Look at Cale — one minute he was hauling some crackhead in for stabbing a kid for his allowance and the next he was eating lunch while appreciating art capable of moving people spiritually. People were complex. Compelling. Confusing. And that was where the answer lay. "What if I wanted to visit Connolly?"

Cale jerked her to a stop. "Hey, what d'you wanna pull a dumb-shit stunt like that for?"

"For answers."

"So wait for the trial. Listen, you've got to walk away from this and get on with your life, or it'll eat away at your work, your relationships, parts of your life you won't believe."

Cale meant well, but if Connolly had stabbed her, she'd want to see the scar; raped her, to discover if she was pregnant; burgled her, to learn what he stole. As it was, she was in limbo. He'd done something, and sure as hell it wasn't only copping a quick feel. She'd come looking for answers, but found only more questions. She was not leaving without at least one lead to go on.

By the time they'd strolled through the gallery and onto Fifth Avenue, she'd convinced Cale her hunger for answers was actually healthy. She described a story she was drafting, a reworking of the Good Samaritan tale: how today the Good Samaritan was as likely to pick your pockets as you lay dying as offer assistance. Cale liked that. He even offered her case histories to support the thesis. Said she wouldn't believe the number of 'Samaritans' who stalked the streets. Finally, he said he'd pull some strings and arrange a visit for that afternoon.

She glanced back at Cale, who was disappearing onto 89th Street. He was very personable, but...? If he wanted to experience beauty to purge the ugliness of his profession, why the Guggenheim? Why not a cozy Italian bistro, where a woman would smile a genuine smile as he approached, grateful for him interrupting his busy schedule just for her? Was he alone? And having a love of art, why was he so eager to share the horrors to which humanity could stoop, instead of praising the heights to which it could soar? Was he so tired of victims and loopholes, bleeding hearts, and repeat offenders? Still, who could blame him? If she had to swill the scum off the streets, day in day out, she wouldn't be cynical, she'd be suicidal.

Yeah, right. Because she was acting so sane right now! Was she 100% sure that meeting Connolly was the right thing to do? No. Was she sure it would lead to anything but more heartache? No. Was she sure she'd find her precious answers? No. So, was she going to go through with it?

***

70 years ago, Rikers Island had been nothing more than the city's garbage dump. Today it was the dumping ground for an entirely different sort of refuse. It was only 11 miles from the Statue of Liberty, the national symbol of freedom, yet it must have felt 11 million miles from the 'Land of the Free' to the 14,000 men and women incarcerated in the island's 10 facilities.

Mary glanced down at the icy East River swirling beneath the bridge. Anyone foolish enough to try to swim to freedom would last about one minute before hypothermia set them free from the world, not just Rikers. Ahead, the mile-long bridge arched, obscuring much of what lay in wait.

A plane thundered out of LaGuardia Airport, so close overhead she could almost touch it. She should be up there, jetting away to some exotic Cayman Islands beach, not wasting her Christmas trailing to this Godforsaken place.

Denied bail, Connolly had been transferred to King's Detention Center to await court. Matthew D. Kramer was warden — 'a man of vision, striving to drag an archaic correctional system into the 21st century through a progressive stance on rehabilitation and rights', or so the jail's website said. His photograph, however, suggested he'd look more at home behind the bars than in front of them — he was balding and fat, with a mustache like an aged rat had crawled onto his face and died. Mary doubted his web browser history would bear scrutiny by the Child Protection Agency. Still, books and covers and all that.

She glanced at her speedometer: 22 mph. She'd felt fine driving through Manhattan. Fine on the Queensboro Bridge to Queens. But once on the Grand Central Parkway and getting smacked in the face by that first mileage marker to Rikers Island? Boy, had she started to sweat. Now, with each passing second, her heart thumped harder, as if she was going to the island to become an inmate herself. She wiped her palms on her black pants, then eased down on the gas again.

The Samaritan's story having grown on her, she'd toyed with a couple of ideas, but could no longer concentrate. She turned on the radio to take her mind off the trauma to come.

A newsreader said, "— U.S. servicemen were killed today in—"

Someone was going to have an unforgettable Christmas. She switched stations.

"— and, over the next decade, 18 million African children will lose at least one parent to AIDS if—"

Did nothing good ever happen? She switched again. A music station would be lighter and take her mind off her worries.

"Forgiveness is not just a word,
Raise your voice and you'll be heard.
One world is so close—"

"Jeez!" She punched the radio's power switch. Like the world needed another pretentious, millionaire rock star preaching about harmony and the wonders of God. What it needed was a God who gave a damn. Why was there so much suffering in the world? Why were places like Rikers still so necessary? Talk about bad things and good people. If God could blast the cities of Sodom and Gomorrah off the face of the Earth for being sinful and corrupt, why couldn't he rid the world of the Taliban, Al-Qaeda, murderers, rapists, pedophiles? Because the only justice was that which you made for yourself. Well, today, she was going to reap hers. She would *not* be a victim. The next hour would provide all the answers she craved. Then someone would pay.

Her car cleared the brow of the arched bridge. Suddenly, there it stood, the key to her future — King's Detention Center. Gray and cold, like hunks of discarded stone from the sculptor's chisel.

Mary gulped. A car honked behind her. Her speedometer read 19 mph. It seemed to be falling one mile per hour for each beat per minute by which her heartrate rose.

Facing your attacker, even if he's cuffed and behind bulletproof glass, wasn't exactly at the top of most people's Christmas wish lists. Unfortunately, she had no choice. She needed this. She drew a deep breath and hit the gas.

***

Mary parked, then headed for the security office, gazing up at the razor wire-topped wall that climbed 18 feet into the air and probably as far into the ground.

A thousand fingernails scraped down a thousand blackboards as gates the size of a bus screeched open. A gold Lexus glided out, receiving a respectful nod from the entrance guard. Mary recognized the driver, and his dead rat — Kramer. With the jail's crest emblazoned on the door, a green SUV prowled out next. A guard was driving with another two in the back, one on either side of a shaggy-haired guy in an orange jumpsuit. If she'd seen the shaggy-haired guy in the street, she'd have been tempted to smile: he had that kind of unplaceable, yet familiar, face. Maybe it was someone who'd made a pass at her in a bar. Thank heavens she'd passed on him.

The entrance guard eyed her. Oh, boy, this was it. She was just seconds away from the guy who'd mauled her, violated her, done heaven only knew what to her. She held her stomach. She wanted to hurl. She swallowed hard at the bile biting at the back of her throat. Aching to run and never look back, she trudged on.

She straightened her jacket. She'd no idea what to expect, so she'd come in her job interview outfit: black jacket, matching pants, lilac blouse. It announced efficiency, professionalism, reliability. But right this moment, she had the nagging fear it screamed, *'I want it sleazy and I want it now!'* to every hard-bitten, horny con on Rikers.

The guard smiled. "Can I help you, ma'am?"

From the acne smeared across his square jaw, he looked barely 20. "Please." Her voice croaked with nerves. She couldn't show such weakness when she confronted Connolly. She cleared her throat. "Please." She handed him her I.D. "I've a visit arranged with John Connolly."

He clucked his tongue. "Sorry, ma'am. That prisoner's unavailable right now."

"Unavailable?" She snorted a laugh. She hadn't gone through all this to be messed around with by some kid barely out of high school. "He's just popped out to the movies?"

The guard's smile dropped. "I'm sorry." He handed her I.D. back. "Maybe if you phone ahead next time."

"But it was only arranged at lunchtime."

"Things change."

How could a prisoner be *'unavailable'*? Surely if it was due to illness, that would be stipulated to avoid confusion. An escape would be hot news. And if he'd died, surely *'unavailable right now'* was somewhat misleading. Something wasn't right.

She pointed toward the Lexus cruising over the bridge. "Was that

Warden Kramer?"

"That it was, ma'am."

"And in the car behind?"

"I'm sorry, I'm not at liberty to discuss prisoner movements."

"Okay. Thanks for your time." She turned to leave, but hesitated. She dug in her purse. "I'm sorry, maybe I should've introduced myself." Smiling, she held out her hand. "Mary Shelley. Reporter for the *New York Standard*." People responded to reporters in one of three ways: treated them nicely to get their names in the paper; treated them nicely to keep their names out of the paper; treated them like crap after previous attempts to achieve options one or two had resulted in the opposite outcome to that desired. A 66.7% success rate. Good odds.

The guard shook her hand. "C.O. Jones, ma'am."

Breaking the handshake, she gestured to his hand. "That's my card."

Her card was indeed in his hand, along with a folded $50 bill.

She smiled. "I'm writing a piece on the efficiency of the correctional system." More pressure for him to play ball. "Tell me..." she toyed with another fifty, "... would Warden Kramer be popping out to the movies, too?"

The guard half-looked over his shoulder. "Warden Kramer," he glanced at Mary's fifty, "usually visits his wife in Bellevue 'round about now, ma'am."

"Thanks." Mary turned away.

"Er, ma'am?"

She glanced back.

"The, er..." He nodded toward her fifty.

"The what?" She raised her voice. "The bribe?"

He cursed and scuttled away, shooting glances for whoever might have heard.

Mary marched to her car. She didn't mind paying for information, but she wouldn't be taken for a sucker. Plus, if it was a one-off, she couldn't help but dig at those who so easily forsook morality for a fast buck. But then, that was the problem today — people weren't interested in living a good life, only a luxurious one. They believed the TV, believed the papers, believed the Web — selectively. Global warming was a myth; AIDS in Africa, propaganda. But the world needed another 50-inch plasma screen. Another SUV. Another cell phone. Needed them despite people's plastic being in constant meltdown. Decades ago, people lived paycheck to paycheck. These days? Credit card statement to credit card statement. Debt held the world together, not wealth. If the banks suddenly called in everyone's markers, the entire 'free' world would go bust overnight. Yet people still consumed. Consumed everything. But what could you do? What could anyone do? Scary.

Mary tracked down Bellevue Nursing Home through Information. As she confirmed she was a relative, Bellevue confirmed Elizabeth Kramer as one of their guests. The nerves were gone now. The entire universe was throwing crap at her to see how much would stick before she fought back. Well, the fighting started here.

***

Jasmine. Mary sniffed. Yep, jasmine. That was a surprise. Not like the home in which they'd had to dump Grandma Tate when Mary was 10. She loved her grandma, but hated visiting Rainbow Fields. It smelt like well-worn sneakers left in a dank cellar. Old. Musty. Rotting. Though that aptly described most of the residents, she'd seen no reason to rub their noses in it. If only they'd had money and Grandma Tate could've ended her days smelling jasmine.

Mary turned onto a corridor so wide she could've driven through it. She jerked to a halt. Kramer!

She'd seen the jail's SUV in the parking lot, so had expected to find him somewhere, but now, only feet away from the pervert who'd attacked her, her heart pounded and her legs wobbled like those of a newborn calf. Resting against the pastel green wall, she feigned adjusting her shoe. She drew a couple of deep breaths. Justice. She would have justice. Connolly was going to give her answers, then pay for what he'd done. Composed, she marched on.

Leaning on the wall opposite door 113, Kramer checked his watch. His gaze roamed the wall, the ceiling, the floor, then fell back to his watch.

Mary strolled between him and two guards, one remarkably porcine.

Near room 116, she sat beside a 5-foot palm and opened *Tess of the d'Urbervilles* at Chapter 12. She rested it in her lap to steady her trembling hands. For all anyone knew, she was visiting a guest who was temporarily indisposed. She read. And time passed the way it does in a waiting room while you await a root canal.

But she couldn't read. What was she doing? What could she possibly hope to gain? And how was she going to gain it if she tried? Bribe these guards to 'soften up' their prisoner for her to question? Boy, this was such a mistake.

She restarted the chapter for the fourth time, '"*By experience,*" says Roger Ascham, "*we find out a short way by a long wandering.*"'. Still, the words couldn't penetrate her anxiety. She was about to give up and leave when the shaggy-haired prisoner slipped out of 113.

Mary's breath trembled — John Connolly!

Looking as if he was going to pee himself with nervous expectation, Kramer burst out, "Well?"

The shaggy hair and scruffy beard belied a voice of velvet. "She's peaceful."

Kramer jerked away, then spun back. "*Peaceful?* What the blazes does '*peaceful*' mean? Is she cured?"

Cured? How could a homeless pervert cure someone so ill she lived in a hospice? What was going on?

Connolly stared at Kramer. "I can't cure her."

Kramer's red face clashed with the green walls. "Can't or won't?"

"It isn't a case of 'can't or won't' — it's a case of what Ellie wants."

Kramer glanced at Schwartz. In a blink, Schwartz snatched his nightstick and pinned Connolly against the wall by his throat.

Mary gasped a breath to scream for them to stop, but relented. Was justice being served or betrayed by these protectors of the people?

Face contorted, Connolly made gargling noises.

Kramer leaned closer. "Now listen up, you scum-sucking sicko. Ellie's so addled with Alzheimer's she doesn't know what color the damn sky is! But you're telling me what *she wants?*" He nodded to Schwartz, who released Connolly. Connolly collapsed against the wall. "Now get your sorry ass back in there, do whatever shit it is you do, and don't come out 'til it's done, or so help me, you'll wish it was you living on borrowed time."

Breath rasping, Connolly massaged his throat. He looked Kramer in the eye. "Ellie—" he coughed. His voice croaked, "Ellie gave me a message for you."

"What?" He glanced at Schwartz, who readied his nightstick. "I'm outside her door, but she gives *you* a message for me?"

"She," Connolly cleared his throat, "she can't talk to you."

"Excuse me?" Kramer leaned down to Connolly, snarling.

"When she tries, it hurts too much, seeing you so upset."

Snorting like a taunted bull at a matador, Kramer looked set to take Connolly's head off. But he turned. Paced away. Shook his hung head. When he stopped, he looked to the heavens as if seeking divine guidance, his situation too dire to bear alone. Finally, he turned and pointed back at Connolly. "I'll say this one last time — get your ass back in there, boy."

Connolly spoke, his voice resonant with tenderness and compassion. "She loves you, Matty."

Matthew Kramer squinted at the sound of his name. "What?"

"She doesn't care about her pain, her dying; the drugs will take care to that. But she can't bear the pain it's causing you. The pain *she's* causing you. No amount of drugs eases that pain. That guilt."

Kramer's eyes sparkled with tears. "Guilt?"

"Guilt she's put you through this for so long."

Kramer held his head. "No, no, no..."

"She's accepted what's going to happen. And she says she's sorry, but you have to accept it, too."

Kramer stared at him. His face twisted like a boy who discovers death for the first time when his dog won't move off his bed one morning. "Why? Why? Tell me why?"

"She loves you, but even another 10 years with you wouldn't be worth seeing you in such pain again."

Tears in his eyes, Kramer turned his back, shaking his head. "Nooo."

"She's afraid she'll get sick again one day and she can't put you through all this a second time."

Kramer stabbed a finger at him. "So you'll save her again."

Connolly shook his head. "We all die one day." He walked over and placed a hand on Kramer's arm. "She'd like you to go in. But don't say anything — just hold her the way you used to."

Kramer leant against the wall, back to everyone. Though silent, from the way his body shuddered, it was obvious he was sobbing.

Connolly squeezed his shoulder. "Go. Hold her."

Kramer heaved himself up to stand tall, drew a huge breath, then trudged into 113.

Mary looked away, wiping her eyes. *This* man had sexually assaulted her?

"Argh!"

There was the loud thud of something crashing to the floor.

Mary whipped around.

Nightstick poised, Schwartz towered over John, who lay sprawled on the carpet. "Big mistake, you no-good, stinking—"

"Hey!"

Schwartz turned.

Standing, Mary glowered. "Lose the stick, asshole!"

"This don't concern you, lady." Schwartz flexed to strike John.

Light flashed. Schwartz looked back.

Holding a tiny digital camera, Mary sauntered over. "But this does concern me. And it'll concern my readers when they see their tax dollars being blown on prison brutality. Now," she glared right in his face, "at the risk of terrifying the city's toddlers by plastering your mug all over the *Standard's* front page, as I said," she glanced at his name badge, "Mr. Schwartz, lose the stick!"

Nostrils flared, Schwartz sneered at Mary. Fury blazed in his pig eyes as if he was going to club her instead of John.

Mary's fingernails dug into her palms, her fists were clenched so tightly. She prayed he was too cowardly to fight someone with the spirit to challenge him.

Finally, Schwartz's baton fell. He didn't break eye contact, but growled at his subordinate. "Get this piece of crap outta here, Duncan."

Duncan crouched to apply John's restraints.

"And you, lady, you better pray we never meet when I'm off-duty."

Mary scowled a smile. "Not likely. I'm not into transvestite bars."

Schwartz's left cheek twitched as if being tugged by a thread.

Her heart hammering so hard she was sure they could hear it in Brooklyn, Mary couldn't resist twisting the knife a fraction more — justice could be so sweet. "I'll have the *Standard's* attorneys contact your prisoner — see if he wants to press charges." She had more chance of winning the Nobel Prize for Literature by penning a horoscope column, but Schwartz didn't know that. So not only would it give him a few sleepless nights, it'd keep John safe for the next few days. After that? Boy, would he be in for it.

Yanked to his feet, John looked at her. "Thank you."

Mary smiled. He had the bluest eyes. The bluest. The kind of blue you see on postcards, or in a movie where some exotic, palm-strewn beach glides into a water so inviting you want to drown in it, knowing it'll wash away your troubles.

Schwartz shoved John to start him down the hall. "Out, Connolly, before your guardian angel makes me hurl."

Turning the corridor, Schwartz glanced back.

Defiant, tall, and proud, Mary glared at him.

He snorted and disappeared.

Mary gasped and crumpled against the wall. She held her forehead with a trembling hand. She'd lived in New York most of her adult life, but that was the closest to a beating she'd ever come.

One hand sliding along the wall for support, she tottered back to her seat and slumped down onto it.

Could someone so compassionate by day transform into some opportunistic sexual predator by night? What had John done that Kramer thought he could heal? Could he? Or was he just an accomplished con man? He certainly had a way with words. But why would someone with a gift for healing live on the street? Even if he had no gift, why would someone so articulate be unable to find friends, a job, a life?

As her breathing calmed and her heart slowed, the world was slowly pulled into focus. She'd come for answers? Come to crucify John. And what? She'd become his savior. No matter where she went, who she saw, what she did, all she ever found was more questions than answers. She knew what she had to do. It would distress people, disrupt people, probably even endanger people — especially her. It was foolhardy, irresponsible, irrational. But it felt right. And sometimes, even though the whole world screamed at you not to, you just had to trust your gut, take a leap of faith, and do the right thing.

***

Over the phone, Cale laughed. "You jerking my chain here?"

Pool balls clacking behind her, Mary gazed across a bar bedecked with chains of gold decorations, but few patrons to admire them. "I'm sorry if it's inconvenient, but I—"

"Inconvenient? That what you think it is? Inconvenient?" He mumbled something that sounded like a curse. "You were lucky, Miss Shelley. But when this guy rapes his next victim, are you gonna hold her hand and explain the 'inconvenience' of it all?"

"Look, Detective, I don't expect you to understand this—"

"Thank God for that."

"— but I believe it's the right thing to do."

"The right thing is what's already been done."

Mary sighed. She didn't want to upset Cale, he'd been such help, but after obsessing for an hour, she was determined to see it through. "I'm sorry, but I'll testify I gave consent if I have to." What would happen to a sexual assault charge then? She waited for a biting riposte. It didn't come. Nothing did. "Detective Cale?"

Cale said, "I'll process the paperwork," then hung up.

Mary drew a deep breath. This had better get her those answers. And one hell of a story. She didn't mind the odd risk, but there was going out on a limb and then there was walking the plank — if the guy really was a sicko, boy, would he exact revenge for his incarceration.

She slunk back to her stool at the bar. She'd felt like such a cow, canceling Amy's second Christmas — she could hear the poor kid bawling in the background — but she had to do the right thing. She stared into the tequila she'd toyed with for an hour. Was this the right thing? Or was Cale right? Would she be solely to blame when John raped someone? Murdered someone? "Oh, hell."

"Excuse me?"

Mary jumped, then turned. A guy with hair so slick it looked plastic smiled at her. "You got the time?"

She glanced to the heavens, then said. "You really want to know the time or what color my panties are?"

He grinned. "Well, if you're—"

"It's 5:25." Mary turned back to the bar.

She threw back her tequila. She grimaced and smacked her lips. Then sniggered. "A healer?" Something weird had happened to her. Something weird had obviously happened at the jail. But a healer? What was she on? She stared at her phone. She still had time to call Cale back before he did anything.

8

Let there be Light

M ary shook her thermos. Empty. Great. She turned the ignition for the heater to warm the car and zipped up her parka. The glass squeaking, she rubbed a window in the condensation-clouded windshield and peered across King's Detention Center's deserted parking lot. The only sign of life was a scrawny dog sniffing a ground mottled white. A snowflake settled on the windshield. She craned her head to the night sky. Heavy snow forecast; she hoped her trip home wouldn't be much longer in coming.

She looked over to the security office. Was it worth the walk to ask how much longer the release process would take? No. After she'd ragged on those C.O.s earlier, they'd stonewall her again. And she could cross poor old Cale off next year's Christmas card list. Boy, had Cale been pissed when he got back to her. Still, what could he do? She wouldn't press charges, and, medically, how John had come to have her blood all over him was a total mystery. Case closed.

She took up her notepad; her story would be a distraction from the cold and boredom. She poised to write, but gazed out at the whitening world, her fingers automatically finding her crucifix. What in heaven's name did she hope to find here? A saint or sinner? One would bolster her worldview but endanger her life; the other would ease her troubled mind but crucify her beliefs. No good could possibly come of this.

But she'd been cured of an incurable disease. Strolled away from a head-on collision without even breaking a nail. You couldn't just turn your back on a miracle. A miracle? Yeah, right. She'd once read of a skydiver whose chute had failed, but he'd somehow survived. That put her miraculous collision escape in perspective. So what of her incurable disease? Cancer patients sometimes went into remission — was that a miracle? No, merely a temporary reprieve. Maybe that's what had happened with her diabetes. Turco wasn't a diabetes specialist, just a common doctor. A hundred bucks said a Google search would throw out thousands of diabetes 'miracles' just like hers. Incurable, her ass! If medical science was so infallible, why was cancer still such a killer?

"To hell with it." She slung her pad onto the passenger seat and yanked the car into gear. The wipers cleared the windscreen...

A lone shadow lumbered for the bridge.

Mary's heart skipped as if she'd approached her building, only to see a strange face staring out of her bedroom window. She squinted. Was it him? Her heart skipped again — Him!

It was now or never. Oh, boy. Should she?

Her hands trembled so much that she fumbled the door handle twice before finally scrambling out. She tottered over, her legs stiff after sitting for so long. "Excuse me?"

The figure plodded on, oblivious.

Louder. "Excuse me?" She scurried closer. With each step her stomach tightened as if she were being laced into a whalebone corset.

The figure in the dark overcoat turned. Snow swirled around him.

Blasting clouds of breath, she stopped before him. Those blue eyes pierced hers. Oh, Jeez, it was him! Now what? "Er, I, er, I mean, it's," she laughed, "er... I'm usually good with words, but..." She laughed again.

"Try one."

"Excuse me?"

"Try one."

"Which one?"

"'Hello.'"

She smiled. "Didn't think of that." Did he recognize her from the hospice? No way. Earlier, she'd been a power-dressing exec; now, a parka and a woolly hat made her look like his best buddy. "Okay. Hello."

He nodded in greeting.

Now what? She blanked. Holy crap, where did she go from 'Hello'? She'd had a whole speech planned, but...

John smiled. "Can I help you?"

A bum, fresh out of jail, face to face with his accuser, and he was offering her help? "Hi, I'm Mary Sh—" she reconsidered divulging too much, "Mary." She jabbed behind her. "My car's over there, if you'd like a lift into the city."

"That's very kind, but—"

Mary pointed to the only route off the island: the bridge spanning a mile of dark, freezing-cold water, now being lashed by snow. "It's a long walk." She prayed he couldn't afford the Q101R bus. "And really, it's no trouble. I mean, if you've friends picking you up, or ... or your hobby's igloo building..." she laughed, catching snow in her hand, "Otherwise, I can drop you at your, er, well, anywhere."

Those blue eyes gazed at her, into her. She gazed back, lost like a child in her first rainbow.

He said something.

She realized she was staring. "Sorry?"

"I said, I'd appreciate that. Thank you."

"Great. Great. It's the car, er—" Turning, she pointed to the only car in the visitor's parking lot. "Ha, yeah." They ambled over. Jeez, what was wrong with her? All her friends envied her grab-them-by-the-balls-'til-you-get-what-you-want attitude. Why was she bumbling like a gawky teenager finding herself sitting beside the school's star quarterback, on whom she had a crush?

Underway, the heater invigorating her chilled bones, Mary regrouped. Okay, first to put him at ease, then to edge in her questions. "I visited Beijing last year. You know, China." She cringed. She'd added China in case he didn't know where Beijing was, but now, instead of sounding friendly, she sounded condescending. Anyway... "I walked the Great Wall at Simatai, where it's still unrenovated — I tell you, some parts it's like you're in Epcot and Disney threw it up yesterday. But Simatai? Oh, just stunning. It snaked over the mountains, all covered in snow, Mongolia in the distance... Oh, straight out of a fairy tale." She glanced over. "Buddhists are weird, though. Like, Buddhism's supposed to teach you such a reverence for life, not just for people, but every living thing, and yet they eat, well, every living thing. Literally. Starfish to swallows, snakes to sharks. You name it. Weird... Have you ever traveled, John?"

No answer. She glanced over, hoping she hadn't offended him, and saw a smirk. "What?"

He said, "John?"

"That's your name, right?"

"But I didn't tell you it was."

"Ah." Damn. Talk about stupid. "Ha, guess I should come clean. Believe me, this isn't my hobby — hanging around outside jails, picking up the first inmate I see." Though considering her love life, that was a viable option.

"It was a brave thing you did this afternoon."

"Oh. Ha. Didn't think you recognized me with the hat and all." So long as he didn't recognize her from the crash. If he did, and wasn't truly so benevolent, she'd probably feature in the *Standard* herself: in the obituaries. But it'd been dark, she'd been a wreck, he'd never realize.

"Thanks again," said John.

"Oh, forget it. My mouth runs away with itself sometimes. If I'd had chance to think about the consequences..."

He touched her arm. Barely. "Don't belittle yourself. Most people would've tried everything to avoid getting involved. But you chose to help. And choice defines us. Those who choose to stand for what's right, against those stronger than themselves, have the strength to change the world."

Okay, there was a compliment in there, but talk about intense. She feigned a smile and nodded. If he was some religious nut on a mission, he was walking.

"Sorry." He turned to his window. "I have some rather firm beliefs and, like you, my mouth runs away, too."

"That's okay." She laughed. "For a moment, I was worried you were gonna ask if I'd been touched by Jesus yet and received the Word."

He shook his head and sniggered. "The Word."

"Not religious, then?"

"People confuse religion with semantics. Any fool can read a book on horticulture and grow a rose, but only the enlightened will see its beauty and smile."

Holy crap! When she'd moved her pad from the passenger seat for

John to sit down, she'd activated her dictaphone. She prayed it was getting this. This was the mother lode of Christmas human interest stories: John was the Einstein of street people, able to communicate mind-blowing concepts in throwaway sentences, with all the pomposity of ordering a burger. If she could get him to really open up, she might find not just her answers, but the most wonderful story. "So you believe in some sort of religion, just not the traditional kind?"

He chuckled. "Hey, don't get me started."

"No, I'm interested."

He shot her a sideways look.

"Really." She smiled.

"Well, it's many of the traditional elements that cause all the problems. The world's evolving, so religion has to evolve alongside, or it loses its relevance. That's why so many in the West are turning to the East for answers and vice versa, each hoping something new will provide solutions. You see, millennia ago, communities were so insular, life so primitive, people needed something to bind them together, give them direction. And the Bible provided that. But now? Now, we get Bible-pounding presidents preaching abstinence, and popes proclaiming it's a sin to use prophylactics, leaving Africa with 30 million AIDS victims. If God had intended the Bible to be an unchallengeable rulebook for all time, and He'd sent His Son to Earth, why didn't His Son write it, in plain language, so there were no misinterpretations over what was meant?"

She snickered. "Tell me about it. Name a war that was fought over food or water, not religion. It's all just assholes killing in God's name. If religion isn't the evilest of Man's inventions, I don't know what is." She realized John was studying her intently. Oh, no, she'd upset him. This was where she ended up facedown in the East River. She shifted uncomfortably. What could she say to placate him? Quick...

"And you believe that?"

Her palms sweaty on the steering wheel, she glanced over. He stared, as if judging her. But there was no threat, merely curiosity. Still, best to deflect things. "Hey, you said it yourself, religion's bull, right? Like Nietzsche said, 'There was only one Christian, and he died on the cross.'."

"Your Buddhists believe 'form is emptiness, emptiness is form', that nothing's separate from anything else, everything's connected. Physics teaches us all matter is constructed of the same basic components:

electrons, neutrons, and protons. Christianity says God is everywhere, in all things... Extrapolate."

Extrapolate? Hell, was she back in Ed Baker's Psych class? But whereas that had been a tedium to be endured for grades, this actually seemed to be going somewhere. "Well, if everything's made of the same stuff, then everything *is* connected, so ... if He exists, instead of being an old guy up in the sky, God's part of us, inside us."

"Each and every one of us," said John. "Religion isn't about deifying an image of goodness, but about living. You see, the Word was never meant to be about '*the words*', but about feeling — the feeling a mother gets when she cradles her newborn; the feeling a guy gets when he wants a girl, but not just with his pecker; the feeling a CEO gets, not when he makes another million, but when he loses one 'cause he stopped to help an old woman who'd fallen. Religion is life. By embracing life, all life, irrespective of color, creed, even species — only then can we truly live, truly realize our potential."

Instead of wanting to reach for a sick-bag, Mary actually felt invigorated. Scary! Since that day 24 years ago, she'd fought against her upbringing. Not easy when you're only eight and your mom's a devout Catholic. But when you've seen the light about what a con religion is, it's like discovering the truth about Santa — there's no way you can ever believe again. "I thought religion was all about worship, not life."

"100 million Bibles are printed every year. Think of all that expense, all that effort. *100 million.* Yet nearly half the planet suffers starvation, disease, and poverty. Are you telling me that's what God calls worship? Or do you think He'd prefer 100 million loaves; 100 million AIDS, measles, or malaria treatments; 100 million Fair Trade deals?

Whoa. Talk about harsh. But John was right. Christ said, '*Love thy neighbor*' — if your neighbor was starving, unless it was edible, what use was a Bible? And it wasn't just Bibles, it was SUVs, TVs, designer labels. Could people say they worshipped God if they were prepared to decimate the whole of creation to satisfy their every whim? Yeah, right.

But there was one flaw in John's argument. Father O'Brien had blamed the world's wickedness on God's gift to man: free will. But millennia ago, when the world wasn't working out to God's liking, God ignored the free will issue and drowned the entire population of the planet — except for Noah and his family — to start over. So what had changed? Why let the horrors committed today continue? Year after year, decade after decade? Why? Because there was no God to see justice done. Simple. So why had John's words moved her? The day she turned happy-clappy would be the day River Rescue fished her body from the Hudson.

She drummed her fingers on the wheel. Damn her luck. She'd come looking for answers and what? Questions. More damn questions. John was no ordinary vagrant. But a healer? Come on! Well, something had cured her diabetes. But that was impossible. Only it'd happened. Damn it! She needed more time.

***

From across the river, the skyline of concrete and glass giants beckoned Mary home, peppering the darkened sky with a mosaic of lights: the beautifully sculpted Chrysler, the Manhattan-defining Empire State, the wedge-topped Citigroup Center. She loved horseback riding in Monument Valley, windsurfing off the golden beaches of California, hiking the hills of Vermont, but, after a rough day, there was no feeling in the world like the warm glow of beloved landmarks beckoning you home. Usually. Mary cursed them. "If you've nowhere else, I can drop you at the shelter on—"

"No. No shelters."

She needed to find him again. If she couldn't get an address, how about nailing him to a few blocks in a specific neighborhood? "So where then?"

"Anywhere, thanks."

Great. She needed her answers. Plus, John could be the greatest human interest story in years, but once he stepped from her car, he'd be lost amongst New York's eight million other residents.

A car horn blared behind her. She blew out a breath and eased her speed over 24 mph. Think, damn it, think! She couldn't stall much longer. Then, inspiration. "You know, I'm starving. What say we hit this little pizzeria I know in the Village? On me."

"You've been too kind already. Anywhere across the river's fine."

Even a vagrant had a patch he called home. Was John trying to hide his 'address'? What could've driven him to such seclusion? "Hey, it's not charity. I was just interested in continuing our chat, is all. If you don't want to eat, you can sit and watch me."

John thought a moment. "Do you like curry?"

If ever a moment needed a high-five...

***

Holding her apartment door open with her elbow, a bag of Indian takeout in her hands, Mary kicked off her shoes. "You'll have to excuse the mess." There never seemed to be enough hours in the day to juggle her job and the upkeep of an apartment. Heaven only knew how she'd cope with a family. "I'll get some plates." Her apartment designed with an open floor plan, she headed into the kitchen. She'd been anxious about bringing John home — getting a story was one thing, but letting it invade your private life was a huge professional no-no — but what choice did she have? Rough it under a tarp in the same alley as him?

Barely through the door, John surveyed the living room. After a moment, he ambled over to her desk. He ran a finger over her files of press cuttings and photocopied journal articles, all neatly indexed and catalogued, then gazed at her two reference bookshelves. He thumbed *The Writer's Encyclopaedia of Quotations*.

Mary sighed at a sink brimming with crockery: one of the drawbacks of not washing the dishes until there was enough to warrant such drastic action. She liked to think she was saving the planet by saving energy, but it was only her own energy she was really conserving. "Sorry, it'll take a minute."

John meandered over to the couch and gazed at the laundry strewn everywhere.

"Oh, sorry." She skipped over and bundled it up. "Please." She gestured to the couch, then scurried to her bedroom. Returning, she smiled. Hell, she must look like such a slob. "Sorry."

John took a newspaper from the trash bin. He opened part of it on the floor and dumped his blood-stained coat on it, then laid the rest over the brown leather couch before sinking into it. The couch was so well worn in that it hugged like a racing car seat. "You apologize too much."

"Well, I, er, don't want you to think I live like this normally."

"But you do."

"Okay, but that doesn't mean I like people knowing it."

"For the past month, I've lived in a box behind a bankrupt shoe store."

"Oh." That put her insecurities into perspective.

But that was the first solid information about himself he'd volunteered. In the car, she'd finally confessed as to her vocation and he'd been unfazed. Now she'd proven she trusted him by bringing him here. Maybe it was time to ease in the odd question. But she had to go carefully. If she spooked him and he bolted, she'd never get her story and, more importantly, never find her answers. She snagged two bottles from the refrigerator. "Beer okay?"

John nodded. "Thanks."

The plates clinked on the glass coffee table as she set places. "So, you a New Yorker born and bred?"

Those blue eyes stared at her. Into her. But instead of making her feel uncomfortable, it felt safe, tranquil, heavenly. Like wallowing in a luxuriant spa bath. And she never wanted to get out. She forced herself. "Hungry?" She slung a rainbow-striped beanbag to the floor opposite John. Boy, she was going to have to tread so lightly.

"Shelley?" said John, looking at an envelope on her table.

"Hmm?" said Mary, bringing the food over.

"Mary *Shelley*?"

"Oh." *The* Mary Shelley wrote *Frankenstein* 200 years ago. This Mary Shelley felt as if she'd been plagued by that fact almost as long. "My mom thought Mary and Shelley just had that ring. She didn't catch on for years."

Mary spooned lamb dopiaza onto John's plate. They'd sauntered into the Tandori Kitchen, but Salim, the headwaiter, had politely informed them that all the empty tables were reserved for a party due to arrive at any moment. She'd tensed to rage against their fascism in rejecting John's custom, but then realized how stupid she'd been to think a restaurant would ever seat him. Okay, he'd washed in jail, but what diner would relish sitting near a bum in a blood-stained overcoat? She'd graciously accepted a takeout, though quickly regretted it when John took what felt like an hour to scour the menu and decide on a dish. That was the moment John the astute, compassionate philosopher had transformed back into John the filthy, whacked-out weirdo. She'd almost run, then and there. But something had stopped her. Compelled her not to abandon him. She'd no idea what. Just an overpowering feeling. She knew what she was doing was crazy, but she just couldn't help herself.

John shared out the mushroom rice.

"Want some?" Mary offered him some chicken vindaloo.

"Is it nice?"

"Gorgeous. But hot."

"Please."

Finally, they dug in. But the instant the first spoon of vindaloo hit John's tongue, he cupped a hand to his mouth and rolled back on the couch, eyes closed.

Well, that's what you got for playing with the big boys. A vindaloo could make a fire-eater cry, so to the uninitiated, it must be like battery acid. She held out his cold beer. "John."

No answer.

"John."

Nothing.

Okay, it was hot, but it sure wasn't life-threatening. Wuss. "You okay, John?"

He chewed slowly, then swallowed. Finally, he removed his hand and opened his eyes.

"I told you it was hot."

He grinned. "I always wondered what it tasted like warm."

"What?" Then, it hit her. When John said he liked curries, she'd never imagined he'd never had a freshly prepared one. Vagrants didn't discover cozy little bistros with authentic ethnic delights; they discovered filthy dumpsters with yesterday's slop. No wonder he'd taken so long in choosing: he didn't know any of the dishes. Something so simple and so readily available as fast food and yet it was so way beyond some people's dreams. Jeez, would she have to reassess life to see it from his perspective? She ripped her naan and offered it. "Keema naan."

John beamed.

She smiled. This must be like the glow a parent gets from introducing their child to life's little wonders.

"Have you any milk, please?" asked John.

"Sure." She fetched a glass.

He washed milk around his mouth, then spooned in curry. He repeated the process. He saw her watching. "It helps neutralize the taste, so each mouthful's as fresh as the first."

"Oh. Didn't know that."

John shrugged. "I read."

"Yeah? Who d'you like?" She pegged him for a Michael Crichton fan: grounded enough to belong in John's world, yet fantastic enough to allow him escape from it.

"Herrington, Schuyler, Xiao Chen Chun..." He continued eating, as if those were the darlings of the *New York Times* best seller list.

"Herrington?"

"*Geomorphism: the Ngorongoro Crater to the Mariana Trench.*"

"Oh." Not something she'd have been overjoyed to find in her Christmas stocking. "You read a lot?"

"Uh-huh."

"Just geology?"

"Philosophy, ecology, math, economics, theodicy..."

Was there no end to the surprises? "So, everything really."

"I've never seen the attraction of *Peanuts*."

He said it with such conviction, Mary burst out laughing.

He winked.

Educated, polite, and a dry wit. And Greta said she could never pick a guy. But a bum? Talk about her luck. "So, you ever had your own place?"

"You know a landlord who takes empty tin cans as rent?"

"Haven't you ever worked? Never found something you're good at, something you enjoy?"

"We can't all be as lucky as you."

"Lucky?"

"Enjoying your work."

"It's all I ever dreamed of." Unfortunately, just because you dream of something doesn't mean you'll excel at it. Her dream featured the editorship of the *New York Times* paying for a penthouse overlooking Central Park — reality was three small rooms and not a single tree in sight. "But what gives it away I enjoy it?"

He nodded toward her desk. "It's the only area that's organized."

"There you go — deductive reasoning like that — a P.I."

"And have to pry into people's lives? Expose their secrets?"

"Find missing persons. Things people have lost. There're all kinds of ways to help people." She wanted that story. Needed her answers. "Don't you think you'd be good at helping people?"

Those eyes stared into her again. For an eternity. Then... "What do you want, Mary?"

His directness surprised her. "Excuse me?"

"What do you want?"

Her cheeks burned. "I, er... Well, like I said, I'm a journalist ... I thought you'd make a good story."

He shook his head.

"Hey, I'm not some hack only interested in sensationalism, I—"

He held up a hand. "What do you really want?"

"A story. Your story. That's what I do."

He put his spoon down. Stood. "Thank you, but I should be going."

What? No! "But you haven't finished." She leapt up.

He snatched his coat up. "You've been very kind."

"I told you I was a reporter. If we highlight the homeless issue, maybe someone might actually do something about it." What had she said that was so bad?

Dragging on his filthy coat, he marched for the door. "You're a good person, with an open mind. Never forget that."

"John, please. Don't leave like—"

John yanked the door open, but turned. "What do you want, Mary?"

Oh, boy. What a good Samaritan she'd turned out to be. Here was someone truly in need, yet all she wanted was to improve *her* life — answers to ease *her* mind; details for *her* story — then to cast him aside. She didn't care. Didn't want to help. And John had sensed that. She gazed down. "That..." Avoiding eye contact, she jabbed at his coat. "That's my blood. I'm the woman from the car accident."

"And?"

"Wh—" She gawked. "You knew?" So why string her along? What did *he* want? Money? Was he just a con man after all? Hell, he was as bad as she was. Except ... he hadn't sought her out. He'd tried to refuse everything she'd offered. If it hadn't been for her machinations, he wouldn't be here now. So it was she who'd got what she wanted: access to the one person who could answer the questions that had plagued her 24/7 since the Christmas Eve crash. She drew a deep breath and, finally, looked John in the eye. "I need to know what happened that night."

"I healed you."

Her mouth dropped open.

Her gaze hung in empty space as her world of science and logic, modernity and fact, crashed around her. Healed her? Impossible. You couldn't heal without drugs or a scalpel. Even Eastern medicine relied on herbs, massage, needles... No one healed with just a touch. Impossible. Yet she knew it was true. Not because it was the only scenario to fit the facts, but because she felt it. Just felt it.

The tornado of her thoughts calming, she realized something. "John?" Gone. She raced down the stairs and through the hall, the mosaic floor icy cold under her bare feet. She yanked open the door.

John marched up the street toward Cloud 9 music store.

"John, please!" Mary dashed down the steps to the street. As she spun to chase him, her feet skidded in the snow. She crashed to the sidewalk.

Sliding, she scrambled up. Her right knee buckled. "*Arghhh!*" She caught the iron railings to save from falling.

She looked up. John was just a shadow flickering between pedestrians dashing through the driving snow. She hobbled after him.

Her knee gave way again. "*Argh!*" She grabbed a streetlight for support, then scanned ahead.

Vanished.

She slumped. "No!" The greatest story of her life, possibly the greatest of the century, had slipped from her grasp. She sank to the sidewalk. Sat in the snow. Gaze lost in the swirl of snowflakes like that of a junkie blasted on smack.

Scurrying by, umbrella braced against the weather, someone tossed her a few coins.

She stared at the holes they left in the snow. Gradually, the holes disappeared and the treasure was gone as if it had never existed.

9

Where Clouded Leopards Lie

Tick. Tick. Tick...
24 years ago, Mary turned her back on the Church, religion, God, the whole celestial enchilada. For 24 years, she'd denied everything spiritual as fakery; the weakness of those unable to accept death as an end; as another form of control over the masses open to those on high. But a healer!?

Her teeth chattered. Cocooned on her couch, she pulled the quilt around her more tightly, leaving only her face peeking out through the wisping steam of a mug of hot chocolate. She slurped her drink. By the time she'd got her head together, struggled up off the sidewalk, and hobbled home, so much snow had fallen that she looked as if she'd been trekking in the Antarctic. Talk about cold.

But if a healer wasn't proof of spirituality, what was? For one person to physically affect another, so profoundly, so quickly, so intangibly was inexplicable by any science she knew. "Damn it!" Had she been wrong all these years?

She glanced at the clock again, but she already knew the time — it was barely a minute since she last looked. John had been gone 48 minutes. He'd be miles away. No chance of finding him. Even if she wanted to. Too late for that now. Far too late. She slurped her chocolate. Glanced at the clock again. Even if she wanted to find him, where would she look?

"Oh, get a grip, girl." She shuffled around, turning her back on the clock. This was ridiculous. She was not trailing out into a blizzard to search for some bum who lived in a fantasy world. Healer? Healer, her ass!

Anyway, she'd be crazy to even consider it, what with the freaks, sickos, and whack-jobs who infested Manhattan's shadows by day, let alone by night. She shivered just at the thought of it.

The wind rattled the window.

And the clock tick-tick-ticked. So slowly. Like Chinese water torture. Tick-tick-ticking into her mind, relentlessly gnawing at her thoughts.

Tick. Tick. Tick.

Plod. Plod. Plod. Each second saw John another step farther away. Her precious answers farther away.

Oh, this was bull. She'd discovered her answers 24 years ago. Straight from the horse's mouth. And what answers were they? When Mary hadn't accepted her explanation, her mother had become irritated and told her to ask Father O'Brien. So she asked Father O'Brien. He'd talked endlessly without saying anything, then told her to have faith in God, that He'd answer her questions. So Mary asked God. And God had said? Not one damn word. No matter how she begged. That very moment, she'd decided if He was supposed to love her but couldn't give her an answer as to why He'd done what He had, either He wasn't all-knowing, or He wasn't all good. Either way, if he'd abandoned her, she'd abandon him.

In 24 years, she'd neither regretted nor questioned her decision. She wasn't about to turn her life upside-down now, just because some lying freak 'said' he'd healed her. No way. No way in hell.

Tick. Tick. Tick.

She slung the quilt off. She'd prove it. She'd damn well prove it. She marched out. On returning to the living room, she opened a tiny travel case in her lap — her diabetes test kit. Healed? Yeah, right. Just because she felt fine didn't mean she was. She'd prove her blood sugar was abnormal; prove it was haywire because her natural insulin levels were way off; prove no one was 'healed'. Then she'd go to bed, forget all this bull, and, tomorrow, get on with her life.

She snatched her pen-shaped lancet. Set the spring-loaded mechanism to fire the pin tip into her flesh. Hovered it over her fingertip...

Stared.

But what if...?

Tick. Tick. Tick...

No. No way. It was impossible she was healed. It was just the freak result of something she'd eaten. Or drunk. Or a virus. Any number of things could've thrown her metabolism out of whack. God? Ha! But what if it was true? She'd have to re-evaluate everything. Everything! Whoa— She would? Hell, the entire world would. Such a thing could bring global peace and prosperity, or just as easily bring chaos, even war. Jeez, a simple cartoon had had the Islamic world in uproar — imagine if the West produced tangible evidence to cast doubts on their whole faith. No, no, no. It was impossible. *Impossible!*

Tick. Tick. Tick...

But what if...?

Damn it. She fired the pin. Blood oozed.

***

Mary knocked the car heater up to maximum. She still couldn't stop shivering. She squinted at a shadow lumbering along the sidewalk into the swirling snow. Damn — just some guy.

John avoided shelters. He had no money, no friends, no food. Of course, he could just bed down anywhere, that being one of the 'perks' of being homeless, but just as she'd felt the warm glow of familiar landmarks, so would he. He'd spent the past month behind a store. That meant he felt 'at home' there. Since he had no Christmas celebrations to be traveling home from, it seemed logical to assume he lived in the neighborhood in which the crash had occurred. So, with the crash site as the epicenter, she'd been combing a five-block radius for a derelict shoe store for 90 minutes, and? Zip. This was her one lead. If she scored a blank, it was game over.

She winced. Despite it being strapped, every time she moved her leg, pain shot through her knee like someone was cracking it with a hammer. And her fingertips were as tender as if she'd scoured them with a wire brush — she'd lost count of how many times she'd pricked them to repeat the blood sugar tests. And for what? Every result the same. Every last one. To try to force her body to react, she'd even drunk three cups of tea so laden with honey they made her retch. What happened? Nothing. Was all she'd endured to be in vain?

She hung a right. Scoured another sidewalk, more storefronts.

Fifteen minutes later, she hung another right. Ahead, the crash site mocked her again. She sighed. She'd lost him. She turned for home.

A snow plow prowled the opposite side of the road. As it passed, she caught movement on the sidewalk beyond. She gasped. A dark figure disappeared down a shadow-drenched alley. She slammed on the brakes.

A Buick blasted its horn and swerved around her.

It had to be him. Had to. "Oh, please. Please, please." She parked outside a darkened deli, then lurched back, her limp leaving dragged footprints in the snow.

At the mouth of the alley, she stared down... Oh, God help her.

A fire escape; trash cans; a Ford pickup with a flat front right tire. And shadows. Deep, dark shadows. If she ventured down there alone at this time of night and got stabbed or raped, who in their right minds would offer one shred of sympathy?

She scanned the surrounding area, praying for a signage proclaiming 'Shoes 'R' Us' or 'Boot World'. Nothing. Left, stood a stationer's. Right, a store plastered with fliers: a boxing championship at the Garden; a global warming rally; Geoff Tanner for President. Unfortunately, though abandoned, the store gave no clue as to its history.

Mary stared into the shadows, shadows heaving with knife-wielding muggers, sex-starved junkies, whackos whose only gratification was derived from violence... From the brief glimpse, it had looked like John. But shaggy hair and a heavy coat wasn't exactly a unique fashion statement amongst the homeless. Hell, it could've been anyone.

She shrank from the alley's gaping mouth. She was going to die. It was that simple. Die! But she had to go on. Her mom always warned her that she should be careful what she wished for. Well, she'd wished for answers and unfortunately got them — now she had to face the responsibility of what those answers had brought. John hadn't merely healed her, changed her life; he'd changed the entire world. Nothing could ever be the same. Overnight, he could rid the world of cancer, AIDS, heart disease, meningitis, tuberculosis. Overnight, by being able to heal others, he could prove that people truly were all connected, all interdependent, all one. Overnight, he could show people something bigger than themselves, something spiritual, something to touch them so deeply it would change their lives forever. Okay, not overnight, not everyone, but over a year...? Holy crap! And John could do it. As easily as she stirred her coffee, John could give a Parkinson's sufferer an extra 10 or 20 years.

But why didn't he realize that? Why couldn't he see the path he'd chosen denied millions life? She had to find him, convince him, share him with the world. But as she stared into the darkness, her skin prickled. If she was wrong, the next few seconds could easily change her life again — by ending it.

Umpteen sets of footprints crawled into the unknown. Oh, boy. There could be anyone down there. Anything. Waiting. She gripped her pepper spray. It wouldn't have much effect on a blade or a bullet, but it was all she had. Her heart pounding like a little girl's on hearing her closet door creak in the night, she took a tentative step into the alley, creeping along the flattened snow of a tire track.

Screeeheeeee.

She jumped; it was only a fire escape squealing in the icy wind. She held her spray up. It shook. She gripped it with both hands, like cops did with their guns on TV. It still shook. Her gaze prowled the blackened nooks. She tried to swallow, but her mouth was too dry. She barely dared breathe for fear every lowlife lying in wait would hear and know her exact location. She shuffled on.

She glanced back at the street. The street lavished in light, in warmth. The street so very, very far away. Her breathing shuddered. Adrenaline surged. Every pore of her being screamed, *Run!* She shuffled another step into the darkness. She had to go on. This was the moment her entire life had been building toward, the moment that would give it true meaning — her one chance to do something truly worthwhile. She barely mouthed, "Please let it be John. Please let it be John." She stumbled farther.

In the dark of a set-back doorway, she spied a shape. A man-sized shape. She gasped. Her breath billowed in a huge cloud of fear. She squinted, struggling for more detail, but saw only lurking darkness. She crept closer. Her steps were so tiny, her footprints were just a shuffled track, while her heart thumped faster than the little girl's when her closet door swung open at midnight. She gripped her spray tighter. It trembled.

70

The darkness hugged the shadows.

Oh, God help her, if this wasn't John, she was dead. "Oh, God. Oh, God. Oh, God." The darkness moved. She jumped. Prayed her eyes had deceived her. But it moved again. A huge black figure loomed out of the shadows.

Mary gasped.

A gravelly growl tingled her spine.

Nooooo! She hit her spray's button.

Nothing.

"Shit!" She threw the canister. Ran.

But her knee buckled.

She scrambled to save herself, but she crashed into the snow. The asphalt knocked the wind out of her.

She twisted around, gagging for breath.

The black shape swooped. Oh, God, she was dead. Dead.

She kicked.

"Mary?"

Flailed her arms.

Louder. "Mary."

She froze. "John?" Her body flooded with relief. She reached up. Clutched him. "Oh, John! Oh, thank God."

He helped her up. "What do you want, Mary?"

"A triple tequila and CPR." She held her chest, gasping huge breaths. "Oh, Jeez... Oh ... I thought that was it." Breath calming, she smiled. "Oh, thank God, it's you." Nervous energy broke a laugh. She glanced down to a black shape beside him — a mangy mutt.

"What do you want, Mary?"

"To find you."

"I'll walk you to your car." He guided her around to face the street.

She pulled away. "Whoa. I've just nearly died trying to find you."

"So what do you want?"

"I—" Realizing something, she stamped her foot. Her knee? No pain. Holy hell, it was true. She stamped again. "How— how did you do that?"

John sighed. And turned back for the shadows.

"Hey." She scrambled in front of him. "What the hell's your problem, John?"

He stared.

"Now ... ha ... stop me if I'm wrong, but you *really can* heal people."

Silence.

"You healed me."

Silence.

"Probably saved my life."

Silence.

"Doesn't that mean anything?"

"Don't worry, you don't owe me, Mary."

"What?" She hit his arm. "Of course, I owe you. But that's not why I'm here."

"So what do you want?"

"Oh, will you quit it with the *'what do you want'* crap, please? Hellfire!"

"Answers?" said John. "A story? A warm glow, believing you've done something good? You should let your mouth run away more often, if that's the only time you help people."

"Now, just a damn minute..." She stopped. On first chatting with him, she'd joked it was only her mouth running away with itself that had made her help him in Bellevue. Her only truly selfless act was defending John against Schwartz. Everything else had been machinations to get what she wanted. Had John based everything around that moment? Judged her 'worthy' because he believed she was a good person, then left when *he* decided she wasn't? Well, screw him — she was a good person.

"Well?" John waited.

"So I wanted answers, maybe a story. That so hard to understand?"

"Couldn't you just accept what I'd done for you? Or do you question every gift you're given?"

"I usually let a scarf or scent go. But walking away from a car crash, getting cured of an incurable disease — kinda raises the odd question, you know."

"Go home, Mary." He tried to push past her.

She realized she was being aggressive. "Okay, okay. I'm sorry. Look, this isn't why I came."

"No? So what do you want?"

"Argh!" She shook her head. "That damn question again."

"So answer it."

She did. "You. I want you."

Silence.

"Don't you appreciate the gift you've been given?"

Silence.

"You can heal. Heal! Yet you hide away in some rat-infested alley like a—"

He shook his head.

She grabbed his arms. "Listen to me! Hiding this from the world's worse than ... 9/11, Belsen, and the Ku Klux Klan all rolled into one."

He twisted away from her. "You've no idea."

"Really? So enlighten me."

Silence.

"John, what kind of world would it be if— if Shakespeare had hidden his gift? If there'd been no Michelangelo, no Mozart, no ... Mother Theresa?"

Silence.

She stared into the shadows that highlighted his face. "You've a gift greater than anything the world's ever known. Not only could you heal people, but through healing them, you'd bring them together. John, you could heal the world." Gandhi, Mother Theresa, Nelson Mandela... they'd all shared their gifts of humanity and the world was richer for it. But John? He was so way beyond anything ever seen, he'd change everything. "Please, John."

But John stared resolutely ahead.

Mary exhaled loudly. What was wrong with him? Didn't he see her vision? Maybe he did. Maybe he was frightened of failure? Or rejection? Even success? So why use his gift at all, if he wanted it hidden? So many questions. But she had to convince him. "Why did you heal me?"

Silence.

She shook him. "John!"

"Because... Because I could."

"No."

He stared at her. "The paramedics wouldn't have arrived in time."

"Nah-huh."

"So why?" he asked.

"Because it was *the right thing to do*."

He snorted. Looked away.

"You knew, John." She shook him again. He looked back. "You knew you were the only one who could save me. And you couldn't stop yourself doing the right thing. Well, I've got news for you — the world's going to hell and there's no one else around to help, John, just you."

"I— I can't."

"You can."

"They'll demand too much. Just like you."

No argument there. Everyone would want to know where he came from, what he wanted, how he did what he did — every microscopic detail of his life.

He pulled away. "I can't... No... You don't understand."

"So you think you can just hide away here and no one will bother you?"

"They haven't. For 19 years."

So that was why he'd dropped out. Why he shunned even his fellow homeless. He was frightened his life would never be his own again. So he'd hidden. Hidden from everyone and everything. Alone. Forever. What a godless life.

"I— I can't, Mary. I'm sorry." He trudged for the darkness, for sanctuary, his dog trailing alongside.

But he was fooling himself, or he wouldn't have healed her and heaven only knew how many others over the decades. But she couldn't force him. Couldn't do anything, but pray. "You're a healer, John. You healed me. You couldn't help yourself. You honestly believe you can just walk away?"

10

The Dawning of the End

Deathly silence... But for the wheezing of breath. And the beeping of machines.

Mary had never seen so many children being so quiet as there were on this ward. But then, wasn't death the ultimate silence?

At the farthest bed from the ward entrance, so least likely to be seen, John laid his hand on little Molly Sullivan's bald head. Her eyes fluttered open. John smiled. "Hi."

Molly's mouth trembled, but no sound came out.

Other than Grandma Tate's, Mary had never been this close to death. But Grandma Tate had lived her life; these children had barely started theirs. And some people believed in God? Okay, bring them on in. Sit them down with these children who were all hooked up to monitors and machines and drugs. Let them explain how these poor angels were suffering so, because it was God's will; being snatched from their loved ones, because it was God's will; spending their last moments on earth surrounded by death instead of running in the sun, playing in the rain, surrounded by love ... because it was God's will!

As John ran his hands over Molly, Mary burned her gaze into them, into Molly, aching for a flicker of a smile, a flicker of hope, a flicker of life from the little girl. She stared and stared and stared, praying to see the pure joy of a child able to once more run, play, laugh. But even as she gazed on, a voice in the back of her mind screamed at her to run, that this was crazy, that they'd get caught. John had been released from jail barely 12 hours earlier after being arrested for groping an accident victim — now he was 'fondling' a terminally ill eight-year-old. Oh, boy, talk about throwing away the key! And guess who'd be in the next cell? Yet, fear tempered by curiosity, she couldn't drag herself away. To witness a miracle? Wouldn't that be the greatest moment of her life? Wouldn't that be worth risking anything?

She glanced at the entrance again, then around the ward they'd sneaked into and back to John. John just standing. Doing nothing. Nothing but touching Molly.

Oh, please don't let anyone come. Please! She'd helped Bobby Cole cheat on his midterms at Columbia. With him caught, she'd come within a whisker of being expelled, of ruining her chances of a decent future, a decent life. Her heart palpitations now hammered harder than on that morning outside the Dean's office, waiting for his seeming 'life or death' decision.

"Come on, John." This was taking too long. Yeah, right. Like she knew how long it took to perform a miracle. She studied John, desperate to see how he achieved the impossible. But she saw nothing. She stared closer. Nothing. Shouldn't there be some massaging, some glory-be-to-God, some ... ethereal glow? How could he heal a cancer victim if he did nothing? *Heal a cancer victim?* Did she hear herself? Bobby Cole had dumped her a week later — he'd just been using her. Blinded by his silver tongue, she'd almost ruined her life. Had she made the same mistake again? Maybe this week John was the Second Coming, but next week he'd be Napoleon. "Oh, crap." And she'd done it. She'd convinced a silver-tongued pervert he could change the world. He'd wanted to be left alone, alone with his delusions, and she'd dragged him into the light. What had she done? What monster had she unleashed?

She studied Molly. No improvement.

And John?

He just stood. Touching a child. Smiling like a loon.

Oh, no. What was she thinking? A healer?! For Christ's sake! And she was his accomplice. They'd get banged up forever. They had to get out. "John, we'd better go."

He ignored her.

Oh, hell, this was her fault. All her fault. But wait. She could still save Molly.

"John, leave her alone." Nothing. "John!" Security would dash in any second, restraints at the ready.

Mary grabbed John's arm and spun him around. "I said, leave her alone!"

He smiled at her. Smiled like a child who liked to play pretend and pull the wings off butterflies.

Oh, no! What had she done?

11

The Race for Life

Mary pushed her metal-rimmed glasses up her nose. Not only did they make everything blurry, her having had laser eye surgery, they felt so cumbersome. She craned her head around the chirpy waitress at the espresso machine and found a reflection in the mirror uncrowded by cream coffee cups. Boy, she looked like the head of some prissy girls' school — glasses and hair wrenched into a bun.

"And at New York's Christchurch Children's Hospital—"

Mary's attention shot to the TV behind the counter. She leaned closer to hear over the masses bustling around the arrivals terminal. The camera panned over children playing on the floor, jumping on beds, chasing around nurses and parents and doctors, all of whom simply gawked in amazement. Children everywhere. Children causing chaos. Children ... bald ... emaciated ... like shadows.

"— doctors are stunned at the recovery of an entire ward of terminally ill patients. Little Molly Sullivan — she's the one using her bed as a trampoline — had a failed bone marrow transplant and was diagnosed with just days to live yesterday." Closeup on a reporter: a black woman with straightened hair, straightened nose, straightened teeth. Perfect. "The children started recovering at 9:15 this morning after a man and woman were seen sneaking from the ward. The couple remain unidentified, but police would like to interview them in regard to today's incident. Meanwhile, doctors confirm all the patients, and yes, I did say 'all', are in total remission, but they have no explanation for what's happened. Parents, however, know what they're seeing and what it's called." A caption read 'Susan Sullivan, mother'. A woman with tears streaming down her cheeks grinned so wide it must've hurt. "It's a miracle. A miracle." The reporter reappeared. "Who says Christmas only comes once a year? This is Leigh—"

"Refill, ma'am?" The waitress smiled.

Mary shook her head. "Thanks." She wished they hadn't had to sneak away from the hospital. Wished they could've stayed to see the miracle for themselves. It was like not being able to attend a spectacular party, then later hearing all the wild anecdotes about what amazing fun everyone had. She wanted to go to that party. She wanted to share that fun.

"Ready?"

Mary turned. Those same blue eyes locked with hers, but the rest was a total stranger. Sporting new jeans and a brown sweater under a ski jacket, John smiled. Now, after a trip to the airport's restroom, his hair lay slicked back in a ponytail, and he was clean-shaven. Despite two decades on the streets, his skin looked as fresh and soft as hers, and she moisturized twice daily. The only remnant of his previous life was a chain of blue stone beads around his neck.

Mary smiled. "We've — sorry — you've just made the news."

He shrugged, not remotely interested.

"Oh, come here," said Mary.

He stepped closer.

She wiped shaving foam from his left earlobe. "John..."

"Hmm?"

She wiped the foam on his sharp nose. "Why'd I end up in hospital? I mean, all these kids were up and playing in minutes, so why wasn't I?"

"Someone disturbed me before I could finish."

"Oh." So instead of her healing in an instant, like all these kids, it'd taken hours. That must have been why she hadn't had a reaction to her insulin shots until after Christmas — whatever John had done was still healing her, but once that had worn off, a single shot had almost killed her. She'd tried to resist, but it was no good. "So how do you do it?"

He pulled back. "Mary—"

"But how—"

"Please."

"John, it's a reasonable question."

"Is it? When you rented your apartment, did you check the architect's calculations for the load-bearing walls?"

"What?!"

"Before our flight, did you question the laws of aerodynamics? Verify the pilot's credentials? Safety check every nut, bolt—"

She waved her hands. "Okay, I get it."

"Do you? So many things in life you accept on nothing but blind faith — why's what I do such a stretch?"

"Okay, okay. I'm sorry." It'd been a long day — preparing for the trip, bathing Mutt before dropping him off at Greta's, dashing about Manhattan — and it was about to get even longer. Still weary after the flight, she could've done with another coffee, but she snatched up her backpack. "Shall we?"

They bustled for the exit.

Faith? Yeah, right, like that was an answer. She hadn't taken anything on faith since she was eight and old enough to think. When people saw some magic act, wasn't the first thing they said, 'How did they do that?'? Okay, this wasn't a trick, but just because she'd seen it with her own eyes didn't mean she didn't want answers.

"Where now?" asked Mary.

"Taxi."

She nodded. John dictating their schedule bit by bit, she'd meant, where was their ultimate destination? But...

***

Driving past the Space Needle, Mary smiled as the *Frasier* theme song popped into her mind. She'd never visited Seattle before, not that this visit would count, being so fleeting, but she'd imagined the tower would be taller.

Roaming unhindered amongst the legitimate visitors to the children's cancer ward at St. Barnaby's, John and Mary ambled for the bed farthest from the door, 12-year-old Eduardo Suarez's bed. Mary wiped her sweaty hands on her jeans. They approached the couple at Eduardo's bedside: a woman whose dark skin couldn't hide the even darker rings under her eyes, and a man who fidgeted with his watch strap, chin quivering.

Clutching a clipboard to her breast to stop her hands from shaking, Mary smiled. "Hi, I'm Meg Planer." She gestured toward John. "This is Professor Simmons. We're from St. Barnaby's 'Live that Wish' program. Maybe you've heard of us?"

The couple hadn't. Mary wasn't surprised, as she'd only invented it 40 minutes earlier at a cyber café.

His parents distracted, John sidled over to Eduardo and held his hand.

"Okay," said Mary, "we're a charity organization that tries to fulfill the dreams of sick children, and, I'm pleased to say, little Eduardo here qualifies."

"You mean we get something? For free?" said the mother.

Mary broadened her smile. "Won't cost you a cent. If you'd just complete these forms, please." She handed them the makeshift forms she'd scrambled together in the café. "Just let me have those back before you leave. And don't forget to 'Live that Wish'."

The couple engrossed in the forms, John leant down and cupped Eduardo's cheek. Eduardo strained a smile. John smiled back. "You're going to be okay." He nodded to Mary.

Bed by bed, John and Mary moved toward the door. This was Russian roulette. Each time they pulled this stunt, that bullet — being caught — cranked one chamber closer. Would the next bed be an empty click or a BOOM! Mary's heart pounded faster and faster. With each glance toward the door, she expected security to crash in, pin them down, and call the police.

But no one questioned their cause; everyone was eager to have something for nothing; all the children seemed remarkably lively as their parents explained they had only one wish, so to make it count.

Natalie Goldman's hand twitched as John took it — her idea of holding hands, but she lacked the strength. She smiled feebly as he touched her shoulder. Obviously feeling something instantly, she hauled her head around to look John in the face. "Are you an angel?"

John leant down and put his finger to his lips. "Shhhh."

Natalie whispered, "A secret angel?"

***

"Doesn't matter who he is, Mike," said Senator Tanner on the TV over the register, "all that matters is he's a hero. Such altruism is a shining example of what makes this country of ours great. I tell you, he's done more for the American people in one day than the current Administration's done in four years, so—"

A dumpy waitress surfed the channels. She paused on the news. "He said what, honey?" Sitting on the hospital bed, Jess Phillips — blonde hair sculpted by a team of top architects — leaned down with her microphone to Natalie Goldman.

Playing with her fingers, Natalie grinned, shy but overjoyed to be on TV. She whispered, "He said he was an angel, a secret angel. But he was so nice, I'm sure he won't mind me telling."

Jess looked into camera. "So there you have it, Kent. New York yesterday morning; Seattle yesterday evening. Where will the Secret Angel strike today?"

In the studio, Kent adjusted his smile. "Just so long as he shows up somewhere, Jess."

Mary smiled. "The Secret Angel, huh? Want I should get you a cape?"

John answered with a raised eyebrow.

Mary sighed, cutting into her bacon. They were changing lives. Changing the world. But it wasn't accolades she wanted, just closure. She'd been healed, but had missed out on all the joy for the surrounding trauma. Now all these kids had been healed, but having to get in and out so quickly, again she'd missed the joy that such a miracle would bring. It was like a dream — half-remembered snatches that seemed so real at the time, but left nothing tangible and were lost forever. Had they performed miracles? Had they really done so much, so quickly? Or was it really just a dream? She wanted to trust John, believe in him, but how could she without proof? She felt cheated. So cheated.

"I get you anything else?" asked the dumpy waitress, her lank hair as lacking in body as she wasn't.

"A glass of orange juice, please," said John, and added before Mary needed to, "and another black coffee. Thanks."

Mary nodded her thanks. The red-eye to Miami, in coach, hadn't been fun, so she needed an early morning boost. "Kids again?"

"Adults."

She nodded. But there was more to chew over than bacon. "How do you choose who to heal?"

82

"Hmm?"

"Don't get me wrong, I mean a dying kid's a dying kid, but couldn't we just've stayed in New York, healed a whole bunch there, maybe some that weren't dying, too, then moved on?"

"Doctors can mend a broken leg, treat kidney stones, medicate a cold. If I healed everything, people would take life for granted. So far from appreciating how precious life is, they'd lose what little respect they have and abuse it even more."

No argument there. People knew the risks of cigarettes — did you see the Marlboro execs cashing unemployment checks? Tell people John could cure everything and Self-Discipline and Caution would be on the next flight to Aruba to party with Gross Excess and Recklessness.

She squirted A1 sauce on her hash browns. "Just so long as there's a plan, and we're not haring all over the country just for the hell of it. I mean, it's not the money—"

"I know."

"— but at this rate, my cards are gonna be maxxed in just a couple of days."

He nodded.

"So?"

"So?" asked John.

"There is a plan?"

"There is a plan."

She waited, her raised eyebrows and open hands asking more than a thousand words could, but no more was forthcoming. Finally, she resumed her breakfast. "Well, okay, then. Just so long as there's a plan." John never hesitated about what to do next — a good indication they were following a plan — but what kind of plan could possibly warrant such extreme and seemingly haphazard measures?

***

Sacred Heart Hospital, Miami, Florida, went smoothly. As a distraction, Mary feigned fainting and was taken to sit at the nurse's station. They made her coffee and fussed over her while John sneaked in and out before anyone knew it.

Their evening visit to Phoenix's Arizona Memorial Hospice went just as well. Another red-eye then whisked them to Philadelphia Mercy Hospital. Its online staff directory provided their cover there — after buying coveralls and a cheap meter, while Mary scrambled under the beds testing electrical outlets, John did his work on the pretext of checking the beds for maneuvrability. Next stop: Duluth.

***

Washing his hands in the pastel green restroom, Tom glanced in the mirror at Simon, who was using the neighboring washbasin. "Glad you could make it."

"Have I ever not?"

Tom looked at his reflection, then Simon's. While Tom had a tinge of dignifying gray, Simon had an old man's mop of it. While Tom had laughter lines, Simon had haggard tramlines. Could the ravages of the mind really exact such a toll on the body, or were they both really so old? Was it really half a century since Simon used to throw pebbles at his window for a midnight rendezvous in his tree house? Really 25 years since Jackson Forge lost that order for 7,000,000 brass rivets, setting them on the path to where they were today? With Simon laid off from Jackson's, Tom had gone behind his too-proud-to-accept-charity best friend's back and paid off a full year's mortgage for him, to stop the bank foreclosing, and so giving Simon time to get back on his feet. Tom had almost cried at selling his one family heirloom — the stamp collection his dad had spent a lifetime collecting — but what was a pile of paper compared to a friendship? And that's where the dream started — good friends falling on bad times. If only Simon's current troubles could be solved so easily.

"Everything go okay?" asked Tom. They'd discussed everything at the hospital. Everything but that which truly needed discussing.

"We let them enjoy Christmas. Told them next day."

Tom dried his hands. "How did Jean handle it?"

"Unbelievable. Amazed me how she held it together, what with all the tears."

Tom turned. "Look, I've said it before, but if there's anything I—"

Simon shook his head. "Thanks all the same." He patted Tom on the arm. "You're a good man, Tom. Jean always says you'll amount to something one day, if you'll only apply yourself." He winked.

In the hallway, as Tom and Simon strolled toward the conference room, someone called out. "Mr. President?"

They turned.

Flashing a smile, a young woman jauntily marched over holding a plain brown paper bag. "Your special delivery, sir."

Tom winced. He could've sworn he'd said to keep it from Beth *and* the staff.

Simon clucked his tongue, shaking his head.

Her smile dropped. "I'm— I'm sorry, sir. Did I—"

"How long you been with us, Tiffany? Three weeks?" asked Simon.

"Come tomorrow." She looked tearful. "But if this—"

Simon held up his hands. "Don't panic. Everything's fine. What with Christmas, it looks like Mrs. Stevens has never gotten around to giving you her talk." He took the bag. Opened it. Sniffed. "Extra cheese, bacon, hold the relish." He snorted at Tom.

Tom's mouth watered. But he said nothing.

"Tiffany," Simon marched over to a trash can, "you're going to love it here at the White House — best damn job in the world — but the President's supposed to be watching his diet, so no more 'special deliveries', okay?" The bag thudded into the bottom of the trash.

"I'm sorry." She looked at Tom. "So, so sorry, Mr. President."

Tom smiled. "It's okay, Tiffany. No harm done." He turned for the conference room. What was the world coming to when the most powerful man in it couldn't enjoy something as simple as a cheeseburger? "Chief of Staff *and* diet doctor? You bucking for a raise?"

Simon ambled alongside, chuckling. "Beth's gonna kill you one of these days."

"Well, cholesterol sure as hell ain't."

They entered the conference room, Tom first. "Morning, everyone. Trust you all had a happy holiday."

Everyone stood, "Morning, Mr. President." Around the table were Gloria, Simon's deputy; Michael, director of communications; and Ryan, press secretary.

Tom tossed a copy of the *Washington Post* onto the table, its headline screaming, 'Who is the Secret Angel?'. "Sorry to call you in during the holiday season, but what can anyone tell me about this guy, and how can we get him off the front page?"

Tom took his usual seat in the middle of the 16-seat table. Most presidents liked to sit at the head with everyone looking up to them; Tom liked to be hands-on, at the epicenter. Plus, the Roosevelt Room had no windows — sitting here, he could gaze at Cezanne's *House on the Marne*, which he'd hung between the rows of the nation's Services flags. He loved the Impressionists. He loved how they'd struggled against dogma, poverty, and public denigration, and, through belief in their vision, left the world such wondrous gifts of color, joy, and life. Without a real slice of nature, Cezanne's vibrant, billowing trees and dancing, watery reflections nourished his soul during many a grinding meeting.

"I saw David Blaine levitate in Times Square, I swear," said Ryan, running a hand through his auburn hair. "I was blown away. Next thing, there's *Magicians Unmasked* on cable, and the trick's so simple an eight-year-old could pull it off."

"Oh, come on, Ryan," said Gloria, clicking her pen as she always did when she thought someone was talking bull, "this isn't some guy standing funny — this is doctors seeing tumors disappear."

"Records can be forged, doctors bribed," said Ryan. "Come New Year, five'll get you 10 he's signed a million-dollar deal with NBC for his own special."

Clearing his throat, Michael said. "That's as may be, but just this morning I had the Saudi ambassador demanding we censure the press, as all this talk of miracles is insulting to Islam."

Tom sighed. Apparently, no one knew anything. "Okay, we have to leak our tax proposal today or we lose the opportunity — and I want it front-page news. New Hampshire's less than a month off, and Tanner's all over the media praising this guy, while we're getting squat. We need some good press, or that 58–31 lead we all love so much is going to disappear faster than you can say 'Ex-President Tom Stevens'. So if we want a second term, we need that front page, people."

The New Hampshire primary was the first in the round of nationwide state primaries to establish which candidate each party would field for the presidency — voting had no bearing on the actual election. Tom and Tanner were battling for that candidacy. The battle had seemed all but won, with most polls giving Tom a 27-point lead, but with Tanner leaping onto the Secret Angel bandwagon, what seemed unassailable today might tomorrow be pitifully inadequate. New Hampshire had such national significance that if Tanner won there, Tanner fever would sweep the nation like a tsunami — nothing rallied support crazier than an underdog coming good. And Tom should know — it had worked for him. So the frenzy the media would stir up could see the presidency snatched from him. He had to stamp his authority on New Hampshire and thereby on the entire nation, with a massive show of support.

Tom looked to the one man who could cut through the bull to nail answers on problems others could spend days struggling with to no avail. "Simon?"

"Aren't we being premature? Other than the fact this guy's supposed to be healing folks, no one knows one damn thing about him. Yeah, Tanner's getting exposure by jumping on the bandwagon, but when you're so far behind in the polls, what you got to lose? I tell you, this Secret Angel turns into a very public devil, hell, is this thing gonna up bite Tanner on the ass."

Tom said, "Yes, but the clock's ticking. With all this miracles malarkey, if this guy doesn't screw up but does stir up the Christian vote, that's a big block to lose."

"I don't know," said Michael. "We pulled in our share with our stance on moral values. So far, this guy hasn't said boo about religion. If he's for real, we could turn the moral aspect to our advantage."

"Come on," snapped Ryan. "Like he's for real. No one performs," he made air quotes, "'miracles' for nothing—"

"Except politicians," said Gloria.

Ryan continued, "— and an act like this, with the right marketing, the guy could be richer than Jesus. The guy's after something."

"I hope you're right, Ryan," said Tom, "'cause if this guy's for real, an inconvenience could become a crisis."

"Give it a week. He'll have a set of demands like Bill Gates's wish list."

Michael cleared his throat again — that used to be an annoying tic, but Tom barely noticed it anymore. "What I don't get is, unless you've got a fetish for air miles, why zigzag coast to coast — New York, Seattle, Miami, Phoenix — instead of just doing a circuit? You'd halve the distance. Just doesn't figure."

Tom nodded. "So he's either stupid or working to a plan. And I know where my money is." This guy was not stupid.

"You ever play the lottery?" said Simon.

Tom frowned. "Occasionally, but—"

"Why?"

Was Simon going somewhere with this? "Same reason as everyone, I suppose. Much as I'd like it to be, 1600 Pennsylvania Avenue won't be my address forever."

"But you're one of the most educated presidents we've had. Don't you feel stupid battling odds of 40 million to one?"

Something clicked. Tom stared at his old friend — as insightful as ever — and broke into a smile. He nodded. "This guy's popping up everywhere. From one end of the country to the other. No one can even guess where he'll be next. So everyone with so much as the sniffles is thinking, 'He could come here. He's got to heal someone — it could be me.'"

Simon smirked. "Exactly. Not only is he creating an enormous buzz with his 'miracles', he's multiplying it tenfold by surrounding himself in such mystery, while still making the guy in the street believe he could turn up in his backyard in the next half hour. Whoever he is, he's one hell of a player."

So even more of a problem. "Okay," said Tom, "let's tread carefully with this. Find out who he is; how he does what he does; what he wants. If we have to bury him, I want it fast and clean."

Miracles? Miracles belonged in the Bible. And the last place the Bible belonged was in politics. The astute might see Beth elbow him in church when his mouthing of the hymns was less than convincing, but to most, Tom was as God-fearing as the next gullible American. Religion was fine as a hobby. But a lifestyle choice? You didn't need religion to lead a moral life, so the sooner people saw it for its xenophobic failings, the better. If Tom needed *guidance*, he'd sooner turn to the local rag's horoscope than religion — at least he could see the stars existed, giving astrology a head start over God any day. No, the country didn't need miracles, it needed a leader. And that leader was him. The economy and foreign policy were in the best shape in years, so he'd be damned if Tanner was going to give the country a good mauling. "Let's get busy, people — I don't care what strings you have to pull, what favors you have to call in, just get me that front page."

***

Their job in Minnesota done, it was at the airport that Mary saw it — 'Who is the Secret Angel?' read the *Duluth Evening Chronicle*'s front page. And there, in grainy black and white, was a blown-up CCTV still of John, from Phoenix, complete with hair slicked back in a ponytail. She recognized him, but only because she knew it was him. All the newspapers had similar features. She thumbed through the *Chronicle*, then a couple of others. They were laden with before-and-after pictures of scans, patient testimonials, and doctors stumbling through preposterous explanations to protect their beloved science. Most stories were relatively factual. But how could they embellish upon the story of a man traveling the country, healing the dying? Of course, there were the obligatory kooks claiming to be John, yet none able to heal so little as a paper cut, let alone Alzheimer's. Not to mention politicians such as Geoff Tanner and fading celebrities jumping on the bandwagon. Then there were the sensationalist stories speculating on John being a modern prophet sent by God. One paper even claimed to have found references to recent events in Nostradamus's writings. As for his accomplice? She was a blonde brunette, 25–45, with a short hairstyle cut long, possibly with glasses or possibly without, and a Scottish accent. Mary recalled everything but the accent. Remarkably accurate for the press. Yet the strange thing was, reading all the stories, Mary realized she knew little more about John than the press did.

She bought three papers and sauntered back to the boarding gate. John had said the media would track them down soon enough and hamper their work, hence the disguises. Well, that couldn't come quickly enough for her. She raked her fingers through her stringy hair, wincing as she tugged through the knots. Wigs made her scalp itch as if she had fleas, and washing in airport restrooms was not the feminine pampering she enjoyed. But then, how could she explain that to John, a guy who'd lived on the streets for two decades? Hell, for him, washing in restrooms and sleeping in padded plane seats must be like vacationing at the Las Vegas Hilton.

"Bitch!" She snickered and shook her head. Her hair? Screw her hair. She was experiencing the greatest adventure in history. And not just experiencing it, but, with John's blessing, documenting every single detail of it. Yet here she was worried about the condition of her hair, while all around her, day after day, people were dying. Dying needlessly. Prematurely. And John could end that. There'd be time aplenty for hair washing when it was brittle and gray. Now was the time to seize the moment.

Approaching John, she did a double-take. "What the...?" A four-strong family, obvious devotees of the Quarter Pounder, waddled past, each swathed in a white T-shirt emblazoned with *I* ♥ *the Secret Angel.*

"Oh, boy." Didn't take people long to turn John's gift into nothing but an easy buck. What next — Secret Angel candy *guaranteed* to shift cellulite? Secret Angel beer *guaranteed* to boost brain power? Secret Angel microwaves, breakfast cereal, deodorant, siding, all guaranteed to have that miraculous Secret Angel touch? Talk about exploitation.

At the gate, his legs pulled up onto his seat, John meditated in the lotus position. She ruffled his hair. By way of disguise, she'd trimmed it in Philly, but, at his insistence, it still hung over his collar.

She tossed the *Chronicle* into his lap. "Never had you pegged as a Buddhist." She'd assumed he was Christian. Understandable, given the circumstances.

He glanced at the headline, his headline, but tossed the paper aside. "The more you open your mind, the more you open your life to unglimpsed possibilities."

"There's your job — fortune cookie writer."

John grinned. "A writer?! Like sitting at a desk, chewing a pen's a real job."

She laughed. Being together for three days, 24/7, sure cut through the crap of getting to know someone. That said, John performed miracles. Miracles! As in Bible miracles. While she made every attempt to avoid even thinking about it, wasn't John the nearest thing to something biblical the modern world had ever known? Didn't that mean he should be all 'Thou shalt have no God but the one true God' bull? "So you're not a Buddhist?"

"We've just had pizza — does that make us Italian?"

"No, but..."

"In the Middle East, around 3,500 BC, the Sumerians invented a basic math. 1,500 years later, China designed the abacus. And 4,000 years after that, the British built the first computer. Now there's a PC in every kid's bedroom. Chips in every phone, TV, car. If we'd isolated ourselves in tiny enclaves..."

"We'd still be living in huts," said Mary.

John nodded. "Without Pythagoras's theorem, Einstein couldn't have constructed a paper airplane, let alone the theory of relativity. He built on concepts developed in ancient Greece, during the Dark Ages of Europe, in contemporary labs across the globe. We're a world of individuals with insatiable appetites for answers, yet our strength comes not in individuality and knowledge, but in unity and questions."

Whoa. Mary blew out. John's ideas had such immensity, yet such clarity. "Pity religion can't see how interconnected we all are. Think of the hell we'd avoid, then."

"Our second President, John Adams, said, '*This world would be the best of all possible worlds if there were no religion in it.*'."

"Amen to that."

John smirked. "If I were to say, it's wrong to steal, wrong to lie, wrong to kill, wrong to commit adultery, what's the first thing you think of?"

"Moses. The 10 Commandments."

"Not Buddhism? The Five Precepts?"

"Ohhh, come to think of it..." She laughed. Not a clue.

"How about Islam?"

All she knew about Islam was 9/11, vindaloos, and face veils.

"Hinduism?"

She shrugged.

"All the faiths draw on the same core values: it's wrong to kill, steal, lie... The problem is, those who aren't religious don't care, and those who are, are biased toward their chosen faith. So instead of religion binding us together, we get so entrenched in its differences, it divides us and builds walls between us. Yet the amazing thing is, at the core, we all believe in the same basic values that make life worth living."

"So we should build on those core values to bring us closer?"

"Exactly."

Made sense. It worked for everyday relationships.

"And the religions already have common values," said John, "so no one has to accept anything alien. That's the beauty of it."

"Yeah, but if there's only one God, which is it going to be? Muslims sure as hell ain't going to want ours. And I can't see the Pope bowing to Mecca every morning."

"Everyone believes they have an innate right to choose their own faith. The American people believe it so strongly, we've even written it into our constitution with all our other rights. But if we're wrong about that right, what else are we wrong about? Should we reintroduce slavery?

Take the vote from women? Close schools and open workhouses? See, at the core of our society is tolerance. But it's not just us. Islam advocates peace above all else, and the Qur'an prohibits the spreading of Islam by force, so the basic teaching for every Muslim is tolerance of other faiths. Tolerance is the key. Homogenizing Mankind, creating a world of brainwashed clones, will stifle Man's search for answers just as surely as building walls."

"Yeah, but it's never gonna run, is it?" said Mary.

"If we all agree murder's wrong, stealing's wrong, lying's wrong, what's it matter if you wear a beard or not, paint a dot on your forehead or not, which book you read for guidance? The purpose of religion, ALL religions, is not simply to worship some celestial being, but to show us how to live together — why do you think Christianity's got 10 commandments but only one's about worship? So, when we all have that same goal, where's the problem?"

Fundamentalism aside, when the logic was so black and white, where indeed was the problem? She hated religious education for children — brainwashing those too young to question it — but if John could deliver his Religion 101, the next generation would, undoubtedly, be vastly wiser than any to live thus far.

John returned to his meditation.

Mary settled down to read *USA Today*. "Holy crap!"

John looked.

"Get this." She held out a full-page Wild West-style wanted poster, then read, "'Wanted: the Secret Angel. Dead: zip. Alive: $20,000. Know his name? Get rich quick. Call KBNY on 800 555 2313.' Oh, that's all we need."

John closed his eyes. And sniggered.

He'd never reacted to a news item before. Did he know something she didn't?

12

A Kind of Homecoming

He scrutinized the taxi outside the Rose Garden Hotel, one of the many hovels in the Times Square area, just as he'd scrutinized every bus, cab, and car to drop passengers there for the past five and a half hours. Would these be the guests he was awaiting? Or another prostitute and a man with less morality than a feral dog? His father was so right about the West — it defiled so much that should be held so sacred. Come the Day of Judgment, Allah would send so many to taste the torment of the Fire.

The Muslim jerked up in his seat as a woman hauled herself from the back of the taxi. Was that she? His stare drilled into the cab's shadowy interior, but he couldn't make out the other figure still on the back seat, bundling up their belongings. The Muslim squinted, breath caught, hands tensed on the steering wheel. Was it he? Was it he?

Finally, the figure clambered out into the chill night.

The Muslim gasped. Him! Yes!

Mary trudged toward the hotel door, which was in such a state of ill repair its varnish was worn to the wood. She was obviously so tired she didn't have the strength to push it open, so she just leant against it and fell in. John followed with the backpacks.

The Muslim laughed. Laughed like a man seeing the last lottery ball fall to complete his set of numbers. He'd done it. Done it! He'd found them. Now to make his move. He patted the bulky, black sports bag in his passenger seat. No one could resist the offer he was about to propose. No one. Not even a miracle worker. Especially after such hectic traveling: they'd be weary, off-guard, easy targets. He had him. He had John Connolly.

***

Mary tramped along the hotel corridor, eyelids drooping. Talk about tired. Six cities in six states in three days, the length and breadth of the country! And she'd been cheated in every last one — they'd healed more than two hundred people, yet had done it so covertly that they hadn't shared in the joy of a single one. It was like carrying a baby for nine months, only to have him snatched away the moment he was born. You'd never know what he looked like. Never know what he grew up to be. Never share his smiles at his achievements, or tears at his failures. You suffered all the trauma, dreamed of all the joy, but were left cradling thin air. Agonizing. Frustrating. Draining. If only she could share the joy of just one person. Just one. So it didn't feel like it was all happening to someone else. So she could connect. So she could ... believe.

Finally in their room, Mary collapsed on the bed. "Ahhhhh."

Rock music screeched.

"What the...?" She jerked up. John was standing before the TV, puzzling over the remote. "John!"

"What do I press for the news?"

John had totally ignored the TV, newspapers, and radio, despite being the lead story for the last three days. Why did he have to choose now to develop an interest? "Argh." She fell back. She'd sympathized with John's perplexity at cell phones, as he'd never owned one, so she hadn't minded demonstrating when he wanted to check that Greta was coping with Mutt okay. But surely he'd used a TV remote? Mumbling, she tramped over and snatched the remote. "Look, either press the numbers, if you know the station, or use the up and down buttons to go through them one at a time."

She shoved the remote at him, then slumped on the side of the bed, but grimaced — a spring stuck into her. Great. "Can't we just go home?" But John was too engrossed in channel surfing. Her cards all but maxxed, why had he insisted they crash at a hotel? Especially when she could barely afford even this dump. The wallpaper seam separating

94

over a dark patch on the wall drew her attention. She peered under the bed. "I see one roach, ONE, I'm outta here."

"— which is why we must stop him now," blared the TV .

"Surely," said presenter Dan Latterman, his hair so perfect it seemed digitally enhanced, "when he's healing dying children, whatever his motive, he should be applauded?"

"You see? Applauded? Should we applaud charlatans, thieves, fraudsters?"

Mary jerked up and glared at the grizzled man with a shock of white hair. "You asshole!"

The old man continued, "If we accept him now, because of some wild claims he's healed the sick—"

"Hardly claims, Father Murphy," interrupted Dan. "All the doctors concur their patients have been cured. And with no explanations, people are understandably using the word 'miracle'."

"Now, that's just the kind of media sensationalism that's causing the problem, so it is. Only the Lord can grant miracles. And as if that's not bad enough, in the press today, I found three mentions of the word 'prophet' and one mention, yes, *one mention*, of the word 'Messiah'. *Messiah*, would you believe? Absolute blasphemy, so it is. Blasphemy."

"But — at the risk of repeating myself — he's healing sick kids."

"But who's to say what he'll be doing tomorrow, if we let him pass himself off as the Messiah today?"

"Should we hold him accountable for what the press writes?"

"So why the secrecy? The disguises? Because he's got something to hide, is why. And let me tell you, it's not just Christians he's insulting — many religious communities are rightfully indignant, especially the Muslims when our press force-feeds everyone 'Christian miracles', thereby denouncing Islam. If we don't end this right now, there *will* be a backlash, just like—"

A finger to his earpiece to focus on listening, Dan gasped a laugh and his eyes popped wide. "Sorry, Father, I'm going to have to interrupt there for a KBNY exclusive. Ladies and gentleman," he beamed like a groom on his wedding night, "KBNY has just received confirmation that the Secret Angel is one John Connolly, a vagrant no less, hailing from our very own New York City."

Mary slumped back to the bed. "Oh, crap."

Dan gave John's age, details of his schooling, even showed a picture from his yearbook — just a pimply boy-next-door teenager. Mary was quite disappointed. But what did she expect, a halo?

Dan paused, receiving an update. "Excuse me, ladies and gentlemen... Uh-huh... And this has been verified?" Back into camera. "We've just been informed that it was, in fact, John Connolly himself who supplied the details to claim KBNY's $20,000 reward—"

Mary gasped. She stared at John, who was glued to the screen. The guy for whom she'd left her life behind, to follow unquestioningly, was only in it for the money? Was that why he'd needed her cell? To blow the whistle on himself? Holy crap. He wasn't doing this to help those in need, but to help himself to fame and fortune.

"— And get this, ladies and gentlemen," Dan smiled, "even though John is one of the city's unfortunate homeless, he's donated every single cent of that $20,000 to Water Relief Africa. Boy, this story just gets better and better..."

Mary stood. How could she have doubted him? She felt guilty. Dirty. Like she'd sold him out. She took his hand. "John, I just want to say—"

"... Mary Shelley," said Dan. "No, not the author of *Frankenstein*, but a writer nonetheless, here at the *New York Standard*."

Mary gawked. That explained why they were in this dump instead of her cozy apartment.

John didn't look away from the TV. "It's going to get harder now, but it was better we make use of the reward. We'll be hunted like celebrities, plagued by questions, hangers-on, for *favors*. But we have to finish our work, Mary," he looked at her, "we can't let—"

Someone hammered on the door.

There was no room service. No friends or relatives knew they were here. Had the haranguing started already?

Louder hammering.

John moved for the door, but Mary barred him. "Let me." She'd say John was in another room, giving them time to flee down the fire escape. She loathed the pseudo-journalists who made people's lives misery by hounding them for the public good — to expose vital facts such as which celebrities got pimples or pit stains just like real human beings. Scum.

She cursed. The hotel was so cheap it didn't even have a spy-hole in the door. She took a deep breath and opened the door.

"Oh!" Mary recoiled, shocked. "Didn't expect to see you here."

"Sorry. Didn't mean to startle you. Is Mr. Connolly available?"

She glanced back.

John nodded.

She opened the door fully. "Please." She turned to John. "This is— oh, of course, you've already met."

"That we have. Hello, Mr. Connolly. A pleasure to meet you under different circumstances."

"Detective Cale." John nodded. "What can I do for you?"

Cale smiled. "See now, er," he ran a hand through his hair, then rubbed the back of his neck, "that's what I was gonna say."

Cale explained he'd followed the story in the media, like most of the world. Once the photo of John appeared, he put together Mary's miraculous car crash escape and her subsequent insistence that John be released. Discovering she wasn't at home or with family, he simply ran a credit card check and discovered payments for airline tickets to all the cities the Secret Angel had visited. The final charge had been for this hotel, just hours earlier.

So why had he come?

Cale said he might be the first to trace them, but the media circus would be close behind, and once that hit town, John would have a hard time continuing his work without someone experienced in security, crowd control, and street smarts. Whatever, wherever — Cale could handle it. While he spoke, he fidgeted, barely making eye contact for more than a second. Someone so confident and worldly-wise on the street wouldn't be flustered by talking to a man in a rundown hotel unless a great deal was at stake.

"But what about your job?" asked Mary.

"Ha, right. My job. Was a time I fell for that old cliché of believing I could make a difference. You know what it's like busting your balls to get some scumbag off the street, only for his wise-ass attorney to get him back out there before you've even finished booking him? I tell you, the whole world's going to hell. Only way I see it being saved is with a higher law than anything D.C.'s got to offer."

"But we're only healing people, not changing the world," said Mary.

"And the two ain't connected?"

They were. But apart from talking to her, John had shown no inclination to share his vision with a wider audience.

Traveling the way they did, Mary wondered if Cale knew what he'd be giving up. "What about your family?"

He shrugged. "I got a Christmas card from my daughter this year — I was gonna frame it."

"No wife?"

He shrugged. "Goes with the job."

John remained silent. Cale looked at him, then Mary. A bead of sweat ran from his brow.

She'd thought it hard anonymously flitting city to city. Boy, would she pray for the return of those good old days. And as if the press wouldn't be bad enough, there'd be the whack-jobs who thought stalking was the ultimate compliment. Reject them, and they were just as likely to turn up the next day with a .38 as an autograph album. Cale was right: he could be very useful. Unfortunately, John said nothing. A pity. Mary shrugged apologetically.

Cale hung his head. When he looked up, his eyes were so sorrowful it was as if the news had just sunk in that a dear friend had died. "Please, Mr. Connolly. I—" He bit his lip. "You don't always get a chance to make up for your mistakes. I... I need this."

But still John just stared. Silently.

Cale's shoulders slumped, his expression dropped. Suddenly the big cop looked so small, so vulnerable, so beaten. Cale heaved a breath. "Well, thanks for your time." Shuffling out, he looked at Mary. "You need anything, just call."

"That won't be necessary, Detective Cale," said John, his hand outstretched.

A grin burst over Cale's face. He grabbed John's hand. Almost ripped it off, shaking it so vigorously. "Oh, wow. Thank you. Thank you so much. And please, it's Ben."

"Oh, I've always liked Benjamin," said Mary.

Ben glanced at her. "Ha, er, Benton, actually. But we don't wanna go there." He continued shaking John's hand. "Hey, I can't tell you what this means to me. Really. God, I was so nervous." He finally wiped the sweat from his brow, obviously believing to have done so earlier would've exposed that secret. "Now, I know you've had a rough few days, so must be dying to get your heads down, but if you give me a snapshot of what you wanna do next, I can nail the logistics and—"

There was another knock at the door.

"You expecting anyone?" asked Ben.

"No," said Mary.

"What did I tell you? It's starting already." Ben stepped for the door, but John caught his arm.

***

Scrutinizing the doorknob for the slightest movement, the Muslim wiped his sweaty palms on his pants, transferring his sports bag from hand to hand in order to do so. Allah be praised, he'd found them.

The door opened halfway. A woman peeked out. A woman named Mary Shelley. Social Security number 078-05-1120. Single. Journalist.

"Yes?" she asked.

"Good evening. My name is Rashid Al-Alawi. I'd like to speak with your companion if I may, please." He fidgeted with this bag.

She smiled politely. "Sorry, you've got the wrong room."

"Miss Shelley, don't demean my intellect or your own. I wish to speak with Mr. Connolly."

Mary eased the door to. "Sorry, wrong—"

It was now or never. Time was up. Rashid barged in, knocking Mary aside. "Please, forgive me but—"

A burly man whipped out a Beretta 9mm and, with a scowl as determined as his gravelly voice, said, "Hold it, fella!"

Rashid jerked back in shock.

"Drop the bag and back away."

Rashid froze, bag clawed to chest. His legs felt as if they'd give way any second. For the love of Allah, what was happening? He stared at the gun, the black emptiness of the muzzle. "Please, I—"

The man grabbed his arm. Spun him around. Slammed him into the wall. Rashid felt the gun muzzle slam into the base of his skull. His eyes screwed tight. Please, no! Not when he was so close. For the love of Allah, no!

"D'you always force your way into a lady's room?" The man snatched the bag and slung it to the floor. Hit Rashid's left arm. "On your head." Kicked Rashid's feet wide apart.

Rashid's eyes popped wide open. His bag. His bag!

His face squashed against the wall, Rashid spluttered, "Please, I– I need–"

Roughly patting him down, the man said, "Save it, fella."

"Ben," said John. "No violence."

"Believe me, John, the number of whackos about today, you can never be too careful."

"Mr. Connolly, I–" The gun jammed harder against his head. He gasped. Oman was a peaceful country. Not like Iraq, Iran, Gaza. He'd never felt the cold horror of a gun muzzle pressed against him. Never felt so close to death. But he'd come here to save a life, not to end his own. His mind, usually so sharp, was a haze – he couldn't think what to do, what to say. His heart raced, breath panted.

Ben stepped back, still aiming his gun, and snagged the bag. He dumped it on the bed. Opened it. Did a double-take. "Holy Christ!"

Unable to see the contents, John said, "Ben."

Ben was too distracted by what was inside the bag.

"Ben!"

Ben looked up. John gestured for him to let Rashid relax. Ben lowered his gun.

"Mr. Al-Alawi?" said John.

Rashid hardly dared turn to look. When he did, sweat plastering his face, John gestured to his bag.

Rashid slumped with nervous exhaustion. "Oh, thank you. May Allah bless you, my friend." He tottered over to his bag, his legs unsteady, as if he'd just run up 10 flights of stairs. His bag was too heavy to lift the first time he tried, the trauma had exhausted him so much. He heaved a breath, then, finally, upended his bag. An avalanche of bundles of $10 bills tumbled onto the bed.

Mary gasped.

Rashid could've brought $100 bills, but with 10 times fewer notes, that wouldn't have had such impact. "$100,000, Mr. Connolly. For just five minutes of your time. Here. Now. I would've brought more, but this isn't a particularly salubrious neighborhood."

John was unmoved.

"Sorry, bud," said Ben, "looks like we're not for sale."

His hammering heart calming, Rashid said, "Everyone's for sale, my friend. Only a fool believes he doesn't have a price."

Ben adjusted his grip on his Beretta.

Rashid twitched a smile across his chubby face, hoping the oaf wouldn't mistake wisdom for insult. "No offense."

John said, "A man isn't measured by what he owns that glitters, but by what he does that matters."

That was truly philosophical. As spiritual as any imam Rashid had ever heard speak. But that was the last thing Rashid wanted to hear. He needed someone who craved money. He looked at each of them warily. This was supposed to have been so easy, but it couldn't be going worse.

John gestured. "Go on."

"Oh, thank you." Maybe there was yet hope. "As I said, I'm Rashid Al-Alawi, and, as you can see, I'm not without substance. Unfortunately, even my wealth can't help my daughter, Aisha, who's dying of leukaemia. I'm hoping, Mr. Connolly, you can rectify that situation." He gestured to the money. "This is merely a gesture of goodwill. Name your price and it can be in your account by noon tomorrow." Finally, Rashid relaxed. The deal was surely struck: John liked to do good deeds — imagine the deeds he could do with $1,000,000.

John scanned the money.

Rashid smiled. "*Any* price."

John looked at Rashid's watch. "Nice watch."

"A Breitling." Rashid fumbled in his haste to unfasten it. "A gift from my wife." He handed it to John. "Please."

John gestured for Ben to holster his gun, then took the watch.

Rashid smiled. A small sacrifice. It was amazing how many deals could be clinched with but a shiny bauble sweetener. He smiled at each of them. "Sapphire crystal glass. Accurate to within a second or two a day. Worth $3,000." He'd built his empire not just with business acumen but gut instinct — John was understandably cautious, but hooked. This deal was as good as done.

John nodded. "To within one second a day?"

"The most accurate movement ever designed. Please. My gift."

John handed it back.

Bemused, Rashid shot a glance around the group. He felt as if he were the one whom the doctors had just said had only weeks to live. "I, er ... If you'll just name a price. Please, Mr. Connolly."

"One second a day?" asked John.

Why in the name of Allah was he so interested in the watch if he didn't want it? Aisha was dying. Second by second. Some days, she needed so much medication she was barely what one could call alive now. He couldn't fail her. "Yes..." His voice trembling, he cleared his throat. "Yes, one second. Now, please—"

"And you miss that second?"

Rashid frowned. Had he misheard? "Excuse me?"

"When your watch loses that second, do you miss it?"

Rashid looked at Mary and Ben, but saw only confusion. "I'm sorry, I..."

"You see," John showed the watch Mary had bought him so that, should she doze off at an airport, they wouldn't miss their flight, "my $30 X-Tech might lose minutes, even hours over a year — I don't know. But as I treat every moment as precious in itself, whether it's 8:21 or only 8:20 and 59 seconds, doesn't matter."

"Forgive me, but ... what does this have to do with my daughter?"

John gestured to the Breitling. "At $3,000, does your watch tell the time 100 times better than mine?"

Rashid fidgeted with his lucky silver cufflinks — a parting gift from his father when Rashid had left Oman nearly 30 years ago to take up his Caltech scholarship. John was a miracle worker, so he could be forgiven certain eccentricities. But Aisha was dying, and he had no idea what John wanted. "I... Please, my daughter."

"Someone who spends $3,000 on a watch that tells no better time than one at $30 must be more than merely 'not without substance'."

"Ah." Rashid nodded, stroking his goatee. Not only was John a healer, he was an astute businessman. What was 'any price'? One million? Two million? Two hundred million? Without parameters, how could John obtain the best price? In Rashid's eagerness to win favor, he'd made an elementary error. Name any price? John might as well have said 'an Oreo and the moon'. Better to make a solid offer, then negotiate around it. But Rashid didn't have the luxury of time. "I'll give you $5,000,000."

John shrugged.

Rashid needed the deal done. "$8,000,000. In your account by noon tomorrow." He didn't have that much cash, but if he had to realize a loss through liquidating stock to raise it, it would be worth it.

But John remained unimpressed. "How much are you worth?"

What!? Did he want everything? "$10,000,000. And I'll have you back here in an hour. $10,000,000 for one hour's work." He couldn't get John back in an hour, but desperation made for wild promises.

John paced slowly away. "If I'm to bare my soul to heal your kin, is it too much to ask for whom I'm doing it?"

"As I said, I'm Rashid Al-Alawi. I own Mouse Incorporated, a software house. And, if you must know, my assets are valued at 92.6 million."

John nodded, eyebrows raised. Was he finally impressed enough to deal?

"92.6 million must make you very happy. Obviously not as happy as if it was 900 million, but 10 times happier than only nine million."

This was the same nonsense as that about the watch. What was wrong with this man? Had he no sense of common values? Or was it quite the reverse? "Look, what is it you want? 15 million? 20 million?"

John shook his head.

"So what? Please."

"Tell me, do you live 10 times better than if you only had nine million?"

Rashid laughed and threw his hands up. "Is that it? That what the *great healer's* doing all this for? One big score?" John wanted 83 million, leaving him with just nine. It wasn't the deal he'd come for, but if it meant Aisha's life... "Fine. Take it. Just heal my daughter."

John shook his head. "I don't want your money."

"What?"

"But I'll take your watch."

"Again, my watch!" Rashid looked at Mary. She seemed equally perplexed. John declined 83 million, but wanted a watch — until he got it, again, then he'd want something else. Rashid's fists clenched. He could be home now with Aisha. Rashid had only ever assaulted someone once — when he was 12 and Tariq Al-Rowas pushed his sister Suhair down. While Islam condemned violence, the Qur'an acknowledged a time and place for it in protecting yourself or others from aggression. He'd given Tariq a black eye. But tonight, how he ached to see John bloody for stealing what little time he and Aisha had left together. Yet he removed his watch. "Take it."

John did. Then he gave Rashid his $30 X-Tech.

Rashid frowned. What was he supposed to do with this piece of junk?

"Put it on."

Rashid sighed, but humored John.

"Now," said John, "what time is it?"

"Are you serious?"

"What time is it?"

Thinking of Aisha, he drew a deep breath, trying to calm his rising anger. If one wanted something from an imbecile, one had to play imbecilic games. But how much longer would he have to endure this lunacy? He looked at the X-Tech. "8:24."

John smiled. He tossed the Breitling to Ben. "Get what you can at McGarry's Pawn, two blocks down, then rent all the free rooms here, and at the Europa."

"You got it," said Ben.

"You know Cardboard City?"

"Yeah."

"It's going to be a cold night," said John. "Don't leave anyone out in it. You've got Mary's number; call when you're done — there's someone needs picking up."

Rashid stared. What fool rejects enough money to buy a chain of hotels in favor of pawning a watch to rent rooms in them? This 'healer' had been blessed with the gift of healing at the expense of intellect.

Ben marched for the door.

"And Ben," said John.

"Yeah?"

"No guns."

Ben nodded and left. John turned to Rashid. "So, do you live 10 times better than if you only had nine million?"

Rashid stared, struggling to comprehend John's rationale. This wasn't the game of some half-crazed eccentric — this had a definite point. But what? Did his Breitling tell better time than an X-Tech? At $3,000, of course his told better— And then he realized. Did his watch *tell better* time than John's? Time couldn't be *told better*. Time simply was. His Breitling was merely a machine performing a function. Yes, it was incredibly accurate, but it didn't matter whether it was 8:21, or 8:20 and 59 seconds. It was what you did with time that mattered, not time itself. Did it tell the time 100 times better than a $30 X-Tech? No, it was just a watch.

So did he live 10 times better with $90 million than if he only had nine million? If you were poor, finding $5 in your pocket wouldn't just raise a smile, it could mean the difference between eating that day and starving. The problem was, the wealthier you were, the bigger that surprise find had to be to raise that smile. He could find $5,000 and not even flinch. Money merely fulfilled a function. End of story. Most people dreamed of wealth, but lived happy, fulfilled lives with a tiny fraction of what he had. Compared to the average Joe earning $40,000 a year, did 90 million make life so perfect that if he lost all but nine million, his family would be suicidal? Did he live 10 times better?

He studied John. A healer was one thing. But a man with such vision married to such charity? Such a man could move worlds. "No. No, I don't live 10 times better."

John smiled.

***

"That's great, Ned," said Tom on the phone, lounging on one of the Oval Office's two pastel green couches. "You won't be sorry, believe me." He listened, then smiled. "That so? $1.2 million in campaign funds should be worth a free lunch at the White House, huh?" He laughed. "And happy holidays to you, Ned. Give Ann my best. Thanks again." He hung up.

People and corporations couldn't make unlimited donations to political parties, but there was nothing to stop a wealthy individual like Ned establishing a group with other like-minded citizens and spending any sum he wanted of his own money on advertising, voter registration, issue awareness... When presidential campaigns could easily demand budgets of $200-$300 million for TV ads alone, groups such as Ned's would be crucial to Tom's candidacy.

But it wasn't just the money. Ned and Ann were good people. Almost his friends. A rare luxury. With the demands of office, a family life was problematic, let alone a social life. Oh, yes, when you were the most powerful man in the world you had no end of 'friends' — friends looking for favors, for support, for advancement. But true friendship went beyond wealth and position. It went to something deeper, something at your very core.

He sighed. Yes, he had so many friends ... who'd stab him in the back this instant if it helped their cause.

Simon marched in, Ryan behind him. "Sir—"

Tom frowned. "Simon? I thought I told you to go home and spend some time with Jean." It had to be torture being so sick, yet being alone so often with nothing to do but dwell on your predicament.

"Sorry, sir, but I wanted to watch Epstein on our tax break first." He grabbed the plasma screen's remote.

Tom checked his watch. "It's that time already?" Epstein was respected industry-wide. A good report from him would whet the press's appetite for more. And the grapevine said Epstein had liked what he'd seen.

The screen showed a bald, bespectacled reporter talking to a man in his early sixties with unusually black hair and mouth crammed so full of teeth, his smile gleamed like the fender of a '50s Cadillac fresh on the forecourt.

Tom frowned. "What in hell is Tanner doing on Epstein?"

Epstein said, "It isn't doing your campaign any harm either, Senator. You've already jumped 12 points on President Stevens in the last few days."

"13 points." Tanner grinned. "But you know, Ted, politics ain't everything. As John's proving. What John's doing goes beyond politics, race, social boundaries. John's showing each and every one of us we're all God's children, and if we work together, for the benefit of all, nothing's impossible for the American people."

"Ryan, I thought Epstein was onboard with the tax-break feature since you gave him the inside track?" said Tom.

"He was, sir. Must've bumped it at the last minute. Connolly's all over every station."

Tom shook his head. This tax leak was supposed to have been a political boost to drive them into the new year and the first round of primaries with a solidified lead and the press behind them. Now, it'd been hijacked by Tanner for more grandstanding.

Epstein said, "So do you believe what some people are saying, that he's a prophet, a savior?"

"Well, Ted, only a fool would see a miracle and ignore it for the sign it is. I think what John's proving is America is God's promised land and the American people are God's chosen people, so other nations better take stock, 'cause it's our duty to bring the world into line according to the Lord's Word."

"Oh, hell's teeth." Tom glanced toward the heavens. "What's this moron trying to do? Incite the entire non-Christian world to rise up against us?" The Middle East was a big enough headache as it was, without stoking the fire. China and the rest of the Far East weren't far behind. And instead of glorifying what Connolly was doing, Tanner had just made him prime target for every religious nut with a grudge. "Hell, it's statesmen like Tanner who give free speech a bad name."

"If only the voters agreed, Mr. President," said Ryan. "They're really going for this religious schmaltz. Connolly's reawakened an old-fashioned morality with his selfless good deeds and a lot of people are saying it's been long overdue in coming."

Simon nodded. "Oh, if there's one thing Tanner knows, it's how to jump on a bandwagon. He's built his career on it."

"He's got that privilege," said Tom. "When you're 27 points down in the polls, you've got to clutch at any straw going. But I'll be damned if he's going to steal this election out from under us by riding Connolly's coattails. We got any figures on our latest phone poll yet?"

Ryan winced. "Tanner's spot on — he's halved our lead to 14 points."

"Halved it! In just three days? Hell's teeth!" Roughly, for every point Tanner gained, Tom lost one, so such a volatile swing had major impact. "*Any* mention of our tax break?"

Simon blew out a breath. "A segment on Fox. A few column inches here and there. Page seven in the *Post*."

"Seven!?" Normally, it would've been headline news.

"It's only to be expected," said Simon. "After all the hype and mystery, now the Secret Angel's revealed, all anyone's talking about is Connolly."

Ryan added, "But even miracles will get old quickly, sir. He's a one-trick pony, and the press has the attention span of a gnat. This time next week, they'll be all over some poor schlep caught with his pants down in the wrong bedroom."

"I don't know. I've a bad feeling about this." Tom drew his hands down his face. "This couldn't have come at a worse time, with New Hampshire just around the corner."

"It's only one primary, sir," said Ryan.

"Ryan, it's *the* primary. In modern history, only two candidates who lost in New Hampshire went on to win the presidency. *Two.* Do we really want to push for a third? Before all this, *maybe*, we could've rode out a defeat there. But now?" He shook his head.

"Sir," said Simon, "we all know Connolly's too good to be true. Well, he's gonna slip one day, and when he does, boy..." He sniggered, shaking his head. "If there's one thing the press likes more than building someone up, it's tearing them down. Tanner wants to jump on the Connolly bandwagon, I say, give him a leg up. It's gonna cost him, believe me."

"I pray you're right, Simon." But somehow... "Okay, I want a full transcript of Tanner's interview — let's look at damage control here. And I want a full profile on Connolly by tomorrow. I don't care if he's healed your own mother, I want options. Or I want him shut down."

13

Uninvited Guests

Jeez." Mary had used the phrase 'how the other half lives' innumerable times but never appreciated its true connotations. John passed her an iced tomato juice from the refrigerator in the front of Rashid's car. Car? Accessorized tank! It was an H1 Alpha, a Hummer: the street version of the multipurpose vehicle the military used. It had a grill like a snarling pit bull and an attitude to match. But this pit bull had been civilized, having all the accoutrements of a limo ... not to mention having been converted to run on vegetable oil.

Mary sat Rashid's laptop on the central transmission/driveshaft tunnel that divided the vehicle in half, giving each seat its own 'compartment'. Since each seat also had arms, the Hummer felt as luxurious as a private jet and as wide as a bus. Using the onboard cellular connection, she emailed her mom and sisters to warn them of the impending media onslaught.

"So I hacked United, Delta, and what have you," said Rashid, driving, "cross-referenced the passenger manifests, and came up with you two. That gave me your credit card details, Mary, so I hacked your bank." He turned and grinned, "Hope you don't mind, but I deleted your outstanding balance."

Mary laughed. "Hey, knock yourself out." Woohoo! She'd have been paying that baby off 'til next Christmas.

"So anyway," said Rashid, "the last transaction gave your reservations for the Rose Garden. Simple."

Simple? Yeah, right.

Struggling to describe their situation in a simple email, Mary paused. John had sold out their anonymity for $20,000, which would make their work infinitely harder. Now he'd rejected a thousand times that, money which would've made their work infinitely easier. He'd said he had a plan. But what plan was so perfect it couldn't benefit from a $20 million injection? John was so much more than every man she'd ever known, except in one infuriating aspect: he wouldn't open up. Why had he rejected so much money? How could they fund their work beyond the next few days? Maybe John had lived rough too long and simply forgotten how crucial money was to doing even the simplest of things. With the 20 grand John had donated to Water Relief Africa, they could've toured the States for months, healing thousands *permanently*, not just quenched the thirst of some Ethiopians *temporarily*. And 20,000,000? Hell, she didn't even want to go there. Everyone made mistakes. Yeah, but how many made $20 million screw-ups and didn't live to regret it?

***

The illuminated water features and sculpted Japanese-themed gardens should've hinted at what was to come, but Mary still never guessed as they approached the huge stone house. She'd expected a computer whiz to live in the ultra-high-tech minimalism of interestingly-angled white concrete and oceans of glass, not the stately grandeur of a mansion.

At the front door, Rashid pressed his thumb to a small plate. He smiled. "I always used to lose my keys." The door opened.

Rashid ushered them up a sweeping marble staircase and along a hall lined with paintings of historic vehicles: the *Spirit of St. Louis*; a Ford Model-T; *Bluebird* skimming over the crisp white plains of Bonneville Salt Flats. Mary noted the lights behind them automatically dimming. So it was high-tech, just high-tech hidden behind a traditional façade.

"At the time," continued Rashid, "all the search engine algorithms were brutally basic, so a couple of the major players were interested, creating something of a bidding war. I sold, invested in the dot.com boom, and luckily got out just before the crash."

Rashid had referred to luck numerous times in answering John's question about his entrepreneurial ventures. There was a modicum of luck in many things. But what most people called luck, those possessing it called perseverance, determination, and a dogged stubbornness not to fail. Luck? How many light bulbs did Edison construct before one lit and stayed on?

With a tray of untouched food, a woman exited a room. While painted henna patterns twined about her hands, her green Gucci outfit suggested she didn't even possess a face veil, let alone wear one.

Rashid introduced his wife, Sana, stroking her luxurious black hair, a contrast to his, which was thinning.

They all entered the bedroom, which was so crammed with high-tech medical equipment that it did indeed resemble the sickbay of the starship *Enterprise*.

Rashid crept to the bed. He kissed Aisha on her sunken cheek. "This is John, the man I told you about. He's going to help us."

Aisha's eyes flicked to John. Her shaking hand sought her father's. He took it.

Mary stared at Aisha. The girl's arm was so thin, bone so protuberant, it looked like it belonged to an Auschwitz survivor, not a 10-year-old girl who should be playing hooky, driving her parents crazy with loud music, and dreaming about what it was like to kiss a boy. God had forsaken another child. Unfortunately, it appeared so had Allah. Of all the world's prayers, were any of them ever answered?

Rashid stepped aside.

John cupped Aisha's hand. "Don't worry. This won't hurt."

Sana pulled close to Rashid, her eyes sparkling with tears. He hugged her.

John smiled at Aisha, then walked away.

Puzzled, Sana looked at her husband. He looked at John. "You aren't going to heal her? ... Why? ... Despite her color, she's as American as you are!"

"Daddy, I'm hungry."

Rashid gasped.

Sana sobbed. Ran to Aisha. Smothered her in her arms.

Rashid turned to John, mouth agape, aghast at his outburst. "I—"

John gestured it was of no concern.

But it was. Rashid grabbed him. "Thank you. Bless you. May Allah bless you."

John patted him on the back. "Don't hug me. Hug your daughter."

Weeping, Rashid dashed to his wife and child, and flung his arms around them.

Hands clasped to her mouth, Mary heaved a great sigh. She'd ached for this moment — no more running, no more hiding. She gazed at a family smiling, hugging, crying. John didn't just bring health, he brought love. He didn't just touch flesh, he touched souls. She felt warm, like the glow you get from watching someone's face as they unwrap a gift and find a treasure they've dreamed of forever. Locking her arms around one of John's, she pulled as close to him as she could. Thanks to him, she'd helped give Rashid, Sana, and Aisha the greatest gift imaginable. She grinned. She couldn't help it. And, through the blur of her tears, she bathed in the joy of a family made whole again — the most beautiful sight she'd ever seen.

***

As Sana left to prepare a strawberry milkshake and a dish of double chocolate chip ice cream for their ravenous daughter, Rashid approached John. "You must've heard this a million times, but if there's anything I can do. Anything."

Oh, thank you. Talk about an open invitation. You'd have to be insane to reject $20 million a second time. After the frenetic cross-country race on her maxxed plastic, $20 million would buy them time, ease, efficiency, privacy. Finally, some luck. Mary looked at John. Why wasn't he snatching the opportunity? Oh, no. He'd one of those quizzical smiles she recognized meant a game was afoot. What was wrong with him? Just take the money.

Rashid smiled. "Please. Anything."

Take the money!

John nodded toward a table, upon which sat a bookmarked copy of *The Lord of the Rings – The Return of the King*, playing cards, and an MP3 player. "Pick a card."

Rashid laughed. "After what you've just done, you want to play tricks?"

"Pick one."

Rashid shook his head. As did Mary. John had performed miracles. Actual miracles. Why did he now want to perform a cheap street hustle? Take the damn money!

Rashid conceded. He cut the deck so only he could see a card.

John didn't hesitate. "Jack of Hearts."

Rashid chuckled, then revealed the Jack of Hearts. "Some trick, but I prefer your earlier one." He gestured to Aisha.

Mary hadn't seen John touch the cards but couldn't swear he hadn't. Still, it was a clever trick. Now, about that money!

"What now?" asked Rashid. "A rabbit out of a hat?"

"Shuffle. Try again." John strolled over to Aisha, his back to Rashid.

The cards shuffled and cut, Rashid said, "Okay."

John whispered to Aisha. She grinned, then said, "10 of Spades."

Incredulous, Rashid revealed it was.

Aisha clapped.

"Now," Rashid smiled, "if you could do that with the price of pork-belly futures, my friend, it'd be some trick. 90 million would look like the loose change in your glove compartment."

John nodded toward the door. "Walk with me."

Rashid accepted.

Mary followed.

John stopped her. "Mary, would you mind excusing us for a few minutes?"

"Wh—, er, ha, no. No, of course not."

They left.

What just happened? Okay, John was the star quarterback while she just ran interference, but she'd thought they were a team. Other than John storming out of her apartment, since she'd picked him up on Rikers Island, they'd barely spent five minutes apart, drawing them together. It'd been a crash course in bonding. She looked on him not just as a marvel, but as a mentor, a friend, a good friend, possibly even more. Now he wasn't there, it was as if something were missing, like someone had shot her best friend. Why was he excluding her?

Whoa, talk about paranoid. She'd spurred John into action, yes. She was documenting everything, yes. But what was she, a jealous school kid frightened someone was stealing her friend? John wanted time with someone else, fine. Anyway, he'd probably collared Rashid to talk money. Yes, but Rashid had openly discussed his finances, so why the secrecy? What was John scheming?

Sana returned.

Devouring her ice cream as if she hadn't eaten for a month, which looked about right from her appearance, Aisha laughed about seeing her school friends again, her pony club friends, even obscure friends she'd met in chat rooms. Strangely, she never mentioned any family — no grandparents, aunts, cousins, nothing. Maybe they still lived abroad. But with Rashid's money, why would that be a problem?

No sooner had Mary's curiosity been kicked into overdrive than John and Rashid returned — John his usual reticent self, Rashid hyper as a child seeing his birthday presents. Rashid clutched an assortment of papers in one hand, the other repeatedly clicking a pen. He announced to Sana that John, Mary, and Ben would be their guests for the foreseeable future. He had an excellent security system to protect them from the press, funds to aid their work, a T3 internet connection, and 308 satellite TV channels from 17 countries for entertainment and information. Anything they needed he didn't have, he'd buy.

Mary was disappointed John hadn't consulted her, but if it was the Rose Garden Hotel or a multi-millionaire's mansion... She phoned and asked Ben to pick up their things from the hotel and gave him instruction on running that extra errand for John before joining them.

Rashid then scurried away to make some 'business' calls. For a multi-millionaire tycoon, late night business calls weren't at all unusual; for a proud father who'd just seen his daughter snatched from death by a miracle... Okay, so her grandparents had slipped Aisha's mind. But wouldn't Rashid be bursting to tell his parents the miraculous news?

So maybe it was business. Maybe a deal he and John had struck. If so, Rashid looked remarkably happy for a man about to give away $20 million. And now they were living here, too. Something was going down, but what?

***

Sana wiped her eyes again, marveling at Aisha and Mutt — the dog rolling around and scampering like a puppy; her daughter giggling and playing like a little girl should.

Ben had run that extra errand — fetching Mutt from Greta's. Sitting beside Mary at the dinner table, he devoured another spoonful of saffron rice and lamb cooked with cinnamon and nuts. "This is beautiful, Sana. Really."

114

Sana couldn't stop smiling. "Thank you, Ben."

Ben looked at Aisha. "Great kid. Can't imagine what it must be like to think you've lost her, then have her back."

"It's... It's..." Sana gasped and burst into tears. Mary squeezed her hand. It was an amazing sight. It must be something like seeing your family off at the airport, only for their plane to blow up — your world imploded. Then later they walked back through the front door, one of them having forgotten their passport. The crushing joy and relief would almost kill you. But questions overshadowed Mary's wonder.

Over dinner, she'd tried to pry into whatever John and Rashid were concocting. Unfortunately, despite having hardly touched his meal, John was even quieter than usual, seemingly content to listen to the debate into which she'd become embroiled with Rashid.

"But it *must* start with education," said Mary, her food going cold, the making of her point more important than the warmth of her dish. "If you don't educate them, they'll be reliant on aid forever."

Rashid waved his spoon. "It's not enough. You can educate all you like, but if they don't have a shared knowledge base, poor countries can never develop on an equal footing with rich ones."

"But if they're handed everything on a plate, where's the incentive to develop?"

"As incentives go, starvation's pretty compelling."

"Look, people have to take responsibility—"

"You can't *eat* responsibility, Mary."

She pointed with her spoon. "One cause of rainforest deforestation in Brazil — which leads to soil erosion, which leads to unproductive farmland — used to be that to claim land, people had to cut down everything on it. That was the law, for Pete's sake. Even if they didn't want to use the land, just own it, they had to raze every damn thing growing on it to the ground. Thankfully, people learned, and the law changed. *Education and responsibility* — people helping themselves."

Rashid shook his head.

"What do you think, Ben?" said Mary.

"Hey, nothing ruins a beautiful meal like politics."

"John," said Rashid, "surely you have views on this."

Mary smirked. Her cunning tactic had worked. She'd involved Ben, only to spur Rashid into involving John. Even if John accepted every syllable of Rashid's argument, he'd push the boundaries of the original premise so far, Rashid wouldn't know whether he'd won or lost. More importantly, she'd learned there was little point in asking John direct questions, so this way he might let something slip of what they'd been scheming.

John turned from smiling at Aisha playing with Mutt. He held up a single rice grain. "What do I have here?"

"Damn fine rice," said Ben.

"Literally or metaphysically?" asked Rashid.

John shook his head, studying the rice. "Everything."

Rashid squinted. "Everything? What do you mean *everything?*"

"Everything," said John, as if it was self-explanatory. "From the cosmic dust that made it, the stars, and all things, to the sun's rays that provided the heat to grow it. From the rains evaporated from the world's oceans to nourish it, to the iron mined to make the blades to harvest it. From the ancestral line of the farmer who nurtured it, to the ancient forests that fell to create the gas that cooked it. In this tiny grain is the entire universe. Everything." He played with his neck chain of blue beads. "You see, matter can't be created or destroyed, only changed, so everything always has been and always will be everything else. Even us. We aren't separate from the world. We don't live in a vacuum. Like this rice, we need the interaction of everything around us to live — air, heat, water. Without them, we'll die. It's a chain that links us in life. Now, the links can be microscopic, like the algae in the oceans that produce oxygen, or gigantic, like the Antarctic, which generates weather. But no matter how immeasurably small or inconceivably big they are, they're fragile, so if we abuse just one link—" He yanked his necklace. Beads scattered across the table, bouncing everywhere.

Everyone stared, mesmerized.

"We each have a responsibility to every person and every thing. Until we embrace that, not one of us will ever be truly free."

Everyone stared at John, at the beads, at each other.

"That's as may be, John," said Ben, "but if you're gonna abuse that rice by talking it to death, I'll be only too glad to take full responsibility for it."

Mary elbowed Ben, smirking.

"Hey, a man's gotta eat."

Sana offered to fetch more, but Ben took John's offered plate and spooned rice onto off. "After a speech like that, you think I'm just gonna let you throw this in the trash?"

Rashid leaned closer to John. "So how would you deal with the Third World? Fair Trade? Unionization? Tax exemptions?"

John sipped his water. "Like an older brother to his younger one."

Mary smiled. She had three older sisters. Without their support, wisdom, and charity, would she have her own apartment, a college education, a career she loved?

Yes, how important family had been in her life? Why wasn't it important in Aisha's? While Rashid was generous and the perfect host, shouldn't they learn more about him before getting into bed together? "So, you get back to Oman often?"

"Not as much as we'd like." Rashid sipped his khawa coffee.

"I bet Aisha's grandparents will be dying to see her now she's better."

"I lost my parents some years ago," said Sana.

"I'm sorry, Sana," said Mary. "So your family, Rashid?"

Rashid and Sana flashed wary glances.

Mary smiled. "Boy, they must be so proud of everything you've achieved."

Rashid nodded. "My mother."

"Oh, I'm sorry. Has your father passed away, too?"

"No."

Sana said. "They had a disagreement some years ago and—"

Head bowed, Rashid said, "I brought disgrace on my family and on Islam." He looked up. "Still, we can't all be the perfect son." He offered the Zinfandel. "Anyone?" While a teetotaler, he kept a well-stocked wine cellar for entertaining.

Disgrace? He was a multi-millionaire who'd offered to help them heal the dying. What disgrace could such a good man possibly have brought? But to pry could jeopardize whatever deal John had struck. Yes, but Rashid had originally offered mere payment – what had John offered that Rashid had now joined them? Mary simply hadn't gone back to work; Ben had taken leave. But that was from crappy, dead-end jobs. Rashid had an empire – you couldn't build an empire without endless hours and immense dedication. For him to entrust its running to someone else, John must have tempted him with one hell of a scheme. What could it be?

Still, why look a gift horse in the mouth? Their work would be immeasurably easier now. Nothing could stop them. So long as Rashid's disgrace was moral, not something criminal that could drag them down with him if he got caught, things couldn't be better.

***

"Goodnight, Ben," replied Mary, as Ben went into his room.

Rashid stepped into the next room. The lights automatically raised to a dimmed level. "L3." The illumination brightened. "You should find everything you need. If not, just ask."

John meandered into a room decorated around a Chinese motif. He stroked a carved oak statue of Sakyamuni standing on a black lacquered table .

Mary waited outside, but Rashid waved her in. She wandered in, looking for a connecting door to her room, but saw only one to a bathroom.

"Well, goodnight," said Rashid, leaving.

"Er, Rashid?"

He turned.

Mary shrugged, open-handed.

"Is there a problem?"

"Ha. Er, I'd say so." She pointed. "*One* bed?"

Rashid gasped. "Oh, please, my sincerest apologies. I thought... You seem so close. Just the one hotel room. I— Please." He beckoned Mary and showed her to the next room. "Forgive me."

"Hey, Rashid, forget it." Mary felt awkward at his embarrassment – he'd made a fair assumption. But it'd been one hotel room for one simple reason: her spiraling debt. "And *I'm* sorry if I opened up old wounds earlier."

"I'm sorry?"

"I know what it's like to lose touch with your father."

Rashid nodded.

Her inquisitiveness overpowering her decision not to pry, Mary waited for Rashid to reply. He didn't. Maybe if she shared, he'd do likewise. "My dad walked out when I was eight. Like a lot of kids, I blamed myself, you know."

Rashid nodded again. And was again silent.

"But I'm sure your father really is very proud. He probably just can't to tell you. It's that guy thing."

She could see he was thinking things over, so held her tongue. Gave him time to choose his words. To share only what made him comfortable.

Finally, he said, "Goodnight, Mary."

She closed the door and leant back against it. She sniggered. What a strange night — the perfect end to the past few days. It was weird how Rashid could be so open about his wealth and business, so accommodating to virtual strangers, yet be so closed about one of the primary relationships in life. Or was it weird? She'd mentioned blaming herself for her parents' split, but that was so generalized, so clichéd, it was no more of an actual disclosure than Rashid's 'disgrace' revelation. But she couldn't just haul a 24-year-old skeleton out of the closet over dinner on first meeting someone. Rashid obviously felt likewise. She sighed. All those years ago, she'd been the spark that lit that fuse which blew her family apart. Without that, her parents might still be together. She'd believed that as a child and, 24 years later, still believed it as an adult. She was the spark, but someone else was the friction. And that was when her relationship with God died. He caused the friction that made her the spark. Caused all those events. Then refused to tell her why. Bad things, good people? She'd given up on that answer long, long ago.

Mary washed, then slipped into a king-size mahogany four-poster with swathes of white chiffon highlighting its chocolatey-brown wood. It felt so long since she'd slept in a bed she thought she'd died and gone to Buddhism's Nirvana, Christianity's Heaven, Islam's Paradise, all in one. Spread-eagled, she waved her arms over the crisp cotton, so cool and icy-smooth against her bare flesh.

She peered over her bed. On the other side of the wall was John's room. He hadn't reacted to Rashid's mistake about them being a couple. Why? Because he appeared to be uninterested in her as anything but a friend! What a compliment that was from a guy who lived in a box? Okay, she was no Jessica Alba, but, hey, was John fending them off with a stick?

But what if he did make a pass? Hmmm... Rashid was right. They were good together. Easy. Comfortable. No pretense. But did street people have partners? If they did, how did they get intimate? Find a bigger box? Beg for months to afford a room for a night? Maybe most of them were celibate. Did that mean John hadn't been with a woman for 19 years? Hell. But that'd put him at 17-years-old. Maybe he'd *never* had a woman. "Jeez! What a waste?" She smiled at her mental image.

Someone knocked at her door.

Dragging on the cream robe she'd found in the bathroom, she trundled over. On opening it, she beamed. "Hi."

"Sorry, I hope you weren't sleeping," said John.

"No, it's fine."

He took her hand. Other than running for the plane in Phoenix, it was the first time he'd done so. He held it tenderly, as you would a newborn kitten. She hoped the dimmed hall lights hid her flushed cheeks.

"I just wanted to say thank you," he said. "None of this would've been possible without you. As much as I healed those people, you did, too."

She squeezed his hand, unable to say anything for the lump in her throat.

"Goodnight," he said.

She watched him walk away. She ached to call him back. Could she?

14

And so, to Arms

With his camcorder, Rashid tracked John and Mary running across the helipad of St. Bartholomew's Hospital, Tampa, Florida, their hair flailing in the wind of the helicopter's rotor blades. He smiled at the demeanor of the greeting party — the hospital's registrar, a delegation of specialists, and six security officers. With a mixture of sternly folded arms or beaming smiles, half looked as cynical as the other half looked excited. Were they all in for a shock.

On the ward, Ben inspected the security arrangements he'd requested when they'd radioed ahead, then instructed the security officers on their duties: deterring onlookers, staff, and other patients, so John could work unimpeded. Ben then disappeared to be their own eye-in-the-sky — a lookout for news crews or increases in traffic — so should word of John's visit leak, he could re-deploy security to ensure John wasn't mobbed like the latest pop sensation recognized in Tower Records.

Rashid filmed the more able patients clapping as John entered.

Dr. Fassbinder pushed his glasses up his bulbous, strawberry-shaped nose. He didn't even look at the patient. Didn't see the tube pumping oxygen up her nostrils. Didn't see her sallow, sunken cheeks. Didn't see her glazed eyes staring into space as the morphine drip, drip, dripped away her life. All he saw was his file. "Emily Thompson. 72. Diagnosed with non-Hodgkins lymphoma 14 months ago. Nonresponsive to—"

"Holy shit!" said Dr. Huang.

Fassbinder glanced at his colleague, then followed his gaze.

Emily's eyes sparkled up at John, her cheeks as full and red as if she'd just enjoyed a bracing walk along a country trail, admiring the first shoots of spring. Fassbinder's file dropped. His jaw, too.

The camcorder image wobbled, Rashid chuckling. He knew just how they felt: mystified, jubilant, awestruck, uplifted.

Unlike some Muslims, he never begrudged his Zakat payments — if Allah saw fit to bless him with wealth, it was only fitting he be charitable toward those less fortunate. Plus, if he fulfilled enough good deeds, he might yet offset the disgrace he'd brought upon Allah and be taken into Paradise in the Hereafter. But merely writing an annual check, even if his ran into six or seven figures, left one totally detached, not really knowing — or indeed caring — if one had actually made a difference to anyone's life. But this? Oh, what a difference! Magical. Utterly magical. He'd never felt a thrill like it. No, that wasn't true. 10 years ago, March 25th, he'd felt just like this. It was raining. So gloomy it was almost night in the middle of the day. Yet his life couldn't have been filled with more light as he cradled Aisha — she was barely four minutes old. A treasure at the end of years of heartbreaking IVF failures. Something miraculous. Something so infinitely bigger than he was. Yet something, intimate, personal, tiny. He'd felt alive. So truly alive.

He zoomed in on Fassbinder telling a nurse to have all the patients scanned. Two other doctors argued over possible medical explanations while a fourth just stood beaming at everyone, tears streaming.

And then came the haranguing: How did John heal? Was it tiring? Was any condition beyond him?... Mary ran interference, but the questions were relentless. Understandable — the impossible suddenly possible. Rashid understood why they'd adopted the covert approach until now.

As John went to his twelfth patient, Mary said. "You getting all this?"

Rashid nodded. "But he's so quick." For someone who lived on the street, John proved remarkably quick in many ways. Earlier, he'd quizzed Rashid on streaming video, bandwidth, podcasts. Finally, he'd suggested Rashid film their healing sessions, then upload them to the Web so people could judge his work for themselves, instead of relying on the sensationalist press. Rashid was overjoyed. But Mary hadn't eaten another spoonful of cornflakes. Rashid had explained his would be a wobbly video-diary, while her documentation would be an in-depth exploration of the greatest event in recorded history. She'd appeared placated, but he felt under her constant scrutiny. That could prove problematic — he'd have to cover his tracks meticulously with an inquisitive journalist so close. The paper trail, electronic trail, communications, planning — everything would have to be as covert as possible, then all but the most crucial evidence destroyed. But maybe there was a more subtle solution. Maybe confiding in Mary about his family would sate her journalistic instincts. At least until it was too late for anyone to do anything about it. Yes, he'd get her alone later. Chat. Confide. Con.

***

After jetting to St. Petersburg first thing, they'd already covered two hospitals there and another in Tampa, all by helicopter, and it was barely past lunchtime. Their Lear jet having rendezvoused with them in Tampa, it was now whisking them to Jacksonville.

Mary stared down at arctic landscape–like clouds: a great plain of white tumbling away to billowing glaciers. But the majesty was lost on her. As was the luxurious ease with which they were now accomplishing their work. Instead of reveling in their sumptuous good fortune, she was anxious, frustrated, plagued by questions. She strained to hear John and Rashid's conversation over the jet's engines and Ben's TV. Impossible.

She closed her pad. Ever since she was a small girl, she'd dreamed of breaking that 'doctor discovers cancer cure'–style hold-the-front-page story. Talk about hitting the mother lode. Having left the guys to the rear seats, she'd sat near the galley to work. But then Ben had moved closer to watch TV. So with the noise and her preoccupation, she couldn't focus to write. And she had to document this. Had to. She'd been devastated when John casually suggested Rashid upload videos to a website. She'd feared Rashid was stealing John's story, what would be the one true achievement of her life. An old cliché haunted her: a picture paints a thousand words. Luckily, she'd realized it didn't. It would show what they did, when, and where, but it could never capture the essence of why, or how. And these were the questions on the entire country's lips. And they were the questions she could answer.

But it wasn't just her writing troubling her: it used to be her and John taking on the world; now, increasingly, it was John and Rashid. Okay, many a patient falls for the doctor who saved them, but she'd felt a closeness to John, which she'd thought he felt, too. True closeness. So, foolishly, she'd dared to dream of what could be if their relationship developed. Talk about dumb! Another man she cared about set to abandon her. She was going to end up just like her mom. Alone and heartbroken. Or alone and bitter. Either way, it was alone. Maybe this separation was a godsend. She'd do well to distance herself. Protect herself.

She gazed at John. He felt a million miles away.

Leaning across, Rashid jabbed at the papers in John's lap. John pointed to something on Rashid's laptop. Rashid punched numbers into a calculator. He grinned, shaking his head, then showed John. John nodded.

John and Rashid had already had a meeting before breakfast. A meeting Mary only discovered while exploring the mansion. The instant she'd walked into his game room, Rashid snatched up the documents laid across his pool table like a teenage boy caught ogling porn by his mother.

That wasn't simply money talk. Not paranoia. Something was going on. Something they wanted kept secret.

Rashid ambled to the galley. "Drink?"

"No, thanks," said Mary.

He took a mineral water, then crouched beside her, his back to the others, creating an intimate space. "I, er, I'm sorry if I was a little short last night — about my father — but it's a somewhat difficult subject."

"I can imagine."

"My father... Sana..." He exhaled loudly. "A Muslim has certain obligations... Not meeting them isn't just ... a trifle to be wished away with a few Hail Marys, but a tremendous insult to Islam. My father's a good man. But... Shame before the community is one thing; shame before Allah?" He shook his head. "My father feared the American culture might corrupt my faith, but he wanted the best for me, so he allowed me to study here. I discovered a whole new world. New possibilities. New choices. And I made one — Sana, not the woman my parents had arranged for me to marry. My father hasn't spoken to me for 27 years."

124

Whoa. And she thought a phone call every few months and the odd, belated birthday card was bad. Talk about harsh. "Your own father disowned you just 'cause he doesn't like your wife?"

Rashid smirked. "If only it was a case of simply liking or disliking someone. I agreed to the arranged marriage, but then not only did I break my word, I broke it by marrying a Hindu without demanding she convert to Islam, something forbidden by my religion, so bringing disgrace on everyone."

"Ah." Nothing said '*love thy neighbor*' like xenophobic hatred. "There no way to put things right?"

"Despite being poor, my father returns the money I send, refuses to even acknowledge Aisha, and turns me away from his door without even opening it. He says I've brought such shame on the family, on Allah that he'll go to his grave with no son, no heir, nothing to say he ever existed."

"Can't your mom smooth things over?"

"He forbids her to speak to me, too. And she respects him as head of the household."

"From what you said, I thought you were still in touch."

"Letters my sister, Suhair, smuggles between us. I think my father knows, but as it's not breaking his will — not direct contact — he turns a blind eye." He stood. "Anyway, I just wanted you to know I appreciated your candor and kind words last night."

She smiled. "You're welcome. I hope one day your father comes around."

"Every day I pray to Allah that today might be that day."

He smiled, drank some water, then meandered to the restroom. Nothing unusual. Except he took the onboard flight phone.

Okay, that was the 'disgrace' mystery solved. And it went some way toward explaining why Rashid was so eager to help them — he was trying to redeem himself in the eyes of Allah. But what of the secret meetings? The secret phone calls? Questions gnawed at her like a snared coyote at its own leg. She stared at the restroom door. How she ached to press her ear to it.

Boy, she had to ignore this, or it'd eat her alive.

John caught her eye and smiled. She reciprocated. She glanced at Ben, who was watching TV, an iced Bud in one hand, a box of Oreos in his lap. She smiled again. Now, this was flying. She'd seen private jets in the movies, but never dreamed she'd ever fly in one. But, boy, was it small! Rashid had chosen a Lear 60 over a 35 because it was 'bigger'. With head room of only 5 feet, 6 inches in the very center of the aisle, she could almost stand up. How 'big' did that make the Lear 35? Not that she was complaining. How they'd suffered in coach, airport lounges, in taxis stinking of cigarettes, sweat, tacos... Now she felt more like a movie star promoting her latest blockbuster than a penniless journalist on a mercy dash.

John had protested the environmental expense of such jaunts, until Rashid pointed out that not only could they cover three or four times more hospitals per day, but it would be far less exhausting for John: flights leaving when he wanted, not to a schedule; helicopters from the airport right to the hospital, bypassing all the traffic; space for in-flight relaxation or planning, not crammed in coach with a screaming kid in the seat behind. When it was so beneficial to the greater good, how could John argue?

"John," called Ben, "your old flame's on TV?"

John ambled over, frowning.

Mary peered over. So John had known women. Pity.

A bleached blonde, belly battling a red blouse 10 years too young for her, gazed past the reporter into the camera. "Yeah, I was John's first sweetheart. He's always been kinda special." She giggled. "I taught him how to kiss."

John stared coldly. "She spat at me. Called me a gypsy 'cause my Mom couldn't afford the latest Nike."

"Oh, I remember John, sure," said an elderly, bald man. "Such a sweet kid. I remember saying to his mom, 'That there boy's gonna do you proud one day, Mrs. Connolly.' I just knew there was something special about him."

"It was January," said John. "My shoes leaked. He told us to leave his shoe store and stop wasting his time when my mom asked for credit 'til payday."

In front of a van marked 'Aldridge's Audio-Video', a guy rubbed his weasel snout of a nose and grinned. "John Connolly? Hell, yeah. I did some work for them once. Little Johnny sat watching me while I fixed his busted TV. I ruffled his hair, like you do with kids, and blow me if a migraine I'd had all day didn't just up and leave there and then. I won 50 bucks on the Lotto next day."

"When he arrived," said John, "there was $30 on the shelf. He left, it'd gone. My mom couldn't prove anything. She cried."

Ben hit the 'off' button.

Mary had learned more about John's life in the last minute than in the past four days. How could someone who'd suffered so much at the hands of others want to now devote his life to helping them? "People are like that, John. They might detest the sight of you, but they'll lie through their teeth if they think it'll get them on TV. It gives them a taste of fame. Makes them special, too."

"Yeah, John," said Ben. "World's full of self-important assholes. Don't let it get to you." He twisted to John. "But here's something that's been bugging the hell outta me: the U.S. is the richest, most powerful country in the world — why'd you wanna heal here, not somewhere like, I dunno, Ethiopia?"

"You've answered your own question."

"Excuse me?"

"Because it is the richest, most powerful country in the world. Think about it. If I healed Ethiopia, who'd care? Would you?"

"Well, er, I..."

"Sure, CNN might run a 30-second snippet," said John. "Might even get buried somewhere in the *Times*. But that'd be it. But I heal the U.S.? Not only does the world sit up and take notice, it jumps 'cause the U.S. tells it to jump. Ethiopia? Who's going to care about a bunch of peasants who couldn't even grow a potato to feed themselves yesterday discovering the secret to world peace today?"

"Whoa, whoa, whoa!" A rush of endorphins shot through Mary as if William Faulkner had risen from the grave and begged her to collaborate on one last novel. "World peace? What about world peace?"

"It's not just people who are sick," said John, "it's societies. And like tumors, societies don't heal themselves."

Mary said, "You're going global?"

"Like I said, we're all links in the same chain. Break one and... So, yes, I intend visiting other countries."

Ben rubbed his chin. "So why not take your time at the hospitals? Talk to folks. Not just the dying, but everyone. Reassure them. Tell them they're doing good, that things are gonna be just fine."

"But are they doing good, Ben? Will things be just fine? Around the globe, 60,000 people die every day simply because they don't have enough food, enough water, enough medicines, enough protection from the elements, from disasters, from violence. *60,000 every day.* Do we hear about it? Yet let just a handful of white, middle-class Americans die 'cause some screening procedure's failed and outrage is plastered all over every newsstand and TV station from the Keys to Alaska."

Ah. Talk about a doozy of an argument.

"Yeah," said Ben, "but that's not just laying your hands on a sick kid; that's governments. And they ain't gonna let you mess with them, buddy. No way."

"Ben's right, John. Famine, poverty, injustice... That's not just healing, that's changing the world."

"And all it would take to change the world and end suffering is for good people everywhere to stand up and say one simple word."

They stared at him. One word? *One* word? What single word could possibly be so powerful it could change anything, let alone the entire world?

John said that one word, 'Enough!'

People had stood up, had objected, had screamed 'enough', yet there was still racism, still the bomb, still inequality. "John, it's way, way more complicated than that," said Mary.

John smirked. "Did I say it was going to be easy?"

***

In the Hummer's passenger seat, Rashid hit 'enter' on his laptop. "Okay. I've uploaded the first video to our website. I'd appreciate feedback before we go live."

"We've got a website already?" asked Mary. Damn, if this guy wasn't a computer genius. "What's it called?"

Rashid shot furtive glances. "Ah. I, er, hope you don't mind, but I used my work-in-progress title." He spun the laptop around on top of the console between the front seats. A video showed John healing Emily Thompson in Tampa on *TheIncredibleJourney.com.*

Very apt. And the first leg couldn't have gone better — two hospitals in St. Petersburg, one in Tampa, and three in Jacksonville. Six in one day. Incredible. And it hadn't gone unnoticed by the media — the airways were alight with John's 300% leap in productivity.

Like a child taking a painting home from school, Rashid stared anxiously at John.

John nodded. "That's great."

"It's pretty basic," said Rashid, "but I think that look works. We don't want all bells and whistles. The content has to speak for itself."

John nodded again.

"Mary?" Rashid turned to Ben at the wheel. Having a passion for rally driving, Rashid had said he hated being driven but had relented in order to complete the website. "Ben, I'll take you through later."

"Bud, I don't know a podcast from a bucket of wings, so don't wait on me."

Mary played with the site. Navigation was easy. Pages uncluttered. Everything immediately accessible. "Yeah. Cool. Really."

"Great." Grinning, Rashid took the laptop back. "I've already started some buzz on blogs and RSS feeds, so if everyone's agreeable, we'll go live."

And, to a small round of applause, live they went.

What a perfect end to a perfect day. Flying to Jacksonville, Mary had harbored doubts after John's 'changing-the-world' revelations, but now she couldn't wait for tomorrow. With Rashid's resources, they could go anywhere, do anything. They were unstoppable.

***

"— so, at the register," said Ben, approaching Rashid's front door, "there's this huge, black woman — I'm talking 300 pounds of pure momma — collapsed on the floor. But she's so big, we have to help the medics get her on the gurney. So while we're heaving here and hauling there, her head scarf falls off, and underneath's a frozen chicken. True as I'm standing here. Turns out she's shoplifted the chicken, but it's so damn cold, she's passed out 'cause it's frozen her brain."

They laughed at the fallibility of people. Even John smiled.

"Ben, my friend, you sure have—" First through the door, Rashid froze at what he saw. It felt like he'd fallen from a boat into icy waters — it snatched his breath away; the shock paralyzed him; he thought his life had ended.

Near the dining-room door, two men pinned Sana and Aisha, shoving guns into their sides. Another two trained guns on Rashid and the others. One man stood in the middle, twirling a stiletto blade between his fingers as if it were a pencil. Rashid gawked, eyes wide as saucers. Surely Allah hadn't just given him back his daughter to now snatch her from him along with his wife?

Tongue lolled out, Mutt lay in a pool of blood on the marble floor at the foot of the staircase. He'd obviously tried to protect his new pack, the only pack ever to care for him, and paid the price.

Mary gasped. She barely muttered, "Oh, God."

Guns or no guns, Rashid had to save his family. He lunged.

But Ben grabbed him. "Easy, buddy. Let's not do anything stupid."

Rashid struggled, but was held fast. "What do you want?" he shouted, his breath panted gasps. What kind of monster held a gun to a little girl?

Crying, Aisha reached for Rashid. Her voice squeaked, "Daddy."

Sana reached for her, but was yanked back. Black streaks gaped from Sana's eyes, her tears having run her makeup.

"Harm them, and I'll kill you!" Rashid's words spat venom, but his eyes were wide with fear.

With chiseled good looks and an athletic build draped in Versace, the man with the blade laughed, dragging on a Marlboro.

A shaven-headed thug waggled his pistol at Ben. Ben showed he was unarmed by opening his jacket.

"What do you want?" asked John, his demeanor both submissive, yet indomitable, like a becalmed sea.

The man stopped twirling his blade. He took one last drag on his cigarette, then flicked it at John.

It bounced off John's chest. John didn't flinch.

The man smiled. A scar that ran from his left eyebrow to just above his jaw twisted the smile into a sneer. His gaze crawled across them: one brown eye; one clouded white, like the scar. "My boss, Mr. Panucci, has some business for you. Thomaso Panucci, Mr. Panucci's brother, took a bullet two years ago. He ain't walked since. Mr. Panucci expects that to change tonight."

"Sorry," said Ben. "We don't do house calls, Vinnie."

"Oh, I think you'll make an exception on this occasion, Detective."

One of the thugs shoved Sana down. She cried out. He rammed the muzzle of his Beretta against her head.

Aisha shrieked, "Mommy!"

"No!" cried Rashid. He struggled frantically to break free from Ben. He'd kill these monsters. Kill them.

John clutched Rashid's shoulder. "Don't worry."

Oh, Allah be praised, John had a plan to save them.

John stepped forward. Mary tugged his arm, but he patted her hand reassuringly.

He strode across the floor. Stared at Vinnie. Then turned for the stairs.

Vinnie raised his voice, "Hey, asshole!"

"Wh—" Rashid gawked. Why was John abandoning them? Why wasn't he saving his family? Rashid felt he was drowning, his life ebbing away into icy blackness.

As if lifting a bowl brimming with liquid gold and not wanting to spill one precious drop, John cradled Mutt and carried the barely breathing dog for the living room.

"Asshole!" shouted Vinnie. "Turn your back on me, you'll find a bullet in it."

"John, please," said Rashid. Why was John risking his wife and child for a dying dog?

John at the living-room door, Vinnie nodded at one of his thugs.

A shot fired, cracking like a bullwhip right in Rashid's ear.

Aisha and Sana screamed. Mary jumped, then grabbed Ben's arm.

A slug blasted into the doorjamb inches from John's head. John didn't flinch. He disappeared inside.

Mouth agape, Vinnie stared.

John emerged momentarily and closed the door. From inside the room, barking erupted as vicious as that of a wolf pack's alpha male on being challenged.

"Please, John." Rashid prayed John would rein in his eccentricities and save his family.

Vinnie puzzled at the sudden lively barking, but then sneered. "You obviously have little respect for life." He stabbed his blade toward John. "Any more games, it won't just be a dog's blood you're mopping up."

John marched over. "If you intended to kill the women for pleasure, you'd have done so. If you intended to kill them as a show of strength, you'd have done so. But they're bargaining chips. Killing them, or any of us, diminishes your bargaining power. That wouldn't be clever."

An anxious doubt fell over Vinnie's cocky demeanor as he glowered at John. Then the sneer returned. He caressed Aisha's cheek with his glistening blade. A dark patch drenched the crotch of Aisha's pyjamas. Her face twisted into a grotesque picture of fear, like a wax sculpture left too close to a fire.

Tears streamed down Rashid's face. His family was going to die before his eyes, yet restrained by Ben, he was so helpless. Useless. Impotent. "No! Please. Please, don't hurt her. Please."

Vinnie snickered mockingly at Rashid, but his smile faded to wariness when he turned to John. "Mr. Panucci doesn't like to be kept waiting."

"Mr. Panucci will have to get used to it," said John.

Vinnie sliced Aisha's cheek.

She screamed. Such a piercing shriek it hurt Rashid's ears. He bawled, "No!"

Mary ran to save Aisha.

Ben grabbed her by the wrist. Yanked her back.

Ben now only holding him by one hand, Rashid broke free. Flew at Vinnie. He'd kill him. Kill him!

But John caught him. "No!"

Rashid screamed. "You're dead!" He clawed at Vinnie, but couldn't reach. "Dead!"

Vinnie leered.

Ben grabbed Rashid, freeing John.

John marched up to Vinnie, so close he must've felt his breath.

"John, please," called Mary, crying.

John glowered into Vinnie's eyes, as if searching for something. Humanity? A soul? The Devil?

Vinnie held his stare, then frowned and looked away. He shuffled back.

John crouched before Aisha. Instantly, the only sign of injury was the blood on the white marble floor.

The thug pinning Aisha released her and crossed himself. She ran to Rashid. He dropped to his knees. Hugged her. Sobbed. Gripped her like a tornado threatened to snatch her away.

John glared at the thug holding Sana.

132

Perspiration glistening on his shaven head, the thug sneered. He clicked back his Beretta's hammer. But Vinnie gestured for him to release Sana. She too ran to Rashid.

As coolly as wiping up spilled water, John mopped the blood off the floor with his handkerchief.

Vinnie towered over him. "Mr. Panucci told me to play nice, but only if you did, too."

As John eased up, he swept a hand over Vinnie's face.

"*Arghhh!*" Vinnie staggered away, clutching his head. His men spun, guns trained on John.

Mary screamed, "No!"

Ben sprang at the nearest thug, but the man pistol-whipped him over the head. Ben crashed to the floor.

Rashid leapt up. Guns turned on him.

"Wait!" shouted Vinnie. Straightening up, he felt his face, checking for what was wrong. He shook his head as if to clear it.

He whipped a semi-automatic Glock 18 from inside his jacket. Rammed it against John's forehead. "I don't know what you've done to me, but if you've got a God, now would be a good time to make your peace with him." He glowered. With two brown eyes and no scar.

15

Open Wounds

Mary glanced at the clock on Rashid's mantel again: 12:34 a.m.. Where the hell was John? He had given his word to help Panucci if Vinnie forsook taking hostages, but it had been a lifetime since he'd left. What if they hurt him? What if he needed her? She should've insisted on going, despite his objections.

"*Ffffff!*" Ben sucked through his teeth.

"Oops. Sorry." She winced at the thought of someone carelessly pawing a wound she had. Kneeling on one of two cream sofas bigger than her bed, she dipped a swab in disinfectant and gently dabbed the sliver of bloody flesh in Ben's scalp. She'd already dressed it once, but it wouldn't stop bleeding. "This really needs stitches."

"No point trailing to ER — John'll be back soon."

Would he? What if he never came back? Oh, this not knowing was hell. The anguish; the crushed hopes; the 'what if' dilemmas... It was like pacing a doctor's waiting room awaiting the results of your scan — like Schrödinger's cat, in the same moment your life was both all before you and totally ended. Limbo. Torturous, never-ending limbo.

She looked at the clock again. "Damn it." Still 12:34.

Mutt whined and paced in a circle, then gazed at the door. Mary knew just how the poor dog felt. When Rashid came back in, she'd ask for some music as a distraction. Her gaze drifted to the two-foot-high

134

portrait of a woman over the fireplace. It was so simplistic it looked as if a child had drawn it in one movement without taking the pen off the paper. While it was great that Rashid loved Aisha so much, the picture was totally out of place amidst such sumptuous furnishings. "Rashid run out of refrigerator magnets?"

So as not to turn his head, Ben glanced at it from the corner of his eye. "How the other half live, huh?"

"Hmm?"

"Picasso."

"That's a Picasso?"

Ben laughed. "What? You thought Aisha drew it?"

"Boy." She gazed at it. Rashid was rich, but she'd never imagined seeing a Picasso anywhere except a gallery.

"You know," said Ben, "much as I despise the Vinnie Constanzas of the world, I wish there were more like him."

Mary pulled back. "What!? You want the streets crawling with animals who'll carve up kids to get what they want?"

"See, when I joined the Department, most of the criminals were like Vinnie. Oh, I don't mean Mafia goons, but thieves, rapists, killers. It was us and them. Now? More and more, it's all internet fraud, identity theft, pedophiles in kids' chatrooms... Used to be the bad guys had faces. Nowadays, so many aren't even present at the crime scene, but sitting at computers hundreds, even thousands of miles away. How do you protect people from that?"

"So you'd prefer them all to wear masks and carry bags marked 'swag'?"

He looked her in the eye. "You know what I mean, or am I just too damn old?"

"I know." She rubbed his shoulder.

Rashid trudged in.

"She okay?" asked Mary.

"She's stopped crying. Sana's sleeping with her tonight. And I've made arrangements for armed patrols with dogs to start tomorrow." He stabbed a poker into the log fire. It crackled and sparked. "Hell! Why didn't I think of that sooner?"

"Don't beat yourself up, buddy," said Ben. "I'm supposed to be the security expert."

"Hey," said Mary, "no one's to blame. If we'd had guards, the only difference would be the bodies littering the place. Now, let's just pray John's okay and put it behind us."

A door slammed.

Mutt's ears pricked.

Mary prayed. Let it be John. Let it be John. Let it be— "John!"

"Well, it's too late for Santa." He strolled in with a cheeky smile.

Mary dashed over. Flung her arms around him. Sobbed into his shoulder.

Tail wagging, Mutt jumped up. John ruffled his neck.

Rashid slapped John's back. "Can't tell you how relieved I am, my friend."

Ben winked at John. "Told you he'd be okay." He shook John's hand.

"I was so worried," said Mary.

John pulled back and brushed away her tears. "I'm sorry I put you through this." He looked up. "All of you."

"Don't you apologize." She let him guide her to the sofa. "It was those animals. They want damn hanging."

"You should've let us call the authorities," said Rashid.

Warming his hands, John crouched before the fire. Mutt nuzzled him. John raked the white flash on the dog's chest. "Mr. Panucci was actually quite upset. Said his men acted beyond their remit."

"Oh, yeah," said Ben, "a real diamond, Panucci. Only last month, he donated Paolo Zanetti's body to medical science. Course, Paolo hadn't exactly finished with it. And like we could prove anything."

"For Sana's and Aisha's sakes," said Rashid, "I'm glad you did, but why help those men so willingly?"

"If someone's sick, why shouldn't I heal him?"

"Because they're violent, damn animals, John," said Mary.

John said, "Sometimes, in a brutal world, the most vicious animal can be your greatest ally."

Ben heaved a breath. "Buddy, you get into bed with these people, you can't just up and walk away. They got you for life."

"There's a saying," said John, "I'm sure you're all familiar with it: 'Let he who is without sin cast the first stone.'... If I only heal the worthy, who will I heal?" He looked at Mary. "Will you judge who deserves to die?"

136

Mary gaped. Who could ever answer such a question?

John's gaze roamed to Ben, then Rashid. "Hmm?"

Silence.

John peered over at a shadow lurking in the doorway. "You?"

They followed his gaze.

Mary gasped. Holy Mother of God, no. Please, no!

Ben leapt up. Fists clenched.

Mutt snarled.

Rashid grabbed the poker.

"Rashid," said John.

Rashid stormed for the door, poker raised.

Mary backed away. Heart hammering. Gripped John's arm. No, no, no. Please, not again!

Rashid swung the poker back to strike.

John shouted, "Rashid!"

Rashid pulled up. Glared at the shadow. "Get the hell out of my house, or in the name of Allah—"

"I invited him," said John.

Rashid turned, face contorted as if John had thrust a knife into his back. "What!?"

Mary gasped in horror. "John, tell me you didn't."

Ben slumped to the sofa, head shaking in his hands.

John said, "Mr. Panucci asked what I wanted for healing his brother."

Stabbing the poker at the shadow, Rashid glowered. "And you wanted him?"

John beckoned. "Please."

Vinnie strolled in.

Breath.snorting, Rashid glowered at Vinnie, the poker trembling with the effort of not unleashing his fury.

Ben dragged his hands down his face. "John. John. John." He sighed. "Big, big mistake."

"For once we agree on something, Cale," said Vinnie.

Ben sniggered. "If John wasn't here, Vinnie..."

"The name," Vinnie glared at each of them, "is Vincent. Not Vin. Not Vinnie. Not Vince. Vincent. You'd do well to remember that."

"Or what?" Ben lurched up.

Vincent lunged.

Mary cowered. She envisioned blood. So much blood. No. Not again. Please!

But Mutt gnashed at Vincent. He jerked back. Scowled.

Stepping between them, John eased Ben back down and held Vincent at bay. "You know the deal. Or should I tell Mr. Panucci you couldn't even last a minute, let alone a month?"

Mary pointed at Vincent. He had Mediterranean good looks and an athletic physique, but all she saw was ugliness. "You want us to put up with that for a month?"

"Hey, I'm as ecstatic as you," said Vincent.

Rashid paced. "I'm sorry, John. This is too much. He breaks into my house. Threatens my wife. Cuts my daughter. And you expect me to welcome him? Why, John? Give me one good reason."

"Because I ask."

Rashid waved his hand, face dark with outrage. "Some things are beyond favors, my friend."

Sighing, John slumped to the sofa. "Before you hired the helicopter, did you check the weather forecast?"

Rashid frowned. "I'm sorry?"

"Did you check the forecast?"

"What's that—"

"Was it right?"

"To a degree. But—"

"A degree?"

"Well, no. It rained."

John nodded. "But coming home, you still checked tomorrow's forecast."

"So?"

"So, it's a sad world where people have more faith in a bad weather-caster, doing the job purely for the money, than in someone who heals the sick, without any thought for recompense."

"That's out of order, John." Rashid stabbed the poker. "You *know* what I'm doing for you."

"And is this so much more?"

Rashid shouted, "He cut my daughter, John. My daughter."

Mary squeezed John's arm. "John, it's not fair to ask Rashid this."

John paused, as if considering their arguments. Finally he said, "At the risk of repeating myself, did I say it was going to be easy?"

Rashid glared. "Then let me simplify things — either he leaves this instant, or come morning, you all do."

Rashid had proven invaluable to their work. It would be logistical suicide without him. Fighting the hordes of paparazzi, fans, protestors, and, not least, fighting bankruptcy — it would be impossible to continue. "Please, John," said Mary, "think of what we'll be losing." She glared at Vincent. "He's not worth it."

John looked at each of them. When he looked at her, she shuddered. It felt like the disappointed glare of a proud father finally seeing the fallen ways of his once beloved child. "Then *who* should I heal, if not the sick?"

Rashid stared resolutely. "I'm sorry you feel that way, my friend."

***

"Goodnight, Ben," said Mary.

Cale exited the living room. Rashid had turned in already, after showing Vincent to the pool room, locking the connecting door, and activating the main house's security system. He'd also booked them all cabs for 9:00 a.m.. It was over!

From the sofa, Mary watched John sitting before the fire's dying embers, lost in the crackling flames. The dream was dead. There was nothing more that could be done. Well, maybe one thing. In the grand scheme, it wasn't much, but it was a start. She slouched over and sank to join John on the floor. The fire enveloped her in its passion like a lover's embrace on a chill night. "I'm sorry."

Orange light bathed his face in shadows.

"I didn't see what you were getting at." She still wasn't sure she understood. Was this something to do with changing the world? Was Vincent a guinea pig? Did John believe if he could alter Vincent's worldview, he could alter anyone's?

John didn't reply. Was he so disillusioned by their lack of faith?

Mary glanced away. The flames licked enormous shadows across the room. John had such clarity, such vision, such charity — it was mind-blowing. But abnormal. If only she could convince him their reactions to Vincent shouldn't be condemned, but seen as normal responses from normal people. Flawed people. But normal people were flawed.

She took his hand. She ached to say the right thing, to do the right thing. "John, we all wish we could see things as clearly as you, but sometimes it's—"

"I'm sorry."

"Oh." She laughed. "I had a whole speech thing going, there."

"It's going to be so, so difficult now, without Rashid."

"Hey, you've still got me and Ben," she added disparagingly, "and Vincent."

He gazed at her, tears in his eyes. "Thank you."

"Hey, we'll be okay." She'd no idea how — her plastic would last little more than a day with four of them jetting the length and breadth of the country every few hours.

He squeezed her hand. "Like I said, I couldn't have done any of this without you, but ... sometimes ... when I see something's so right, I forget about the implications for everyone else and mess up."

"John, with everything you've done, no one could ever say you've messed up."

He stared into the fire. "I just wish ... I could be more normal."

"Hey," she cupped his cheek, turned his face toward her, "don't ever change, John Connolly. You're the most incredible man I've ever met, and I don't mean just the healing thing, I mean you. Now, promise me, don't ever wish to be less than you are." She gazed into his eyes, his blue, blue eyes.

16

Whispers in the Dark

His thoughts as engulfed in shadows as his bedroom, Rashid lay, eyes wide open. Hour after hour after hour.

What if he continued helping John? Which meant accepting Vincent! When the Day of Judgment came — when the seas burned, the sky peeled away, the mountains were pounded into dust — when all were judged on their good deeds and their sins, where would Rashid find himself? Tasting the rivers of wine in Paradise? Or tasting the torment of the Fire in Hell?

In Allah's eyes, allying oneself with a wrongdoer made one no better than they. Despite his good deeds, Rashid would suffer the same fate as Vincent — an eternity in the Fire.

But the Qur'an taught love, charity, tolerance. Allah repaid good deeds tenfold and took the worthy into Paradise. Could Rashid's charity, his helping John, outweigh the sins of accepting Vincent?

Rashid heaved a sigh.

Islam condemned violence. Condemned people who employed evil for their own ends. If John chose to associate with such men, the right thing was to abandon him.

But what of forgiveness? Was that a teaching to be ignored at one's whim?

He heaved another sigh.

Forgiveness? If he had his way, he'd have retribution for the pain his family had suffered, as the Qur'an allowed. Forgive? No. He'd already lost his mother and father; he couldn't risk losing his wife and daughter, too. This was over.

He plumped his duck-feather pillow, then nestled into it, his path finally clear to him. Yes, he'd made the right decision. He was doing the right thing.

His mind at ease, he drifted into sleep.

***

Rashid's phone rang.

17

The Spark

Rashid knocked, then entered the darkened bedroom. "Good morning, John. L2." Dimmed lights raised as he marched for the window. After yesterday's troubles, he'd left it as late as possible to wake everyone. Most people weren't early risers, but that wasted so much of the day. As the seasons changed, if the sunrise wasn't too early, he'd often stay up after his daily pre-dawn prayers and squeeze in an extra few hours of work. It was one contributing factor to his success — all those extra hours gained him an edge over so many would-be entrepreneurs. "It's late. We're going to have to hustle to shoehorn in Cleveland, Detroit, *and* Columbus, my friend." He ripped open the drapes. "Breakfast in 15 minutes." He turned.

Mortified, John stared from his bed. As did Mary, her sheepish smile poking over the covers pulled up to her chin.

"Ah." Rashid marched for the door. "So, maybe make that 30 minutes." He smiled and left.

***

"Hey!" Mary shouted. She was embarrassed but way more curious.

Rashid poked his head back in.

"What's going on?"

"We're going to Ohio, aren't we?" said Rashid.

"Er, Vincent — the whole *he goes or we go; it's all over* thing?"

Rashid grinned. "We made the midday news in Oman."

"And?" Surely they'd made the news all over the world. Why did—Mary gasped. She bolted up, holding the sheet against herself for modesty. "Your father saw it. Did he call?"

Tears sparkling in his eyes, Rashid beamed. "Allah be praised."

"Oh, Rashid, that's fantastic."

He bowed his head, then ducked out.

"Oh, I'm so pleased for him." Rashid had regained his family by redeeming himself in the eyes of Allah and was obviously eager not to undo the good he'd done. They were unstoppable again!

She smiled. "And that'll save us having to spill the beans." The turn in hers and John's relationship could've been awkward to broach over breakfast. She rolled over to John. Giggled. "Do you think he wears a suit to bed?" Rashid was always impeccably dressed, but always formal.

Silence. John's stare was nailed to the ceiling.

Oh, hell. That was never good when you'd just slept with someone for the first time. Maybe if she beat a hasty retreat, they could pretend it had never happened. Yeah, right. Damn, had she screwed up this time? She rolled out of bed. "I'll, er..." What? Give you a call sometime? Oh, hell, she'd ruined everything.

"I'm sorry," said John.

"Hey—" her breasts bounced as she hunted for where her clothes had landed, "— shit happens." Damn it. She knew she should have distanced herself. She knew it! She bit her lip, determined to hold in those tears.

"No, it was wrong."

Tears? This had just gone way beyond tears! "Excuse me? *Wrong?* Am I unclean or something? Not worthy to touch the miraculous John Connolly?"

"No," he pushed up, "I mean it was wrong to take advantage of you like that."

She laughed. "What!? *You* take advantage of *me?* Baby, a gorilla gorged on Viagra couldn't have abused you more than I did last night." She jumped back on the bed. "You're not very good at this, are you?"

He shrugged.

She brushed his hair. "You never date in high school?"

"School wasn't good for me. Everyone thought I was strange."

"Awww... I'd have been nice to you."

"And have your friends turn on you? No."

Hmmm. Peer pressure could make monsters out of the best of people. She'd seen kids ostracized at school — had she helped them? "Was it so bad?"

John stared at the ceiling and sang the way girls do while jumping rope:

"Johnny Connolly — he's got warts,
Johnny Connolly — pees his shorts.
Johnny Connolly — so poor he cries,
Johnny Connolly — let's hope he dies."

And John wanted to help people, not climb on a mall roof with a sniper rifle? "Jeez, they sound proper little darlings."

"They didn't know any better."

"Oh, that's what they say when some kid unloads a .38 into his classmates. Believe me, they know. That why you dropped out, to get away from people?"

He shook his head. "'Cause I couldn't help people."

"With what you got? How could you not help?"

John stared at the ceiling, brow furrowed, as if making a tough decision. Finally, he said, "The day after my fifteenth birthday, I found a pigeon on the roadside — blood and guts everywhere. The poor little thing was terrified when I went near it, but it was almost dead, so couldn't escape. I bundled it in an old newspaper and carried it to a bush, so it could die peacefully, in the shadows, away from cars and kids prodding sticks. No sooner had I put it down than it flew off into the trees — no blood, no injury, nothing." He sniggered. "Boy, was I freaked. But once I'd got over the shock, realized the power I had, I thought I was going to change the world." He smiled. "Oh, the dreams I had."

"So what went wrong?"

"Adrian McCarthy."

"Who?"

"The only kid in school less popular than me."

"So?"

"So I didn't help him."

"Hey, don't beat yourself up. Probably made the kid bulletproof." She ran her fingers through his hair. He was just as frail as she was in some ways, yet in others, he was the strongest person she'd ever met.

"He's probably CEO of some pharmaceuticals giant and gets his kicks rubbing it in people's faces on classmates.com."

"If only."

"I bet you. Those kids always bounce back."

"He hanged himself in the gym, one Wednesday afternoon."

"Ah." Damn her big mouth.

"That's when I realized I couldn't help people."

"But look at what you're doing now. Look at all the lives you've saved... I mean, it's not like you gave him the rope."

"But I didn't help him. And I could have. And that's the problem: we're all little Adrian McCarthys, all Johnny Connollys. We've all got gifts and fears, dreams and needs. And that's what we play on. Whether it's bragging about a new car, being an ogre at work, giving a store clerk a hard time, why is it that so often we can only feel better about ourselves by making someone else feel worse? I needed a friend. Adrian needed a friend. Together, we could've made each other's lives infinitely better. Yet I just saw someone weak, someone in need, someone slowly dying, and chose to look the other way. And that's the world we live in."

She ached to be supportive. But it was true: evolution, democracy, nature, business... only the strongest survived. That was as may be, but true strength embraced compassion, charity, cooperation. And change needed uncompromising heroes, stubborn visionaries who possessed that inner strength. History was littered with them: Lennon with his bed protest against war; Dr. King and his 'I have a dream' for racial harmony; JFK's 'Ich bin ein Berliner' stand for freedom. Could John be such a catalyst?

She snuggled on his chest, hoping the comfort of togetherness would ease his troubles. "It'll come good. You'll see."

"Will it? The law *and* religion are there to protect us. But they don't, 'cause people don't respect them. The law says it's wrong to kill. So do Christianity, Islam, Buddhism, Hinduism, all the faiths. Yet people still kill. Why? Because they can't see themselves in someone else. To most people, the world's populated by objects, with them at the center, the only real person."

"Yeah, but it's not as if you can get inside someone else's head to know how like you they are."

"What do you hear?"

146

She puzzled. "What do I hear?"

"Uh-huh."

"Birds... A plane in the distance ... er—"

"Closer."

"Ben's radio."

"Closer."

"Er... My breathing. Your breathing." She smiled. "Your heart."

He stroked her hair. "When you see a man in the street, you don't see him as a person, just as 'a guy': no history, no future, not even a present. Might as well be a mailbox. But when you hear someone's heartbeat, feel the softness of their skin, the warmth of their breath, suddenly that mailbox vanishes and there's a real person. Someone complex, alive, unfathomable, just like you. Once you see someone just like you, even if you don't see them for another 50 years, they can never ever be a mailbox again."

"But you can't listen to everyone's heartbeat."

"Why do you have to? Listening to just one tells you that *you aren't* the center of the universe. It's as if someone's lifted a blindfold: you see the world's full of people. Wondrous people, just like you."

And once you saw people just like yourself, you'd understand the pain they'd feel if you hurt them would be just like that if they hurt you. Pure empathy. Brilliant. "And you think the world's ready to take off its blindfold."

"No."

"No? So why are we trying?"

"Because if we don't, who ever will?"

John could heal, was a philosopher, had such tremendous humanity... A question had niggled her for what felt like a lifetime. A question she'd felt too ridiculous to ask. But the longer she spent with John, the more it seemed the only question that mattered. She pushed away to look him in the face. The moment she did, she felt stupid.

"What?" he asked.

Unable to look at him, she twisted the white sheet with her fingers. "It's... No." She laid back down. "It's stupid."

"What?"

Curiosity gnawed. She pushed up again. "Well..." she sighed, "it's the things you do, things you say... It's like... I don't know... Like you're the Second Coming or something." She glanced up, half hoping to see him laugh. He didn't.

He stared at her. She twisted the sheet again. Finally, he said, "Do you believe in what I'm doing?"

"You have to ask?"

He arched his eyebrows.

"Totally."

"But you still feel the need for that question?"

She shrugged.

"So if I say no, will you stop believing in me?"

"Course not!"

"It won't shake your belief at all?"

"Hell no! I'm with you 100%. Nothing could ever change that."

He nodded, staring down. He finally looked up. "So, if you believe so strongly, what could possibly be gained by me answering?"

***

C++, HTML, Tommi Makinen, Monaco, NASCAR... the bookcase in Rashid's study groaned with his favorite topics: computing and racing.

Mary handed him the disk onto which she'd burned her story. He put it in his safe. She wasn't paranoid, but in a world of hackers, viruses, and thieves, it was prudent to keep a backup.

Mary couldn't stop puzzling over John's answer. Dreamily, she trailed a hand over a battered, leather-bound book on Rashid's desk.

"The Qur'an," he said. "Have you read it?"

She hadn't read the Christian Bible for 24 years — why would she read Islam's? She smiled. "Not recently."

"Just as well. You can't say you have unless it was in the original Arabic."

"Oh." She'd knock that off her 'to do' list then.

"If you don't mind me saying, you don't seem overly religious, Mary."

She laughed. "Not *overly*, no. What gives it away?"

He pointed. "So why the crucifix?"

Her smiled dropped.

"I'm sorry. One's religion is—"

"No. No, it's okay. It's just kind of a long story."

Rashid sat on the edge of his desk, waiting.

148

Ah. She'd thought that a conversation stopper, not starter. Still, he'd shared his family problems with her; perhaps sharing would bring them closer, and who knows what he might divulge in return.

"A gift from my dad."

"Ah. You said you'd lost touch."

"Yeah, for years. And it was all my fault."

"Surely not."

"Oh, believe me, it was. I made his life hell for walking out on us."

"Another woman?"

"Oh, no. That would probably have made it easier to handle." She paused. "See, he hated religion, but loved my mom — unfortunately, a devout Catholic. He doted on me and my sisters, but let Mom have her way and take us to church every week. 24 years ago, January 22, was to be my confirmation — a very big day for a little Catholic girl. Unfortunately, January 21, I was diagnosed with diabetes."

"I didn't know you were diabetic." He slapped his forehead. "John."

She nodded. "Anyway, being told you've got to stick needles in yourself every day for the rest of your life is traumatic as hell to an eight-year-old. I mean, needles? Every day? Come on! What kind of God does that to an innocent little girl he's supposed to love? So, next day, at the church door, I refused to go in. Screamed the place down about what a monster God was. Mom was horrified and tried to haul me in, but my dad hauled me out. Said if I was old enough to question God, I was old enough to choose to worship him or not. Mom went ape. That morning we were a loving family; by lunch, we were halfway to being just another divorce statistic."

"He left you there and then?"

"No, but that's when the problems started. But they hid it, so when it finally came, all I saw was my dad simply abandoning us. So at every possible opportunity I made his life absolute hell. For years. He moved to Tulsa in the end — I suppose it was too tough being so close to us yet so far away."

Rashid nodded.

"Anyway, he started a new family, left us behind."

"I'm sorry."

She shrugged.

"And your crucifix?"

She toyed with it. "He knew how much my confirmation meant to me, so gave it to me that morning. The last thing he ever gave me while we were a proper family. Course I threw it right back at him later, along with everything else I could find he'd given me."

"And you blamed God."

"After all the crap I'd been force-fed about love and goodness? Damn right. He couldn't tell me why He'd given a little kid an incurable disease, then taken her dad away, so I thought, 'Screw Him.'."

Rashid shook his head and blew out a breath.

"Wasn't 'til college my dad and I got our relationship back on track. And the damnedest thing was, he'd kept this," she wiggled her crucifix, "hoping one day he could give it to me again."

Rashid laid a hand on her shoulder. "I'm pleased things worked out."

Mary smiled. "So, hey, your dad, too, huh?"

He beamed. "Because of the good we're doing with John, he said if Allah had seen fit not to turn his back on me, he had no right to, either."

She patted his arm. "I'm thrilled for you, Rashid. Really."

He bowed his head in thanks, then saw her frown. "But?"

"Hm? Oh, nothing."

"No, go on."

"Well ... you ... helping John."

"Ah, you mean, why am I, a Muslim, helping a Christian perform miracles?"

"Uh-huh."

He smiled. "Mohammad, peace be upon him, said if we see a wrong, we should move Heaven and Earth to right it. If we can't, we should speak out against it. And if we can't even do that, we should hate it with all our heart." He sighed. "For so long now, I've dreamed of redeeming myself after bringing such shame on Allah. Well ... now, I think I know how. And I think if I don't do everything in my power to ensure John succeeds, it'll be an even greater crime against Allah."

She smiled a twisted smile.

"You don't agree?"

"No, go for it. It's, er, just ... well ... I never figured it was all down to Allah."

150

"You don't know anything about Islam?"

"Not a thing."

"So you've never heard of Noah, Moses, Jesus?"

She sniggered. "Yeah — they're main characters in the Bible."

"Really?" He smiled again. "I know a billion Muslims who'll swear they're main characters in the Qur'an. See, we're not so different, after all." Rashid shrugged. "Allah, God, Ganesh... When all the gods are safely tucked away in bed at night and we're all alone in the dark, don't we all pray for the same things — to be healthy, safe, loved?"

"That's something John would say," said Mary.

"That's something John did say. And that's why he'll achieve great things if..."

"If?"

"Forget it. Too many years in the cynical business world."

"Rashid?"

"Well, peace and goodwill to all. Do you really think everyone's going to be as enlightened as we are?"

Mary had been so entranced by John, she hadn't considered others might not be. Apart from a minority of protestors, the Secret Angel had received nothing but praise. Yes, John would upset fundamentalists. But normal people would see the wonders he performed for the sick, hear the wonders he revealed of life. Surely? Yes, but did the opinion of 'normal' people matter? What would become of politicians if there were no more arguments? Armies if there were no more wars? Corporations if there was no more greed? Take away fear, need, and greed, you've pretty much got a utopia. But would the power-crazed, the hate-mongers, the empire-builders stand for a utopia? Oh, hell!

***

"Bin Laden?" said Cale.

"Yes," said John.

Staring out of the Lear's window, Vincent sipped his scotch, the ice clinking on the glass. He hadn't bargained on there being in-flight entertainment — a comedy double act. Hilarious. He picked up his paper napkin and, barely looking, resumed folding it.

"Okay," said Ben, "it's 1939 and Hitler's got cancer. You couldn't heal him."

"Why not?"

"The man gassed 6,000,000 people!"

"And?"

"And!? John, come on, man!"

"So, even though I could heal him, I shouldn't, just because I disagree with his politics?"

"Politics? We're not talking an extra cent on tax here, buddy. Gassing 6,000,000 innocent people is not politics."

"If you fight evil with evil, haven't you already lost?"

"Hitler, John, Hitler. Biggest monster in history."

"If I could know a man, see into his heart, and *really* know his future was as black as his past, could I heal him? Is that the question? Or is the question this: could a man so healed ever see the world so black again?"

"But Hitler?"

"Around the U.S. there are over 3,000 inmates on death row, yet if a single one of them gets sick, what happens?"

"That's different."

"Why? Because it's acceptable to shock 2,000 volts through a guy's skull and fry his brain, but it's obscene to withhold painkillers and leave him suffering a migraine?"

"Those guys didn't gas 6,000,000."

"So is it morality we're arguing over, or math?"

"Come again?"

"At what point do you qualify as a monster? Six million? Six thousand? Six?... Was Hitler a monster after his second victim? His third? His 4,028th?"

"John, the man was evil. Ain't no getting away from it."

"A man's only the sum of his two parts: what he's done and what he'll do. Unfortunately, you can no sooner predict his future than you can change his past. You might as well try to blow out the sun."

Vincent set down an exquisite origami rose. He smirked. The Secret Angel was a bleeding-heart, psycho-babbling pussy. Big surprise. Anyone who pulled off what he did and wasn't king of his own Caribbean island just had no handle on the world.

He saw Mary eyeing his rose. He scrunched it.

He glanced at Rashid hammering at his laptop — a man who probably did own his own island. So why wasn't he enjoying it, instead of wasting his time here? Mary? Hot, yes. But weird. Supposedly John's woman. Supposedly a writer. So after an hour, why was her page still blank while she stared at Rashid? And fat cop Cale? Man, what a bunch of losers. He reclined his seat, cradling his drink. A month of this? A vacation.

"Sorry, John." Cale stood. "We're gonna have to agree to disagree on this one." He knocked Vincent's arm, spilling scotch all over him.

Vincent jerked. "Oh, for Christ's sake!"

"Hey, sorry there, V-man. Turbulence." Cale winked at Mary, then gestured to Vincent. "Refill?"

Vincent sneered. Mr. Panucci had been very clear on how he should behave while John's 'guest'. "One month, Cale. Just a month."

Cale grinned. "That's a whole heap of days. You want I should count them off for you?"

Vincent glared, unblinking.

Cale meandered off to the galley.

One night the fat cop would waltz down a street and feel a sudden stabbing pain in his back. Vincent would watch him grin then. Not that he was some sicko who got his rocks off on pain and gore — it was just part of the job — but sometimes work and pleasure coincided. Not that society valued his craft. Why? If a supermodel could use her talents to get what she wanted, why couldn't he use his God-given gift? And it was a gift. He'd discovered he had a flair for violence when big Tommy Greenhalgh had bullied him in sixth grade. One kick and Tommy's knee busted like a toothpick. But the gift hadn't come easy. It'd taken years of hard graft and sacrifice to develop, to work his way up to where it could do the most good. But it was worth it. Thanks to spirit and enterprise — what made America great — he was a self-made man at the peak of his profession. He could hold his head high in any company.

John crouched beside him. "Ben *is* a good man."

Vincent snorted. "Like you'd know."

"I know. So if anything was to happen to him, I'd be upset. Probably so upset I'd mention it to Mr. Panucci. And he's so appreciative of my help, he'd probably be upset, too."

Maybe true. Maybe not. Mr. Panucci was indebted to John, so even though he was big on respect, would he appreciate Vincent's retribution as a matter of honor? "So I'm just supposed to sit here and be everyone's whipping boy?"

"You're my guest. You'll be treated as such."

Vincent nodded. "You muzzle your pet and I won't lay poison."

John turned. Vincent caught his arm. "You ever want the lowdown on your 'good man' there..."

John left.

Pouring orange juice, Cale looked up. "Want some?"

John shook his head. "I know this goes against the grain, but for the next month, Vincent's a member of the team — I'd like you to cut him some slack."

Ben heaved a sigh. "Like I said, John, big mistake. If you'd—"

John laid a hand on his arm. "But it's my mistake, Ben. So let me take responsibility. Hmm?"

"You know the problem with responsibility?" said Cale. "It usually ups and bites you on the ass."

18

Quicker than the Eye

From the ward's doorway, Vincent gawked at the vacated beds in Cleveland's ICU. He stared at an old man who'd been hooked up to a ventilator and who was now snorting great lungfuls of fresh air at the window, like a wine connoisseur savoring a particularly aromatic Riesling. Yes, he'd seen Thomaso Panucci walk, but his problem could've been all in his head: Thomaso believed it would take a miracle and so had given up trying – along comes Mr. Miracle and hey, presto... He'd seen the dog healed. Rashid's kid. Then there was the healing of his own face. And what was it with his cigarettes? Every last one tasted like burned skunk! And *all* these people, *all* with different illnesses, *all* healed? And the doctors *all* clueless. One even weeping. Another shooting video on his cell phone.

But ... this was impossible. Yes, but it was happening right before his eyes, so maybe... No. No, no, no. It was impossible. He shut his right eye and peered through his 'healed' left. He saw. Normally. Shit! No... Impossible. It had to be mass hypnosis or something. It was a scam. Had to be. There was no God, no miracles, no celestial 'big picture'. You were on your own in this world. If you didn't look out for yourself, you'd be eaten alive. Used, abused, and screwed. Yeah, well, not him. He grabbed what he could, when he could. Screw everyone else. It was the only way to guarantee you survived. And, man, did he know what to

155

grab now. He gazed at John. Maybe with the right handling, the greatest cash cow to ever live had just waltzed into Vincent's life.

With skin so wrinkled and sagging it looked like a bag of prosthetics for a zombie flick, a woman tottered toward Vincent. Obviously unused to being upright, she crashed to the green concrete floor. She floundered.

"Vincent!"

He turned.

Mary nodded to the old woman, while helping an amputee on with her checked blouse.

Vincent gazed at the woman. As if. Mr. Panucci's instructions related to the inflicting of violence. Nothing about becoming a geriatric's wet nurse. Like he was gonna let some old hag who couldn't even stand drool over his Armani suit.

Dashing to help the woman, Mary cracked him on the arm. "Asshole." She helped the lady up. "Muzzle his pet? If there's an animal around here needs muzzling...!" She glared at him. "Or gelding."

Vincent sniggered. Losers. They didn't know what an opportunity they had here. And people who didn't know what they had were reluctant to fight for it. And if you weren't prepared to fight for something, you didn't deserve it. What they had here was pure gold. Well, Vincent would fight for gold.

John and Rashid were forever poring over Rashid's laptop. There had to be secrets on there. Vincent had seen Mary using it for email earlier. If he could get a look at it, maybe he could piece together enough to grab his share of this cash cow.

A slight, dark-skinned orderly bumped Vincent's arm as he passed. Vincent glared as the guy scuttled over to John and Mrs. Kenyatta, a white-haired shell who Vincent could barely picture even blinking, let alone walking or talking.

A huge glob of phlegm splattered on John's cheek.

Then a tirade of Middle Eastern gibberish showered him, too. What was this? Some Islamic protest crap because John was white and Christian, yet pulled off god-like stunts? Or the results of the pro-Christian frenzy the media had whipped up?

So where was Rashid when they needed him?

Two doctors grabbed the orderly, but he fought.

Hell, talk about needing to smell the coffee. Vincent muttered, "Get a life, asshole. It's just a scam."

Not wanting to let the old woman fall again, Mary couldn't dash to help. She shouted for the security guards at the far end of the corridor.

Struggling, the orderly lashed out at John. John didn't react. He said something in that calming voice of his, but it was buried under the shouting.

Mary bawled, "Vincent! Vincent, do something!"

He did.

He left. He needed options. Not hassle.

He ambled into the restroom.

"And what's my back end on that with—" Rashid glared. "Sorry, I'll get back to you." Flipping his cell shut, he stormed into the end stall. The stall beeped with the sounds of texting.

Vincent smirked. Money talk. Illicit money talk. But how could they make money without actually charging people? What was their angle?

***

From the center of the ward, Vincent frowned. One by one, the dying children of Detroit's Park View Hospital leapt from their beds like kids on Christmas morning. Too weird. And he'd seen some real pros: Shuffles McGee could draw an ace from any deck of cards; Malcolm R could pick a guy clean, blindfolded; and as for Dr. Lamb's accounting skills? Hell, he deserved honorary membership of the Magic Circle. But John was something else. Vincent couldn't spot his trick. John seemed to use no medication, no therapy, no 'message from God', nothing. Most of the time he barely even touched people, barely spoke. An amazing scam. Amazing. Of course, it was only a twist on the Emperor's new clothes — everyone was so desperate to be healed; if one believed it, who wouldn't play along in the hope of being healed, too? — but what a twist. Psychosomatic bull. And like there was any way in hell Vincent was going to be the one to stand up and shout, 'Look, the Emperor's naked!'. There was way too much money to be made to risk that. If only he could figure how the scam worked.

He glanced at his gold Rolex. He liked Panerais — so cool — but who'd ever heard of them? Rolex? Even a sap mopping a Burger King's floor knew you were someone with one of those babies. He timed how many seconds it took John to heal a little girl with all kinds of tubes sticking out of her.

But something clicked in Vincent's mind. He gasped. Spun to a nurse. "What was wrong with her?" He pointed to the girl.

"Little Stacey? She needed a lung transplant. But look, isn't it wonderful?"

"Yeah, yeah. Wonderful. So how much would something like that have cost?"

"Oh. Er... It's not my area, but, er, with all the aftercare, I suppose two, maybe three hundred thousand, but—"

"$300,000!" He turned away, grinning like an idiot. Heaven! He'd died and gone to heaven. Heart transplants. Bone marrow surgery. Chemotherapy. If it cost 300 grand to treat a cancer victim, what was it worth to an insurance company to see that patient healed? $50,000? $100,000? $200,000? Oh, man, this was inspired. What a scam. That had to be the money angle — why else would Rashid, already a multi-millionaire, waste his time unless there was a massive return? But how about the healing? How did John make all these people well for long enough to see the payout? Didn't matter — he obviously could. But this current scam was worth peanuts. With the right setup — charging say, a flat 50 grand a time, and a production line, not all this trailing all over the country — John could heal four, five, maybe six hundred per day. Whoa, Vincent would be richer than God. Private jets, luxury villas, cars... Oh, and women! Man, he was going to make your average rock star look like a damn choirboy!

Something hit his heel. He turned.

A ball lay at his feet. Eight feet away, a child with not a hair on his head gazed at Vincent expectantly.

Kids. If they weren't leeching your hard-earned cash for food, the latest cell, or college, they were your Achilles heel, making you vulnerable to even your weakest of enemies. So, okay his bachelorhood broke his mother's heart. Hey, hearts were meant to be broken. If not, no one would ever die.

He ignored the boy.

"Vincent!"

Her again! Hot, maybe. But boy, would he soon tire of giving Mary a slap to keep her in check. He glanced to the heavens and turned away, straight into Cale.

Cale picked up the ball and slammed it into Vincent's stomach, then glared, nose to nose.

Vincent had killed 11 men and put enough in the hospital to keep John busy for a week. Any other time, he would've struck already — only a white-hatted cowboy or a fool lets the other guy 'draw' first — but he knew Cale was way too decent to start anything surrounded by kids. Vincent smiled. Let the enforcer do his worst.

Cale raised a happy voice for the boy. "Don't worry, buddy, he didn't know the game, is all. But he gets it now." Cale pushed the ball harder and growled softly. "Throw the ball, Vinnie." He released the ball.

It dropped.

Cale scowled.

Vincent sneered. "I could take you apart like that kid would an insect."

"And John would heal me and then I'd break your legs," said Cale. "And then he'd heal you. And then, and then, and then... Wonder who'd cry uncle first? So why not be a good boy, throw the ball, and save John a heap-load of trouble?" He smiled.

Cale had a point. Where was the fun in busting someone up if he didn't stay busted? He could take Cale apart, yes. But how many times would he have to do it? John must've healed upward of 80 people today and he hadn't even broken a sweat. Whether Vincent quit through boredom, exhaustion, or frustration, it would still be *quitting*, letting the cop win. Better to play nice. For now. Get what he wanted. Break the rules later.

He ran the ball backward under his sole, then flicked it onto his instep, once, twice, three times, and into his hands.

Cale strutted away. He winked at Mary. She grinned.

Vincent tossed the ball.

The boy clapped his hands together too late. It bounced off his chest. He stopped it rolling away, but when he tried to mimic Vincent's soccer skills, he stood on the ball. It shot away. He crashed to the floor.

Vincent strolled away, chuckling and shaking his head.

***

"Actually, sir," said Michael in the conference room, "you've already met her."

Tom squinted at the photo clipped to the biography in his file. He didn't recognize her or the name Mary Shelley from his press dealings. "Nope."

"Christmas Eve? When you neglected protocol and gave the Secret Service palpitations going on your mercy dash?"

Tom frowned. "That's her?" No way. "She was all but dead. Connolly didn't start healing 'til two days later."

"She was his first." Michael turned to the next page. "He spent the intervening two days in jail — Connolly's the pervert you had arrested."

"What!?" Tom turned to the page. It was John's biography. "Please tell me this is some kind of sick joke."

"Seems he wasn't feeling her up, sir, but healing her."

Tom shook his head. How wrong could you be? He sighed, then scanned John's details. "There's no father listed."

Michael shrugged.

"Find one," said Tom. "I don't care what the more sensationalist press is writing, this was not an immaculate conception. The more info we have, the easier he'll be to deal with." He looked at Rebecca Wormsley, who sat at his far right. Professor of theoretical science and comparative theology at Harvard and author of 'God: Supreme Being, Alien, Myth, or Monster?'. "What's the Church's and academia's take on these so-called miracles, Professor?"

"The Church is quite clear on miracles, Mr. President." With a pelican-crop double chin and a shock of dyed red hair, she looked more suited to a trailer park than a seat of learning. "Lourdes, France, for example, has documented over 7,000 healings over the last 100 years, but the Catholic Church only recognizes 67 as being authentic miracles, the most recent being Jean-Pierre Bely, an M.S. sufferer, cured in October 1989." She twitched her nose and sniffed.

"So there are miracles outside the Bible?"

"Oh, yes," she said, "but after authenticating only 67, less than one in 100, from the world's most celebrated source of healing, the Church won't look kindly on Connolly's claim of performing upwards of 67 a day. As for the scientific community? Their knee-jerk reaction will be guilty 'til proven innocent, so to speak. Without lengthy, controlled studies, they'll pretty much draw the same conclusion as the Church."

160

She sniffed. "Sorry. Rhinitis. Too many years with dusty books in musty libraries."

"So if the Church and the eggheads won't buy it," said Ryan, "what are we so worried about?"

"What are we worried about?" asked Tom. "Last month's Gallup poll says 45% of people believe Genesis over the Big Bang theory of creation. 45%. Here's a guy straight out of the Bible, performing miracles at the drop of a hat. That damned ambulance chaser, Tanner, has already shaved another three points off our lead, drawing almost level with us, despite Connolly never having even opened his mouth in public. What happens if Connolly comes out as supporting Tanner?" It'd be the greatest routing of a president in history.

"Ah."

"Has anyone asked?" said Simon.

"Excuse me?" said Tom.

Simon twirled his pencil. "Let's get it out in the open. So there's no nasty surprises further down the line."

Gloria stopped doodling a flower to point with her pen. "Yeah, who's to say he doesn't support us?"

"We can't find any political affiliations," said Michael.

"So? Everyone wants something," said Gloria. "We find out what he wants and negotiate."

Michael held up Rashid's photo. "And that takes us to Rashid Al-Alawi. What do you get for the guy whose friend's got everything?"

"Nuh-uh. Everyone wants something," said Ryan. "There's been healers as long as there's been whores — you ever heard of either giving it away for free?"

"There was one," said Simon.

"Really?"

"It's in an obscure text, but maybe the Library of Congress could help out."

Ryan poised his pen. "Got an author?"

"Matthew — that's double 't'..."

Ryan wrote. "Uh-huh."

"Mark..."

"Yeah."

"Luke..."

161

Ryan tossed his pen down and winced a smile at Simon.

Tom shot Simon a stern look. "I agree, Ryan. A dealer doesn't give school kids freebies 'cause he's a nice guy. Give your customers something for nothing. Get them hooked. You've an income for life."

Michael referenced his file. "He doesn't endorse anything. No evidence he's accepted a single cent in donations. He's not affiliated with any organization or charity. Water Relief Africa got that 20-grand reward, but he could just have stuck a pin in the phonebook."

Wormsley gazed into space. "*We saw the risk we took in doing good, but dared not spare to do the best we could.*' Oops. Sorry. Frost — one of my favorites... If Connolly's modeling himself on the Saints, one would imagine he'd be spreading some sort of doctrine, as well as healing. It's possible he thinks he's acting totally altruistically, but sometimes even the best of us care more about that warm glow *we* get from doing something good than any benefit to someone else."

"You mean he gets off on doing good deeds?" asked Ryan.

"It's possible."

"So, say, he won't play ball," said Ryan, "how about nullifying the religious aspect? Dig up something from his past to discredit him."

"Nuh-uh," said Michael. "He has no past. Went straight from high school to new Messiah."

"Hey." Tom slapped his hand down. "Sensationalism stays in the gutter press. We start talking like that, what the hell's Joe Public supposed to believe?"

"Sorry."

Tom drummed his fingers — pinkie to index, then the reverse. Years ago, he'd read it was a good dexterity exercise for those hoping to create dazzling guitar solos. Worked like a charm — on tables. His guitar? Another story. But the habit stuck. He sighed. An A-list celebrity batting for you could easily boost your ratings. But it wasn't John's political affiliations that concerned him. 45% of people believed Genesis. If John played on that, to what figure could that soar? 60%? 70%? Science would take a pummeling. But what else? Would anti-Semitism rear its ugly head? Post 9/11 and Iraq, what would happen to tolerance of other faiths if someone wanted to pack the religion powder keg and light the fuse? Whether John truly was healing people wasn't the issue — the interests of a couple of hundred people were incidental when you had 300 million to look out for. Tom had to protect them. But how? A newborn baby might never get meningitis, but that didn't mean you didn't inoculate against it. "The last thing we want is to victimize him and create a martyr, but there any law he's broken, to tarnish his whiter-than-white image?"

"Not a thing," said Michael

"Anything we can leak? Like he's healed twice as many whites as blacks, or never goes near Jews?"

"Demographics are so even, you'd have a problem busting him on eye color."

Tom looked to Wormsley. "Could we nullify the religious aspect?"

"Depends on whether you believe the research into Vmat2."

"Excuse me?"

"Vmat2. A gene. Supposed to make 50% of us more receptive to spirituality. So it's not just what he does, it's what's preprogrammed into us that matters."

Tom sighed again. Campaigning was hard enough without some Messiah wannabe to contend with. "Okay, it's getting too close to New Hampshire to let this run and see where it's going. First, under the auspices of service to his country, we invite Connolly to receive the Presidential Citizens Medal — it's always easier to fight someone you've met, got a feel for, than a total stranger. Second, it'll look like we're in his corner, giving us some much-needed exposure. Third, I'm bringing in Bob Schecter — I don't like setting the dogs on anyone, but we don't know where Connolly's going, so if we can't resolve this amicably, the CIA's the next best option. Finally," he held up a list of healed patients. "I want every case scrutinized by the country's best. And I mean the best. I know it's the holidays, but throw whatever money you have to at this to get it done. We need to know if this is a hoax or ... well, who knows. Okay?" Positive press, neutralizing Connolly, resolving the healing issue. *That* was a plan. New Hampshire felt safer already.

"In poker," said Simon, staring at John's photo, "the game never just goes on and on and on. No matter how big the bankrolls, at some point the pot always reaches a critical mass and..."

"And?" asked Tom.

Simon broke his pencil and looked up. "There's only ever one winner. He's just waiting for the right pot."

***

Ben laughed, up front in the Hummer, with Rashid's laptop. "Get this: 6,628,109 hits before the website crashed. If only we'd charged a buck a pop for downloads."

Mary clapped. "Yes!"

"Incredible," said Rashid, driving. "I'll increase the bandwidth tomorrow."

Mary grinned. Yesterday, they'd gelled as a team, bonded as characters, laughed as friends. They knew they could change the world. Then the world set them to task by presenting Vincent. Yesterday was filled hope, camaraderie, giving; today broiled in a mire of loathing, lies, secrecy. As if that wasn't bad enough, there'd been the Muslim orderly's protest. And nothing was scarier than a religious nut on a crusade — those types would stop at nothing. They just had to thank God he didn't have a gun. So, after such a day, Mary and everyone else needed something to pull them all together — boy, was the website success ever it?

"Hell, John," said Ben. "You can't buy publicity like this. You sure about NBC's offer?"

NBC wanted John to host a New Year's Day spectacular tomorrow, featuring live healing. John had rejected $1.5 million.

"I don't know," said John

Second thoughts? Thank God. "Really?" said Mary.

John sucked through his teeth. "1.5 million's 1.5 million. Okay, NBC'll probably make a hundred times that in global sales. But... maybe corporate sponsorship wouldn't be that bad. Be kind of cool to see official Secret Angel lunch pails, get some action figures sculpted of all of us, maybe even release a CD."

Rashid and Ben laughed. Even Vincent sniggered. Mary hit John. "John! 1.5 million's no joke. Think what charities could do with it."

"And that's worth adding to the world's problems?"

"How's it adding to the problems?"

"Because business *is* the problem. Corporate America's only interest is in selling you garbage you don't want, while withholding the essentials you actually need."

"1.5 million would be pretty essential to most people," said Mary.

"How much did that T-shirt cost, Mary?"

Had she missed something here? "Excuse me?"

"Your T-shirt?"

It wasn't even a label. Even John couldn't make a big deal of this. "I don't know. Maybe 20 bucks."

He shook his head. "It costs 130 gallons of water to grow and process the cotton for one simple T-shirt like that. Yet in many parts of the world, people are dying of thirst. 130 gallons. And if that isn't cost enough, there's all the fuel, pesticides, dyes, and chemicals needed to get it from a seed to a hanger in a mall. Not to mention the pollution each one of those causes along the way. Yet how many times will you wear it before slinging it in the back of your closet? 15? 20 maybe? That's just one T-shirt. Imagine the cost of a car... Now, when was the last time someone redecorated 'cause the paint was peeling; got a new PC 'cause their old one had blown; new shoes 'cause all their others had holes? *Everyone* treats *everything* as totally disposable. It's criminal. So don't ask me to help corporate America brainwash people into blowing all the world's resources as if the four-minute warning just sounded."

It was unlike John to condemn something so vehemently. Yes, businesses manipulated the population into buying what they could easily live without, but even John couldn't change that. So why not climb onboard and milk it for all he could?

"I wanna send an email." said Vincent, alone at the very back of the Hummer. The standard vehicle was a four-seater; Rashid's customization incorporated remodeling to allow an extra seat to be bolted to the top of the driveshaft tunnel whenever needed. It didn't look the comfiest place to sit, but everyone wanted Vincent as far removed from the group as possible, including Vincent.

Ben laughed, passing Rashid's laptop back. "Someone gave *you* their email address? Who smuggled it out the psych ward for them?"

"You must remember my little sister Therese, Detective," Vincent sneered. "She's the one as kneed you in the nuts when you tried to nail Paolo Zanetti on me. What a cop — floored by a little girl!"

"Rashid," said John, "what if I wanted to hire Madison Square Garden? Tomorrow?"

"Tomorrow!"

"Ben's right — there are things I need to say."

"Hey, what d'you know," said Ben.

Vincent sniggered. "Yeah, 'cause railing against the evils of Gucci is really gonna stick it to corporate America."

While it stuck in her craw, Mary said, "Vincent's got a point."

Ben smiled. "I dunno — say, 30 bucks a pop, that'll be some night."

"No," said John. "No charge."

"You're not expecting Rashid to foot the bill again?" said Mary. They had no income, and John declined donations. Until now, Rashid had cheerfully covered all their expenses, but even he'd have limits.

"Ben's provided the money."

Ben gazed around. "I get a Christmas present I don't know about?"

"Pay per view," said John.

Mary threw her hands up. "But you said you won't do TV, 'cause they'll edit it and fill it with beer commercials."

John smiled. "That's why we'll stream it online."

"And all the people who don't have access? You'll decimate the audience."

John squeezed her hand. "Web's worldwide, Mary."

"Now you're talking," said Ben.

Okay, Mary had to admit the plan had merit. At least they'd have an income to hold in reserve for when Rashid either went bust or went away. In fact, at only a few dollars a time, in one night, they could make as much as Rashid was worth. "So how much? Five? Ten bucks a time?"

"A penny."

"One cent?" Ben and Mary cried in unison.

"To cover costs."

"But it'll cost... Heaven only know's how much," said Mary.

"And we'll have millions logged on."

She blew out a breath. "Well, I suppose live healing will—"

"No. No healing," said John.

"Buddy," said Ben, "don't take this wrong, but people have never heard you speak — you might be some gibbering idiot for all they know. They're only interested in your healing. You don't give them what they want, they're gonna be pretty pissed."

"I want to help people, Ben, not entertain them."

"Hey, you've got some great ideas, but that ain't what gets people hot. They want lifestyle advice, they'll search Google, or ask their buddy over a beer."

Mary took his hand. "I'm sorry, John, but Ben's right."

He gazed into her eyes. "Within your lifetime the Arctic will melt, the seas' fish stocks will collapse, and the rainforests will disappear. Will Google help then?"

The media was so full of 'the end is nigh' sound bites that people were blasé, if not downright bored. John's public premiere would just leave them cold. "John, that's all well and—"

He held up his hand. "Imagine you're at the top of the Empire State Building. You look out. And all you see, in every direction, is utter devastation. No buildings. No roads. No cars. No boats. Total destruction. The nearest building still standing is your mom's house in Philadelphia — 120 miles away... That's the area of rainforest we decimate every single year."

A few trees getting cut down in South America was one thing, but the equivalent of a nuclear blast in your own backyard? Mary shuddered. Maybe John did have something to say.

Rashid glanced back. "So what do you intend, my friend?"

John looked at Mary, his greatest dissenter. "You know how your mom's always dreamed of seeing Paris? Climbing the Eiffel Tower; enjoying a lazy cruise on the Seine? So you and your sisters booked her a holiday as a Christmas present. And she was so thrilled she cried. So you cried, too."

She nodded. She felt her eyes welling now.

"That's how I feel every time I heal. The joy of giving someone something they dreamed of is one of the greatest gifts we ourselves can receive. That's what I intend to do."

"Come again?" said Ben.

"You don't need a doctorate in philosophy to know it's wrong to steal, to cheat, to kill. They're all moral givens. But that's where people draw the line. They know it's wrong to take something from someone else, but they don't appreciate it's equally wrong not to give someone what they need. Well, I'm going to change that. I'm going to give more than anyone's ever given and ask for nothing in return. I'm going to teach by example. I'm going to teach the world to give."

Without looking up from Rashid's laptop, Vincent sniggered. Unfortunately, Mary found herself doing something she'd never dreamed of: agreeing wholeheartedly with him. "John..." she blew out a big breath, "er, Live 8 was, er, a free event to change the world. The greatest stars on the planet, stars most of us have idolized for years, decades, reached out and touched a billion people. Is there still famine in Africa?"

"Mary's right, John," said Ben. "While I'm ashamed to admit it, I had a great day at Live Earth, especially seeing one of my all-time heroes – Roger Waters – but am I still driving a beat-up, gas-guzzling SUV or a compact, eco-friendly Jap job? Sorry, bud, but people'll just grab what they can get for themselves and skedaddle."

"Initially," said John. "But once they feel the joy of receiving without asking, they'll want to reciprocate, and, slowly, it'll transcend the individual, permeate society, and actually become part of our nature."

Vincent laughed.

Oh, God help them. John was going to blow everything with some half-assed, pseudo-philosophical bull. No one outside a sick bed would ever take him seriously again. "John, people know—" she counted on her fingers, "—smoking, junk food, unprotected sex, no exercise, can all kill them. Do they care? Do they, hell? So how are you going to stop them destroying the rainforest to grow cattle feed just 'cause it *might* displace some tree frog that *might* be found to secrete some enzyme that *might* one day cure acne? People can live with a zit; they won't live without cheeseburgers."

"Yes, they will."

Mary laughed. "No, John. They won't."

"Trust me." John smiled.

Oh, no. That was probably Nixon's last remark at the Watergate, Lewinsky's parting words to Clinton, Captain Smith's instruction to the look-out on the *Titanic* who screamed 'Iceberg!'.

They were screwed. Screwed!

19

Dead Man Standing

The flames flounced and the smoke plumed high into the stage lights — lights that had illuminated Hendrix storming through 'Purple Haze', Mohammed Ali battling 15 rounds with Joe Frazier, and the first perfect '10' for Olympic record-breaking Nadia Comaneci. Center stage today, Madison Square Garden, stood a 6-foot-tall potted rubber plant, ablaze in a blur of dancing yellow flames.

People jostled in and took their seats. All 19,000. Like children lining up for Santa's toyshop, they scanned this magical domain, straining for a sign Santa had arrived, while musing over the wondrous gifts he'd previously bestowed and those he had yet to deliver.

From the wings, Mary gazed into the cavernous arena. Everyone saw the burning plant, but after a moment's puzzlement, ignored it. As a burning bush, God talked with Moses. Was John hoping to capture the audience's attention with a biblical air? It wasn't working. And it wasn't needed — He'd captured the world with his healing; he didn't need this pathetic gimmick. The event was going to be a disaster. She stared at the fire extinguisher beside the plant, praying no one would climb on stage and use it. With any luck, the smoke would activate the fire alarm and an evacuation would shock John out of this ridiculous course of action.

Her prayers were answered in part — no one climbed on stage.

"Come on. Burn, damn you." She glanced at her watch: 4:28 p.m. Night in Europe. Morning in the East. Just two minutes for a blazing inferno to halt the disaster. It was bad enough John had insulted the President by declining an award at the White House — now he was going to blow his credibility trying to 'convert' the masses. "Burn!"

But the amount of smoke was inconsequential in an arena the size of a couple of football fields.

Rashid clapped, hunched over his laptop. "Incredible. Incredible. 178 million logged-on. Incredible."

178,000,000! That had easily covered the costs of readying the arena in just 24 hours. But it meant John was going to die in front of an audience that would make the Super Bowl envious.

A line of security guards marched out and encircled the stage. There was to be 'Strictly NO Healing', as the plethora of flyers, Web announcements, and posters stated, but people would still try. Besides, John wouldn't risk another protest ruining everything. The guards' appearance an obvious sign, the crowd roared. They weren't kept waiting.

From a trapdoor, John rose onto the stage.

The arena erupted with whistles, cheers, clapping, and screams, as if the Beatles had just strolled on with a guest appearance by Elvis.

"Oh, boy." Mary clasped her hands over her mouth, heart hammering. When she was seven, she'd been in her school nativity play as her namesake, Mary. She'd been so excited. Couldn't wait. Couldn't stop smiling on the day. Then... finally standing before all those people, all those eyes drilling into her, she'd blanked. Just stood there staring back, tears streaming down her cheeks. Tonight, possibly half a billion eyes were drilling into John. Talk about stage fright. This would be a disaster. Absolute disaster.

"Hey, it'll be fine." Ben slung his arm around her. "Has John put a foot wrong yet?"

For the past five days John had worked miracles, both real and metaphorical. Ben was right. She smiled. John would stun the world.

But it wasn't the world that stood stunned. It was John. He froze.

"Oh, God, no." Mary cringed. Whatever possessed John to think talking to millions would be as easy as chatting to them?

John didn't move. Didn't speak. Just stared.

The cheering flagged, the audience sensing something was wrong.

"Come on, John." Maybe she should run on. Say he was exhausted after today's flying visits to two NYC hospitals and one in Allentown, Pennsylvania. Beg their understanding. "Please, John."

Finally, just as the top half of the plant toppled over, John shuffled stage front. Applause burst forth. John gestured for quiet. A tattered air of hushed voices descended as they awaited the wisdom of one so blessed.

As if someone had flicked a switch, John burst into life. He thrust his arms upward. "Is God in this house today?"

"Amen!" "Yeah!" "Hallelujah!" Whoops of delight rained down. He punched the air.

"Is God truly with us?" shouted John.

Clapping and stamping. "Yes!"

John punched the air.

"And are we doing God's work?"

Whoops and screams and clapping thundered down as if God were breaking through the very roof to be with them himself.

Aghast, Mary stared from between her fingers. Apart from alienating all non-believers, John had become the very thing he hated: a preacher pandering to the lowest common denominator. Had stage fright made him lose the plot? Or after two decades of shunning human contact, did he believe this was how to woo an audience? What now? Some pantomime of talking to the burning bush to spread The Word?

"Boy, are we boned," said Ben.

John let the cacophony die, then strolled to the plant. Snatched the extinguisher. Doused the flames. So much for talking to God through a bush. What the hell had he hoped to gain with that feeble stunt? Mary bit her lip. It was a train wreck. A train wreck even John couldn't save them from.

Licked by yellow flames, one leaf still flickered. John picked it up and turned it so the flame grew. He marched to the front left of the stage.

"Oh, what now?" This couldn't get any worse. Then she saw where he was heading. Oh, yes, it could get so much worse. "Oh, no. No, John."

Mutterings rumbled around the arena.

John stopped before an 8-foot American flag, which, like its three counterparts, stood guard on the stage corner. He scanned the faces studying him. Slowly, he lifted the flame up to Old Glory.

People cried out, "No!"

Fists hammered the air. "Don't!"

Face twisted in outrage. "Get away!"

Some of those in the front rows jostled for the stage. Security held them back.

Cries bombarded John as if he were about to behead the firstborn of every parent present. Mary shouted, "John! No!" They'd hang him. Didn't matter if he'd healed Jesus himself on the cross — they'd hang him.

The flame crept closer.

The screams grew louder.

The fire barely a hair's width from the cotton, John dropped it and stamped it out.

"Oh, thank you." Mary clutched her chest. Most of the audience did, too.

Head bowed, John ambled center stage. "I love America. I love the American people. I love the American way of life. But this," he pointed to the flag, "is just a piece of cloth. Symbolic, yes, but of no intrinsic value. My love is here—" he thumped his heart, "— not there." He stabbed at the flag.

"You should've seen your horror, your outrage, when you thought I was going to burn that flag." He pointed to those near the front. "You'd have lynched me, if not for the security. Just to save a piece of cloth." He meandered over to the plant. "How many of you fought to save this plant?"

"It's just a plant," bawled some guy.

John smiled. "Very astute, sir. But the plant's real. What you feel for that," he jabbed at the flag, "is illusory... Don't believe me?" He signaled the sound engineer. The house P.A. system cut to a recording: 'Is God in this house today?', 'Amen!', 'Yeah!'. The opening questions and euphoric responses played back to a confused audience. They'd come to see miracles, not listen to the ramblings of a loon.

Muttered rumblings once more crawled around the arena.

Mary stared at Rashid. Was this their secret scheme? Rashid shrugged, as baffled as she was.

"If the other faiths will indulge me for a moment," said John. "It took God six days to create all this." He swept a hand over everything before him. "Six days. The most powerful being in the universe needed six days... Not..." he snapped his fingers, "that. Not..." he checked his new X-Tech for six seconds, "that. Not an hour, two hours, not even a full day, but *six days*... That," he pointed to the flag, "took a seamstress in South Dakota 14 minutes to stitch... So tell me, which truly deserves to be revered? A piece of cloth? Or the whole world?" He paused to let the question resonate. "It's strange how we choose to see God in America, but not in this plant; in ourselves, but not in the things we do; in our lives, but not all around us. Yet who do we turn to, to protect us from disease, from sorrow, from terror? God, the celestial Prozac... Is the best way to worship the creator to destroy everything he created?" John gazed at them. They were confused. Spellbound. Silent. "So next time you take the kids to the zoo, or you enjoy a picnic in the park with your partner, pause to think that in just 100 years, every second cage in that zoo will be empty; every second flower in that park simply won't exist. Why? 'Cause that's how quickly we're killing species because none of us has grabbed an extinguisher to put out the fire of deforestation, pollution, climate change..." He weighed his hands. "Six days." He looked from one to the other. "14 minutes." He shook his head. "It's all about perspective.

"But please, I'm not here to bash anyone's beliefs. I'm not going to ask you to forsake your country, or start worshipping a tree, a mountain, or a goat. All I'd like us to do, together, is open our minds to possibilities we might never have imagined. So tonight, I'm not going to talk about religion, or America, or politics. Tonight we're all nation-less and culture-less. Because tonight, the only thing I'm going to talk about is the one thing we all have in common: life."

Mary smiled, staring at the bewitched crowd. Why had she ever doubted him? He was just messing with people's heads, dragging them into his world of answers and clarity.

"Before I go on, I want to thank you for coming tonight. It means a lot to me. And that includes those on the internet, too. For though we might be divided by distance, by language, by religion, you all believe something special's happening, something that's worth being a part of. And that makes you special, too, because you're open to new possibilities. You've taken the first step. Now, I'd like us to take the second together. So, what new possibilities? Well, let's start with the most important one: how to live happier lives. And I'm not just talking about charity for the disadvantaged. I'm talking about you, me, every man, woman, and child living a happier, easier, richer life. So come on — let's not just make today the start of a new year, let's make today the start of a new age." He clapped the audience. "Come on."

They clapped back, louder and louder, as the gravity of his words sunk in.

Ben beamed at Mary. His lips moved, but she couldn't hear. She didn't need to. John had them. Had the whole world. A miracle.

"Thank you." John let the euphoria subside. "I tell you, I was so nervous about speaking to you all, I haven't eaten all day." He patted his stomach. "So please ignore any rumbles or squeaks — they aren't part of the show."

Laughter lightened the air.

"Anyone else hungry?"

Replies shouted from the sea of faces.

"Glad I'm not the only one. Believe me, after this, I'm gonna be stuffing my face all night. But we've all been hungry some time, only to find nothing in the refrigerator. Just like we've all been broke, after blowing a wedge on the latest Nike. And sick? Who hasn't suffered in bed, while some good Samaritan brought us chicken soup? Talk about life? Life really sucks at times, and don't we know it?"

People cheered and applauded.

Cameras on booms, cranes, handheld worked inconspicuously to capture each nuance.

John held his stomach. "Jeez, I could eat a horse." Smiling, he pointed to a man with a red shirt straining over his gut. "Bet you know what I'm saying, huh?"

"Yeah."

John pointed elsewhere. "You looking forward to your credit card statement arriving?"

A bushy-haired woman shook her head.

"Ever had a sore throat so bad everyone had to wait on you hand and foot?" He pointed again.

A man laughed, then nodded.

"Yep, life sure can suck." John's smile dropped. "In Africa, people just like you and me die of starvation. In Russia, people just like you

and me die of cold. In India, people just like you and me die of disease."
He pointed at the red-shirted man. "You really hungry?"

The man shook his head.

John pointed to others. "You broke? ... Been sick?"

No one answered.

"You see," said John, "in this great country of ours, even though I lived on the streets for 19 years, I can no sooner say I've been hungry, poor, or sick, than a blind man can marvel at a sunset... But I don't have to experience it. I can imagine. See, that's the wonder of being human: we don't need to experience something first-hand, we can empathize, see what's wrong, and know, *truly know*, we have the power to change it."

"Around the world, someone dies unnecessarily almost every second. That means," he checked his watch, "while we've been shooting the breeze, 288 people have died. Sorry, 289. No, 290. In fact, they're dying so fast that by the time I've told you how many, I'm already wrong. And in case you're having difficulty picturing what one person dying per second actually means, take a look around you..." He paused and scanned the packed arena, as everyone else did. "There are 19,000 people here today, but not a single one of you would live to see one second after midnight tonight." A deathly hush fell. "Now, before anyone starts edging for the door, I'm asking no one, I repeat, *no one*, to dip in their wallet." He grinned, beckoning into the audience's depths. "Yes, ma'am, hurry on back before someone steals your seat."

Everyone laughed. Not for long.

"The two World Wars killed 69 million people. *69 million*. They're thought of as the greatest human atrocities in history. *The greatest human atrocities*." He pointed at a woman in a flowery dress. "Where'd you rather work — the Naval Base, Pearl Harbor, 1941, or an AIDS-infested brothel, India, today?"

"Pearl Harbor."

To a fat guy guzzling soda with his kids. "Where'd you rather see your family — France under German invasion, 1916, or famine-stricken Ethiopia, today?"

"France."

Mary nodded. The prospect of oppression, a POW camp, even a bullet in the head was far less scary than the certainty of a lingering death to poverty or disease.

"Very wise." John paused. "Here, if someone puts a .45 to a little girl's head and blows her brains out, people are outraged. Yet every single second of every single day, we put guns to the heads of those in Ethiopia, in Haiti, in Afghanistan. Guns loaded with tuberculosis and HIV, loaded with contaminated drinking water, loaded with poverty and hopelessness. Where's our outrage now?"

He paced across the stage. "I know. I know... It's a huge problem. A gigantic problem. A real monster. How in hell can we, just ordinary people, stop it? So we fall back on procrastination. And putting it off brings on indifference. And not caring gives us memory loss. So everything's hunky-dory again... A huge problem. A real monster. Hell, I must be crazy to even mention it." He pointed to the crowd. "You must be crazy to even listen."

He stopped pacing. Stared intently. "Was it crazy to believe in the fall of slavery? Hell, no. Our forefathers slew that monster. Was it crazy to believe in the fall of the Nazis? Hell, no. Our grandfathers slew that monster. Was it crazy to believe in the fall of segregation, communism, apartheid? Hell, no. Our fathers slew those monsters. So, I ask you, are we the weakest generation America's ever bred? Are we to shame our fathers, our grandfathers ... *our children*? Or are we to stand together, tall and proud and united, and shout, 'No! We *will* be heard! We *will* make a difference! We *will change the world!*'?"

The audience erupted.

***

Alone in a den cluttered with Knicks memorabilia, Tom jabbed his beer at the laptop on the coffee table. "Hell, if this guy's not good." It took him and his team years of experience and days of drafting to write something so stirring — John had been living rough barely hours ago.

A personal 'underdog' joke between Tom and Simon, the *Rocky* theme tune played on Tom's cell. He answered. "Yeah, I'm watching."

"Can you believe this guy?" asked Simon.

"Tell me about it. He ever decides to run for office, we might as well hire a U-haul there and then. I'll get back to you when it's over." Tom hung up.

He lounged back on the cream sofa, a tobacco sunburst Strat beside him. Tom had witnessed Hendrix mesmerizing the Garden all those years ago. Awestruck, he'd bought his first guitar the very next day.

Hendrix was a genius. Innovative. Visionary. But John...? John was a whole other level.

***

John waited for quiet. "Now, I know what you're thinking: 'How are we, just ordinary people, going to change the world? That needs heroes!'. Well, I'm going to make you heroes. Each and every one of you."

He strolled along the stage. "But if I tell you the lowest 10% of wage earners in the U.S. are still better off than two-thirds of the world's population, you're going to think I'm going after your wallets. If I tell you half the people on earth, yes, *half*, live on less than two bucks a day, you're going to think I'm after your wallets. And if I tell you one-sixth of the people on the planet don't have clean drinking water; that one woman dies in childbirth *every minute*; that for every healthy, well-fed American there are 10 people suffering in poverty, you're going to think I'm after your wallets... Suddenly, being a hero doesn't look so attractive, huh? So if I tell you that without sacrificing one red cent from your wallet, you could end disease," he pointed to a fat, mustachioed man, "would you be a hero?"

"Hell, yeah!"

"If I tell you that without sacrificing the tiniest scrap of bread from your family's table, you could end hunger," he pointed to a heavily pregnant woman, "would you be a hero?"

"Yeah!"

"If I tell you that without sacrificing your plasma screens, your gym memberships, your two weeks vacation, you can still end poverty..." he swept his hand across the audience, "would you be heroes?"

"YEAH!" A 747 flying inches over Mary's head couldn't have thundered louder.

Mary jigged up and down with joy for John. She'd no idea how he'd ever deliver, but John's specialty was to deliver the impossible. She gazed at the sea of smiling, whooping, and waving. John's healing was incredible. But this? This was something else. And that's when she saw...

Someone not smiling, not whooping, not waving.

Someone shuffling down the aisle toward the stage.

Someone clutching something under her shawl.

Wearing a black sari, a slim, 30-ish woman approached the security line, her face a determined glare.

25 yards from her, Mary puzzled. What was she doing? What did she want? What was she hiding?

As she puzzled at the Hindu woman, Mary's smile faded. She remembered the pastor on TV: '... many religious communities are rightfully indignant...'. She remembered the hospital orderly's fury. And she remembered Rashid: *Do you really think everyone's going to be as enlightened as we are?* Images flashed of great men who'd tried to change the world — Martin Luther King, Gandhi, JFK. Great men. Dead men. Assassinated men. "Oh, no!"

Mary grabbed Ben.

Stabbed a finger at the woman.

Screamed, "It's a gun."

Ben shouted, "What?"

Panic snatched Mary. Her heart pounded as if she'd seen the gun drawn, aimed, and the slack taken up on the trigger. She shrieked, "A gun! She's got a gun!"

Ben followed Mary's finger. He snatched his radio. Barked commands.

Mary clutched her mouth as security swooped. Quick. Quick. Get her quick!

Guards the size of redwoods pinned the woman. Ripped open her shawl. Snatched what was inside.

Safe.

Mary heaved a breath. "Oh, thank you. I thought that was it."

Security bundled the woman for the exit.

"Wait!" A voice thundered. "Wait!" John's voice.

The crowd calmed from curiosity.

Security waited.

"You ... didn't come to listen," said John. "You came to speak." He waved for her to be released. She was. She snatched her property: a coffee jar–sized ornate box.

John beckoned her.

Mary bit her lip. "Please, John, don't." There was something wrong about this woman, a woman so grim amidst such jubilation. This would end badly. So badly.

Rashid shouted to the sound engineer. Using a joystick, the guy maneuvered a boom microphone toward the woman.

Heavily, yet determinedly, she trudged up the steps to the stage as if they led to the gallows. Her fingers clawed her box to her chest.

John went to greet her.

Finally on stage, John but feet away, she ripped open the box and hurled the contents. A cloud of gray powder engulfed John.

A gasp exploded in the arena.

Then ... silence, as if a box of anthrax had been released and everyone had dropped where they stood.

Everyone stared. Agog. Agape.

Finally, the woman spoke. "You talk of changing the world to end suffering. What do you care about suffering?"

John stood statue-still. Covered in powder, he looked like a ghost.

Her voice faltered. "Asif, my husband, died Christmas Day. Since then, while all the world celebrated the birth of a 'great healer', I've had to watch my little Asra and Kamal," her voice broke, but she struggled on, "cry so hard I thought their hearts would break and they'd join their father. And you have the nerve to talk of heroes!" She hurled the box.

It bounced off John's shoulder.

Another enormous gasp shook the arena.

John didn't flinch. Just stared.

The woman sobbed. "You could've saved him..." she sniffed away the tears, "but you didn't. And I just want to know why? Why you saved all those other people, but you let my Asif die. Let Asra's and Kamal's father die."

Motionless, John stared.

"Why?..." her voice squeaked. She gestured to the powder. "That's all I have left."

Oh, holy hell. It wasn't a box; it was an urn.

***

His beer frozen at his lips, Tom gawked at the screen. "Talk about a train wreck." Connolly was as good as dead. After all the man hours and tax dollars they'd thrown at this problem, a single woman had buried him in a moment's grief. Excellent.

***

Teary-eyed, Mary ached to run to John, to run to the woman ... but words could never ease the pain of such loss. How devastated must a woman be to throw her husband's ashes over someone?

Obviously drained by the trauma of attending the rally, the woman sobbed. Her voice was barely a whimper. "Why?"

John was still. So deathly still.

"Oh, please, John, say something," muttered Mary. Even walking off-stage would be kinder than simply reveling in her suffering. Was he so angry? So offended to be covered in Asif's ashes? "Please, John."

The woman was so consumed with pain, with questions, that her knees buckled and she sank toward the floor.

Finally, John moved. He grabbed her. Saved her. Raised her up again.

Crying, she gazed into his blue, blue eyes. "Why?"

"I'm sorry," said John.

"Sorry?" She shot him a mocking smile that was little more than a grimace. "Well, that's all right, then." She picked up her box. Turned. Stumbled down the stairs.

"I'm sorry anyone suffers."

She stopped, but didn't turn.

"That's why I'm here. And if there were any way I could change what happened and save Asif, I would."

She half-turned. "But you could have."

He sat on the top step, so he was no longer looking down on her, but into her eyes. He reached out to her. "I can't save everyone." She took his hand.

He said, "Love can nurture us, nourish us, give us pleasure beyond our dreams and strength beyond our imagination, but if we lived in a world where nothing bad ever happened to those closest to us, would there be a place for love? You see, it isn't just companionship that strengthens love, it's the threat of losing it. Wasn't Asif frightened for you when you went into labor? Weren't you afraid for him whenever he was unexpectedly late coming home? If life wasn't so fragile, filled with such fears and anxieties, could love exist? No, because it's that empathy, that fear, which binds us stronger than any drug, contract, or law ever could. Take fear away, make us indestructible, and what happens to love?"

"But why did he have to die?"

"You mean, why didn't God intervene? Why doesn't he rid the world of cancer? End poverty? Halt an earthquake, a tsunami, a mudslide?"

"Why?"

180

John sighed. "If your daughter, Asra, fell off her bike, should God be there to save her from breaking her neck?"

"Yes."

"And if she went over the handlebars and damaged her eyes, should God be there to save her sight?"

"Yes."

"And if she only broke her arm? A finger? Grazed her knee?"

The woman sobbed.

"Once it starts, where does it stop?"

"I just want him back."

"If we know God will protect us from disease, stay a mugger's knife, turn away a tornado, how do we nurture the respect for life that everyone and all things deserve? Isn't it only through loss that we truly know we're alive?" John laid a hand on her shoulder. "I could take away your pain, your loneliness, that longing which gnaws day after day ... but won't that just be taking away your love?"

She sobbed and fell toward him. He hugged her.

***

Tom snatched his cell. "Yeah?"

"We got a problem," said Simon.

"Damn right, we've got a problem. No excuses — I don't care what day it is — I want everyone here by 7:00."

"Already taken care of."

Tom hung up. Threatening his campaign was one thing. But inflaming the people into believing they could change the world? This guy was no nuisance, he was a damn time bomb! Anyone else coming out with this garbage would be little more than light entertainment. But this guy performed miracles; was the hottest story in the world; had charisma, intelligence, a magic way with words — the stuff of which heroes were born. A hero like that could command armies. And, boy, had the American people been clean out of heroes for way, way too long. Could they resist the lure of the promised land?

20

Aftermath

Sipping orange juice in Rashid's conservatory, Mary gazed out at the koi pond bathed in ice. Between the bare cherry trees, icicles cascaded down the rock waterfall and sparkled in the nightlights. Such stillness. Such starkness. Such a contrast to the evening's Garden spectacle. John couldn't have been more of a success if he'd planted that woman. A disaster? The world was reeling under his spell. It would've given him anything. Anything. And what had he asked for? Nothing.

Well, that wasn't strictly true.

He'd described his path to a better world: education, rights, and freedom; the elimination of poverty and famine; a sharing of innovation, knowledge, expertise... In return, he'd promised gifts for the American people: a lower cost of living for a higher standard. How? He wouldn't yet say. But after his performance, they'd have followed him into the crater of an erupting volcano if he'd said he could stay its might. And that was what he'd asked of them: to follow him when the time came.

Cryptic as usual.

That was why he'd refused to heal. His healing was like a movie trailer — to get people intrigued; get them talking; get them hooked for the real ride: his philosophy.

Behind her at the walnut table in the kitchen, Vincent's knife screeched on his plate as he sliced his steak, snapping her from her thoughts. She meandered in. She hated to talk with him there to sneer, but he seemed engrossed in his paper. "John?"

"Hmm?" Sitting opposite Vincent, John didn't look up from Rashid's laptop and a demographics report on the webcast.

"It's not just a dream, is it? I mean, you do know how to do all these things?"

"Mmm."

"But how?" She didn't like to doubt him, but her vocation, natural curiosity, *and* common sense were hard to ignore. "The world's corporations own, well, the world, and the only time a politician listens is when he's looking for your vote. You really think they're just going to sit still for all this?"

He clicked the mouse. "Will they have a choice?"

It wasn't Vincent who sniggered. "What?"

Finally, John pushed the laptop aside. "Who ended segregation in the '60s? A government task force, or the people? Who ended the whaling industry? Corporate policy, or the people? Who ended the Vietnam War? The President, or the people?"

Everything he'd promised would cost a fortune. The government wouldn't pay. So that only left one source. "But none of those involved your average Joe sticking his hand in his wallet. Even you can't conjure billions out of thin air."

"The average person has no idea how powerful he is," said John.

"And this 'power' can get him a better standard of living *and* save the world, but cost him absolutely squat?"

"To ensure its existence, big business has to constantly convince us that what we bought yesterday is so inadequate we'll only be happy if we buy something new today, which is an endless spiral, 'cause they'll only find something else to 'guarantee our happiness' tomorrow. And while people are fickle, there's one universal — they don't like being told what to do. Once people realize corporate America isn't selling them the things *they* need, but brainwashing them into buying what *it* needs purely to exist, they'll rebel. It's the biggest secret in the business world: we don't need big business, it needs us. So all we have to do is make business work how we want it to work."

Yeah, right. Like that would ever run. Mary couldn't count the shoes, jewelry, scent she'd bought — particularly after a hard week or a bad break-up — only to lose interest once their novelty wore off. But, like everyone else, she liked the thrill of something new, something different, something to add color to her life. And pleasure aside, people weren't just brainwashed — they bought to replace outdated fashions, obsolete equipment, stuff that bored them. No, John needed more. "People like the thrill of buying new stuff, John. You'll never change that."

"No? Even with its speed governor, your car will do 95 mph; without it, it'd probably hit around 110. The limit's 65! What suckered you into wasting money on all the mechanics to make your car hit speeds you'll never use — then into paying *even more* for extra equipment to stop it from ever reaching those speeds? And everything's the same: DVD recorders, PCs— This." He showed his watch. "Water resistant to 200 meters? Who am I, Jacques Cousteau? Think of the resources wasted in producing so much stuff we don't need, compounded by those wasted in throwing out something that's not defective, that we're only changing 'cause some marketing campaign told us to. Now, think what we could do with all those resources."

Logical. But people would never buy it. You couldn't live in a consumer society without consuming! And, boy, did the American people love to consume. To change that would take a major shift in ... well, everything. But, as the Garden event had proven, John knew exactly what he wanted and how to get it. He had to have a plan. Was that what he and Rashid were plotting?

***

Mary sidled out, brow furrowed. Vincent sniggered. Some people were just such easy targets. His nightfall-blue Lotus Elise did 150 mph. Was so responsive, it felt like a part of him. That wasn't brainwashing; that was awesome. But if people preferred John to tell them what to do instead of corporations, like he cared. But there was something he did care about.

Vincent looked up from his paper. "You know," he forked his French fries, "I get where you're coming from — refusing the NBC gig."

"Good."

"With what you got going, 1.5 mil was a damn insult."

"Is that so?"

"I tell you, with the Vegas contacts I got, you'd make a deal like this," he gestured to the house, "look like a skid-row soup kitchen."

184

John merely stared.

"But I know you're not interested in that."

John stared still.

Vincent held his gaze — that 'John stare' wasn't gonna faze him! "So here's the deal: if people are dying every second 'cause they can't afford food or medicine, give them the money. Save them."

"Go on."

Hooked, yes! Now for the kill. "Start a foundation for good causes."

John nodded.

"And I'm not talking the whole Siegfried-and-Roy thing in Vegas. I'm talking classy, you know. You do your spiel, some healing, and before you know it, we're shipping cargo planes of food to Ethiopia. Simple."

"We?"

"Like I say, I got contacts." See, just tempt the guy with the right deal — John was only human.

John nodded. "And your cut would be?"

Whatever his Magic Circle accountant, Dr. Lamb, could make disappear. "Hey, no way." Vincent held his hands up defensively. "I got an image to keep up in front of those guys," he nodded toward the other room, "but I got heart, man. You musta seen that, or I wouldn't be here. Right?"

"But I'd only heal those wealthy enough to pay for it?"

"Ah, no," Vincent smiled, "See, like big law firms, one day you'd heal for a ticket-buying audience, the next you'd do pro bono work wherever you want. Feeding the starving *and* healing the sick — two birds, one stone."

John gazed into space, obviously considering the idea.

Vincent finished his wine. Hell, he was gonna be King of Vegas. Richer than Jesus. John was good with the speech stuff and Rashid was good with the logistics stuff, but when it came to scams? Man, Vincent was in a different league!

John shook his head. "Somehow, I don't think—"

"Hey, think about it, man. Rashid's not gonna foot the bills forever. And anyways, you really wanna stay here if you don't have to?"

"Why wouldn't I? Rashid's a generous friend and a good man."

"A good man who prays to a false God."

"He does?"

"Excuse me?" Vincent sniggered. "You saying Allah's the true God?"

"Do you know a better one?"

"John," Vincent frowned as if wounded, "don't be pulling that crap on me."

With a tip of the bottle, John offered Vincent more merlot.

Vincent preferred Bordeaux to this Chilean 'merlot' mouthwash, but with Rashid being a teetotaler, was it any surprise his wine cellar sucked? Still, he accepted, squeezing more ketchup on his fries.

John poured Vincent wine. "If you think of religion only in terms of God, as something outside of you, you'll always be outside of it."

"What?"

"If someone treats you as they themselves would wish to be treated, does it matter to whom they pray?"

"So you don't care if someone's Hindu, Jew, Buddhist..."

Without looking, John continued pouring wine, overflowing Vincent's glass. "Any fool can pray for a better world, but it takes a wise man to know it's only what's in his own heart that can change things. The Torah, the Sutras, Ganesh, Muhammad, atheism — every one agrees happiness can only come through empathy and morality."

Vincent pointed to the wine pooling across the table. "You might wanna stop."

John gestured to the spilled wine. "You don't want this?"

Vincent glared.

John put the bottle down, then nonchalantly held up his glass. "Religion is only as good as the vessel that carries it. The more you dwell on what's outside, the more you miss what's inside." He drank.

Vincent snorted. It was enough to make his brain hurt, yet ... it kinda made sense.

"As for Islam?" said John. "Islam springs from the same roots as Judaism and Christianity."

"So what...? All religions are the same? God is God is God?"

"Some would say. Though never in a church, a synagogue, or a mosque."

John gazed at Vincent for a moment. "If I asked him, Rashid would write you a check, right now, for $5,000,000."

"What?" Did he hear right?

"$5,000,000. No Vegas. No healing. Just one small job. Then you can leave. Get on with your life."

Vincent sniggered. "Yeah, sure. Like there's no catch."

"No catch."

"So what's the job? Something ridiculously impossible?"

"If it is, you've achieved the ridiculously impossible 11 times in the past."

He'd done it 11 times already? John was scamming him. Had to be. "5,000,000? You're shitting me."

John just stared.

"Okay, call him in. Get it signed."

John said, "There's just one condition."

Uh-oh. Here you go.

"The check's only good for 24 hours."

"I said call him!"

John did. Rashid argued, glared at Vincent, double-checked that Vincent would be gone forever if he did this, then, finally, wrote a check. He handed it to Vincent. On John's insistence, he then left.

Vincent smiled. "Just like that?"

John nodded.

Unbelievable. Okay, Vincent could maybe cream off four times that in Vegas, but how many years would that take? Whatever the job, he was set for life. He grinned. Tonight he'd hit a club, a couple of lines of coke, get laid — wash all that do-gooding crap out of his system. "The job?"

John smiled. "I want someone killed."

Vincent laughed. "I figured it wasn't selling Girl Scout cookies." John was just a normal guy, with normal needs, normal grudges. Someone must have cracked his scam and John wanted him silenced. Easy money. "I knew this was all just a scam. But that's cool. So who's the mark?"

"Don't you want to know why?"

"Why would I need to know why? Just give me a name, an address."

John clicked Rashid's laptop, then turned it around to Vincent.

Vincent's jaw dropped.

John stood. "Don't be fooled into believing all you care about is money. You do have heart, Vincent." He left.

Vincent stared at a photo of Therese. Therese, who'd idolized him since she was old enough to talk. Therese, who'd struggled to understand him when everyone else had given up. Therese, the only person who could make him smile just by being herself. Therese his sister.

***

"— and Ambassador Zhang says his government is livid we're allowing such events to pollute the internet," said Ryan.

"So tell Ambassador Zhang the Chinese government can sever all its lines to the Web if it likes, but the day we censor Google and Yahoo's the day we close for business," said Tom. He gazed through the French windows, away through the bare oak branches wavering in the night breeze, to the Retreat's rolling hills. How he ached to be out walking with Beth, throwing sticks for Bruno and Red, instead of imprisoned here with the problems of the world. "Anything else?"

Ryan checked his file. "Rabbi Kushner, Imam Haaris, Bishop Applegate, and a whole bunch of others are demanding to know what we intend doing about the blasphemy he's spouting."

"Well, hell, let's rip up that pesky First Amendment, now, huh?" said Michael.

"Sorry, Ryan," said Tom, "it's a while since I attended Sunday school, but don't the Torah, the Qur'an, and the Bible all teach 'love thy neighbor'?"

"Matthew 22:39," said Simon. "Connolly's talking tolerance and the Church is talking Holy War." He sniggered. "Same old, same old."

Bob Schecter smoothed down the few wisps of hair desperately clinging to his head like refugees to a raft. "Is it our problem some Bible-pounding beak brains are buying into this crock?"

Tom shook his head. "So Connolly wants to show people how to forget their differences and live happily together, and for that the Church wants to crucify him?"

"Only the more fundamentalist sections," said Ryan.

"Only the fundamentalists?" said Tom. "Well, thank God it's no one liable to do anything stupid. Jeez. Anyone else on our case?"

"Not so vehemently." Ryan slid a list over to Tom's place at the table.

Gloria stood up from crouching before the Frank Lloyd Wright–style fireplace. "If the guy would just be up front about what he wants. But oh, no, we got the only evangelist *not* asking for donations parked in our backyard."

188

Ryan nodded. "But why are so many people buying into it before they even know what it is? It's like buying a CD before you even know whether the artist can sing."

Simon meandered over to the onyx coffee table for some coffee. "It's called faith, Ryan. They don't seem to advertise it on MTV these days no more."

Slumping against his chair back, Tom gazed at the 7-foot Christmas tree, its ornaments sparkling in the flickering firelight. Christmas seemed an age ago. Everything seemed an age ago. How it had all seemed so much easier all those years back, before it had all started — him and Simon righting the world over a beer; in the interval of the game; over dinner 'til Beth and Jean screamed at them to quit. So easy. And, boy, how he'd laughed when Simon suggested running in the forthcoming Mayor's election. He'd laughed the next day when Simon phoned, too. But Simon hadn't let up. Then, when the laughter finally died, Tom realized anything was possible. And the more they talked and studied the opposition, the more they realized they couldn't lose — their policies were better, their goals more achievable, their administration more transparent. But lose they did. People didn't want the goals, the policies, the transparency; they wanted the razzmatazz, the feel-good factor, the spin and ballyhoo. They didn't want an honest bean-counter; they wanted a dynamic leader — an invaluable lesson Tom had learned well. Climbing to the presidency through successive campaigns had given him a deep understanding of the people and how to protect them. For it wasn't those armed with a bomb or a gun who were to be feared; it was those armed with charisma and a silver tongue. "Well, Connolly might be nothing but smoke and mirrors, but he delivers like no one I've ever seen. I ask you, watching him, can you say you didn't wanna jump up and holler 'Yeah, I wanna be a hero!'? 'Cause I sure as hell can't."

Clicking her pen, Gloria shook her head. "You notice he kept saying it wasn't a scam to empty people's wallets? You ever see a street hustler show you the queen just before he mixes the cards and cleans you out?"

"Common hustler or not," said Tom, "Tanner's using him as a mouthpiece and getting the election handed to him on a plate. Yesterday we still had a 49–40 lead, but I dread to think where we stand now." He shook his head. "Hell's teeth." He snorted. "You dug up anything usable, Bob?"

Bob said, "Al-Alawi's been selling off his assets like there's no tomorrow since meeting Connolly. The money's obviously going somewhere, we're just not sure where, though we are looking into Connolly's association with Vincent Constanza and the Panucci family—"

"Oh, come on," said Michael, "Like the guy heals by day and supports organized crime by night."

"Well, they're stashing the money somewhere," said Bob. "If it's on the up, why not in a bank, like normal people?"

"I hide my wallet at night," said Michael. "That make me a hood?"

"Okay. Okay," said Tom, "so you're telling me that despite a $30 billion intelligence budget, the CIA can't find it?"

"I'm telling you, Mr. President," said Bob, "Al-Alawi's not only a shrewd businessman, but a hacker as good at any we got at Langley. But we've tapped everything we can, so it's just a matter of time."

John was too good to be true. Whether his angle was to con billions out of the gullible, create a religious backlash against consumerism and damage the economy, or incite an international crisis, it was tantamount to terrorism. They had to discover what he was up to, how, and why , then preempt any attack against America or its people. While this was a domestic issue and therefore not the CIA's domain, surveillance had to be covert so that, should anything or anyone be discovered, there were no leads back to any government department. Everything had to be eminently deniable. Only the CIA had those Black Ops resources.

Gloria stretched. "If he's some sort of communist, maybe he's just giving all the money away. Redistribution of wealth and all."

"Rawls," said Michael.

"Rawls? What's rawls?" asked Tom.

"Not what. Who," said Michael. "Connolly's ideas aren't communistic. It's Rawls's Difference Principle: as long as the poor become better off, the rich can get disproportionately richer without any moral dilemma. Everyone's richer; everyone's happier."

"But where do the resources come from if everyone just gets richer and richer and richer?" asked Tom.

"And there's your problem. Jobert, Fukuyama, Grof, everyone agrees a 'global society' would benefit the world. Economically and philanthropically. But there just aren't the resources to go round. For example, a team at Yale estimated that to give every single person on

190

the planet a developed standard of living — electricity, water what-have-you — would take 1.7 billion tons of copper. Problem is, there's only 1.6 billion left. In fact, in *The Moral Dimension*, Seric argues—"

Tom held up his hand. "So it won't fly?" He ambled back to the window.

"Not without major lifestyle sacrifices."

"It's unworkable bull," said Bob.

Tom stared out at the leafless trees swaying in the breeze. When beleaguered by problems, he found it soothing to watch the wind rustling the oaks and willows. Some of his best ideas had come while lost in their gentle to-ing and fro-ing. "Just what would happen if we tried to give every backwater Indian, African, and Chinaman a microwave, SUV, the latest PC?"

"You could kiss the ozone layer goodbye for a start," said Michael. "Skin cancer would rocket; weather patterns would go haywire; more famines, floods, droughts. Mines would dry up. Oil, too. Deforestation—"

"Okay, okay," said Tom. "So basically, for me and you to keep our beers nicely chilled in the refrigerator, half the world needs to live in disease-ridden poverty?"

Michael nodded. "In a nutshell."

"What about alternative energy?" asked Gloria.

"Yeah, right." Ryan snorted. "Who's gonna buy an electric car with a 40-mile range, that needs charging all night every night, when your gas guzzler roars like a lion and there's a gas station on every corner? Like all this 'one world' spirituality crap is ever going to fly."

Simon smirked. "Buddha, Muhammad, and Christ all believed it'd work. Or are you saying the teachings that keep over six billion of us living together in peace, that promote harmony and cooperation, that demand a universal ethic, are essentially hogwash?"

Gloria frowned. "So you're saying it's a good thing?"

"I'm saying many things have merit; still don't make them practical."

"Thing that gets me," said Gloria, fidgeting with her pen, "is he's just walked off the street, literally, yet expounds ideas like he's chair of the philosophy department at Harvard."

Simon smiled again. "A library's one of the coziest spots in a city."

Tom rested his forehead against the glass. It was hard, cold, unyielding.

"But of course, with no address, he won't have borrowed anything for his record to give us a handle on where he's heading."

"We could check the libraries' servers," said Bob. "See which websites were visited recently. Might take some time, but it's doable."

Excellent. Tom turned. "Now, that's a start. What else?"

"Freeze Al-Alawi's assets for an IRS audit?" said Gloria.

"Too much," said Tom. "If we victimize Connolly, he'll turn it to his advantage."

"So we don't focus on him or his team."

"I'm listening," said Tom.

"Runways develop potholes; planes, hydraulics faults; air controllers have strikes. If we can't stop him, we can at least slow him down."

"Good. Anything else?"

"Well," Ryan fanned the list of healed patients, "we any closer to nailing him as a fraud?"

"We've only a handful of case studies back," Michael shrugged, "all pretty much saying he's kosher."

"Some years back," said Tom, "there was footage uncovered of an alien autopsy in Roswell. Biologists, special-effects gurus, photographic experts — hell, half the world — studied it in minute detail and all swore it *had* to be authentic. Then some Brits owned up to filming it in a London apartment. So if you wanted to pull a hoax like Connolly's, how would you do it?"

Various suggestions came forth: hypnosis, narcotics, bribery, pain blockers, body doubles, coercion...

"You know," Michael laughed. "Forget it."

"Michael?" said Tom.

"No, really."

"Michael, we got squat..."

"Well, I know this is straight out of left field, but ... maybe he's for real."

Bob threw his pen down. "What is this? Open mike at the comedy club?"

"All those patients are still up and walking."

Bob sniggered. "So what? He's the Second Coming? 'Cause that's just what we need — some sandal-wearing bleeding-heart telling us where we're going wrong."

192

"I think we can safely discount him being the Second Coming, Bob," said Tom.

"So what d'you mean, 'for real'?" asked Gloria.

"Michael means, Gloria," said Tom, "that maybe Connolly really does heal and really does know how to make a difference."

"Exactly," said Michael.

"Now I've heard everything." Bob slumped on his elbows.

"You see, it could be a win-win situation." Michael laughed. "Instead of trying to stop him, we help him."

"Help him how?" said Tom.

"Well," said Michael, "look at the alternatives: either Al-Alawi backed him in a hoax involving every medical practitioner this side of China, or the guy's for real. Al-Alawi's worth 100 mil, so what's in it for him? And 'til six days ago, Connolly was eating out of a dumpsters. You telling me a guy who can mesmerize an audience of 200 million couldn't even get a job selling fries to get off the streets?"

"So you want we should just hand the country over to him? Watch him run it into the ground?" said Bob.

"Of course not," said Michael. "But if he can heal, we help him. If he's got sociological insights, we use them."

Tom paced the polished oak floor. Not many people would decline an invitation to the White House. Tom wasn't angry, more curious — that showed not arrogant stupidity, but a calculated confidence that he needed no help from any quarter to achieve his goals, no matter how high. "Help him?" He sighed. "Call me crazy, but somehow I doubt raising the minimum wage and passing a bill for everyone to love thy neighbor is what this guy has in mind. Like Simon said, he's playing for big stakes — he ain't gonna like what we're prepared to bring to the table."

"That's right," said Simon. "And that's why we've gotta take him out of the game."

Everyone stared at Simon.

"No matter what recessions we have to brave, we brave them. No matter the hurricanes or quakes or droughts, we brave them. Al Qaeda? Bombings, shootings, hijackings — we brave them. Why? 'Cause through it all, adversity gives the American people strength and only furthers our resolve to triumph. But this? This is deadlier than any bullet, ruined harvest, or stock market crash. The American people will take on any

adversary and defeat it through unity. But if that unity rots to the core..."
Simon shook his head. "Whether this guy's for real or fake is academic.
He's eating away at our unity from within. Forget Bin Laden — this guy's
the most dangerous man on the planet."

Simon was right. And it was Tom's duty to protect the country. At
any cost. So why did he feel people would see him as the guy who shot
Bambi's mother?

***

Tom waved. "Goodnight, Simon. My apologies to Jean." Simon and
Jean had little enough time without impromptu meetings. Still, personal
sacrifices were part of the job — guilt at neglecting your family for the
nation's interests was one of the first things a statesman had to learn
to cope with. He turned to Bob, who was collecting his papers way too
slowly. "Something on your mind, Bob?"

"There's, er..." Bob clucked his tongue.

Reticence was unlike Bob. "Yeah?"

"There's one option we haven't considered, sir."

"We've been at it the best part of six hours, Bob, so I doubt that.
But...?"

Bob checked the door, as if ensuring they were alone. "I, er, have a
team, a specialist unit, trained to clean up messes like this."

Tom laughed. "Holy hell, Bob."

"Mr. President, it's the only sure way of guaranteeing—"

"That we're all impeached? That this guy becomes a martyr? That
the entire administration ends up in Attica?"

"Sir, I—"

Tom held up his hands. "What's that word you like, now? Ah, yes,
'Disappeared'. So much nicer than garrotted, or poisoned, or blasted in
the head with a .38. Hell, Bob." He snickered, shaking shook his head.

"With respect, sir, the interests of the nation must come before any
personal considerations," said Bob.

"Personal considerations? That what it is? So nothing to do with
justice, rights, free speech, the Constitution?" Tom laughed, turning
Bob for the door. "Hell, Bob, you might be head of the CIA, but thank
God you've no aspirations for public office."

21

From Grace to Fall

No—" As Rashid drove them home, Mary snorted into her cell. What a day. On trying to depart Lexington Private Airfield first thing, the tower had grounded them for an hour due to problems receiving their Lear's radio signal. Then, when they arrived over Kansas City, Missouri, a fuel spill on Runway 1 kept them in a holding pattern, wasting another hour. Second stop, Springfield, had gone okay. But after jetting to Memphis, Tennessee, their charter helicopter hadn't shown, so they'd had to hire cabs. They'd covered only three of the planned seven hospitals. A disaster and everyone was truly pissed.

"Look, it's not—" Mary snorted again. John glanced up from a CNN report on a demonstration by fundamentalists outside the hospital at which he'd first healed. Eight arrests had been made after violence broke out following the burning of an effigy of John. Mary rolled her eyes. "Really, the money's not— Oh, to hell with it." She hung up. "CBS. Offering a Dr. Phil-style show." She shook her head. "They just don't get we're not for sale." It was the latest of the relentless media offers, none of which served John's purpose.

Ben hung up his phone. "More bad news." He jabbed at the news report. "Some of these clowns have gotten hold of Rashid's address. Our security's holding them outside the grounds, but it don't sound pretty."

Ben suggested they wait for the police. But John insisted they push on. He seemed to enjoy making things difficult. Or was even he as desperate to see the day ended as everyone else?

***

The 7-foot wrought-iron gates swung inward. Barking as mean as Cerberus, four German shepherds dragged their handlers into the throng of protestors sixty to seventy strong. The mob parted, hurling abuse and jabbing banners proclaiming allegiance to Christianity and the one true God.

Moments later, the guards' appearance confirming John's imminent arrival, the mob easily guessed John was in the approaching Hummer. The protestors scowled with outrage, pounded the air with their fists, stabbed placards at the car.

A stone shattered the windshield.

Mary gasped. Grabbed John's hand.

The horde at bay, Rashid floored the gas, shooting for the open gates.

The hounds barked. Curses rained. Stones pelted.

With so many strangers so hungry to lynch her, Mary's adrenaline exploded. She squeezed John's hand as if she were trying to crush it. A voice in her head screamed, 'Run! Escape! Hide!'.

A placard slammed into her window. She jumped. Cowered from her door. Crushed John's hand even harder. That voice screamed louder. Louder! 'Get away!' All she saw was a blur of hatred. All she heard was a blur of hatred. Her world was a deafening, chaotic blur of hatred.

It felt as if time had frozen.

Finally, Rashid hared up the drive, gravel spitting at the guards as they backed inside the perimeter.

It was over. Mary panted, clutching her chest. "Oh, thank God." Never had just a few seconds lasted so long.

"Stop, Rashid!" said John.

Rashid turned from squinting through the crazed windshield. "Someone hurt?"

"Stop!"

Rashid hammered on the brakes. The tires churned dark furrows in the drive.

John leapt out and dashed for the closing gates.

196

Oh, no! "John!" Mary knew what he was going to do, now his friends were all safe: reason with the mob. Holy hell, they'd tear him apart.

Ignoring her, he shot for the gates' narrowing gap.

Jeering, the crowd swelled forward.

Ben clambered out and lumbered after him. "John! John!"

"Oh, hell." She had to do something, but what? She grabbed Rashid's camcorder and scrambled out. If there were trouble, she could at least document it for the police.

The mob's fat ringleader saw John approaching. Comb-over flailing in the wind, his weathered Bible thrust skyward, the fat man shouted, "*And Jesus said unto them, 'Take heed lest any man deceive thee. For many shall come in my name, claiming "I am Christ", and shall deceive many.'*"

The mob screamed, faces red in twisted hatred, fists clenched in endorphin rush.

Just as the gates closed, John squeezed through.

Brandishing a placard proclaiming '*Thou shalt have no other Gods before me!*' a blond-haired man spat at John.

John stood. Silent. Defiant.

Ben shouted at the guards. "Open the gates. Get the dogs out there!"

The fat man spat his message more fervently, the devil now before him, "*For false Christs and false prophets shall rise and show great signs and miracles to deceive. So be on thy guard. Be on thy guard!*"

Someone shouted, "If thine eye offend thee, pluck it out!"

A stone glanced off John's temple. He barely flinched. It would've been wiser to fall and not taunt them.

The first stone cast, more pelted. Then fists and feet as the mob engulfed John.

Oh, no. They'd kill him. Mary threw the camcorder to Vincent, who'd climbed into her seat for a better view. She backed for the gates. "Get this! Get it all!"

She sprinted for John. Fear? There was no fear. Just as a woman seeing a knife-wielding maniac threatening her child isn't paralyzed by fright, but energized by the primal instinct to protect those she loves, so Mary raced to save John.

The gates glided open. Ben barged through and leapt at the mob. He heaved them off John like a farmhand tossing hay bales.

Right behind him, Mary yanked the blond man back by his hair.

He spun. Face red with fury. Fist raised.

Oh, no, he was going to kill her! Mary cowered, pulling her arms up for protection.

But the guards were out, too. The dogs gnashed, straining to attack.

The protesters shrank back, courage deserting them in the face of adversaries prepared to retaliate.

Rashid backed the Hummer up.

Mary dashed to the battered, bloody ball in the mud — John. "Oh, no." How could people abuse someone so innocent, so good?

Floundering, John struggled to stand. She hauled him up. Blood gushed from his right temple, covering half his face. Filthy, he collapsed over the Hummer's hood.

Mary shouted, "You fucking animals!"

Someone pointed a camcorder at her, obviously wanting a sick trophy to show the good ol' boys back home.

"*Fallen!*" cried the fat man, triumphantly. "*Fallen is Babylon the Great, that hath made all nations drink the maddening wine of her fornication.*"

"I'll give you fallen!" With a giant of a haymaker, Mary cracked him in the mouth. He reeled into his followers.

The crowd surged to retaliate, but the dogs strained at their leashes. A standoff.

Rashid dashed to help John, while Vincent filmed through the window.

Sirens blared. Three squad cars screeched toward them. Red and blue lights smeared anger-twisted faces.

Ben ran to the nearest car. After a brief exhange, Ben, the guards, and six patrolmen converged on the mob.

The lead patrolman shouted, "Okay, drop your banners, your stones, and back up." He turned to Ben. "You aiming to press charges?"

"Damn right we are."

"No." John pushed off the hood.

"Let Ben handle this, John," said Mary.

"Please." John gestured for the police to halt.

The fat man saw it as weakness. "*The time has come for judgment, for rewarding thy servants, and for destroying those who destroy the earth.*"

John spat blood to clear his mouth, blood drenching the right side of his face like a mask. "You want scripture?" He stalked toward the fat man. "James 3:13: *'Who is wise and understanding among you? Let him show it by his good life, by deeds that come with the humility of wisdom.'* Matthew 5:10: *'Blessed are those who suffer persecution for their righteousness, for theirs is the kingdom of heaven.'* John 3:12: *'I have spoken to you of earthly things, yet you refuse to believe; how then will you believe if I tell you of heavenly things?'*"

The mob shuffled, uneasy at their doctrine used against them.

The fat man sneered. "Do not test the Lord thy God, lest He test thee and thee be found wanting."

John shouted right in his face. "I test *no one*. I heal; I help; I put right what's wrong. If a man can't be judged by his deeds, what can he be judged by?"

"By God."

"To a hate-mongering pariah like you, there is no God."

22

The Dogs Unleashed

Simon dashed into the Oval Office. "Excuse me, sir, but you're gonna want to see this."

Tom slung away a report on Connolly's healed patients that confirmed his worst fears — they all appeared healthy. "You sure?"

Simon grinned. "Oh, yeah." He hit the remote for the plasma screen TV. Outside Rashid's gates, in blood-free left profile, John glared at a fat man with a wispy comb-over, a Reverend Wilmore of Saw Flats, Alabama. John spat, "There is no God!"

Tom gasped, then punched the air. "Who's your daddy!"

Simon winked at him. "Told you he'd slip one day."

Dan Latterman, of KBNY, stared into camera. "There you have it, ladies and gentlemen, straight from the horse's mouth." The screen-in-screen showed protestors peacefully waiting outside Rashid's gates, then cut to dogs gnashing at women, children crying, Mary punching Wilmore. "Over the past seven days, this nation has taken John Connolly, the Secret Angel, to its heart as a healer, a prophet, some have even said Messiah. But now, as this footage shows, isn't it time we listened to the cynics who've said, all along, it was just too good to be true? Yesterday, Connolly said he healed for the love of others; said he wanted nothing in return; said he could heal the world. Today, his followers turn to violence; he sets his dogs upon women and children, then proclaims there is no God. Is this a man we should encourage our children to look to for guidance? Invite into our lives like an old, trusted friend—"

Tom applauded. "The voice of sanity at last!" He sauntered over to his liquor cabinet. "Thank God." Pouring two scotches, he glanced back. "For a while there, I tell you, I thought the whole world had gone to hell and we were the only sane two left."

"Me too, sir."

Tom handed him his drink. "To sanity."

They toasted, Simon adding, "And the power of the press."

"Amen to that."

***

"You absolute asshole, Latterman!" shouted Mary at the TV, from beside John on Rashid's sofa.

"So we release our camcorder footage," said Ben. "Show what really went down."

"It's not enough, my friend." said Rashid, clicking off the TV's power switch.

"They're not interested in the truth." Pacing, Mary jabbed at the TV. "That crap's much bigger than the truth... Damn it!" Why did the media take such pleasure in building someone up, only to knock them down? Why? Money — once good stories went stale turning them around into something bad guaranteed to hold people's interest 'til the next ad break.

"There must be something we can do," said Ben.

"Why?" asked Mary. "We'll heal those who need it. To hell with everyone else."

She saw Rashid flash an anxious look at John. Holy crap, even now they were still playing games? "Hey, if there's anything we should know...?"

Rashid buried his face in his laptop.

Mary pushed. "John?"

John sighed. "*Though seeing, they cannot see; though hearing, they cannot understand.*"

"Excuse me?!" Was he kidding? "We walk away from *everything* for you and you take the piss?"

John shook his head. "Mary, I—"

"Well, forgive a dumb bitch like me for giving a damn!"

"I wasn't referring to you."

"Oh..." she glanced at Rashid. "Well, maybe if you let everyone else in on your plans, we wouldn't be in this mess. Holy crap." She paced. "Have you any idea how difficult it is to win the press back once they think you've screwed them over?"

John said, "Mary—"

"I mean, I wouldn't mind if we'd milked them for all we could, but to let them have free rein, then get shafted—"

"Mary—"

She shook her head. "Jeez, I should've known. If only—"

"Mary!"

She looked at John.

"Call KBNY. Tell them they've just got another exclusive."

***

Propped up on her elbow on her pillow, Mary lightly brushed the steri-strips over the gash in John's forehead, then over his bruised eye. "Why don't you heal it?"

"Some women say the hottest thing about Harrison Ford is the scar on his chin."

She tutted. "One knock on the head and now sex appeal's top priority."

"A soldier wears his scars proudly after battle."

"And no harm in going for the sympathy vote, either." John had declined payment from KBNY, his only stipulation being Vincent's camcorder footage must be shown in its entirety, or no deal. Such a major coup, how could the station refuse?

"We will be able to turn this around?" asked Mary.

John shrugged.

She almost wished he'd said 'no'. A week ago, she'd have given anything for a chance at a meaningful life. Now... Now, she'd give anything for a mortgage, the school run, mundanity. But there could never be a life of mundanity with John — the needs of the many outweighed the needs of the few, or the one. Could she handle sharing him with the world? Yes. But that wasn't how it would work. Could she handle coming second to everyone in need, everyone suffering, everyone wanting? If she couldn't handle that, she'd lose him. Simple. She exhaled loudly. What had she done? What had happened to distancing herself for self-preservation? Even if it were for such a worthy cause, could she bear to be abandoned? If only he'd reassure her. Share his plans. Promise to be there. She couldn't hold the question in any longer. "You and Rashid."

"Hmm?"

"There anything I should know?"

"Nope."

"Nothing?"

"Nope."

Hell. Was that a 'nope, there's nothing going on', or a 'nope, there's nothing I feel you should know'? In the future, she'd construct her questions more carefully.

***

At his desk in the Oval Office, Tom pushed away a budget proposal on subsidizing cattle feed in the Midwest. Now the Connolly crisis was over, they could get back to running the country, and maybe he could get back to stealing quality time with Beth. He gazed across at Monet's *Morning on the Seine, Good Weather* above the fireplace. The green and blue fusion of trees and water was an absolute delight. Most presidents felt obliged to hang a somber portrait of Washington or Lincoln, but in a room so often imprisoned by the solemnity of office, was a little color, light, life, too much to ask for? Yes, all he had to worry about now was an election, budget cuts, the Middle East... It was heaven.

Simon strode in. "Evening, Mr. President. Got some news on our boy Connolly."

"He's revealed the hoax? Moved to Canada? Joined the circus?"

"He's not gone quite so far, but it's good for us, all the same."

"Oh?" Connolly's declaration that God didn't exist was to their campaign what winning the lottery would be to a trailer park family. Yes, his 'miracles' had converted half the country, but fortunately it was mostly the half that saw miracles as divine acts of God. Talk about shooting yourself in the foot. And that's just what Tanner had done by backing Connolly. Simon had been right, thank God. The story would run a few days, then bury itself, leaving the press open to matters political. Anything now could only accelerate that process. Excellent.

"Late press release." Simon waved a paper. "KBNY is hosting an exclusive tomorrow. A kinda right to reply."

"Connolly doesn't do TV."

"He does now. But that's not the best of it."

"Oh?"

"The program's in the form of a debate."

"A debate? What's to debate?"

"Not what. Who?"

It didn't matter at all. This was the act of a desperate man. Tom shrugged.

Simon smirked. "Senator Geoff Tanner."

"Tanner!" Talk about desperate acts.

"Didn't I say every cloud has a silver lining?"

"No," said Tom, "as I recall, you saw the color of that cloud and rushed out to build an ark... Tanner?"

"Live. Nationwide. 9:00 p.m. eastern."

Tom laughed. "So Tanner's burned himself backing Connolly, so thinks if he gives him a whupping on national TV, he'll redeem himself in front of the voters?"

"Shall I bring the popcorn?"

"Tanner may well salvage some support but, ha, he's not the sharpest tool in the box, while Connolly, whoa – he'll rip Tanner a new one, just to reclaim a little dignity."

"It'll be a bloodbath." Simon winked. "Lose-lose."

"It'll leave the voters reeling."

"And we just mosey on in and pick up the pieces. Sweet or what?"

Tom smiled, twirling the end of his pen in the corner of his mouth. He had approaching $200 million pledged to his campaign coffers already and Tanner had been his only real rival. The way things were going, Tom could spend a tenth of that, give the rest to charity, and still be behind this desk for another four years. Connolly would perform one last miracle: presenting Tom with the greatest landslide victory in history. He laughed. What could go wrong?

23

The Voice of Reason

At the foot of the hospital bed, Vincent twisted to see if John had palmed some drug or something to 'heal' a little boy who wheezed like a geriatric chain smoker. Nothing. He snorted. He caught Mary smirking at him. Yeah, right. He'd seen how suspicious she was of John and Rashid — like she, a journalist, didn't want John strip-searched the first time she saw him pull this scam. Scam? Go figure. All these children, *all* these children, were seemingly healed. Events at Charlotte General, North Carolina, were paralleling those in Rock Hill, South Carolina, Atlanta, Georgia, and everywhere else. Vincent had once seen a guy on TV have a vasectomy without anesthetic, using hypnosis alone — hell, made him cringe even now — proving the mind could control the body. It'd been another hellish day of delays and problems, so John had only healed 100, maybe 110 people, yet not one had keeled over dead. Hypnosis and drugs could aid pain management — they couldn't do crap for a lung full of cancer.

What if... What if John was the real deal? "Oh, come on." He ambled away, shaking his head. He was starting to think like all those other losers. He pulled up. Stared. Children jumping, laughing, playing, smiling. Everywhere. He rubbed his head. It was impossible, but what if...

He sniggered. So what if it was real? Like it was the healing that counted. It wasn't the mechanics of a scam that mattered, but the payoff.

He'd figured the money angle: Rashid offered insurance companies John's services for a percentage of what they would have spent on treating people. Hence all Rashid's phone calls. That part of the scam was simple. But to demand his cut, Vincent needed more information. Whenever he borrowed Rashid's laptop for email, the internet history and recent document list were wiped, and every file asked for a password. There were secrets there, if he could just unlock them. And he would. Information was leverage, and leverage was the key to his cut. He'd google 'break passwords'. Maybe he could find something to sneak him past Rashid's security — payback for John's $5,000,000 stunt.

Something rolled against his foot. He glanced down. A ball. Mary grinned, crouched beside a little boy in Spiderman pajamas.

Oh, for the love of... Okay, so he'd humor her to keep her off his back, then get back to studying the scam. Two kicks and he flicked the ball into his hands.

Spiderman clapped.

Vincent tossed the ball. The boy caught it. An improvement over the last loser.

But the boy immediately threw it back and shouted, "Again!"

As if. Vincent trapped the ball under his foot. He flicked the ball up, bounced it on his knee twice, then up to his head. Once. Twice... 'Somehow' he lost control and the ball shot out of the ward door. He shrugged to the disheartened boy, then turned for a closer look at John.

Something tugged his jacket. He looked down.

Spiderman. With two other boys. And two more balls. "Again!" shouted Spiderman.

Vincent scowled at Mary.

She laughed, Rashid behind her, recording him.

Fantastic. Here he was on the brink of being richer than Jesus, and what? Damn kids were crowding out his action.

"Pleeeeeeease," said Spiderman.

Vincent sighed. He looked at the boys, all beaming up at him like he was some kind of hero. Ten minutes ago, they'd had as much chance of ever leaving their beds as he had of becoming Pope. They'd been given a second chance. Was that what John was offering him?

Sucker! Once this month was up, he'd— He looked at John, who was 'healing' another child. One thought gnawed at him — what if John was for real? Vincent couldn't spot the healing scam. And, regardless of their illnesses, *all* the people *every day* made miraculous recoveries. Miraculous? You didn't get miracles no matter how good your medical insurance. Miracles were God's crap. Okay, a wild idea, but suppose there was a God. Wouldn't that mean there was a Devil, too? And a hell? Ah... Considering Vincent's history, that wasn't a particularly appealing idea.

Vincent's Glock 18 was the best pistol ever built. Easy to use, sturdy, accurate, reliable. Yet he still carried a Glock 26 as backup in case something went wrong. God was a crock. Vincent was positive. But what if he was wrong? He wasn't the kinda guy to be polishing the local church's altar any time soon; he was more likely to be filling up its cemetery! So wouldn't it be wise to have a backup plan?

Vincent snorted, staring at the ball. Would it hurt so much to play nice once in a while?

***

Driving from Lexington Airfield to KBNY, Rashid glanced in his mirror at Vincent who was typing an email with his index fingers on Rashid's laptop. Okay, Vincent wouldn't be first on the list for the Santa suit in the next Macy's parade, but something had clicked. He'd spoken to Ben without masking it as a threat, said 'thank you' to Mary when she'd passed him a soda, and displayed his soccer skills for a good 20 seconds to his three-strong audience. Vincent-wise, that was as significant a breakthrough as most of the doctors had witnessed with their patients today.

But was it wise to allow him free rein? Rashid glanced at him again. What remained of the paper trail was ensconced in Rashid's safe. The sensitive files on his laptop were protected with 128-bit AES encryption. And Panucci had guaranteed Vincent's compliance, safeguarding both Sana and Aisha from harm. So how much damage could Vincent do?

John had said the only way to triumph over evil was not by becoming it, but by countering it with good. He was right. It was one of the teachings of Sura 41 of the Qur'an. After all, Rashid himself had been redeemed in the eyes of Allah, and to his parents. So much so, his parents had invited him to visit once John's plans came to fruition. 27 years he'd waited. What a glorious gift John bequeathed to all those he touched. So if Rashid could be saved, why not Vincent?

At a round oak table with Dan Latterman and John, Tanner nodded, smearing a smile over his fat face. "— and that's why we give 29 billion in foreign aid, of the American taxpayers' money."

"It's not enough," said John.

In the wings, Mary smiled. When John had walked on stage, the audience had bayed for a lynching. After seeing the footage of John's assault, however, they'd welcomed him back like the proverbial prodigal son — leaving Tanner backtracking on plans to crucify him.

"John, the American people have mighty deep pockets when it comes to charity, but they work hard for their money. That's why, if elected, I'll slash $360 billion off their tax bill. Ha. Only the Stevens administration or a communist would persecute them with even higher taxes."

John locked Tanner's gaze. Recognizing that look, Mary smiled. Tanner was all spin and sound bites. This would be fun.

"That's a nice shirt," said John.

Tanner nodded. "Why thank you, John. Now, the solution as I—"

"Ralph Lauren? Levi Strauss? Tommy Hilfiger?"

"Something like that, but while I'd love to talk fashion, John, the question is—"

"The Chinese sweatshop worker who made that shirt probably earned around 30 cents, while the CEO of the corporation that sold it could've got $10,000 an hour or more. You've got to have mighty deep pockets to take home a paycheck that big."

"Well, John, I wouldn't know about that, but—"

"Don't you think you should know? Isn't it your responsibility to know?"

"Son, the global economy's a might tricky creature. If you—"

"It isn't the American people who hoard the world's wealth in their deep pockets, it's corporations. If you cap the profit you—"

"Whoa there, John." Tanner laughed. "Cap profit? Hoard wealth? What about R&D, expansion, innovation? Hell, son, you'll have us back in the Dark Ages. What's next? Cap wages?"

"Yes."

Tanner threw up his hands.

Mary covered her eyes. America was enterprise, freedom, hope. Capping wages was tantamount to telling people they'd always live the same crappy lives — killing their dreams. John had blown it.

John was unfazed. "If you capped profits to the needs of the company — salaries at, say, $1 million a year, think what you could achieve with that extra revenue. Or are you saying *you* couldn't live on only a million bucks a year, 'cause I'm damn sure I could? So why should some get five, 10, 20 times that?"

Tanner smirked. "Cap everyone's pay and ship it all off to Ethiopia? That why the American people trail out to work five days a week?"

"That's why I'd reduce the working week to four days. Why I'd use the extra revenue to provide free education for all, free utilities for all, free health care for all."

The audience whooped and applauded.

Tanner just squinted. "You a communist, son?"

"So you have to be a communist to care about poverty, disease, inequality?"

Tanner stabbed a finger at John. "Don't be putting your trash in my mouth, boy."

"So tell me why the American people should have to pay for life's essentials: water, power, health care, education? Or will the Tanner administration consider them luxuries people can forgo if they can't afford them? Why not charge for air?"

Tanner paused, then smiled. "I care very deeply about poverty, disease, and inequality, but I believe in a fair day's pay for a fair day's work. We didn't build this great nation of ours by giving everything away for free, son."

"And we didn't build this great nation because someone paid us. We built it to create beauty where there was only ugliness; order where there was only chaos; triumph where there was only failure. The American people built this great nation; now it's time for them to build a great world."

The audience applauded.

Mary bit her lip. More fancy ideals, wild promises. People would only swallow so much poetic rhetoric before they demanded John deliver — what then?

"Nice speech, son, but the American people ain't the fools you take them for. Once they see all the facts, they ain't gonna let such ridiculous notions fly."

"This country's built on freedom, but people only have the freedom their consciences allow," said John. "Tell me, do you leave your TV on standby?"

"I've read the legislation, son. In fact, I've written a lot of it. And last I looked, leaving your TV on standby ain't exactly a felony."

"No, but instead of just polluting the environment, if the American people turned off their TVs, DVD players, PCs, all those little red lights we love to keep glowing 24/7, there'd be enough electricity saved to power every home in Zambia for a year."

Tanner sniggered. "Is that right?"

John stared into him. "Sixty percent of Zambians live on less than a dollar a day. One in five children won't see their fifth birthday. And life expectancy's 38. Isn't that worth bending down and clicking a switch?"

Mary shook her head. Heartfelt rhetoric, yes, but of no substance. John never gave details of how he'd change the world because there were none. Just rhetoric and dreams. Oh, God help them.

"Great sound bites, son. But people resist change — it's human nature."

"So you're so lazy you'll leave your TV on standby while Africa lies in darkness? So selfish—"

"Now, just one darn minute—"

"— you'll drive cars that burn a gallon of gas every 20 miles, destroying the atmosphere, while one in two Australians gets skin cancer? So ignorant, stupid, and callous—"

Tanner lurched out of his seat. "Who in hell—"

"— you'll claw money from your screw-you-buddy,-I've-got-mine job, while millions suffer, not just in Africa, but here in the U.S. — in our schools, where weapons can be as common as textbooks; in our hospitals, where treatment depends, not on your illness, but your bank balance; in our lives, where success isn't measured in awards, but in holding down two jobs to cover bills, stave off eviction, feed our kids?" The audience clapped and whistled. John stood. He stabbed a finger at Tanner. "And it's people like you who let it happen."

Red-faced, Tanner sneered. "Who in hell d'you think you're, boy?"

John scowled. "The voice of reason. And I've been silent too long."

"Gentlemen, please." Dan waved them into their seats.

"Oh, no," said Mary. John had lost it. Ridiculing Tanner might be good sport, but John had backed himself into a corner. This was beyond even him.

Tanner snorted like a raging bull but sat, mopping his burning red face with a handkerchief.

John slammed a bound document onto the table. He skidded it across to Tanner.

What was that? Mary gasped. Could it finally be her answers? What else would John document?

Tanner flicked his gaze to it, then ignored it. He stared at John.

Mary had waited so, so long. "Come on." Each second hung in the air like an hour. "Open the damn book."

From his temple, a bead of sweat crawled slowly, slowly, slowly down the side of Tanner's face. Finally, he ripped the book open.

Tanner's snorting breath transformed. Into a chuckle. He shook his head, then turned to another section. He chuckled again. "And this is how you're gonna change the world?"

John barely nodded.

Tanner read, "All new noncommercial production vehicles, imported or U.S. manufactured, to have a minimum fuel consumption of 35 miles per gallon within five years. The limit to be raised by two miles per gallon each year thereafter."

Mary slumped. This was John's wondrous plan to save the world? God help them.

Tanner smiled. "This ain't changing the world, it's taking away people's choice."

"No. It's taking away people's greed."

Tanner tossed the document aside. "Just how dumb d'you think the American people are? They'll never buy this."

"No?" John counted on his fingers. "Free education. Free utilities. Free health care."

Tanner's smirk dropped. "You'll not find one senator, congressman, or governor who'll give you the time of day. They see a crock like this, they're gonna laugh like it's raining tequila."

"Then it's good I won't need them."

"You gonna replace them?" Tanner laughed. "Hell, I'll give you credit, boy, you got spunk. But why not go the whole hog? Why not install yourself as P—" His smile vanished. Wide-eyed, he stared back at the book, then John.

John smiled. He turned to the audience. "Ladies and gentlemen, I'd like to announce that I, John Connolly, will be running as an independent candidate in this year's election for President of the United States of America."

A breath gasped around the audience, then ... the studio exploded with cheers, applause, and whistles.

***

Tom stared at the TV, mouth agape.

Simon stared, agape.

Gloria stared...

Ryan...

***

Mary gaped. Oh, God help them. John's secret plan, the plan to save the world, the plan he'd spent every other second concocting with Rashid ... was to be President!? They'd thought they'd suffered a backlash with the protests, media maligning, even the hate mail they'd started receiving. That was a backlash? Yeah, right — when your average Islamic fundamentalist got upset, was he happy to simply pen a scathing letter? Corporate America? Oh, they'd be just lining up to give back the billions of dollars they'd prized out of the people. The Orient? Human rights were stepped around like dog crap on the sidewalk.

She buried her face in her hands. Realistically, it was probably the only way John could deliver everything he'd promised, but ... while half the world would love him, the other half would love to see him dead. And not just John. If America was running rampant over everything and everyone to forge a new world of equality and prosperity, it too would be a target. This could be the end. Literally. The Apocalypse. John wouldn't be seen as a savior, but an anti-Christ.

24

Heroes for Ghosts

At 33,000 feet, Air Force One's four General Electric CF6 engines droned as if they were God chanting 'Ommmmm' to maintain Nirvana. But despite being so much closer to heaven, Tom was no nearer enlightenment.

He bustled into the wood-paneled conference room. "You better have something good, 'cause President Jiang's so pissed, he's canceled their Boeing order to prove it. Says Connolly's candidacy is a direct assault to enforce western ideology on China to corrupt the Chinese people." It was only minutes since Connolly's announcement, yet Tom's problems had multiplied tenfold.

"They don't mind the 'direct assault' of Wal-Marts and KFCs when there's a quick buck in it for them," said Michael.

"Tell me about it," said Tom. "They didn't even let their own people into the Forbidden City for 500 years — now there's a Starbucks slap bang in the middle. Hell, if cross-cultural enterprise is such a cash cow, maybe I should stick a noodle bar in the Oval—" He pointed at Ryan. "Oh, my... What the hell is that?"

Ryan's face burned red. He clutched a file to his chest, hiding an 'I ♥ the Secret Angel' neck tie. "Oh, er, Chloe bought it for me. Made me, er, promise to wear it. Sorry, sir."

"Chloe?"

"My daughter."

"I know who Chloe is, Ryan. I just didn't appreciate the White House dress code was being set by a seven-year-old."

On his cell, Simon scurried in. "Yes— Ye— We'll— I'll relay your concerns myself. Thanks for coming to me first, Lyle." Simon flipped his cell shut. "Sorry, sir. General Motors. Another satisfied customer."

Tom sighed. "Don't tell me — Connolly's 35-mpg proposal."

"And all the rest," said Simon. "Still, can't blame GM, it'd cost them millions."

"Ten 747s?" said Gloria, "That's, what, 5-600 million? Boeing can handle that."

"Try 2.4 billion," said Tom. "But, yes, they may struggle, but they'll handle it. Of course, many of the suppliers Boeing outsources to could go to the wall."

"That's the least of the problem," said Michael. "If the Saudis hold good to their threat to cut off our oil, we're talking major recession."

"Didn't I ask for something good?" said Tom. "Should I go out and come back in?" Connolly was set not to merely sink Tom's hopes of a second term, but the entire country so badly it would take decades to recover. "In the last election, 110 million people voted, 59 million for us. Problem is there are 120 million regular churchgoers in this country and most of them believe Connolly performs miracles. Do you wanna do the math, 'cause I sure as hell don't."

Ryan rattled his pen between his teeth. "Maybe he's not serious about running. Maybe he's bluffing to force us to implement changes."

"If it's a bluff, kid," Bob Schecter's voice blasted from the speakerphone, "why in hell is Al-Alawi selling off all his assets? He's worth 90 million. He ain't shopping for socks."

Gloria clicked her pen. "Ninety million's not enough to run a campaign, but it sure could give one a damn good kick start."

"And I don't know about anyone else," said Tom, "but free utilities, education, and health care? Hell, I'm tempted to vote for him myself."

"You got anything for us, Bob?" asked Simon.

"Collating what we can, but it's mighty patchy."

Simon slid over a list of cities Connolly had visited.

Tom read, "Allentown, Atlanta, Charlotte, Cleveland, Columbus, Detroit, Duluth...?" Nothing new. He shrugged.

"Naturally, we alphabetized the list. Now look." Simon passed another sheet.

"Well, I'll..."

"Exactly," said Simon. "We thought he was zigzagging the country for maximum publicity, but he's settled into a nice, easy pattern now."

Tom looked at the list of states. "Georgia, Missouri, the Carolinas, Tennessee – The Bible Belt."

Simon nodded. "It gets better." He passed a final list over.

Tom read: Arizona, Florida, Michigan, Ohio, Pennsylvania, Washington. Eyes closed, he rubbed his temples. "Swing states."

"Bible Belt and swing States – all the major population areas in the states with the most electoral votes." Simon tutted. "Guy's a genius."

"He's been campaigning and we didn't even know it," said Ryan

"Oh, Lord help us." The high percentage of undecided voters in swing states was often where elections were won and lost. As for John's miracles and the Bible Belt... "He visits three cities in one day and changes people's lives; we show up once in a blue moon and expect the red carpet rolled out."

Michael scanned the lists. "He's only visited 11 states, but if you include New York, that's 197 votes. If he pulled in the big ones, California and Texas, too... Jeez."

"That'd be 286," said Simon.

"But that means—" said Gloria.

"We all know what it means, thank you, Gloria," said Tom. It meant Connolly would have 16 more votes than he needed to win the Presidency. Tom raked his hands down his face. "There *any* good news?"

Simon toyed with his pencil. "A long time ago, there were these two guys. The first had a dream of uniting the world and ushering in a new age of peace and prosperity. The second, Dietrich Bonhoeffer, had a different dream, so different he was hanged for it. All he wanted was to stick a bullet in the first guy's brain. That first guy was Adolf Hitler."

"I don't get it," said Ryan.

Tom said, "I do, and I don't like it."

"I'm just saying, there's more than one way to skin a cat. As I'm sure Bob will agree."

"And the CIA will back whatever action you feel is necessary, Mr. President," said Bob.

In his bid to create a perfect world, Hitler killed 55,000,000 people and brought the planet to the brink of Armageddon. One guy with a gun could've ended untold suffering in a second. But could evil ever be justified in the name of good? Tom hammered the table. "And couldn't the Nazis have made the same argument for assassinating Roosevelt or Churchill?"

"Oh, boy," said Ryan.

Simon held up his hands. "Just illustrating a point, not advising a course of action. See, if you can't sack your opponent's quarterback, you better make damn sure you keep possession of the ball."

But of course! Until now, John had chosen the game and made the rules. How could they compete with 'miracles'? But now? Tom couldn't heal the sick, but he sure could legislate, work the system, muster the people. They had the experience, the expertise, the resources. Now, John was playing their game, their rules. "Any ideas?"

"Free utilities, education, health care? A four-day week?" said Simon. "*We* see it'll run the country into the ground, but your average Joe won't. All he'll see is what's in it for him. We just gotta put it in such a way he'll get it, too."

"Actually," Michael cleared his throat, waggling his pen at Simon, "it, er, er, wouldn't."

"Excuse me?" Tom frowned. If juggling figures were a spectator sport, Michael would be an Olympic champion.

"Connolly's figures ... they, er, add up."

"You yanking my chain, Michael?"

Michael smiled like a boy who'd spent a year's allowance on baseball cards and finally found that elusive pitcher to complete the set. "Oh, it's beautiful. His capping percentages leave enough for business to operate, for contingencies and expansion, yet yield enough revenue to cover all the costs."

Bob blurted, "What? Hell, we won the damn Cold War, boy. We won! We just gonna hand the country over to this new brand of communism now?"

Simon laughed. "A rose by any other name."

"Sorry?" said Michael.

"It's a tax. Plain and simple."

"A tax that only affects 1% of voters," said Michael. "Sure, the

216

Microsofts, the ExxonMobils, the Time Warners are going to feel it like a 2x4 to the head, but the guy in the street? Ha. Be like Christmas Day every day. If you accept the paradigm shift from profiteering to social responsibility, it really could transform the world."

"If?" said Tom. "But whether the figures add up or not isn't the point. The point is implementing such drastic policies would cripple the U.S."

Michael shifted in his seat like a child not wanting to admit he'd misbehaved. "Not if, er, if everywhere adopts the same policies. As Connolly wants."

Tom laughed at the absudity of it. "So the entire world's suddenly gonna stop craving Ferraris and Gucci and Chanel. Even things as simple as remote-controlled TVs? Overnight the whole world's gonna turn into *The Waltons?*"

"Actually, it was only the standby button, not the entire remote." Michael sank in his seat under Tom's glare.

Tom held up his pen. "This is a nice pen: smooth ink flow, well-balanced, comfortable grip. All you could ask for in a pen. And only 99 cents. But if the workers pulling 12-hour shifts in the Asian factories that produced it suddenly wanted a 9–5 day with an hour's lunch, wanted two weeks annual vacation, wanted plasma screens, cars, iPods — everything we expect here — how much would it cost then...? Three bucks? Five? Ten?" And there was the problem: if wages rocketed in Taiwan, Thailand, China, their products' prices rocketed proportionately. Everything from light bulbs to silk, electronics to chicken, CDs to purses. So when the cost of living soared in the U.S., what would the U.S. worker want? Higher wages... Higher wages meant higher prices. And the vicious circle expanded into a black hole that swallowed fiscal policy and vomited up hyperinflation, unemployment, and people carrying their wages home in wheelbarrows like in 1923 Germany.

Humanitarian-based globalization was an aspiration to all in office, but it would take decades of meticulous planning; treaties; cooperation; and very, *very* gradual transformation.

Tom threw his pen down. "Thanks to investment, economic expansion's topping out at over 4%; unemployment's down for the fourteenth consecutive quarter; and we're the first administration to raise the minimum wage in a decade. *We are driving America forward. We are!*"

"And we still can," said Simon.

Tom gestured to him to elaborate.

"See, a meal ticket like Connolly's, who wouldn't buy it? The American people will go for any carrot you dangle as long as the spin's good enough. And we should know. Spin's the only thing gets most presidents elected, 'cause it sure ain't their policies. Present company excepted, of course."

"So what?" said Tom. "We out-spin him?"

Simon clucked his tongue. "If someone believes he's Napoleon, do you salute him? Hell, no. You lock him up to protect society from his delusion. Connolly wants to live in a fantasy world? No problem. We can't lock him up, but we sure as hell can show people what'd happen if he implemented his crazy ideas. No spin. Just facts. Straight down the line. We'll be the first candidacy in history to campaign on nothing but the truth."

Bold.

Risky.

Direct.

Could it work?

They had nothing else.

***

Tom's hot chocolate steamed into the chill night air of the Western Colonnade. He sipped, his gaze drowning in the shadows of the White House rose garden. In the distance, the 555-foot-tall obelisk of the Washington Monument pointed to the star-studded glory of the heavens. Beyond, the illuminated neo-classical dome of the Jefferson Memorial seemed to float majestically on its marble columns. Tom thought of the phrase carved within the Memorial, a phrase in which he often found strength to see through his most difficult decisions: *'I have sworn upon the altar of God eternal hostility against every form of tyranny over the mind of man.'*

He twisted his wedding band. Whenever tough decisions beckoned, he imagined Beth, Courtney, and Danny living ordinary lives in suburbia. If the impact would be good for them, it would be good for America. But this time... He drew a long, breath. A thought gnawed at him like a starving rat chewing at the bars of the trap that imprisoned it. No matter how he struggled to dismiss it, it continued to lurk, scurrying where it would, spreading disease and filth like a plague amongst his thoughts.

"Sir?"

Tom turned.

Simon marched over with a file. "Those numbers."

"Thanks."

"Goodnight, sir." Simon trundled back toward the Oval Office.

"Er..."

Simon looked at him expectantly. But Tom said nothing more. "Mr. President?"

"Er... what you said earlier."

"About?"

"Bon—"

"Bonhoeffer? Dietrich Bonhoeffer?"

"Yeah... You *were* just illustrating a point?"

Simon meandered back, rubbing his chin. He drew a slow breath. "It was our first morning on St. Vincent, just before breakfast, when Jean found the lump in her breast. She showed me, but I couldn't feel anything. Anyway, it'd been a hard few months, what with moving house, her mom dying, getting that tax bill through, so we kicked back, forgot about it 'til we got home. Later, the doc said if Jean could've been treated earlier, even so little as a couple of weeks, maybe..." He locked Tom's gaze. "If I could go back to St. Vincent that morning, I'd hack that damn lump out myself."

Tom sighed. "I'm sorry I keep you here so long."

"Hey, I can type a resignation easy as the next guy. Truth is, Jean wants things to go on as normal. Says it's easier for her than everyone putting on a show."

Tom gazed back into the shadows. "I... I can't help wondering..." He shook his head. "D'you know not one of Connolly's healed patients has dropped down dead?"

"So you're thinking maybe he's the real deal?"

He looked at Simon. "What if..." But he blew out a deep breath, the idea too preposterous to voice.

"If 'what if's were diamonds, we'd all be billionaires." Simon rested a hand on Tom's arm. "What we do, we do for the country, Tom — not on a whim, or for personal gain... What must be done, *must* be done."

"But ... what if we're wrong? What if..." He didn't even want to think it, let alone say it. He lowered his voice. "Do I wanna go down in history as the guy who crucified Christ for the second time?"

"I..." Simon blew out his cheeks. His gaze drifted over the shadows, as if deep in thought.

Tom waited for the wisdom with which Simon always nourished him. And he waited. And waited...

25

Of Deeds and Darkness

Mary rolled over. Again. Thumped her pillow. Again. Nestled into it. Again. But still she couldn't even close her eyes. She blew out a breath.

"What?" said John.

"Sorry. Nothing."

"What?" Her back to him, he caressed her shoulder.

She closed her eyes. Bathed in the glow she knew would soon be lost to her. This was all their life would be now — the odd smile, the odd word, the odd caress in the depths of the night. She'd dreamed of falling in love since she was old enough to talk, just like every little girl, but she couldn't do this — have him and yet not have him. Be slowly pushed further and further away as more and more demands were forced upon him. Be abandoned. Because he'd meet those demands. Even if it killed him. And she couldn't be there to watch that, either. The people would love John, but they weren't in control. Those who were... She couldn't be there to watch John destroy himself. No matter the good cause. But she wouldn't stop him. Even if she could. His work was far more important than she was, than their life together. The world would die without him. Without him, only a part of her would suffer the same fate. She'd stay until he saw his dream for the presidency fulfilled, then leave. Melt into the background as if she'd never existed.

She whimpered, a tear moistening her pillow.

John rolled over to her. "Hey. What is it? The presidency?"

"Nothing. Go back to sleep."

"Mary, I have to do this."

"I know."

"No. I *have* to do this."

"I *know.*"

He put the nightstand lamp on. "Do you want to talk?"

"No. It's okay."

"Mary?"

She sighed. "It's... Why the presidency? Why can't we just travel the world healing people?"

"I have no choice."

"You think that's how China and the Middle East are going to see it?" She bit her lip. "I don't want to lose you."

"And I don't want to lose you? Do you think I want to be president?"

She rolled over to him. "So get out now, before it's too late."

John paused, as if considering the option, then finally said, "Could you sleep here, now, if you heard the screams of a 12-year-old girl being raped by armed militia in the next room ... if you heard the screams of a man being beaten for his beliefs in the attic ... if you heard the screams of starving children in the hall?" He stroked the hair from her face. "That's all I hear — day and night — the screams of the innocent."

"Oh, John." She cupped his face. She'd imagined he lived in a world of light, love, serenity, but it couldn't be more nightmarish. "I'm sorry. I'm just worried. I mean, healing in this country is one thing, but meddling in the affairs of another... John, they just won't take it. So now we've public opinion behind us, why we can't just leave it to the politicians?"

"How long did it take public opinion to end the Vietnam War? The Iraq War? To tear down the Berlin Wall? 60,000 people die needlessly every single day. What if public opinion takes a year? Two years? Five? How many millions have to die before we shout, 'Enough!'? Or should we start saving lives today, this very second? The last thing I want is to be president, but can you give me an alternative?"

She couldn't. The president of the richest, most powerful nation on the planet could easily change the world. But foreign powers would hate John's in-your-face justice. This would end badly. So badly.

Aglow in the light of the open refrigerator, Ben half sang, half muttered, pouring a glass of milk, "So, so you think you can tell, Heaven from hell."

Padding across the darkened kitchen, he mm-mm-mm-ed and da-da-da-ed Pink Floyd's 'Wish You Were Here'. In the conservatory, he stared out at the tree line's ragged veil of blackness, now barely lit by a crescent moon. "Do you think you can tell."

He farted. "Oops. Too much spicy lamb again."

"You're telling me."

Ben jumped, milk slopping down his robe. He spun. "Oh, Jeez... John nearly had a cardiac arrest to deal with, there."

Curled up in the high-backed wicker chair, Mary peered from the drenching shadows. "Sorry." She stroked Mutt beside her.

"Can't sleep?" He sank into the green and white striped cushions of the wicker couch opposite her.

"Nuh-uh."

"You ever been to Manchester?"

"Nuh-uh."

Ben pushed up. "Sorry. I'll leave you in peace."

"I'm sorry, Ben. Got a lot on my mind." She gestured to the couch. "Please."

Ben sat. "Wanna talk about it?"

What was there to talk about? She loved a man who regularly achieved the impossible. Barely a week ago, he'd been holed up in a box behind a shoe store; this time next year, he could be holed up in the White House. And that terrified her.

"He'll do it," said Ben. "Don't worry about that."

"That's the problem."

"Sorry, Mary, you've lost me."

If she kept the problem hidden, bottled up, locked in a box buried so deep, so dark ... that was where it might stay. But if she sneaked even the tiniest of peeks under the box's lid... She sucked in a broken breath. Even in the shadows, it must have been obvious she'd been crying.

"Hey." Ben leaned nearer.

Maybe she was overreacting. Maybe not every box was once Pandora's. She took a deep breath. "You can protect him, can't you, Ben?"

"We're doing okay so far, ain't we?"

"But really. You can?"

He held her arm. "Hey, sure I'll protect him. I promise you. As God's my witness."

She smiled and patted his hand, then wiped her eyes. While John remained merely a healer, the world's only bone of contention was which heavenly force had imbued him with such a gift. Now, however, John had aspirations to be the most powerful man in the world. But even John was only one man. One against six billion. Six billion was one hell of a lot of people to placate. All it took was just one to object. One with a gun, a knife, a bomb...

But what could she do? Three options plagued her.

Reason with John — once John set his mind to something, however, there was no changing it. Option one down.

Let events run — the only way the world would be ready for John was if it were already close to his ideals and just needed a gentle shove. Barring barely a handful, every single one of the past 100 years had seen war somewhere around the globe. Was that a world on the brink of Utopia? Option two down.

Only one option left. One she didn't want to think about — which was why she could think of nothing else. Of all the people in the world, she was closest to John, the most trusted. If anyone could sabotage him, she could. Wasn't it better she did it with a word, than some whack-job with a bullet? But what if she was wrong? What if John was Mankind's best hope for a world where dreams were lived; where hunger, poverty, and disease were resigned to history; where the peoples of all nations tirelessly toiled to achieve unadulterated freedom? Sabotage? Should the entire world die in a seething rage of violence, pestilence, and malevolence for the sake of one woman's love?

She sighed. "What made you find us, Ben? Want to help us?"

"I told you. The cop thing... I just wasn't making a difference no more, so ... I figured maybe I could by helping John."

She remembered how Ben had begged John to let him help them, how he'd said you didn't always get a chance to make up for past mistakes. And something Vincent had said on the plane: 'You ever want the lowdown on your "good man", there...' "You knew Vincent before, didn't you?"

224

Ben sniggered. "Oh, believe me, a lot of cops know the great Vincent Constanza."

"Yeah, but he knew you, too."

Ben shrugged.

"Did you arrest him? That why you hate each other so much?"

"Look, Mary, I don't wanna seem—"

"Okay. Sorry... Being a journalist's like being cop: always looking for answers."

A little chilly, she tucked her feet under her and pulled her robe over them. Ben was a good man, a good friend. She didn't want to upset him purely to satisfy her curiosity. She gazed into the blackness. Even though the sliver was so thin, the moon was dazzlingly bright. "Nice moon."

"My wife," said Ben, "she was called Mary, too. In fact, she was a lot like you, except maybe for an extra 40 pounds. But a good woman; a kind woman; a woman who knew right from wrong. She, er, left me six years ago come June..." He gazed wistfully away. "Anyway, we'd just come back from celebrating our 15-year anniversary on Aruba and, er..." He shrugged.

Mary waited. He didn't continue. She didn't want to pry, but if he didn't want to share, he wouldn't have started. "You were having problems and Aruba was to put things right?"

Ben laughed. "I wish. That would've made it a whole heap easier. Er, no. No problems. Well, short of the usual: work, kids, money... No. No problems. It was my fault. All my fault."

Oh, no. What was it? One beer too many; a colleague's smile; the grass is always greener? Some couples work through infidelity. Others? Once that trust is lost, everything's destroyed. Poor Mary. Poor Ben.

"Anyway," said Ben, "two months after we got back, the Visa bill arrived, and Mary asked how I'd cleared the entire balance for the holiday."

Now this she wasn't prepared for.

Ben drew a long, slow breath and exhaled equally slowly, as if trying to purge himself of the badness he felt within. "That's how I know Vincent. It's not only violence he orchestrates, but 'favors'. Ten grand to look the other way. So I looked... I knew it was wrong, but I loved Mary. I wanted to give her a taste of the life she deserved. One she could've had if only she hadn't lumbered herself with some dumb cop."

Mary padded over and knelt beside him. She held his hand. "You couldn't reconcile?"

He sniggered. "I couldn't even reconcile it with myself. How the hell could I with Mary?"

"I'm sorry."

"I gave what was left to the Cancer Foundation. Earned what I'd spent and donated that, too, but... So that's why I hate Vincent. Every time I look at him, I see me."

"Ben, you're nothing like Vincent. You made one mistake. He's a killer, for Pete's sake. Gets his kicks slicing up little girls."

He smiled and patted her hand. "No... We're the same. A cop's entrusted to protect people, not turn a blind eye for them to be exploited. See, it wasn't only Mary's trust I broke ... it was God's. I mean, all I know of the Bible is from old Charlton Heston movies, but I know enough to know just how bad it was I did."

Mary stroked his hair, seeing tears glinting on his cheeks. "Oh, Ben."

"So I figured, if I helped John, God might forgive me. And if He can, maybe one day Mary can, too."

They sat in silence: Ben lost to the dreams of what could have been; Mary lost to the demons of what could be.

26

The Closeness of Friends

In Rashid's kitchen doorway, Vincent froze. What in the name of...?

Putting slices of bread on a plate, Aisha said with a whiny twang, "Yi, er, san, si, wu..."

Rashid stood at the island, chopping mushrooms on a marble board while exchanging similar whiny-sounding gibberish with Sana. What in hell was going on?

Aisha gasped. Rashid and Sana glanced at her. She stared at Vincent.

Sana pulled Aisha closer. Rashid stopped chopping. "Yes?"

Waltzing in, Vincent pointed at the refrigerator. "Juice."

"I'll bring you some." Rashid stepped toward it.

"I can manage." Vincent yanked open the brushed steel door and snagged a jug of freshly squeezed orange juice. "So what's with the..." He waved his hand at them.

"If you must know, it's Mandarin," said Rashid. "China's going to be the next superpower, so it makes sense to learn something of its people, its culture."

And this loser had built an empire? Pouring juice, Vincent sniggered. "Yeah, right. 'Cause the whole world's gonna stop speaking English."

Rashid slapped his forehead. "Oh, why didn't we think of that?"

Aisha said something whiny again. The three of them laughed.

Vincent scowled at the mocking face. He turned to leave. But didn't. He sat on a high chromed stool at the island and took a slow swig of his juice. He glanced at his newspaper's headline — *Gas Prices Rocket!!!* — then tossed it aside and looked at the family.

Aisha clawed at Sana.

Vincent stared at Aisha. Her eyes widened. Chin quivered. Voice whined, but not Chinese, "Mommy."

"Why don't we go sit with Ben, huh?" Sana guided her away.

Vincent smirked as he watched them leave. But his smirk dropped. Was this all there was to life — the pleasure of terrifying a 10-year-old girl? He sniggered. Hell, with thoughts like that, had he been around these losers way too long? Pussy! Whoa... What had happened to that 'playing nice' backup plan? He heaved a breath. Hell, life sure could throw you a curveball when it wanted to.

Rashid hacked at a mushroom. And again. He threw down the knife. "I've accepted you into my home; it doesn't mean you're accepted into my life." He clattered a steel skillet onto a lit burner.

"And why is that?" asked Vincent. He eyed Rashid's blue apron over his suit. So much money, so little style. Criminal.

Rashid smashed eggs into a bowl. "What?"

"You've accepted me into your home. Accepted all of us. Why? You really think they'll ever let a Muslim influence the Oval Office?"

Rashid whisked the mixture. "After all you've witnessed, you still think the only things in life are power and money."

Vincent laughed. "Isn't that what John wants? Why he befriended you?"

Rashid poured the egg into the skillet. It sizzled. "Go taunt Ben, Vincent. Someone who enjoys your games." He swept the mushrooms into the egg.

"So you don't figure it's a coincidence you got 50-60 million, enough to get a presidential campaign up and running?"

Rashid groaned and slumped against the counter. "Okay, what do you want? What do you really want?"

The insurance money scam was genius. Why ruin it by running for office? Or was there more to the con than he'd figured? "How long you known John intended running?"

228

Rashid glanced at his X-Tech. "Eleven hours."

Vincent stared at him. But Rashid didn't look away. What were they scheming? What had he overlooked? "You already live like a king, so why do all this? What's in it for you?"

Like a child teasing another with a secret, Rashid smiled.

"Well?"

"Contentment."

Vincent studied him.

Rashid said, "It's like happiness, only it lasts longer. You might want to try it some time."

If a multi-million-dollar fortune didn't buy you contentment, what did? There was something illegit going on between Rashid and John. Not the election, the healing, but something else. What? "You really believe John can pull this off?"

"Tell me, if everyone had free education, power, health care; had less need to work, more time for family, friends, interests, don't you think the world would be a happier place?"

The streets of the Lower East Side had provided for all Vincent's formative needs: how to intimidate, extort, maim, kill. Once, long ago, he'd turned his back on that life, out of love. Then that life had caught up with him. And her blood had splattered over all those little origami animals she loved to line up on their dresser. All he got was his scar. His life wouldn't let him turn his back on it, so he'd chosen to embrace it all the more. A week ago, he'd have said it was the best way — indeed, the only way — he could've made something of his life. Today? He wasn't respected, only feared. Not learned, merely literate. Not successful, just more cruel. On his deathbed, could he look back on a life of achievement? But if there'd been guidance, less struggle, more freedom? He didn't like to admit it, but John's vision wasn't just bleeding-heart bull. "The night in your hallway, when we came for John..."

"What of it?"

"I... I, er," He snorted. When it was so difficult, how did people cope? "I'm sorry."

"Pardon?" Rashid squinted as if he'd misheard.

***

Fist raised at the study's paneled oak door, Mary hesitated, hearing Rashid.

He said, "... and that will be transferred to the Cayman account by noon?"

The door ajar, she eased it open a fraction more. Standing at his desk, Rashid fed another document into a cross-cut shredder. "Good... Okay, I'll get back to you about the CBS deal. Thanks, Glen." He hung up.

CBS? John had been emphatic – no more TV. What was Rashid scheming? She knocked and waltzed in.

Rashid spun, eyes wide.

She smiled, holding up a disk. "Latest backup for the safe, please."

"Oh, er..." He snatched the last few papers and rammed them in the shredder, then punched the power switch of his PC's monitor. "Yes, of course." But he didn't move, just watched the shredder.

"Busy?" asked Mary.

"No, just, er," he smiled, the shredder devouring the last inch, "tidying." He took the disk. "How's it coming?"

"Good. I think."

He lowered himself into his black leather chair and spun to the safe.

"How's your business these days?" asked Mary.

"Mouse? Fine."

"Must be a shock realizing you're not indispensable."

"I'm sorry?"

"Well, devoting so much time to John, must be a blow to have built an empire, only to find it doesn't need you anymore."

He locked the safe. "I took a back seat years ago, to spend more time with Sana and Aisha. Life's too short to spend it chasing money."

Easy for a guy with 92.6 million to say. She glanced at the shredder. What she wouldn't give to see its contents whole again. Or what was visible on that computer screen just seconds ago. But this was Rashid, their friend. Despite her suspicions, he'd done everything imaginable to help them. Still... "I spoke to John last night. Tried to convince him to make better use of the media for his campaign. He mention anything?"

"Nothing. But I could make a few calls."

"No. It's okay. I just wondered."

She left. So Rashid was moving money to offshore accounts in the Cayman Islands and had some deal to finalize with CBS. Highlights of their camcorder footage were uploaded to the website daily, but Rashid had free rein to select those 'highlights'. Was he cutting his own movie to sell to the highest bidder, intending to flee the country to avoid retribution? An inside exclusive on John would be worth millions. But Rashid had millions. What could he possibly have filmed that— Under its conservative guise, Rashid's house was a showcase for the most sophisticated electronic gadgets available. What if his security system incorporated hidden CCTV? What if Rashid's movie included footage of Vincent and his henchmen's attack? Her heart-to-heart with Ben? Oh, God ... her and John...

She'd assumed John and Rashid's plotting had concerned the presidency, but it seemed Rashid had a plot all of his own. She'd trusted him, valued his friendship and judgment. Just as John had. But John had enough to contend with. She couldn't burden him with this, too. She'd enlist Ben's help. With their investigative expertise, they'd clear Rashid beyond any doubt. Or crucify him to protect John.

***

Mary tramped into the bedroom. "Why are we trailing to New Hampshire already, instead of going healing? It's just a primary." Voting didn't count toward the election, but merely established which candidate ran for each party.

"40% of voters are undecided," said John, pulling his jeans on. "40%. Think what message it will send if a third-party candidate pools more votes than both the Republicans and Democrats in the most important primary in the country." Sitting on the edge of their bed to put on his shoes, he shot her a smile.

Yes, it would send a message. A dangerous message. Not that that was the immediate problem. She didn't want to be right about Rashid. "Rashid says CBS isn't playing ball, but he's sure they'll cave sooner or later."

He dropped his lace. "What?"

"You're not doing more TV?"

"No."

She tutted. "Sorry, must've got the wrong end of the stick." Hell! Rashid really was plotting something behind John's back. But she couldn't accuse their benefactor without proof and risk blowing John's entire plan. She strolled over and ran her fingers through his hair. Maybe there'd be other rich benefactors. Or John could accept donations. Hell, worst-case scenario, he could sport a jacket emblazoned with 'Pepsi' if it got them what they wanted. But it wasn't just Rashid. The problem was far deeper ... far, far darker.

He obviously sensed something was wrong. "What is it?"

"I..." She glanced around the room, before coming back to him, "I'm worried."

He slung an arm around her waist. "About?"

She shrugged.

"Come on."

"Well..." She pulled away and slunk across the room. "How do we know who's on our side?"

"We have sides? Isn't it simply what's right and what's wrong?"

"Is it? You aren't worried who's going to jump on the bandwagon? Try to manipulate us? Push some hidden agenda?"

"Mary, it doesn't matter."

"What do you mean, it doesn't matter? Of course it matters."

"Yes, people will exploit us. But every second of every day, someone dies who needn't. Isn't ending that worth sacrificing anything?"

He obviously hadn't seen the bigger picture. She walked back, knelt, and hung her arms around his neck. "Listen to me. You might see it as healing the world, but others will see it as corrupting it. They'll see the power you have and fear it, fear you, the way they fear a suicide bomber who believes he's making the world a better place. And what people fear, they destroy."

He cupped her cheek. Smiled. "Should the whole world suffer just so I can sleep safely in my bed at night?"

"John, there's no—"

"Shhhh." He put his finger to her lips. "I've been blessed with the power to end suffering. If I don't try, shouldn't I burn in hell for all eternity?"

Mary hugged him. He'd tried to run away from the world. Tried to run for 19 years. But every second of every day, he'd been planning for this moment, planning how to rescue Mankind. He'd tried to live another life, but couldn't for his yearning to make a difference. And wasn't that what life was all about? If you left nothing behind, was there any point to you ever having lived? Maybe they really could do it.

232

Maybe ordinary people could overthrow the despotism that dominated governments. Maybe John really could usher in a new age of reason, plenty, and caring... But the more she battled to convince herself, the more the lengths to which those in control would stoop haunted her like a stalker in a nightmare whom she couldn't outrun.

She clawed his back. She didn't ever want to let go.

***

While John was with Rashid, finalizing travel arrangements to Manchester, New Hampshire, Mary slipped away. Ben wasn't in his room. Nor bingeing in the kitchen. Nor lounging in the conservatory. But on opening the door to the game room, she gawked. What the...?

The cue ball slammed into the eight ball and rocketed it over the blue baize into the left corner pocket.

"Damn it." Ben slammed a 20-dollar bill down on the pool table.

Smirking, Vincent jabbed his cue at the middle pinball machine — Space Invaders, an '80s classic. "Double or nothing?"

Ben laughed. "Oh, your ass is mine now, boy."

"Ben?"

Ben turned. "Hey, Mary. Wanna play?"

She beckoned him.

Ben toddled over, while Vincent fired up the pinball. "What's up?"

"Me, what's up?" It was Ben who was acting strange. She nodded at Vincent.

Ben shrugged. "He asked for a truce, so..."

"And you trust him?"

"Yeah, right. But John does."

Wasn't Vincent further evidence of John's misjudgment? Didn't that justify her suspicions about Rashid? It was as if John was daring trouble. Wanting to battle it and win. Or did he want to win? Was he really courting martyrdom?

"Look, er," said Mary. But now that it came to condemning Rashid, someone who'd become a close friend, she hesitated. But she needed to protect John — especially as he seemed oblivious to the need to protect himself. "I think there's something wrong."

"Oh?"

"Er..." She glanced over at Vincent. From the pinball's bleeping,

clattering, whirring, and whooshing, he obviously wasn't eavesdropping.
"I think... I think Rashid's hiding something." Oh, no, she'd said it. It
sounded so ridiculous now. Talk about a dumbass! She waited for Ben
to make some crack about paranoia.

"You mean the secret phone calls?"

"Oh, thank God. I thought it was only me."

He sniggered. "Me, too."

"Listen, he's just been discussing some sort of deal with CBS, but
John knows nothing about it. Do—"

"Cale!" called Vincent, his ball lost.

"Look, there's no time now." said Ben. "We'll get together in
Manchester, go over what we've got. Okay?"

"Yeah." Finally, she was getting somewhere. It wasn't just paranoia
— Rashid was plotting something. Whatever it was, they had to stop it,
had to protect John, even if it cost them everything.

***

Tom trudged for the Oval Office. He glanced at Mrs. Shepherd, his
personal secretary, a woman who, metaphorically, had taken more bullets
for him than the entire Secret Service for all the presidents put together.
Unfortunately, even she couldn't take this one. "They here?"

She peered over her heavy-rimmed glasses and gave a single nod.

Tom's heart raced. On a good day, this would be a strained meeting
he'd struggle through with courtesy and aplomb. But it wasn't just *them*.
OPEC had already ensured today wouldn't be a good day. Yesterday,
its Muslim founders had convinced their fellow members to halve oil
shipments to the U.S. Just as Ganesh, the elephant-headed Hindu god,
appearing in Times Square would demolish the foundations of Christianity by proving its god wasn't the one and only true god, the Middle East
believed John posed such a threat to Islam they were prepared to wage
an economic war to silence him. And, religion aside, who could blame
them? Amongst John's campaign planks was the enforced improvement
of fuel economy in cars and a gigantic investment in alternative energies.
If John became president, the biggest gas-guzzling customer on the planet
would take its business elsewhere. That was bad enough, but what would
happen if other nations followed America's lead? Who could blame the
Saudis for being worried? Oil was all they had. If it became worthless,
they'd become just another barren Third World country.

So breakfast had been greeted with soaring gas prices, lines at the pumps, and inflation, with everything from ice cream to neck ties rising in price as manufacturing and transportation costs rocketed. A great start to any day. But now, *they* were here. Could the day get any worse?

Tom entered the Oval Office. "Gentlemen."

It was an indication of the level of their concern that they were here together. Not many things could drag three of the world's wealthiest entrepreneurs away from polishing their billions.

Michael nodded, gripping the figures Tom had asked him to scramble together for this impromptu meeting.

Tom marched across the rug emblazoned with the nation's seal — a bald eagle clutching an olive branch and arrows. Which would he be clutching today? War or peace? "Ned." He offered his hand. "Holding me to that free lunch, huh?"

"Let's hope so, Mr. President." Ned Lynch smiled, but his chubby face showed more anxiety than warmth. Myzopan's triumph over cancer was only superseded by its triumph in transforming Triton Pharmaceuticals from a modest corporation into a global phenomenon. The last thing Triton and its CEO wanted was a miracle worker.

"Morning, Mr. President," said Gustav 'Zig' Ziedlebaum. Zig was to the internet what Bill Gates was to the PC.

Ushering them to the couches, Tom finally greeted Leon Arnold.

Leon reciprocated. LandComber Inc. had had a huge technology base when Leon inherited it. But he'd seen realty as the future and gambled everything on developing a global property empire. And everything paid off, making him the sixteenth-richest man on the planet. He sat, crossing his gangly legs. No amount of Armani could make him look elegant.

"Well, I'd like to say how pleasant this is, but..." said Tom.

"You understand we don't enjoy this, Mr. President?" said Ned.

"Surely you saw the crisis looming?" said Zig. "It could've been avoided."

Did they honestly think he'd just been hiding his eyes, hoping the problem would magically disappear? He'd bent some laws, broken others. But John having announced his candidacy, Tom's hands were now tied. Implication in the obstruction of a presidential campaign would mean a major scandal. "Short of slamming Connolly inside on some trumped-up charge, what do you expect?"

Leon didn't flinch. "Slam Connolly inside on some trumped-up charge."

Tom smiled. "You want a martyr? The nation on our backs?"

"And what would the nation do?" said Zig. "Write to its congressman? March down Pennsylvania Avenue? God forbid, boo your State of the Union address? Still, if you prefer the economy going to hell and the American way of life being under threat..."

Tom had expected a confrontational situation, so he was prepared to make allowances. After all, corporate America would lose billions if Connolly was elected. But success over Connolly would only come through unity, not panic. He paused to allow everyone's thoughts to settle. "Gentlemen, you're funding groups to aid my campaign again *not* for the good of the nation, but because my policies are good for your bottom lines. Now, I lose office; you lose a couple of zeros off your net profit."

Ned smiled. "It's January, Mr. President. Election's in November. Dangle some bright, new, shiny thing in front of the voters, they'll soon forget Connolly."

Tom shook his head. "Don't underestimate the American people, they'll—"

"Oh, please," said Leon, "they'll do what they always do: look after number one. Just like the rest of us."

Michael rummaged for papers from his file to hand out. He cleared his throat. "Gentlemen, if you'll look at—"

Tom held up his hand. "Last week, I had an approval rating of 83%. Today it's barely 40. With no scandal involved, there's been no slide like it in history. You see, Connolly isn't some C-list celebrity pushing his latest diet book, he's a charismatic guy with remarkable insight and rhetoric, someone people identify with because he talks about their problems: health, bills, a better life. Now, I don't know much about biochemistry, e-commerce, or hotel chains, but I know the power of the human spirit. Hell, we'd still be a British colony if not for the American people's fortitude when it comes to fighting for what's right."

"Very romantic, sir," said Zig, "but we aren't asking only for our own sakes. Think of what his policies will do to our culture."

"Screw our culture," said Leon. "We want him buried now, one way or the other. Or are we backing the wrong horse in this race?"

236

One way or the other? Backing the wrong horse? Tom glared at Leon. Tom was the most powerful man in the world, but it was these men and those like them who'd helped put him there. They donated millions from their personal fortunes and raised millions more, money that paid for advertising, voter registration, phone banks, mail shots — everything needed for a successful campaign. To reject their support could be political suicide. Could Tom afford such high principles?

Trying to sweeten the medicine, Ned patted Tom's knee. "What Leon's trying to say, Mr. President—"

"Oh, believe me, Ned, I've no doubt there. So allow me to reciprocate: your contributions are much appreciated, but they don't buy this office. You want that, boy, you really are backing the 'wrong horse'." He stood, gesturing toward the door. "Now, I've a busy day, gentlemen."

Zig grimaced, then stood. As did Ned. "We've known each other a good long time, Mr. President," said Ned. "But you drop the ball now and we'll have to take the game elsewhere."

Tom didn't reply. He would be no one's puppet president.

Leon remained seated, staring at the grandfather clock.

"Leon," said Tom.

Leon glared. "You'll bury Connolly if you know what's good for you."

What the— Tom stabbed at the door. "Get the hell out of my office. Who in hell d'you think you're talking to?"

Standing up to tower over Tom, Leon glowered. "The next ex-president."

***

Even crammed with over 80 people and the front swathed in a Stars and Bars–motif banner, the last thing the disused Thompson's hardware store resembled was the campaign HQ of a presidential candidate. John had stipulated his deeds would speak for him and that producing all the usual flag-flier-poster paraphernalia was an unjustifiable waste of resources. Everyone got a 'I'm doing THE RIGHT THING' button — John's slogan — but nothing more. Considering the primary fervor that gripped Manchester, the lack of flags and banners adorning its buildings was a huge testament to the support for John.

Ambling toward a crossing on Elm Street, Manchester's tree-lined main avenue, Vincent carried a box of doughnuts. He nodded to Mary, who stared from the storefront's window on the opposite side of the street.

Meandering along with two children, a man nodded hello to Vincent.

Vincent ignored him. There seemed barely a building over a handful of stories, let alone ones that scraped world records, and Elm Street had single lanes of traffic politely tootling along, not gas guzzlers growling at each other. Manchester was so small. So personal. So damn ... 'nice'. Made his skin crawl. It wasn't natural for people to be so pleasant without the promise of payment or threat of violence. The sooner they left Niceville, USA, and got back to smog and muggings, congestion and noise, the better.

Vincent barged into HQ, hitting a chubby woman in the back. Despite his apology, the woman pulled her two kids closer to her.

"But won't that encourage people to leave lights on all day and waste even more?" asked a gray-haired guy.

John was sitting on the counter at the far end. He could've stood on it and towered over everyone, but this level was high enough for everyone to see his face, while low enough to retain a personal air. "Everyone will receive a generous allowance for all their utilities. But as an incentive not to abuse it, if they go over their allowance, they'll pay double for everything they've used that month, not just the extra."

"I get it. You set the limit low and we end up paying double what we pay now."

"Please," said John, "you have my word. Anyone who uses their utilities responsibly will *never* have another bill."

The crowd applauded.

"Gas is already up 10 cents a gallon," said a guy in filthy coveralls. "You swore you wouldn't hit people's wallets. What d'you say 'bout that?"

"I say, I'll quadruple the budget for alternative energies. America will have renewable energy so the American people will never again be held to ransom by the Middle East. I'll give our great nation her independence, her dignity, her freedom."

More applause.

"Now, I can't stop your lover leaving, your job sucking, or trade your in-laws for millionaires, but here's what I can do. Many of society's problems stem from the disintegration of the family and of values. A four-day week will give families more time to enjoy together. Free utilities and health care will relieve the stress of providing for them. And free education will allow everyone to pursue their dreams. Better jobs, better health, better living, lower divorce, lower crime, lower stress. Now, don't you deserve a better life? Don't our children deserve the best possible start we can give them?"

More applause.

"This tolerance for other faiths?" shouted a woman with arms barely able to fold over her heavy bosom. "Would that be tolerance for the Buddhists that murdered 2,000 when they bombed Pearl Harbor? Or the Muslims that butchered 3,000 on 9/11?"

***

Devouring one of Vincent's frosted doughnuts, Ben caught Mary's eye and nodded to the door. They squeezed out.

The timing was excellent. Rashid was ensconced in the store's back room, phoning Oman: his mother had been beaten in the street because some moron believed his helping John brought shame on Allah. Rashid was desperately making arrangements to ensure his family's safety. Awful for Rashid and his parents, but lucky for them — he wasn't around to be suspicious of them forsaking John in mid-flow. Leaving Vincent in charge of security had worried Ben, but Manchester was a haven of tranquility, so that was soon forgotten.

And it was a haven. Elm Street's fashions would never set catwalks alight, its eateries would never attract world-renowned chefs, and its scenery would never turn a poet to tears, but Manchester's petite buildings and cozy avenues oozed that homely warmth which the forest of steel and glass giants of Manhattan had destroyed decades ago. Mary wished they could take a timeout to bask in the sense of community.

"— but," said Mary, "John didn't know anything about it."

"CBS is as big as you can get," said Ben. "But why's Rashid chasing money? Hell, he's already Manhattan's answer to Bill Gates."

Mary shrugged. "Maybe it's all a sham. Maybe his business is in the toilet and he's stashing cash offshore. Getting out while the going's good."

Ben nodded. "I've caught odd snatches of money talk, and acronyms and companies, but hell if I know what he's up to." He tutted. "Rashid seemed such a stand-up guy."

If only they could access Rashid's private files. "Don't suppose you arrested Vincent for safe-cracking?"

"Would you trust him with what's in there?"

Mary sniggered. "I'm surprised that Picasso's still on the wall... So what now?"

"Give me a couple of days. I got a buddy works surveillance — he'll maybe have something we can use on Rashid's phones. Or if we can get hold of his cell for long enough, I could run a trace on his phonebook numbers."

Great! If only she could match that. "I've tried names, anniversaries, birthdays, everything I can think of as passwords, but nothing's unlocked his laptop files." It'd been a long shot but...

"Okay. Whatever you hear from now on, make a note. You keep trying his laptop, and I'll work on the phones. If we get enough pieces, we might hit lucky and see a picture of what's going on."

Finally, a plan. It wasn't much, but it was a hundred times more than she'd had yesterday. The sun felt warmer, the air zestier. Today would be a good day. John didn't know it, but she was going to save him.

27

The Best of All Possible Worlds

Peeking from the locker room-cum-dressing room, Mary gazed into Manchester's Roosevelt High School's gymnasium. It seethed with expectant townsfolk and a ravenous media. It was the first public address of an 'unknown' independent candidate, yet the atmosphere was as electric as that of the president's victory party — the people sensed change; the media, blood.

She scanned the jubilant faces, the homemade banners. If only Rashid were their only problem. Yes, this would send one hell of a message to the Republicans and Democrats. Unfortunately, it'd also send one to corporate America, the Orient, and the Islamic world. Talk about pissed. Oh, boy...

John took the dais at the end of the basketball court, beneath a 20-foot 'The Right Thing' banner. "A great statesman once said, 'Ask not what your country can do for you — ask what you can do for your country.' Free utilities, free education, free health care — I think you know what America can do for you. Now, what can you do for America?" John surveyed the gym, which was crammed with eager faces. "Nothing!"

The crowd cheered.

"Not higher taxes. Not higher prices. Not higher productivity. A higher standard of living is going to cost you not one cent more, because everyone's going to do...?" He pointed to the banner.

The crowd shouted, "The right thing!"

John grinned. "And that's why I believe this nation of ours is the greatest nation on Earth."

More applause.

"Unfortunately, with greatness comes even greater responsibility. Responsibility for what? Well, that's the biggie, isn't it...? When we saw the East Europeans demolish the Berlin Wall, we cheered them as heroes fighting for freedom. When we saw that lone Chinese student defy a marauding tank in Tiananmen Square, we cheered him as a hero fighting for freedom. When we saw the Iraqis tear down the statue of Saddam Hussein, we cheered them as heroes fighting for freedom. Just ordinary people. Ordinary people achieving the miraculous. And that's why we identified with them, wanted them to succeed. Yet the next day we were back to being fearful of the yellow peril, the red under the bed, the nation of suicide bombers... Why? Why can't we remember their heroism?

"Why? Because we've got enemies. People who call us weak. Ignorant. Evil. So how can we turn enemies into allies?

"Well, I believe in America. Not because of our technology. Our wealth. Not even because of our Constitution. No, I believe in America because of you, the American people. Why? In the 1940s, who liberated Europe, indeed, the entire world, from the yoke of Nazi tyranny...? The American people."

His audience cheered.

"Who defied the odds to attain Man's greatest achievement by conquering space to walk on the moon...? The American people."

More cheering.

"Who's empowered the whole of Mankind with planes to span the globe; power to light homes; transplant surgery to repair lives; human rights to protect every man, woman, and child from tyranny, oppression, slavery...? The American people."

Thunderous applause erupted.

"As our forefathers have done so many times in the past, let us, the American people, lead the way into a new age of justice, freedom, and equality for *all* people of *all* nations. America will give the world the greatest gift of all — America will give the world *life*!" John shouted over the jubilation. "America will not be defined by the future — America is the future!"

The crowd leapt up and down, screaming support.

Clapping, Vincent whistled. Mary's jaw dropped. Fetching them donuts; games with Ben; applauding John. Was this the same man who'd thought nothing of carving up a little girl to get what he wanted? Mary stared at him. Was she wrong? So very wrong? If Vincent could be so changed, was there hope for everyone?

Arms aloft, John shouted, "On polling day, what are we going to do?"

"The right thing!"

***

The rally over, Rashid parked the Hummer in front of HQ. They dashed in and locked up. Despite the mild night and expectation keeping the streets a-buzz with well-wishers, they couldn't afford to be interrupted now. In the back room, they turned on a TV. Sitting bolt upright, toying with her crucifix, Mary fixed on the screen. Behind her, Vincent leant against one of the huge metal storage cabinets, repeatedly flicking its handle. Normally it would have been annoying, but she was so tense she barely noticed.

Finally, after a mouthwash ad, the President appeared. Mary leaned forward onto her knees. Every time they hit a problem, John produced the goods to triumph. Time after time. He was unstoppable. This was the White House's first response to his candidacy. President Stevens would be pissed, but what could he do?

Smiling, Tom strolled along a leafy lane of picturesque clapboard houses. "We all wish life could be so good." He held his hands out to either side. Buffing a Mercedes in the glorious sunshine, a man waved as his neighbor cruised by in her sparkling BMW. Nearby, a mother and her tiny daughter sat in their immaculately kept garden enjoying an impromptu picnic, blossom dancing on the light breeze. Tom continued, "But could we *all* live the dream, *really*, for just a little sacrifice?"

The dreamy suburban backdrop metamorphosed into a derelict high-tech laboratory smothered in cobwebs. Leaving a track in the dust, he ran a finger over a robotic arm, its hand dangling by loose wires. "This was one of Intel's clean rooms, a room 10,000 times cleaner than an operating theater, where engineers developed future generations of chips." A rat scurried over a keyboard before a broken monitor. "But without profits to reinvest..." He shrugged.

The lab morphed into a manufacturing plant of rusted machinery, gloom seeping through broken windows. "And, because of environmental legislature, this," Tom splashed through pools on the floor, water dripping from the ceiling, "is the Detroit plant where the last American automobile rolled off the production line."

Having morphed again, shrouded in the shadows of storm clouds, Tom shuffled along a street of boarded-up stores. "All over America lay the crushed hopes and dreams of good people. Good people who fought our wars. Good people who powered our economy. Good people who made this nation what it once was: great." He stopped beside a gas station. A sign creaked in the wind, 'Special offer – Gas $50 a gallon'. "It would be wonderful if everything in life was free. But the money would have to come from somewhere." He turned as a rusted ambulance, siren wailing as if it were clockwork and running down, lumbered past, being pushed by three paramedics. He smiled. "Just a little sacrifice."

Mary cupped her mouth. "Oh, hell." Yes, some industries would be adversely affected by John's policies, but the health, education, leisure, and alternative energies industries would explode. Book sales to solar panels. Ski lessons to hydrotherapy... Boom, boom, boom, boom, boom. Once, America had had armies of migrant farm workers, but as technology advanced, they moved into other areas. Now, the same would happen. It was the natural evolution of developed countries. But they'd have a hard time convincing people of that after such damning images.

Rashid patted John's arm. "Well, my friend, we never imagined the government would just roll over on this,"

"It's a cliché," Mary sighed, "but a picture paints a thousand words – and that's one hell of a picture." They needed a counter campaign as quickly as possible. But John wouldn't court the media except as a last resort, so what could they do?

"We need to get out healing again. Remind people we're the good guys," said Ben, as he opened the store door for Mary.

"Thanks," said Mary. "Ben's right, we—"

Ben shouted, "Get back!" He yanked Mary back as if she was a rag doll. As she flew backward, she caught the dazzle of car headlights careering straight for the store. Ben kicked the door closed and, dragging Mary, lunged at the others. Everyone crashed to the floor.

Glass shattered. Wood crunched. Then... A roar like the world was ending. And the earth shook.

The wall exploded. Mary clamped her arms over her head. Screwed her eyes shut.

The metal cabinets crashed over.

Wood and cinderblock blasted through the air.

Flames burst overhead.

Mary whimpered. It *was* the end of the world!

But, almost instantly, the thunder died.

Mary lay. Gasping. Eyes clenched. The ground still. Everything silent — but for the ringing in her ears. She dared to peek from under her arms. Screamed. Scrambled away from a charred, severed arm.

Something grabbed her.

She screamed again.

"Are you okay, Mary?" said Rashid.

She panted for air, her gaze whirling around the devastated room of flames, debris, and smoke. Mind as deadened as her ears, she just stared.

"Mary!" Rashid shook her.

Snapping back to reality, she gasped. She stared wide-eyed at Rashid. His words finally pierced the groggy confusion in her head. "Yeah, yeah, I'm okay!" But what had happened? She scanned the room, desperate for an explanation. She saw Vincent. His face bloody, he tried to push up, but fell back. Rashid offered him a hand. Vincent shook his head to clear it, then hauled himself up. He stood, swaying.

Then Mary's gaze fell on... She gasped. "Ben!" She scrambled over.

Ben lay on the floor. Motionless.

She reached for a hunk of jagged metal protruding from a bloody gash in his back. "Ben!" He'd saved her life. Saved all their lives. He couldn't be dead. Please, don't let him be dead!

Rashid grabbed her hand. "Wait for John."

But John was nowhere to be seen.

"John! ... John!"

Jarring her teeth as metal screeched against metal, one of the cabinets pushed up, then fell back down. Vincent and Rashid heaved it off the floor. John scrambled out, grasped Rashid's arm, and clambered up. The cabinets had taken most of the blast. Probably saved their lives.

"John, it's Ben!" Tears streamed Mary's cheeks. "It's Ben!"

Shaken, John lurched over, veering to his left as if drunk. He crashed down beside Ben.

On John's nod, Vincent hauled the jagged metal from Ben's back. Ben cried out. Mary grimaced, looking away. John laid a hand on the wound. The screaming stopped.

Rashid hoisted Mary up by the arm. "We've got to get out."

She wavered, dazed. "What– what was it?" It was as if she was doped up. Her thoughts waded through mud, and her limbs fumbled as awkwardly as a newborn foal's. Usually so sharp, she just couldn't fathom what had happened. Then she saw it through the ragged hole in the wall. She clutched her mouth.

In the middle of the store, the window and wall demolished behind it, stood a burning car. Its whole rear end was a mass of twisted metal, as if the Devil himself had been locked in the trunk and fought his way out. Manchester had joined the ranks of Belfast, Baghdad, Bali... Someone believed the way to bring peace to the world was to blow it up, starting with peace's greatest advocate: John. Thank Christ the bastard was dead.

With Rashid's support, Mary tottered over the debris.

She felt another arm around her.

"Are you okay?"

She turned to John's blue eyes, so filled with concern. "I'm okay. Ben?"

"He'll be fine."

Behind them, Vincent helped Ben clamber over the burning rubble.

Mary scrambled over the jagged remains of the store front. Safe. She turned to help Ben. Thank God they were all safe.

Staggering, Ben shook his head. Waved her away. Grunted.

"I'm trying to help."

He grunted again.

She shook her head. "I don't–"

He glared. "Run."

Run? He had to be in shock. She forced a reassuring smile. "Ben, it's okay. We're safe."

Lumbering out, Ben shouted, "Run!"

Tires screeched.

246

Mary spun to the sound. From a side road, a silver Honda Odyssey minivan tore onto Elm Street.

Rashid shouted, "Into the Hummer!"

They piled in. For everyone to get in as quickly as possible, Mary scrambled along the driveshaft tunnel to the rear seat. She looked back. "Oh, God help us."

A dark-skinned man leaned out of the minivan's passenger window, another at either side from the back seat. All brandished assault rifles.

Their Hummer was built more like a tank than an F1 racing car — they'd never outrun a minivan, not with 0-60 mph taking 13 seconds. They were going to die.

Rashid shouted, "Hold on!" He slammed his foot down. The 6.6L turbocharged engine roared like an erupting volcano. But instead of shooting forward, away down the street, the Hummer lurched backward. It jerked over the curb.

Dat! Dat! Dat! Dat!

Everyone cowered as bullets peppered the bodywork.

The Hummer crashed through their HQ's jagged wall and battered the burning car aside. With its massive ground clearance, it careered over the rubble like a tank battling an assault course.

The back wall hurtled to crush Mary. Pulling her arms up to shield herself, she screamed.

Cinderblock and glass burst in all directions as the Hummer blasted out onto the road running parallel to Elm Street. A red Buick swerved into a parked Ford.

John reached back. Grabbed Mary's hand. His eyes flashed anxiously, but he was so calm. Too calm. As if it wasn't him being attacked, merely a character in a movie he was watching.

Hitting the gas to tear down the street, Rashid shouted, "Where's the police station?"

Punching 911 into his cell, beside Rashid, Ben nodded behind them. "That way."

Mary spun to see if she could spot it. Oh, no! The Honda minivan screamed around a corner. "They're coming!"

***

From behind Rashid, Vincent called, "Cale." Cale turned. Vincent handed him his small backup weapon, a 10-round Glock 26.

"No!" John grabbed Vincent's arm.

Vincent wrenched free. "I don't tell you how to heal." He snapped back the slide on his Glock 18, racking a round. If some asshole was looking for a killing spree, shit, were they in for one hell of a bad day. It was a pity he'd only one standard 17-round clip, not a couple of 33-round high-capacity ones — with one of those and his Glock set on automatic, he'd almost cut Paolo Zanetti in half. "Make them count, Cale." With no spare mags, they couldn't waste a single shot. He leaned out of the window, twisting back. Aimed. Gently squeezed the trigger...

Shit! With the car bouncing down the road, five would get you 10 he'd hit a bystander by mistake. Time was, that wouldn't have even crossed his mind, let alone mattered.

He jabbed Rashid. "Next right, slew around, then brake hard."

Rashid glanced back, face drenched in sweat. "Dead stop?"

"For a second."

As the next right tore at them, Rashid yanked the wheel. The Hummer skidded around. He slammed on the brakes.

The Hummer sideways on, Vincent leaned out of the window and over the roof to steady his aim. Cale rested on his windowsill.

Bang! Bang! Bang! Bang! Bang! Bang! Bang!

Slugs tore into the passenger hanging from the minivan's rear left-hand window. Blood and brains splattered onto the street.

Leaning out for a clear shot, the front passenger jerked as bullets ripped into him, too, then toppled from the car.

Vincent hammered the roof. "Go! Go! Go!"

Hands trembling on the wheel, Rashid hit the gas.

Vincent swung back in. The exhilaration of being back in his own world raised a smirk. Feeding the poor? Healing the sick? Yeah, right. If he'd known doing God's work could be such a rush, he'd have signed up years ago. Now, if the Almighty would just see fit to give him one or two more clear shots, he'd do a job to make God so pleased He'd grin like He was loaded on coke.

Vincent glanced back. As the minivan flew around the corner in pursuit, someone threw the rear passenger out and took his place. Someone else climbed into the front passenger seat. "Shit!" And that was how good deeds were rewarded?

"How many are there?" said Mary.

"We've only to hold them off 'til the cops show," said Cale.

And Vincent had thought he'd never be pleased to see the boys in blue. He'd used three bullets, Cale four. "We've 20 slugs left. They've bombs and M16s. Do the math." They couldn't outrun them. Couldn't outshoot them. But, with two of their number gone, at least the terrorists would treat them with a little respect — there was a huge difference between the glory of a suicide mission to serve Allah and the disgrace of blindly rushing into a hail of bullets. Cale was right — they only had to hold them off 'til the cavalry arrived. But how?

Cale jabbed across the street. "The mall. Go for the mall."

If Vincent was going to buy it, it was not going to be in Toys 'R' Us. "Cale, what the—"

"Hunting store!"

Rifles. Ammo... It was possible. And with the mall now closed, there'd be no bystanders to get caught in the crossfire. Vincent slapped Rashid's shoulder. "Go!"

Brakes screeched and cars swerved as Rashid whipped the Hummer across the on-coming traffic. The Hummer jerked over the sidewalk. Pulverized a fence. Tore down a grass embankment toward Sunny View Mall.

The minivan bucked the sidewalk after them.

Mud splattering up its wings, the Hummer thundered through a stream and up and over a verge onto the deserted parking lot.

The minivan careered down the banking, but, designed for the school run, not off-roading, it lost traction and the boggy stream snatched it. Tires spun. Mud flew.

The mall's entrance rearing out of the night, Rashid floored the gas. "Hold on!"

Metal screeched as the Hummer ripped through the security shutters. Glass doors exploded. The Hummer tore into the foyer and blasted into an ornamental fountain. Crunched to a stop.

Water spouting everywhere, they scrambled out.

Rashid collapsed. On all fours, he vomited.

Vincent glanced to the heavens. "Oh, for Christ's sake."

John crouched to Rashid.

Vincent snapped. "Get it together, you pussy. Now!"

Rashid nodded, mopping his face. John helped him up.

John was always unflappable, but this? He was so cool it was as if he wasn't being hunted down like a rabid dog, but merely being pulled over for speeding. Didn't this guy ever lose it?

Hearing the Hummer's engine gun again, Mary turned. "Ben!"

From the driver's seat, Cale shouted, "Go!"

She made to run to him, but Vincent jostled her away. "He'll hold them off. Give us time."

"No!" Mary struggled.

Vincent clutched her. "You wanna help him, find a gun store."

Mary dashed for an information kiosk beside a staircase to the second floor. While Cale reversed into the hole in the shutters, she scoured a list of stores. "Upstairs!"

Shots blasted the Hummer barricade.

"Ben!" shouted Mary.

Cale's Glock thundered.

Vincent shoved Mary. "Move!"

As gunfire erupted, Vincent rushed them up the stairs. If Cale could just hold the terrorists off for another minute, he could grab enough firepower to blow these mothers all the way back to Mecca.

Rashid slipped. Toppled to the concrete stairs.

Vincent bawled, "Move it!"

Mary dragged Rashid up and they stumbled on.

The gunfire stopped. Oh, hell. Did that mean Cale was morgue meat?

Atop the stairs, Vincent looked down.

Cale tumbled out of the car and hugged the wing.

Thank God.

Cale scoured the mall, then dashed for a pillar from which to launch an ambush. But he didn't have his Glock. Out of ammo? Should Vincent run back? But he had limited ammo himself. He could only protect Cale for a minute or two, then they'd all be dead. No, they needed weapons. He chased the others, but pulled up. He dashed back to the balcony. "Cale!"

Cale looked.

Vincent tossed his Glock toward him.

But a terrorist burst in.

Cale hugged the pillar.

The terrorist shot blindly at the clatter of Vincent's gun on the tiles. Slugs hit the gun. It skidded away. The terrorist scanned the foyer.

Shit! If Cale broke cover, he'd be sliced in two. Having disarmed himself, Vincent glanced around for a weapon. He snatched a potted plant. Flung it.

The terrorist saw it hurtling down. Scrambled away. It smashed into the Hummer.

Vincent ducked as bullets sprayed the balcony.

But the diversion worked.

Cale smashed the terrorist to the mosaic floor. Straddling him, Cale pounded his fists, turning the dark face into bloody pulp.

Vincent raced after the others.

Automatic fire roared below. Vincent prayed Cale had retrieved the terrorist's gun and let rip, and not that another terrorist had caught him unawares.

Dashing past the stores, Vincent scoured their windows for any hint of weaponry. Where was this damn store!?

"Vincent!"

Ahead, Mary pointed to a store with shutters. A store named 'Gun World'. He sprinted. They were saved. Grab some 9mms, a couple of shotguns. Hell, would these motherf—

Bang! Bang! Bang!

A deli's window shattered.

Vincent dove behind a metal bench. "Shit!" A terrorist reaching them meant two things: Cale was dead, and Vincent was alone in this battle against God only knew how many others. Of course, this could be the last terrorist, but there could easily be more searching elsewhere who'd come running at the sound of gunfire.

John turned back. Vincent waved him on.

From the lack of return fire, the terrorist obviously guessed Vincent was unarmed and no threat, so blasted at the primary target: John.

Everyone dove for cover.

With hair and beard so well groomed he'd look at home in a bank's boardroom, the terrorist smiled, obviously eager to see the horror in the infidel's eyes and the extent of Allah's gratitude. He swaggered toward them.

Vincent dodged from behind his bench. His hand flashed out.

The terrorist clutched his throat. Blood spurted between his fingers. He crumpled to the floor. Twitched. Then, lay still, a stiletto blade protruding from his neck.

Vincent darted for the terrorist's dropped M16. If there were any more of these sons of bitches, he'd slice the mothers in two! He reached for the gun.

Bang! Bang! Bang! Bang!

Vincent crashed to the tiles, blood gushing from his stomach.

***

The greasy, pot-bellied assassin retrieved his comrade's gun. An M16 in each hand, he stalked toward John.

Mary scrambled for John. He pushed her away. "Rashid!"

Rashid grabbed her. "Don't, Mary."

Tears streaming, she mouthed, "No, please, no." She looked for rescue. "Vincent." He had to get up. Save them. Save John. Had to! But Vincent lay in a bloody heap. There was no rescue. No cavalry. This was where the dream died.

John stood up. Proud. Defiant. Unflinching.

The assassin sneered.

Mary screwed her eyes shut.

Bang! Bang! Bang!

She screamed, "No!" She looked.

But John didn't fall. Another miracle?

The assassin spasmed. Blood burst from his mouth. He looked at the blood splattered on his chest. Puzzled, he looked at John, then toppled forward.

From the stairs, a smeared trail of blood led to their savior.

"Ben!" Mary bolted from Rashid.

John raced after her.

The exertion too much, Ben crashed to the floor.

Mary fell to the tiles. "Oh, Ben." She eased his head into her lap. Blood oozed from his chest.

"I—" he coughed, "I promised you, Mary. Now—"

"Shhh, Ben." She shouted, "John!"

John crouched to Vincent. In an instant, Vincent's eyes flickered open.

"Stay wi—" Ben spluttered blood.

Mary stroked his hair. "Shhh, you're gonna be okay." She shrieked, "John!"

His hand shaking, Ben took hers. "Stay— stay with John."

"Of course I'll stay with John, Ben. We'll all stay."

"Prom—" cough, "promise."

She squeezed his hand. "I promise. But everything's gonna be fine." Ben was talking as though he was going to die. She wouldn't let him. "John!"

John skidded down beside her. He'd save Ben. Everything *would* be fine.

John went to lay his hand on Ben.

But Ben caught John's wrist. "I..." Ben coughed blood.

"John!" cried Mary, as Vincent lurched over, drenched in blood.

Ben coughed. "I..."

Mary grabbed John. "John, quick."

John lifted Ben from Mary's lap. "Please, Mary, leave us."

Tears blurred her world. Why was Ben still bleeding? Why was he still dying? Why wouldn't John save him? "Save him. Please."

Vincent shook his head. "Better move fast, John."

"Rashid," said John.

Rashid stood at John's shoulder, tears in his eyes. "I'm here."

"Please." John nodded at Mary.

He couldn't be serious. "What?!... No. No!" Mary shook John. "John, it's Ben. For God's sake, it's Ben!"

Rashid gripped her arm. "Please, Mary, come with me."

"John, please!"

Rashid dragged her. Mary squirmed, but was so traumatized she didn't have the strength to fight. This was Ben. Ben who'd befriended them. Ben who'd helped them. Ben who'd all but given his life for them. Why wouldn't John heal him? As sirens wailed outside, she kicked like a petulant child trying to disobey an ogreish parent. "No. No! Heal him. Heal him!"

Vincent knelt. "What the fuck, man? Heal him!"

John looked down. "Ben?"

"I..." Face grimacing with determination, Ben gripped John's wrist harder, keeping John's hand at bay. "I did good today... I ... might not tomorrow."

A tear ran down John's cheek. He nodded, smiling. "You made a difference today, Ben. Thank you."

Ben smiled. And died.

Mary screamed, "Nooooo!"

Guns scanning the area, police raced toward them.

"I'm sorry, Mary," said Rashid, hugging her.

"Get off me!" Flailing, she broke free and raced to Ben. She cradled him, "No, Ben. No."

John reached for her. "I'm so sor—"

"Don't." She pulled away.

He tried again. "Mary, I—"

She glowered. "Don't you touch me!"

Paramedics arriving, Vincent crouched and slung his arm around her shoulders. "Time to go, Mary."

Mary stared at the killer she'd loathed for so long, the killer Ben had loathed for so long, and yet, the only person who'd tried to help her save her friend. She fell against Vincent's shoulder and sobbed.

When it came time for Ben to be wheeled away, Mary buried her face in Vincent's chest. Seeing Ben crammed inside a black bag, like yesterday's garbage, stabbed her heart like a knife. Then Vincent steadied her as she lumbered down the stairs. But in the foyer, she froze.

John was crouched over a lowered gurney, over the terrorist that Ben had beaten to a pulp.

No... He couldn't be...

But the terrorist stirred.

Mary shrugged Vincent off. Marched for John. "Get away from him!"

John stood. "Mary, don't think—"

She slugged John in the mouth. He reeled back. "Touch him again, and I'll kill you myself!"

Trembling with the effort, the terrorist pushed himself up.

Mary screamed, "You fuck!" She kicked him, mashing his nose across his face. He cartwheeled onto the floor. She flung the gurney aside and dove at him. Kicked again. Vincent and Rashid hauled her away.

Struggling, she screamed at the terrorist, "I'll kill you. I'll find you and I'll fucking kill you!"

28

The Joy of Darkness

I'm sure I speak for the American people when I say my heart goes out to Benton Cale's family and to John Connolly and his friends," said Tom at a lectern on the small stage in the White House's James S. Brady press briefing room. The White House seal behind him on the blue backdrop, he solemnly gazed into the six rows of seated journalists: *L.A. Times*, CNN, *Washington Post*... "Mr. Connolly is a remarkable man, and, though I might not agree with his ideology, he, Benton, and their associates have done this country a great service through their healing work, and for that, I thank them. But we live in a dangerous age. An age when an ability to heal and poetic rhetoric are scant defense against the terrorist threat. As we saw in Manchester yesterday, that threat can come at any time, to anyone, anywhere. There is a great evil in the world and only by standing together can we defeat it." He gazed sincerely into the hearts of each and every American. "And I promise you today, as your president, that this administration will not rest until the freedom of the American people — indeed, the freedom of people everywhere — is guaranteed safe from such atrocities." He hammered his fist to emphasize each of his three final points. "We will not bow. We will not break. We *will* overcome!... Thank you. And God bless America."

Refusing questions, Tom marched off stage right. Using the death of an innocent American to jump a few points in the polls sickened him, but he wasn't just fighting for his presidency, he was fighting for America itself. If Connolly gained power, not only would the economy be in the toilet, religious and political outrage over his policies would make terrorist attacks so commonplace that the evening news could feature forecasts the way it did for the weather. Luckily, while the attack had rallied a sympathy vote for Connolly, it was also a wake-up call to terrorist-paranoid Americans everywhere. But was it too little, too late?

"A cheap shot, but it went well," said Simon. "What do they say about a gift horse?"

"Careful it doesn't bite you while you're not looking."

They strolled down the cream corridor, past bustling offices.

"So, you want the good news or the bad news?" said Simon.

"You mean there's a choice today?" It felt as if it'd been only bad news forever.

"Our campaign support network has taken a hit."

Oh, damn that Leon and his cronies. "How bad?"

Simon winced. "Some heavy hitters must've put together some hellish arguments."

"How bad?"

"Bad."

Tom stopped and grabbed his arm. "How bad?"

"Ballpark? 31 million."

$31 million! "Hell's teeth." Tom cupped his face.

"Five of our support groups, headed by Leon Arnold, have formed an alliance to back Moses Williams. Must think young, hip, black, and Christian covers enough demographics to beat even Connolly."

To lose the backing of groups worth $31 million was bad, but manageable. But if other groups followed suit, Tom's re-election hopes could be ended. He needed those groups to buy advertising, raise awareness, mobilize voters. Tom dragged his hands down his face. "Please say you weren't joking about the good news."

Simon smiled. "Guess who's back playing doctor."

Tom gasped. "He's pulled out of the running?"

Simon handed him a photo of Connolly with a patient. "Twelve minutes ago. Houston."

"Yes!" Even with Leon's backing, Williams was minor league. If Connolly had forsaken his candidacy, the country was safe, and, after devastating Tanner on TV, the presidency was as good as Tom's. "I want electronic surveillance and 'round-the-clock protection for Connolly. From now on, he doesn't fart without we got it in triplicate first." Because of Connolly's media profile, Tom had to be seen to be protecting him — an excellent opportunity to monitor everything the man did and, in the interests of public safety, 'guide' his actions whenever necessary. Tom shook his head. "I never thought I'd say it, but thank God for Islamic extremism."

29

When the Mourning Comes

Do you mind?"

In the wicker chair, Mary looked up. Vincent gestured to the couch, which was a-glow in the morning sunshine flooding into Rashid's conservatory. She shrugged. Having declined accompanying them to Texas and California, to get away from everything on a two-day healing jaunt, she'd barely spoken to anyone since Manchester. They'd all tried to talk to her. Especially John. But like he had anything to say that she wanted to hear, after what he'd done?

She stroked Mutt, who lounged half in her lap, half on the chair, and gazed out at the bare trees. Such bare, lifeless trees. With not a breath of wind, the world lay still, dead silent, but for the ticking of the kitchen clock.

Her eyes puffy and red, Mary stared, her mind as bare of dreams as the trees of leaves.

It was over. She'd known John would abandon her one day — she just hadn't bargained on it being so soon, over something so vital. It wasn't just Ben who'd been killed, it was them. Their dream. Their future. Yes, John could wow people with his healing and speeches, but in the end, people wanted to know that when they turned off the lights and curled up in bed at night, someone was watching over them, keeping them out of harm's way. But if John wouldn't save someone so close, why should the American people, total strangers, believe he'd save them? It wasn't those terrorists who'd killed them, killed Ben — it was John.

Vincent spoke. "You understand why Ca— why Ben did what he did?"

Some testosterone-fueled bull about making a difference and going out in a blaze of glory instead of a whimper of guilt. Very romantic. Very heroic. Very Hollywood. But this was real life. Mary merely shrugged.

"I don't know what he told you, but we did know each other already."

No answer.

"A long time ago, he made a mistake. One mistake. But it seems he never stopped beating himself up about it. And that was an even bigger mistake. See, he was a good cop, and respected and feared for it."

She stared at the trees.

"Just thought you should know." He meandered away.

"One mistake?"

Vincent turned back. "Huh?"

"Just the one mistake?"

"Far as I know."

Mary stroked Mutt, returning to the bare world. One mistake? What kind of a world was John building where a man was condemned for one mistake?

Mutt's ears pricked. He jumped down. His claws tap, tap, tapped on the limestone tiles.

"We're leaving, Mary."

She shook her head at John's voice. When would he get the message and leave her alone? In the window, she saw the reflection of him ruffling Mutt's fur.

"Sure you won't come? We could drop in to visit your mom on the way back from Washington."

He'd refused to heal the only person she'd cared about being healed — why would she want to see a bunch of strangers jumping for joy?

John said, "If you need me, I'll stay."

If she needed him? Where the hell was he three nights ago when she needed him? She snorted. From the corner of her eye, she caught his hand moving for her shoulder. She glowered at it. It withdrew.

"If there's anything, just call." John slunk away. They left.

Ensconced in her own room when they'd arrived back last night, she hadn't spoken to John since... If only she hadn't promised Ben, she'd have been out of here. Why had he made her promise? She snorted again. Because he knew she'd want to run. And while she'd only promised to stay, the spirit of the promise was implicit: stay, help, protect. "Shit!"

But it wasn't just John letting Ben die, it was him then healing the terrorist. Turning the other cheek was all well and good, but there had to come a point when enough was enough and you meted out punishment befitting the crime. John was hot on all things scriptural — had he never read the Book of Revelation? Never read of the sun turning black, the seas turning to blood, fire raining from the sky to scorch the wicked off the face of the earth? Not that she wanted Armageddon, merely justice. Except there was no justice. No justice but that which you made for yourself.

She leapt up. Some cancers couldn't be cured with healing hands and rousing rhetoric; some cancers needed cutting out with fire and brimstone. And if no one else did, she knew just where to start slicing.

Eighteen minutes later, she was sitting in her car, the engine idling. Toying with her crucifix, she stared at her passenger seat. There sat the hard drive from Rashid's study and the contents of his paper shredder. Could she really do this?

She hammered the gas. Her promise? Yeah, right. A promise founded on lies was a promise made to be broken. John wasn't the only one prepared to sacrifice everything to do the right thing. They'd be gone all day — plenty of time to find answers. Then someone would pay for Ben's death. She didn't much care who. And then she was out of here.

***

"Evening, Mr. President."

Lounging on the right-hand couch in the Oval Office, Tom didn't look up from Connolly's planks. Connolly might have caused panic worldwide and come within a whisker of crippling the U.S., but his proposals on alternative energies were fascinating. "This couldn't wait 'til tomorrow's meeting, Bob?" He gestured to the couch opposite.

"I'm sorry, but this won't take long." Bob sat. "I thought it best you be informed as soon as possible, in private, for reasons which will become self-evident." He opened his briefcase.

"Oh?" Intriguing. Had Bob finally discovered something to bury Connolly beyond all redemption should he ever air his ideology in public again?

Bob smiled triumphantly, handing Tom a file marked 'classified'. "Seems one of Connolly's associates is more patriotic than we gave them credit for."

Tom adjusted his glasses. "We got a source?" He read. "And this is reliable?"

"From our analysis so far, it would seem so."

Tom looked over the top of his glasses. "And what's on the table in return?"

"New I.D. Relocation. Income for life. The usual package."

"And there's more to come?"

Bob winced. "That's the 64-thousand-dollar question. This could be just to whet our appetites, or it could be all there is and a bluff. I can't see a guy as savvy as Connolly making it easy for anyone to back him into a corner, even one of his own. But it looks promising."

"Good. Keep me apprised." Tom stood. "Well, thanks for your time, Bob. I'll—"

"I'm sorry, sir, there's more."

"Oh?... Oh, sorry." Tom sat again. "I've always time for good news."

Bob shrugged. "Then I'm sorry to disappoint, sir."

This was very cloak and dagger. Not like straight-to-the-point Bob at all.

Bob fished in his case for another file. "Seems we might not be the only ones to have an insider." He handed Tom another file.

What? Someone inside the White House had betrayed them to Connolly? The whole fabric of Washington would unravel if not for the occasional leak, be it orchestrated or not. But for Bob to be involved, this was not simply someone letting slip the contents of a confidential memo, but a serious breach of national security. Tom opened the file. But he didn't need to read it. One look at the photo of the culprit was sufficient. He slung his glasses aside. "This someone's idea of a joke?"

"I'm sorry, sir, but—"

"Sorry?" Tom jerked up, brandishing the file. "What the hell is this?"

"Sir, in the interests of national security, potential leaks—"

"Potential leaks? National security? What in the name of hell are you talking about, Bob?" He threw the file down.

"Sir, if you'll just let me explain—"

"Oh, there's actually an explanation why the CIA's spying on my chief of staff, is there? Well, thank Christ, 'cause for a second there, I thought the whole damn world had gone to hell. Hell's teeth, Simon's done as much for this country as any president I can name. Me included."

Bob said, "His wife attended Washington Memorial Hospital late this afternoon."

"I know."

"Simon went with her."

Tom snorted. "I know."

"Connolly visited Washington Memorial late this afternoon."

"Excuse me?"

Bob pointed. "If you just turn the page, sir."

Tom did. He found more photos — Jean's makeup streaked her face with tears, while Simon hugged John. Tom slumped. "Oh, no."

***

Hand raised at the oak door, Mary hesitated. She turned to leave, but stopped. When she was eight, she'd refused to let her dad explain why he'd walked out on them, just hated him for abandoning them. Had she learned anything in the intervening 24 years, or was she still just a petulant child who saw the world only in the black and white of how it affected her? She toyed with her crucifix. And this was why she now wore it — to remind her not to accept things on first appearances and condemn out of hand, but to seek answers, especially for why those you loved could betray you so easily. She couldn't reclaim those lost years with her dad, but she could give John the chance to justify his actions, though she doubted he could. She rapped at the door. Just keep cool.

The door opened.

"Can I come in?" she said.

John stepped back. "I never asked you to leave."

Mary marched in. "I'm sorry I punched you."

"And I'm sorry I upset you."

She spun to him. "Upset me? ... *Upset me!* Is that—" She turned away and drew deep breath. Cool. Keep cool. "John, you let our best friend die."

"No. I didn't."

"Excuse me?"

"I honored our best friend's final wish."

Her adrenaline pumped. "Don't pull that... You can't..." She gazed into space, breath snorting. How in hell did you argue with someone who couldn't even grasp what the argument was about? "That's not the point, and you know it."

"Freedom over your own life isn't the point? So what are we fighting for?"

She rubbed her forehead. Male logic — was there anything more dumbfounding? "John, you could've saved him. We could've helped him. He'd have been thankful in the end."

"So I should force my judgment on people, whether they like it or not, and to hell with the consequences?"

"If it's for their own good, yes."

"And I'm the best judge of what's good for someone else?"

Mary paced to the window, the drapes hiding the night. "If a little Amish boy gets heart disease, he's as good as dead 'cause his culture forbids modern medicines. Is that doing the right thing? Or should the authorities intervene, ignore his parents, and heal him?"

John slumped into a billowing red armchair. "If you destroy a person's faith, his ideals, his dreams, everything he lives for, don't you destroy the person, too?"

"We're talking about a child, for Pete's sake."

"I thought we were talking about Ben?"

Mary clasped her head. "Oh, I can't do this." If they couldn't get beyond this, there was no hope. If John would just take responsibility and admit he did wrong, maybe, *maybe*, they'd have a point from which to start over.

John stared at the floor. "When I was 13, my mom died. I didn't know I could heal then, so... She'd fought for three years. Had seven operations. Chemo. But... When she got really sick, my grandma came to help out, but it was really all over, bar the crying. Not that I knew. One Wednesday I came home from school to find my cousins, my aunt, and two uncles just arrived. Even my mom's old college friend had traveled up from Baltimore. Everyone my mom ever loved... She died two hours later. And I cried all night. I'd have given anything for just one more week, just one more day with her. And I could probably have had it, except she knew she'd never be surrounded by such love again, never have such a glorious day again, so she stopped fighting..." John looked up. "And all I could do was curse her for leaving me, for being weak, being so selfish."

"I didn't... I'm sorry."

John sighed. "Would I have healed her? In a heartbeat. I could've guaranteed her endless days of love and companionship from friends and family... But Ben? ... Could I have changed his past? Brought his wife back? Could I have guaranteed him another day when he'd make such a difference he'd change the very world?" A tear rolled down John's cheek. "You think it was easy to let him go?"

"Oh, John, I..." She'd only thought of her loss. She'd never considered it might actually have been right for Ben; never dreamed how it would hurt John to honor Ben's wishes, hurt him to deny his very nature and not heal. Her voice trembled for Ben, for John. "Can we be friends again?"

John strode toward her. She met him halfway. They hugged. Mary clung to him, feeling his warmth, safety in his arms. "I'm sorry."

"It's okay."

After a few seconds, she pulled back. "I know you talked about not fighting evil with evil, but I just couldn't stand that you healed that ... that guy after he tried to kill us."

"You know what a vaccination is?"

An odd question at such a time. "You mean like a flu shot?"

"Exactly. That's a tiny dose of flu that neutralizes the effect of the full-blown virus."

Wow. John really picked his times to talk in riddles. "I don't follow."

"One microscopic speck neutralizes the destructiveness of billions of others."

"Ohhh." He was hoping a healed terrorist would change his worldview and have a domino effect on others. Well, it'd worked with Vincent, but only after prolonged exposure to John. She doubted Al Qaeda would be playing nice any time soon. Thank God John had forsaken politics for healing. "I'm glad we're not campaigning anymore. Couldn't see me in dresses, lording it over the White House."

264

"Lao-Tsu said, '*To see beauty as beauty means one must also know ugliness; to see good as good means one must also know evil.*'"

Way too deep. Mary blew a breath. What was he getting at? That if everyone knew right from wrong, there should be no more suffering in the world?

"I'm making an announcement tomorrow," said John.

"An announcement? What announcement?"

"About your little Amish boy."

"My little Amish boy? There is no little Amish boy. I was making a point."

"A very good point."

Mary stepped back. The Amish embraced modern medicine. She'd invented the scenario to win the argument. What had she started? "I thought you'd decided running for president was too dangerous, too detrimental to your healing."

"No. But that's not the announcement."

Mary held her hands up. "John, Che Guevara fought for freedom, and they assassinated him for it. Now he's just a nameless silhouette on kids' T-shirts. That what you want to be in 10 years?"

"I won't let Ben's death be in vain."

"Oh, Jeez." She buried her face in her hands. With John returning to the 'simplicity' of healing, she'd considered coming clean about investigating Rashid, as John would have the time to give the subject a fair hearing. But if this announcement eclipsed the presidency, she'd better hang fire 'til she knew what was going on. Talk about out of the frying pan!

30

What Dreams May Come

A haunting guitar soared into the church's nave, caressed in a slow dance with a melancholy keyboard. Slowly bending from one mournful note to another, the guitar wept as mellow as honey one moment; the next, like the clash of shattering glass.

Mary had never liked Pink Floyd. Anything without a dance beat seemed to go against the very essence of music: movement, life. But 'Shine On You Crazy Diamond', Ben's favorite song, had a hypnotic sensitivity.

The moment of remembrance over, John looked up, standing beside Ben's plain pine casket. "Ben Cale was one of the dearest friends I'll ever have. There are countless clichés to describe my grief, but, suffice it to say, I'll miss him 'til the day I die.

"Ben had a dream. A dream that drove his life. A dream many of us share. Ben dreamed of making a difference, of changing the world for the better. On the journey through life to achieving one's goals, one meets many who'll help and many who'll hinder. Without Ben, my journey would've ended. Without Ben, that dream for a better world, that dream so many of us cling to, would be dead. Ben Cale made a difference. A difference greater than he'll ever know.

"But Ben became an innocent victim of our times. He died for no other reason than someone was educated with a doctrine poisoned by religious zealots. But we don't have to turn to atheism, or the homogenizing of the great faiths, to end such horrors. We just have to turn to empathy. Because it's empathy that made us abolish slavery and dismantle apartheid. Empathy that makes us give to famine victims, cancer charities, disaster appeals. Empathy that will help us forsake the dead aspects of our religions and allow them to evolve in our global society. You see, it's empathy that binds us together, not laws, not religion. Empathy." Hand on heart, John gazed at the casket. "Ben, I swear to you now, the world will change. It *will* change."

John joined Mary in the front pew.

As the bearers wheeled out the casket for the crematorium, Mary drew a shuddering breath. "Bye, Ben."

Rashid, Sana, and Vincent following them, John and Mary shuffled from their pew. From the crammed pews, the mourners stared. She recognized some as people they'd healed. Toward the back, police officers in dress uniform packed the pews. Vincent was right. Ben was a good cop and respected for it. She prayed he knew. Prayed he could see the tributes heaped at Rashid's gate.

As John and Mary trudged for the door, the nearest officer nodded respectfully. Then his colleague. Then others. They obviously saw her and John as the closest thing to real family Ben had. She felt tears running down her cheeks again, but she also felt incredible pride. Ben had not only made a difference, but left a legacy to inspire others to do likewise. She, for one, would not fail him.

Nearing the door and the ordeal to come, she squeezed John's hand to reassure him he wasn't alone. Whatever his announcement, she'd honor her pledge to Ben and back John 100%.

The enormous black door creaked open and sunlight flooded in.

Flashes blasted. Microphones thrust. Held behind metal barriers all the way down the steps to the curb, reporters barked questions.

John stood motionless. The cacophony gradually died. Finally he said, "I want you all to imagine you're newborn babies, with no concept of into which culture you've been born. Now, imagine the world you'd like to grow up in... Is it the dust bowls of India? The war-ravaged hills of Sierra Leone? The ice fields of Siberia?" He let his words resonate. "Every year, two million babies die on the day they're born. *Two million!* Two million souls who'll never know even a single day of life, let alone a lover's kiss, laughter with friends, the sun warm on their face and birdsong in the air. Two million... Doesn't every child deserve to grow up in that same world you imagined?" He paused. "Two million. Every year. On they day they're born." John snorted. "Well, not anymore.

"I request an audience at the United Nations in one week's time to establish a series of referenda across the world. Any country whose people freely vote to join a new world order will do so. *Will* do so."

Mary shivered. Something bad was coming. Real bad.

"Any nation that opposes the wishes of its people will be brought to justice. I will topple governments. I will cripple economies. I will decimate any power that stands between Mankind and its rightful life. If need be, I will not hesitate from bringing the entire planet to its knees, to rebuild it anew." Eyes widened. Jaws dropped. The people stared, aghast. John continued, "I love America. I love the American people ... so it pains me to have to do this." John scanned the media standing transfixed before him. "Today. 3:00 p.m. Let the world look to CNN."

John marched down the steps amidst the deafening thunder of the press. In a state of shock, Mary stumbled after him. Topple governments? Cripple economies? If John said it, he could do it. And that was the problem — John had lost his mind if he thought the world's powers would sit back and let him.

***

The Hummer scrap, Rashid's new 53-mpg diesel Peugeot revved amidst a strained silence. Mary stared at the stores flying by. Would tomorrow see the dawn of a new age, or would it see these stores boarded up, livelihoods decimated, lives destroyed? John was playing a dangerous game. Dangerous for him, for her, for America.

"You know—" In the front passenger seat, Vincent twisted around to face John, "— I don't wanna rain on your parade, but the warm glow of doing the right thing ain't gonna feed people's families. And while I'm not exactly what you'd call a conscientious taxpayer, you screw with the economy, you're gonna hurt more people than you help."

John said, "We've got computer chips that process 10 billion calculations per second; satellites that can photograph any person on any street; medicine that can re-attach a hand, replace a heart, rebuild a face. Why? Because the developed world gave it to us. But the developed world's only 20% of the world's population. 20%. What if you only had five letters in the alphabet, three notes in a scale? What masterpieces could Shakespeare or Bach have created then? If 100% of the population was healthy, safe, and fed, think of the wonders we could conjure into reality. But instead we let half the world starve."

"And toppling governments, crippling economies is gonna solve that?"

"The guy who invented the wheel," said John. "Did he do it to buy a castle and live like a king, or just so he wouldn't put his back out humping goods to market?"

Grimacing, Vincent rubbed his chin. "See, you heal someone, I'm with you. Say you can give people all the free stuff they need to live, I'm with you. Spout a load of Zen crap, I just wanna whack you."

Mary smiled. Vincent did have a way of cutting through the garbage. Refreshing.

"Despite democracy and elections, people don't run the world; they don't even run their own lives — governments and billion-dollar corporations do. It won't be the people I hurt."

Vincent glanced at Mary. Was he expecting support after the whole Ben affair? He looked to John. "Do this, and it won't just be a bunch of assholes in a rented minivan who come after you."

"As much as I don't want to be president, I *don't* want to do *this*. But sometimes, in order to do what's right, you have to do what could be seen to be wrong. If the world's governments refuse to listen, should we just forget about helping people and go back to our old lives? Should a patient die because we object to killing his cancer?"

Mary grasped John's hand. She ached to believe him, support him, but... "Vincent's got a point. You're not planning anything drastic, are you?"

John smiled. "Trust me."

Oh, hell!

31

To the End of Days

Tom studied the gold medallion on the Roosevelt Room's mantel. Teddy Roosevelt had dreamed of peace and had been awarded the Nobel Prize for his efforts in ending the Russo-Japanese war. Now someone else was striving to bring peace to the world, only it was Tom's dream to stop him. Would history see Tom celebrated? Or would his presidency suffer worse condemnation than that for Clinton's affair, Nixon's Watergate, and Kennedy's Bay of Pigs combined?

Behind him, a door opened. "Morning, sir." Ryan, Gloria, Michael, and Bob greeted him. But no Simon. Simon had phoned to apologize for his tardiness. A stomach bug. After the initial paranoia with which Bob had infected him had dissipated, Tom had tried to phone Simon, overjoyed his best friend had his wife, his life back. Phoned innumerable times. Left innumerable messages. But heard nothing back. Simon wasn't stupid. He'd know it was impossible to keep something like that secret, so why didn't he come clean? Tom sighed. Oh, no.

Twenty-one minutes into the meeting, Michael sniggered. "So to hell with global warming 'cause the world will end anyway if you can't do 0-60 in three seconds?"

"Four point six," said Bob. "And I don't see you cycling to work."

"That's 'cause, unlike your Porsche, my Toyota gets upwards of 45 around town."

"You turning all bleeding-heart green on us there, Mickey?" Bob smiled. "So what happens to the American way of life when we've wasted all our resources developing the Third World? It our turn to live in mud huts then?"

"Okay," said Michael, "one: ending poverty? Not a waste of resources. And two: er, ha, you even bothered to look at this?" He brandished John's platform documentation. "Wouldn't your quality of life, your kids' quality of life, be better with less pollution? Just 'cause you don't like Connolly's philosophy doesn't mean his ideas on," he counted on his fingers, "sustainable forestry, green energy, reversing climate change, renewing the water table won't pan out. But hey, you don't believe me, you do the math." He skidded the document across to Bob.

Tom barely registered the to-ing and fro-ing — he had other worries. Simon knew as much about running the country as anyone. If Connolly had info from Simon, he really could pose a significant threat. But it wasn't that. This was Simon, for God's sake. Simon who'd carried him home after Tom had fallen out of McCluskey's apple tree and broken his leg. Simon who'd set Tom up with Helen Buchanan — his first girlfriend. Simon who'd convinced Tom he had the vision and moral fortitude public office so needed. This was Simon, who'd always been there. How could he not be there now, when Tom's need was greatest?

Tom snorted. "Okay. Okay. When recess is finally over... Now, if we can't take Connolly out of the game before 3 o'clock, is our only hope damage limitation, or have you got something else for us, Bob?"

Panting, Simon burst in. "Morning, sir. Apologies everyone."

"How's the stomach?" asked Tom.

Simon only made eye contact for the briefest moment. "Better, thanks."

"Jean?"

"Best you don't ask, if that's all the same, thank you, sir." Simon placed a paper in front of Tom. "I've just been handed this on the way in." He took his seat.

Bob shot Tom a sideways glance.

Damn! Tom couldn't give Simon a more open invitation to come clean. Could Simon's loyalty really be in question? Simon could never be bought with material wealth, but 'faith' could turn the clearest of minds. But that would have to wait.

Suddenly drained, Tom picked up the paper as if it weighed 100 pounds. When he read it, it became so heavy he dropped it. He massaged his eyes. "The Chinese have withdrawn their diplomatic corps from their consulates in L.A., Chicago— hell, everywhere." Everyone shuffled uncomfortably in their seats. Tom sniggered with nervous tension. "What next? Trade embargoes? Deportation of U.S. citizens? A declaration of war?" Today it was sick joke. But tomorrow? "Hell's teeth." If ever there'd been an eleventh hour. God help them. Tom gestured to Bob. "Bob?"

"Okay, on page three," said Bob, sliding a file over to Simon, "you'll see we've found five account numbers: one belongs to the First Bank of Grand Cayman; another to the Treasury Bank of Antigua. From our analysis of the data, it seems an automated password generator's used after each time an account is accessed via the Web. We've got our best teams trying to hack these accounts, but it's gonna take time. Two of the other accounts we got zip, but the last is for Morrison and Pitt, a Wall Street firm dealing in equities, properties, commodities — you wanna buy your own Caribbean island, it's these guys you call."

Ryan tapped his pen on the padded leather arm of his chair. "And I'm guessing you can't get to that account without a subpoena and you can't get a subpoena without evidence of a crime?"

"The CIA can get to whatever it wants." Bob grimaced. "Problem is, Connolly's so high profile, if we're not gonna create a martyr, everything has to be cleaner than the Pope's mother."

"So where's that leave us?" asked Tom.

"We've more info coming in today, so hopefully everything'll slot together."

Skimming his file, Simon said, "We're confident of getting more information?"

Bob nodded. "So long as we hold up our end."

"Okay," said Tom. "We any ideas of what Connolly's actually threatening?"

Bob sniggered. "So, Al-Alawi's worth a 100 mil; even if Connolly blows it all, what's he gonna achieve? Topple governments, cripple economies, my ass."

"Thank you, Bob," said Tom. "Nothing like a soundly balanced argument to quell one's fears."

"Well, I'm sorry, sir," said Gloria, "but I agree with Bob. Seriously, a 100 mil to finance a global revolution? Please. These days, you'd be lucky if it got you a five-year deal on a decent quarterback."

Maybe Bob and Gloria were right. But with only four hours and 20 minutes until Connolly's 3 o'clock deadline, they needed to be prepared. But prepared for what? Running for the presidency was the greatest threat Connolly could've made and, with 100 million, he had the funds to see that through. But to cripple an economy? Short of nuking Fort Knox and destroying its $6 trillion in gold bullion, the U.S.'s single biggest reserve, Connolly could do squat. Surely? Maybe he was bluffing. If he was, he'd seriously miscalculated. "I'd say, before the funeral, Connolly had us beat in the polls by maybe 15 points. After his little speech, he'd be lucky to be in double figures. If there's one thing turns the American people cold, it's being threatened. Now, can we build on that?" Tom gestured to Michael.

"The dollar's the strongest it's been for three years, and after climbing steadily for the past nine quarters, just yesterday the Dow hit an all-time high. He wants a go at us, I say, bring it on — let's bury him once and for all."

Ryan nodded. "I agree. We sit back and let the guy crash and burn. Get China, the Saudis, everyone off our backs. Especially corporate America. Hell, if I get one more pissed lobbyist on the phone, I swear..." He shook his head.

Tom nodded. It sounded as if they could just kick back and enjoy the show. But that was undoubtedly what Goliath's comrades thought when they saw David. Bob, Michael, Gloria, Ryan ... almost everyone believed Connolly was going to bury himself. Almost. "Simon?"

Simon gazed at the table. "Wise men speak because they have something to say; fools because they have to say something."

Tom frowned. Where was Simon going? "Plato?"

"Uh-huh... See, it's not a fact we like to highlight in our history texts, but for the sake of profits, we continued trading with Germany 'til 1942. 1942! World War II started in '39! What were we playing at? Without us sourcing them oil, Germany would never have been able to invade France."

"So what are you saying?" asked Tom. "Connolly's right?"

"You bet your life I am."

Bob threw up his arms and blew out a heavy breath.

Simon continued. "And that's the problem. The little guy doesn't run his life, we do. And we only get to decide the odd bits and pieces the multinationals let us. It's the buck. Everything revolves around the damn, almighty buck."

"Mr. President," said Bob, "could I suggest we reconvene after a short break?"

After a short break to haul Simon in for interrogation. It was only Tom's order which had stopped that happening last night. Tom held up his hand to Bob. After all Simon had done for the country, he deserved to have his say.

Simon tapped his file. "This guy's no dumb schmuck. If there's one thing we know about him, it's that he does the impossible. So, we wanna sit back and watch someone crash and burn, we better be wearing helmets and fireproof suits, 'cause it sure as hell ain't gonna be Connolly. But we wanna be sitting here tomorrow, we better do something — but fast."

"And what d'you suggest?" said Michael.

"We put a team together — the best legal minds we can find: criminal law, international law, fraud, tax, internet crime, civil rights. We are the most powerful group of people on the planet. We can topple governments. We can cripple economies. But not in one day. Not legally. So why do we imagine Connolly can? It's impossible. Even for him. So we haul in every damn lawyer in D.C. if we have to, and if this son of a bitch holds good to his threat, we nail him to the wall."

While Simon may have been throwing them a curve ball, it seemed logical. No way could a lone individual legally pull off something on such a grand scale in a day, a week, even a month. They had Connolly. Forget martyrdom. Forget miracles. He was going to be just a common criminal. Or a common hoaxer. Either way, they had him!

Tom delegated the work and adjourned the meeting for an hour to assemble the legal team. One problem down. Unfortunately, there was another: Tom would have to confront Simon, and risk losing his best friend and most trusted advisor. Or had he already lost that? He rubbed his temples. Some days, this was the best job in the world. Others...

"Mr. President?"

Tom looked at Simon.

274

"Could I see you for a few minutes, please? In private?"

Did Simon know about the photos? Would he preempt an attack? If he had nothing to hide, he'd have returned Tom's calls. Or been here first thing to explain why he hadn't. Even with two broken legs. Stomach bug? Like hell. Tom said, "Would you give us the room, please?" Everyone else shuffled out.

Good God. Bob had him being as paranoid as he was. Simon was as out-and-out American as the Fourth of July. Yeah, but so was Connolly. And Connolly believed he was doing what was best for America. As Simon said, everyone had his price. Was another 20 years with the woman he loved too much for Simon to resist?

Tom heaved a breath, trying to calm the butterflies in his stomach. Not Simon, please. Anyone but Simon. How could he ever order the arrest of his best friend? "What's the problem?"

"I want to make this as easy as possible for you, sir." Simon placed an envelope before Tom.

Tom stared at the letter, heart pounding. He didn't want to open it. Didn't want to read it. But he ripped it open. He hardly dared look at the letter inside, but didn't need to read far. "What the hell is this?"

"I'm assuming Bob's apprised you of yesterday's events."

Tom shook his head. "The country's facing its worst crisis since 9/11 and my chief of staff thinks it's a good idea to resign?"

"Sir, some people might perceive a conflict of interests."

"And would those people be right?"

"I have been, and always will be, your friend and the country's servant, sir."

Oh, thank God. Tom heaved a sigh of relief, then shredded the letter. "Then let anyone who says otherwise go hang."

Simon smiled. "Thank you, sir."

"No. Thank you, Simon." What kind of dumbass was he to let Bob's paranoia cast doubts on his best friend? "So, Connolly?"

Simon blew out a breath, eyebrows raised. "I tell you, despite all the hype, this time yesterday, the guy was nothing but smoke and mirrors. Today, watching Jean make breakfast, hearing her laugh, seeing her face without that damn oxygen mask ... I cried. I honest to God cried."

This was bad. "So you're saying he's the real deal?"

"I'm saying, people ain't wrong when they use the word 'miracle'."

Tom raked his fingers through his hair and drew a slow breath. "So what are you telling me? That he is the Second Coming, for Christ's sake?" Oh, God help them. Could they be so wrong? Could Connolly really possess the secret to drawing the world together into an age of peace and plenty? Michael said Connolly's figures added up; his moral ideology was beyond reproach; his philosophy cut down boundaries of faith, race, creed... Had they read this situation so totally wrong? "So where do we go from here?"

Simon heaved a breath. "We've already got China and the Middle East on our backs. Now Europe's screaming about his threats. If we cut him any more slack, he's liable to bury the entire country. So, like I said, we put a team together and bury him first."

There was more. Something Simon wasn't saying, whether because he didn't want to burden Tom, or because his duty to his country came before any personal concerns he might have. But if Connolly truly had a gift to heal the dying, Tom wanted to be burdened. He needed answers. To know he was doing the right thing. "Okay, that's what my chief of staff says. Now, what does Simon Rorschach say?"

"Honestly?"

"Have I ever wanted it any other way?"

"I, er," Simon shuffled like a schoolboy explaining his behavior to the principal. "I'd tell the rest of the world to go hang and ask Connolly what he really wants."

"We know what he wants: world peace."

"Sir, with respect, he ain't out to win Miss World. And even the Son of God enjoyed having his feet washed in exotic oils."

Simon was right. Everyone had their price. And maybe they already knew Connolly's. "Our foreign aid budget's 29 billion. Instead of just throwing money at countries to blow as they will, what say we establish a new agency to direct funds into specific projects as it sees fit?"

Simon smiled. "And let Connolly head it."

"Let him go build all the roads, hospitals, power stations he wants. Give him the power to change the world. Let him play God."

"And if he won't play ball for 29 billion, we unleash the lawyers."

Tom smiled. They retain the presidency; the world retains stability; Connolly gets to make a difference. Win-win-win. Some days, this was the best job in the world.

32

When the Sky Falls

2:57 p.m.
The White House ground to a standstill. The U.S. ground to a standstill. The whole world ground to a standstill. Television had cast a spell over the entire globe. This was the fall of the Berlin Wall, the assassination of Kennedy, and the death of Princess Diana, all rolled into one.

A bead of sweat ran from Tom's temple.

CNN's weathercaster predicted storms. Gone was his usual professionalism. His movements were edgy, voice tense, manner distracted, as if he had a gun trained on him.

During the 1960s, the USSR tried to deploy a nuclear arsenal on Cuba. With missiles only 90 miles from Florida, the U.S. would have had scant time to 'duck and cover', let alone launch a retaliatory strike. They'd have been fish in a barrel. Kennedy demanded Moscow withdraw. Moscow refused. The world teetered at the threshold of Armageddon. Every hour of every day, people gazed skyward, expecting death to rain down in a fiery thunderstorm. Thanks to God, the world survived. But Tom knew how those Floridians felt, scouring ever upward for that first sign of doom. He stared up at the wall-mounted TV as the seconds crawled by like hours.

2:58 p.m.

Someone handed Tom a glass of water. He'd no idea who, unable to wrench his attention from the screen. He gulped it down, but within seconds his mouth was parched again. Connolly had declined their offer. Declined $29 billion. Declined the opportunity to change the world. Why? At best, if Al-Alawi sold his business assets, house, every stick of furniture he possessed, Connolly could only wield $90 million. He couldn't topple governments. Couldn't cripple economies. This was bull.

2:59 p.m.

Yet, if it were a bluff and they'd offered him an attractive alternative, why hadn't he grabbed it? What did he know that they didn't? It didn't matter. He only had $90 million. A king's fortune to the man in the street, but in global terms? Bob was right. Cripple the economy? Like hell.

Tom tried to lick his lips, but his dry tongue just stuck to them.

Oh, God...

3:00 p.m.

No phones rang.

No keyboards clicked.

No staff stirred.

The world froze.

As though he was prey being stalked, Tom barely breathed for fear of how close death might be...

He stared at the TV. And the world stared with him.

The on-screen clock all but froze. Some evangelists proclaimed that the fall of governments and the collapse of economies would herald Armageddon. Were they about to witness the biblical apocalypse from which only the worthy would be saved? God help them.

The clock's second hand laboriously creaked around like a windmill's sails on a breathless day.

Then...

She smiled, eyes crinkling. "It's one minute after 3 o'clock and you're watching CNN. Hi, I'm Trisha Daily. Well, for those tuned in expecting reports of the sky falling, we're pleased to tell you, apart from the usual floods, famines, and hardships, all's well in the world. Coming up..."

Pens and papers, shrieks and whoops, flew into the air.

"Oh, thank God." Tom laughed with nervous energy. They'd escaped.

278

Talk about relief. It'd all been a hoax. But why? To show even by doing nothing, Connolly could control world events? But that was a one-time trick. Now they had his number. Now—

Tom's grin fell. "Quiet... Quiet!"

Trisha's newsreader chirpiness fractured. "We're just receiving reports of..."

Oh, Lord, please no. Oh, dear Lord, no.

33

Now You See It

Panic...

Screaming...

Fear...

Destruction...

Nowhere to run.

34

And so the End, Beautiful Friend

The old man who smelled of pee shuffled away from the 7-Eleven's checkout. The clerk, a young black guy, looked at Mary. Avoiding eye contact, she dumped bottled water, prepackaged sandwiches, shampoo — a selection of basics — beside the register.

Behind her, sporting a kick-ass black suit, a Latino dude craned to see her face.

Head bowed, she hid behind her straggly hair.

"Hey, don't I know you?"

Oh, no. That was what she'd dreaded. Why she hadn't left the room for days. Mary gestured to the clerk scanning prices. "Could you hurry, please."

No reaction.

"I do know you." The dude laughed. "Yeah."

Mary turned her back, her heart pounding. "Please, I'm in a rush."

But the dude wouldn't give up. "You're that Mary, right?"

Finally, the clerk said, "$18.85."

Mary rooted in her purse. But the more quickly she tried to fish out her money, the more flustered she became, 'til she couldn't think what she was doing.

"Hey," the dude turned to the other customers, "it's that Mary chick, used to be with the healer guy."

"No, I'm not." Customers gawked at her. She could feel their stares burning into her. She fumbled with her money.

"$18.85."

"Yes. I've got it. I just..." Finally, she found her money. Thrust it at the clerk.

"So what's the story, Mary? Where's all the loot?"

Everyone in the world was staring at her. Judging her. She couldn't breathe. She had to get out. Get away. She grabbed her groceries. Dashed for the door.

"Your change," called the clerk.

She ran out into the darkness.

***

Panting, face glistening with sweat, Mary dashed in and slammed her room door at the Rose Garden Hotel — strangely, the room she'd booked with John so, so long ago. If only they'd registered under a different name then, or forsaken their booking and stopped elsewhere, Rashid might never have found them, and John might still be with her now. She fumbled with the security lock, then slumped against the door, tears streaming. She couldn't go on like this. She had to get away. But where? Anywhere! Anywhere but here.

This was all her fault. She couldn't cope with that. She'd tried to convince herself that it was John's fault for doing what he did instead of accepting the President's $29 billion offer. But even such a huge amount could only change a tiny part of the world, not all of it. So it wasn't John's fault. He had to show corporations, show governments the power he had with which to crush them if they dared ignore their people's needs. No, it was her fault. She'd thought she was doing the right thing, but she couldn't have done anything worse. Why couldn't she have left Rashid's hard drive alone?

She trudged to the bed and collapsed. She had to get her head together. Devise a plan. She couldn't spend the rest of her life hiding in seedy hotels. She clicked on the TV as a distraction from the guilt that haunted her.

Jerry Flashman Tonight beamed from the mock backdrop of Manhattan's nighttime skyline. At his desk, Jerry smoothed a hand over his blond hair, checking to ensure it draped with as much style as his suit. "Okay, my next guests are investigative journalists just back from the Colombian jungle.

They've reported for *National Geographic*, CNN, and last year, produced that mind-blowing *Animal Planet* documentary about swimming with Great Whites. Yep, these guys get around. Now, I know recent events have left a sour taste in people's mouths when it comes to miracle workers, but these guys claim to have found another one." He held his hands up. "And before everyone groans and goes channel surfing, I assure you, this is no John Connolly. No millionaires. No politics. No world domination. Yep, the whole Bond super-villain thing's out. In fact, this one's not even a man. So please, greet Phil Werbernuik and Sal Goldstein."

What!? Mary just gawked.

To applause, two thirty-something guys strolled on. Phil's black leather trousers squeaked on the leather couch as he sat. Sal ran a hand through his slicked-back hair.

Jerry smiled. "Now, guys, a woman? You're not gonna wheel out Connolly's mother, then pass the plate around?"

They laughed, then told their tale. Whilst researching the Colombian drug cartels in the hills of the Caqueta and Putumayo departments in southern Colombia, they heard tales of an old woman who lived deep in the jungle and possessed magical powers. Initially, they wrote it off as simple folklore. But as they traveled, they gleaned more and more about a Mother Maria who ran an orphanage and healed local villagers. Supposedly, no one below the age of 70 had died for the past three decades. They were so intrigued, they set out to find her.

"And you saw her heal?" asked Jerry.

Phil brushed his hands over his ponytail. "Oh, it was the damnedest thing we've ever seen, believe me."

"Strangest thing was," said Sal, "the villagers were so used to it, they didn't get why we were so blown away."

"We've got a clip, I believe?" Jerry looked to his plasma screen.

Sal nodded. "The second session we filmed."

Mary wiped her eyes and slid to the foot of the bed, nearer the TV. What was going on? Jerry Flashman was a reputable journalist. Was this for real?

Insects chirped. Children played on a scrap of cleared land. Two nuns tended a vegetable patch growing maize and cassava. Unshaven, hair stringy with grease, Sal stood before a rickety, single-story wooden building barely the size of two buses side by side. "32 children live and go to school here. The entire structure was built by one person, Mother Maria Hernandez-Gonzalez, with her own sweat and blood, when she came here 42 years ago. The daily running is now left to Sisters Isabel and Sofia, as Mother Maria is simply too old and fragile, and conserves her strength for her biweekly healing sessions."

A howler monkey cried. Blue and red macaws flew overhead. Dirty and dressed in tatters, a man and woman trudged up a dirt track. Between them, a hand in each of theirs, tottered a little boy, his face scarred with lesions, eyes discolored. Sal's voiceover said, "This is five-year-old Luis Herrera. He's been blind for six months after contracting Onchocerciasis — river blindness, caused by a parasitic fly laying eggs under his skin. With his parents, he's just walked for two days, hoping Mother Maria will see him."

In a tiny, candlelit wooden chapel, his parents led Luis to a hunched figure draped in brown robes — Mother Maria. She was sitting on a chair, its bare unpainted wood rough where it had been hand-cut. Behind her, a 6-foot sculpture of Christ on the cross gleamed in the flickering light, polished by decades of adoring hands. Luis's parents knelt him before Mother Maria. Frightened, he grabbed back for a reassuring hand. His mother obliged.

Mother Maria laid her left hand over his eyes. She muttered Latin. Crossed herself. Then removed her hand from Luis.

"Mamma!" Beaming, Luis spun around, his eyes completely healed.

His mother fell to her knees. Hugged him. Sobbed.

Oh, Jeez. No way. NO WAY! Mary leaned forward, scouring the image of the boy for trickery.

The audience clapped.

Jerry let the applause die. "Okay, guys, I've seen this three times and I'm still blown away. What was it like for you just stumbling upon it?"

Sal grinned. "I tell you, when we did the whole swimming-with-sharks thing in South Africa — Whoa! Talk about chills. But this was something else. The hairs are standing on the back of my neck even now."

Jerry nodded. "Mine, too."

Mary gasped. Another healer? So John ... wasn't unique? Not that special? No, this was bull. A con. She snagged the remote control from behind her, but hesitated.

"So, let's welcome the lady herself." Jerry raised his voice. "Mother

Maria."

Mother Maria shuffled on. Sal and Phil dashed over. She hugged them, then, supported between them, toddled over, her back so hunched she barely reached their chests.

Jerry offered his hand, but she reached out to hug him instead. He obliged. Finally, she sat and smiled, teeth missing in her top set.

"So, Mother Maria, I understand it took two full days to get here – I hope the journey wasn't too arduous."

While Sal translated into Spanish, she studied Jerry, her face as dark and cracked as parched clay, but her eyes sparkling like those of a teenage girl. She replied. Sal laughed, then said. "It was a long, long way, but after 40 years of sitting on wooden planks full of splinters in the jungle, our beautiful American toilets made it worthwhile."

The studio erupted with laughter.

As the interview progressed, Mother Maria bewitched everyone with her sensitivity, passion, and *joie de vivre*.

Finally, they came to the highlight: Mother Maria would heal. Live.

Jerry explained she'd never done this before, as it was an abuse of the gift she'd received from God, but her orphanage's generator had broken – not only was NBC providing a replacement, it was furnishing the orphanage with eco-friendly toilets and plumbing for indoor running water. How could she refuse such gifts for her children?

Of all the conditions she treated, Mother Maria liked to heal blindness the most. In western culture, it was debilitating, but people could still lead active, self-sufficient lives. In the jungle, however, blindness could be life-threatening – you couldn't farm, couldn't forage, couldn't work, couldn't live. To that end, Mike Waterstone was introduced. Young, athletic, square-jawed – the epitome of manhood. Alongside, guiding him, strolled Dr. Marshall Strong, senior ophthalmologist at St. Mary's Hospital. His bald head beading with sweat, Dr. Strong confirmed Mike had been blind since birth. Mike chatted but wasn't animated, his head and hands never moving.

Mother Maria squinted into Mike's normal-looking eyes. She patted him on the shoulder and grinned her gappy grin. She spoke Spanish.

Sal said, "She says not to worry. It won't hurt."

Mother Maria kissed the tiny crucifix hanging from her neck, then laid her left hand over Mike's eyes. She muttered in Latin.

Jerry looked to translator Sal. Sal shrugged.

Mother Maria crossed herself. She removed her hand from Mike's eyes.

Mike gasped, eyes wide in shock.

"Is everything okay?" asked Jerry.

Mike's head jerked to look at him. "I— I can see!" He laughed. He whirled his head, taking in all the new, wondrous sights.

The audience thundered applause. Mother Maria smiled, but waved a hand at them, as if the adulation was too much.

"Yeah, right." Mary sniggered. Like that proved anything. Stick him in the middle of the FDR Drive — let dodging the rampaging traffic prove he was healed.

"Okay," said Jerry, "for you unbelievers, we've a little test for Mike. Of course, we could just have him read aloud, but where's the television in that? So, Max, if you please?"

His shaggy hair graying, Max wheeled out a crossbow on a shoulder-high stand. Mike leaned around to watch.

"Okay, Mike, it was explained what you'd have to do if Mother Maria was successful, yeah?" said Jerry.

"Can't wait. This is incredible." Beaming, gaze still whirling to take in all the wondrous new sights, Mike marched over to Max. He stood at Max's shoulder while he demonstrated the handling of the crossbow. Max then corrected Mike's technique when he tried.

Across the stage, two men brought on a 2-foot-diameter, helium-filled balloon and a 6-foot-square wooden board with a target painted on it, to catch the crossbow bolt. Tethered to a weight, the balloon bobbed.

While the balloon and board were aligned, Mike pointed the crossbow at the floor.

"When you're ready, Mike," said Jerry. "Good luck."

A drum roll.

Mike raised the crossbow. Taking great care, he aimed through the telescopic sight. He swung the crossbow left. Nudged it right. Left. Right a fraction... Aimed.

Fired.

The bolt shot.

The balloon exploded.

286

The bolt splintered into the target's outer ring. The burst balloon released smaller ones, which drifted up in a shower of glittery foil.

Cheering and applause.

Mary stared. A healer. Another healer!

"Wow. What can I say?" Jerry clapped. "And, as if that isn't enough, Mother Maria has promised one more miracle tonight. If we can have a volunteer from the audience? A lady, please? No illness necessary."

Hands shot up.

"Er..." Jerry's finger roamed the rows. "The lady in the cropped black top."

Everyone clapped as a beautiful young woman bounced on stage, not an ounce of fat jiggling on her taut belly.

Jerry sidled over and put his arm around her, as more equipment was wheeled on behind a screen. "And you are?"

"Judy." She smiled.

"And you've been on TV before?"

She shook her head.

"Okay, there's nothing to be worried about. We'll take good care of you." He took a piece of fruit from his pocket. "Now, if you'd just stand over there with this apple on your head." He turned. "Ready, Mike?"

She pulled back and stared warily at Jerry.

Everyone laughed.

"What? He hit the target, didn't he? Okay, it wasn't a bull's-eye, but he's been blind all his life. Give the guy a break." Jerry laughed at her look of anxiety. "It's okay, Judy. Just kidding. Now," he looked at her flat stomach and gold navel piercing, "is it safe to say you're not heavy with child?"

She laughed, nodding.

"Ideal. Come this way." He guided her behind the screen, then headed back to his other guests, Mike now back with them. "Mother Maria, if you please."

Sal helped Mother Maria over as the screen was removed. Judy lay on a gurney. A matronly woman in a lab coat stood beside some medical monitoring equipment.

"This is Doctor Elizabeth Childs," said Jerry. "Head of Obstetrics at New York General, am I right?"

The woman smiled and nodded.

"Okay, Dr. Childs, if you'd be so good as to scan Judy for us." As she did, an ultra-sound image was relayed to the audience's monitors and Jerry's plasma screen. The image showed nothing in Judy's womb.

Elbows on her knees, Mary leaned forward. "Oh, you got to be kidding." This was too much. Even John had never done anything like this. Who in hell was this Mother Maria?

"She's not pregnant," said Childs.

"You're sure."

"100%"

"Okay," Jerry scanned the audience, "let's have a number between one and 9."

"Two."

"Nine."

"Four."

"Four is good," said Jerry. "And male or female?"

"Male."

"Okay, Mother Maria. Four months pregnant with a boy, please... And no fries with that."

The audience laughed.

Sal translated.

Jerry shook his head. "If this works, I'm joining a seminary."

More laughter.

"Hey, with my history, I've a lot of catching up to get in the Big Guy's good books." Jerry pointed to the heavens.

Her hand on Judy's stomach, Mother Maria spoke Latin, then crossed herself.

Judy's stomach swelled.

Judy gasped.

The audience gasped.

Jerry gasped. "Ohhh, you gotta be joking!"

Judy's catwalk-flat belly looked like she'd swallowed a watermelon.

Jerry looked to the doctor. "Doc?"

Childs scanned again. She clutched her mouth. A second heartbeat thumped. The audience gaped at the image on their monitors of a large head and spindly limbs, complete with fingers and toes.

"Holy Moly," said Jerry. "And it's a 16-week-old boy?"

Speechless, Childs nodded.

288

Mary clicked the TV off. She shook her head. Incredible. This little old lady could achieve the impossible as easily as John. But whereas John demanded world peace in exchange for his gift and would sacrifice everything and everyone to get it, all this miracle worker wanted was a few bucks' charity for a handful of kids. If only John had kept a sense of proportion, he wouldn't have ended up where he was. And it was Mary's fault. What had happened to him was all her fault.

She stared at the darkened TV screen.

She'd avoided commitment all her life to avoid the pain of abandonment, yet John had all but abandoned her long ago for his quest to save the world. If she hadn't been so stupid, so blinded by love, she'd have left already. How the hell had she got trapped in this mess — alone, no job, no future?

There was nothing left for her here. Nothing and no one. Tears streaming her cheeks, she grabbed her few belongings and her car keys. She had to get away. Far, far away. Only more pain could come from staying.

***

From the shadows of the studio wings, someone peered. Someone plotting.

"Jeez," said Jerry, "if I live to be a hundred, I'll never—"

Judy gasped and clutched her stomach.

"It kicked again?" said Jerry.

"Yeah."

He hovered his hand over her stomach. "May I?"

An unknown voice blasted over the studio speakers. "Hold it! Hold it! Hold it!"

Everyone glanced around, even Jerry. "What— What's going on?" Brow furrowed, he looked off-stage. "Rick?" He held out his hands, gesturing for an explanation. "What's happening?"

"Hold it right there." A man marched on from the wings, carrying a football. "Mike! Heads up." He hurled the ball. It hit Mike on the head and bounced away. "Didn't see it coming, huh? Wonder why?"

Jerry gawked, then scrambled over. "Sir, I... Nobody said... It— It's an honor, sir." He turned to the audience. "Ladies and gentlemen, President Tom Stevens."

Wild applause.

"Evening, everyone. Jerry." Tom jabbed at Childs. "Could I borrow that scanner, please?"

"Of— of course, Mr. President." She offered it, hand trembling.

Tom marched over. "Jerry, a number between one and 9."

"Er, six."

Tom scanned Judy. All the screens showed six tiny figures and sounded a cacophony of heartbeats. Excellent. Just like in rehearsals. Those tech guys couldn't have done a better job. "What's your favorite Disney character, Jerry?"

Jerry floundered. "Donald Duck."

The screens showed Donald Duck in Judy's womb. Donald waved.

Tom flipped the equipment off. "Judy?" He pointed to her bulbous stomach.

Her stomach flattened. Then grew. Then flattened and grew and...

Tom addressed the audience. "Everyone can distend their stomach, some just more than others. There's no magic, no miracle here." He helped Judy off the gurney. "Thank you, my dear." She nodded and scurried away. "Jerry here was simply instructed to pick a young, slim woman. We seated Judy directly in his eye line to camera, ensuring there was no one else fitting that criteria around her, and, being the beautiful, young woman she is, hoped hot-blooded Jerry here wouldn't be able to resist. Thanks, Jerry."

"You're welcome."

"As for this?" Tom waved the scanner. "Motion sensors relay its movement to a PC, which transposes them onto a CGI movie we had a little company called Industrial Light and Magic knock together. You saw the results." He handed the scanner to Childs. "Thanks. Sorry for having to dupe you and Dr. Strong." Tom glanced at Mike. "And sorry for the ball thing, Mike."

"That's all right, sir," said Mike.

"See anything yet?"

"Not a thing."

"Fancy another turn as William Tell?"

"No, thank you, sir."

"Jerry, can I get the feed from the crossbow scope on the monitors, please?"

"Sorry, sir, I've no idea what— Oh, there you go."

No sooner had Tom asked than the screens showed a picture of crosshairs aiming at the floor. Tom took a video game controller from his pocket. "This isn't exactly standard Xbox gear, but it's not rocket science." He manipulated the controller. The crossbow raised itself and swung around. The picture on the screens followed its line of sight. "Just hit the Magic Messiah button and..." Tom hit the X button. A bolt slammed into the bull's-eye. He grinned. What he and Simon wouldn't have given for one of these back in the day. Still, stick this one on the White House lawn, a few beers... If only. He smiled at the audience. "Amazing what you can do with a few servos and Bluetooth."

"As for Mike? Well, he could have a fine career in Hollywood. But there was no miracle. A fishing line got him to the crossbow." Mike held up a barely visible line. "We just reeled him in, 'til he hit the right spot, then Max did the rest with his," Tom made air quotes, "'lesson'."

"And," Tom bowed to her, "who could forget our star? How long have you had the power to heal, Mother Maria?"

Mother Maria's hunched back straightened. She spoke with a thick accent, but in English, "About 11 minutes."

"So your children? Your orphanage?"

"A 14-hour shoot in Belize, yesterday."

"Thank you, Mother Maria— or should I say, Mrs. Estevez. You've done your country a great service."

Tom turned to the audience, both studio and home. "Until she received a call from her agent two days ago, Maria Estevez was just a semi-retired actress. Yet today, thanks to the miracles of technology and the power of suggestion, she can make the sick walk, the blind see, the virginal receive an immaculate conception. Just two days, and she can fool a nation. Imagine the wonders she could achieve with two weeks' preparation, two months, two years... John Connolly dropped out of society for 19 years to plot and scheme. Is it any wonder he fooled us all so easily?

"So why tonight's elaborate hoax? To show how easily well-loved celebrities, like Jerry here, the media, even doctors, can be fooled with the simplest of gimmicks. No one's immune. So this goes out as a warning to us all, so we don't fall victim to unscrupulous sharks again."

"And that brings us to the villain himself: John Connolly. What can I say? Intelligent, commanding, charismatic. Everything you look for in a leader of people. Unfortunately, his campaigning was merely a sleight-of-hand trick to mask his true operation: creaming over $1 billion from the stock market through insider trading. We're only now piecing together how he did it, but the Dow plummeted 237 points in a half hour, sparking a selling frenzy around the globe, which cost in excess of $620 billion and destroyed more lives than we can imagine. And for that, I thank God he's behind bars awaiting due process, looking at jail time of up to 25 years, and we can finally wash our hands of him.

"You see, my fellow Americans, we live in a dangerous world. But the greatest threat to our nation doesn't come from the terrifying might of climate change, doesn't come from the nuclear arsenals of China, doesn't even come from the terrorist cells of Al Qaeda. No, the greatest threat to the American way of life comes from within, disguised as a work colleague, a neighbor, a friend. Yes, the greatest threat comes from us ourselves if we allow such charlatans, such false prophets, into our lives and grant them the power to disrupt our great nation and all it stands for.

"I believe in America. I believe in the American people. Together, let us rise to this challenge. Together, let us drive out this threat. Together, let us ensure the American way of life remains the benchmark for right, for justice, for freedom!"

The audience leaped to a standing ovation.

"Thank you. And God bless America." Tom strolled off stage, smiling and waving at everyone.

Connolly was buried.

The country was safe.

They'd done the right thing.

So why did he feel like crap!?

35

A Time for Dying

From the 5,800-foot-long steel Peace Bridge, Mary gazed down into the dark, churning waters of the Niagara River. She was doing the right thing. She'd struggled with it on the night-long drive, but she was certain now. Downtown Buffalo to her right, Canada to her left, she heaved a sigh as she ran a hand over her precious notebook. Change the world? What had she been thinking? She had to put this mess behind her. Forget and be forgotten. She tossed John's story — her life — into the raging river. "Goodbye, John." The icy darkness snatched it away, and it was gone.

She scurried back to her car.

As the first fingers of dawn seized a new day, she hit the gas, and seized a new life. Canada — a gigantic country, most of it still wilderness. The ideal place for a nobody to disappear.

The knotted tension in her neck muscles eased. Finally, she was free.

36

A Time for Rejoicing

In the corridor to the Roosevelt Room, someone said, "Morning, Mr. President."

Tom didn't register who, but smiled anyway.

Last night's hoax couldn't have gone better, so why did he still feel so soiled, so downright sleazy? Like he'd just accepted money to do the wrong thing. What choice had he had? Yes, Connolly appeared to have healed 1,822 patients. How? Who knew? But Tom couldn't celebrate for those 1,822 souls, only mourn for the other 300 million he was responsible for, whom John had betrayed, ruined, cheated, and endangered. The well-being of the few had to come secondary to the survival of the many.

Connolly crashing the world's markets by simultaneously dumping multi-hundred-million-dollar bundles of stocks onto the New York Stock Exchange had sent waves of panic selling surging around the globe. Such a sum wouldn't usually affect prices so much, but the world had been awaiting disaster at 3:00 p.m. on January 8, so the instant the slightest glitch appeared, everyone jumped ship. The FTSE lost 697 points; the Nikkei, 2,886; Dax, 1,039. The Dow could've crashed farther than any if not for the circuit-breaker system instituted after 1987's Black Monday. It was beside the point that no one would've lost a cent if they hadn't panicked. Beside the point that minimum-wage earners didn't hoard stock portfolios, so only the well-to-do, those greedy to line their pockets further, had lost money. Beside the point that the market couldn't rise and rise and rise, but had to crash sometime.

Investigations had revealed Al-Alawi had liquidated $63 million of his assets. Connolly turned that into $1.2 billion in stocks with which to 'topple governments' and 'cripple economies'. And he'd come damn close. How he'd transformed so little into so much was still a mystery, though the FBI and the Securities and Exchange Commission were looking at everything from insider trading to cyber crime to eco-terrorism. And to think, if he hadn't gotten so greedy, he could well have been the next president and had it all. What an ass.

Simon joined Tom. "Wonderful performance last night, sir."

"You should see my Macbeth. Any news?"

"Couldn't be better. His honor, Judge Harold S. Stanton."

"Oh, he hates us."

"Uh-huh." Simon nodded. "Only last week he lambasted our proposals on prison reform."

"Excellent. And he understands the case has to be fast-tracked?"

"Can't wait to get started, by all accounts."

Tom nodded. If they dithered and Connolly was able to heal so much as one person, or make just one of his rousing speeches, it all could start again. If they didn't capitalize on the situation immediately, Connolly would become a martyr, untouchable. The world would be at his mercy. And God help them then. So, to see things done, they needed to appear whiter than white. A judge with a reputation for speaking his mind and by-the-book lawgiving, Stanton was a gift from God, proving the White House hadn't simply drafted in one of its heavy hitters to nail Connolly at any cost. Connolly would get a fair trial ... then go directly to prison. Stanton was fair, but he was a patriot.

"Hope we're not rushing things," said Simon.

"With such a slam-dunk case?"

Simon winced. "Well..."

"Hell's teeth, if only half of what we know is true, you could cram a dozen of Connolly's healed patients in the jury box and even they'd find him guilty by lunchtime. No. He's dead in the water. People are deserting him faster than rats off the *Titanic*. We need him buried. Now. Hell, he hasn't even denied it. It's like he's taunting us to try him." He turned to Simon. "Throw as much money at this as necessary. I want this case heard yesterday."

It could take years for the stock market to recover. But considering the alternatives of Middle East oil embargoes and aggression from superpower China, it was small potatoes. And all because of that one human frailty which was the downfall of so many: greed.

That said, it was greed which had saved them. Their source had provided the few vital pieces needed for an investigation. Without those pieces, it would've taken time to trace the Morrison and Pitt account, proving Connolly's connection to the crash and he'd have had time to disappear to some Caribbean paradise with a billion bucks in his pocket. The insider's information was priceless. Yep, thank God for greed.

Simon stared at the floor as they walked, his gait a trudge, not the bounce of someone rejoicing at having his wife back. Did he feel as sleazy as Tom? "You wondering if we're doing the right thing after all the good Connolly's done?"

"Aren't you?"

It was no surprise Simon was conflicted. Connolly had saved his wife, giving Simon back his private life, but he was also the most terrifying threat the nation had ever faced, giving Simon the greatest professional challenge of his career.

Simon stopped. "Tom?"

Tom pulled up. Faced Simon. Waited, while his friend struggled to find the words to express the thoughts that were eating at him.

Finally, Simon said, "Can you look me in the eye and say, hand on heart, burying Connolly is what's best for the American people — hell, best for the entire world?"

While anonymous, Connolly had done immeasurable good with his healing; even Tom had to admit that now. Then Connolly had gone public and his philosophy had wreaked immeasurable damage. Finally, the stock market crash had proven how ruthless and dangerous he was. So would the world sit back and let Connolly turn it into a paradise? Or would it fight tooth and claw to stay just the way it was? Yes, Connolly had the power to shape the world, but how many tens of millions would die in the struggle to resist his version of a utopia? Tom stared Simon in the eye. "A wise man once told me, 'What we do, we do for the country. What must be done, must be done.'"

296

Simon shook his head at his own words quoted back at him. He stared at the floor. Thought. Then grimaced and looked up. "Don't make it any easier. If only he'd taken the 29 billion."

If only.

Pleasantries exchanged in the Roosevelt Room, Tom looked for solace, determined to be uplifted by his good deed. "So, what's anyone got for me?"

Michael slipped a paper across the table. "OPEC's confirmation that the first oil shipments are underway as normal again."

"Excellent." Nothing made Joe Public happier than falling prices, especially gas prices.

"The Chinese diplomatic corps arrived back just in time for your performance, sir," said Ryan.

"Good."

Gloria slid a statistical analysis over to him. "Your approval rating's leapt back up into the eighties. In fact, it's two points higher than before all this started."

Tom nodded. He'd thought he'd lost the American people there for a while, thought he'd lost everything. But nothing won back trust like swift retribution against a common enemy. Thank God, China and the Middle East thought likewise. He dreaded to think where it could've ended if Connolly hadn't been nailed.

"And here's the one we've been speculating on." Gloria passed a second paper.

Tom scanned it. He grinned. "Tanner's officially withdrawn his candidacy."

Simon winked at Tom. "Congratulations, Mr. President."

Tom bowed his head. It was generally accepted that his party was heading for success again and now his candidacy was virtually unchallenged. Connolly had crucified Tanner and created such a cross-partisan following that New Hampshire would've sent an undeniable message to the entire nation. And if he'd moderated his ideology, he could actually have made one hell of a president. Instead, he'd just be an inmate with a dream, staring at a gray cell wall year after year. Thank God. Tom might be the most powerful man in the world, but Simon was right: Connolly was the most dangerous. A mad dog if ever there was one. And a mad dog, you either muzzle or shoot. It was the only way to ensure people's safety. Well, Connolly would be well and truly muzzled. Americans could sleep soundly in their beds tonight.

Yes, the entire world agreed Tom had done the right thing. Sleazy? That wasn't over Connolly, it must've been over duping the American people to get his point across. The world was safe. His presidency was safe. What a glorious day.

37

A Wolf at the Door

Approaching the prison's walkthrough metal detector, Mary wiped her sweaty palms on her jeans. Armed guards everywhere, her breath came in sharp pants. It had been four days since she was slammed against a wall, cuffed, and dragged into a van in Rashid's drive. The FBI had battered down Rashid's front door, stormed the house with guns drawn, and hauled everyone away. She'd seen such things on TV, but nothing prepared you for the real-life nightmare. Four days, yet she still trembled at how she'd been manhandled. Still felt sick at how she'd been caged — alone, so alone — the gray walls of her cell closing about her like a noose. Then there were the hours she'd been grilled in that interrogation room, 'til the air was so thick, so stale you had to all but chew it to breathe. Utter hell.

A guard glared at her. Her gaze shot to the floor. She shoved her hands deep into her pockets to keep them from shaking.

For four days, she'd struggled to justify her actions to herself. She'd thought she was doing what was best, but in her ignorance, she'd done the worst thing imaginable: left John vulnerable to his enemies. All those secret meetings; all those secret files on Rashid's hard drive; and all those secret phone calls. All secret. Secret for a reason. Why couldn't she have left them that way? Without the information she'd handed them on a plate, the authorities would probably never have been able to even hold John overnight, let alone incarcerate him in this hellish hole awaiting trial. And the damnedest thing was, it was only her ignorance that saw her free. She knew nothing. Despite the endless questioning, that was the conclusion the FBI had drawn. If only she could go back and put right all she'd made wrong.

Just ahead, a woman stepped through the detector. *Beep. Beep. Beep.* Guards swooped. Mary looked away. Her heart raced so much, she thought she was going to keel over. If the metal underwire in her bra set the detector off, she'd run. If they thought she was a terrorist and shot her in the back, she didn't care — she'd have to get out; she couldn't be manhandled, couldn't be caged again.

Her legs unsteady, breath held, she cringed as she stepped through the detector. Waited for that screeching alarm. For rough hands to try to grab her.

Nothing.

The relief that flooded through her almost dropped her where she stood. But she tottered on toward the visiting room.

She'd glimpsed freedom across the Niagara. But she couldn't cross that bridge to grasp it. All the way to Buffalo, she'd been determined to put her disastrous life behind her and start over. But she could no sooner turn her back on John than she could turn her back on breathing. She needed him. He was a part of her. Without him, she might as well be dead. If she abandoned him, she abandoned herself.

She gazed around the gray visiting room. Before her lay a row of cubicles partitioned from the other side of the room by Plexiglas. Handprints smeared the glass. Lives so close, yet torn so far apart.

Searching for cubicle 11, she shuffled along.

It was her fault John was imprisoned here, surrounded by murderers, rapists, pedophiles. All John had wanted was to help people, and now he was the one needing help. If only she hadn't taken matters into her own hands. The world could've become the paradise God always intended, if only she hadn't been so tempted. Would the world be damned for one woman's self-righteousness?

Then, she gasped. Froze at what she saw.

Her breath shuddered.

She struggled to control her quivering chin.

From behind the glass of cubicle 11, John stared. He looked so

300

small, so vulnerable. The last time she'd seen him, it was as he shot her a glance while being hustled into the back of a black van, shackled like a mass murderer. Overwhelmed by shame and guilt, she'd had to look away. She hadn't been able to face him since — what could she say? How could she tell him she'd destroyed his dream, condemned the world to everlasting poverty, hunger, and disease?

She tottered to the cubicle. A trembling hand took the gray phone. She plastered her other to the glass. "John, I'm sorry. S—so sorry," she blubbered.

He pressed his hand to hers. "Mary—"

A voice blasted over a speaker. "Off the glass, Connolly."

Tears ran into her mouth. Her nose ran as she sobbed. "I'm sorry."

"Mary. It's okay. It's okay."

She couldn't stop sobbing. "I'm s—sorry. It's all— all my fault. Everything's my fault."

"What's your fault?"

"Everything. I'm sorry. I'm— so sorry." She scrubbed her face with the palm of her hand. "I— I thought I was doing the right thing."

"You did, Mary. You did."

"No..." Without her meddling, John would've shown the world's governments his might, forcing them to award their people true freedom, so unshackling the world from the chains of greed. "It's all my fault."

"Mary, you haven't done any—."

"John, I— I went to an investigation company. About Rashid. You're stuck here 'cause of information I paid them to find, which they must have given to the authorities."

"I know."

Her breath jerking, she looked at him. "Wh—what?"

"I know. One of Rashid's guards followed you to keep you safe, then called us. We paid the company off. They didn't find anything."

"So ... it isn't my fault?"

John pressed his hand to the glass. He smiled. "No."

She smiled. "Oh, God, I— I thought it was all 'cause of me." She pressed her hand to his. Thank God, it wasn't she who'd sold them out. She ached to hug him. Feel his arms around her.

"Off the glass," thundered the speaker.

They complied.

"I'm sorry, Mary. It's my fault for hiding so much from you, but I couldn't risk you ending up like," he gestured to the prison, "like this."

But if she wasn't to blame, had she been right all along? "So Rashid—"

"Did only what I asked of him. How is he?"

"I, er... I don't know." She'd been too ashamed to seek anyone out on being released, and after being recognized in the street and spat at, she'd holed up in the Rose Garden. But if she hadn't betrayed them, and Rashid hadn't betrayed them...

***

Versace forsaken for ripped jeans and a threadbare sweater, Vincent raked his fingers through his bangs, sitting at a diner's counter. His hair brushing his forehead instead of being waxed back felt strange, but needs must. Chewing gum, a waitress poured his coffee. He nodded. Three seats along, a bushy-haired woman eyed him. Her gaze shot to her *Daily News* when he caught her looking at him. Had she recognized him? Doubtful. He barely recognized himself. Still, best to play safe.

Pulling a Mets baseball cap farther down on his forehead, he slunk to the farthest booth and slid across the cracked brown vinyl seat to the wall. He sipped his coffee. His lip curled. It tasted so cheap. Cheap as he looked. He checked his watch. Sighed. If this guy Decker didn't show, this could well be his lifestyle from now. John might be forgiving, but five would get you ten Mr. Panucci wouldn't be.

But like Vincent had any choice. If John could let Cale die, someone who'd abandoned everything to support him, he wouldn't think twice about Vincent. For all John's good intentions, he was seriously screwed up. Vincent wasn't about to become his next victim. So what choice had he had but to protect himself and safeguard his future by selling out John?

A guy wearing a black suit sauntered into the diner, his hair as glossy as his shoes. Way to blend in. Recognizing him from the photo he'd been emailed, Vincent nodded. Decker ambled over.

Aiming his Glock under the table, Vincent sipped his coffee.

"Mr. Anderson?" said Decker.

Vincent nodded. His favorite movie was *The Matrix*. The problem was, a 'Neo' or a 'Morpheus' wouldn't exactly see him inconspicuously blend into a new community. But Thomas Anderson — Neo's alter ego — Tom to his friends? That was a strong name that said honesty, reliability. He could pass for a Tom.

The waitress appeared.

"Coffee. Black," said Decker. She left. He slid an envelope to Vincent.

Vincent peeked inside.

Decker said, "Social security number, passport. The cash to be transferred on completion of business."

Vincent tucked the envelope inside his belt, then skidded a memory stick to Decker.

The waitress placed a coffee on the table and smiled. Decker ignored her, opening his briefcase and booting up a laptop. "From Al-Alawi's laptop again?"

"Uh-huh."

Decker plugged in the memory stick. "What was it? Keylogger?"

"No. I stood behind him 24/7 with paper and pen."

"So you installed it...?"

The moment Vincent discovered the opportunity for leverage to get in on the scam. "January 3." He'd downloaded the tiny piece of software from the Web to covertly record every single keystroke of Rashid's laptop. And that was the problem — the only keylogger he could smuggle past Rashid's security measures was so basic it had recorded one gigantic string of data: Mary's emails, stock info, HTML code for their website, John's planks... If Vincent could've deciphered it himself, he'd have been long gone with millions, instead of selling it for peanuts.

Decker processed the data through his own application, then nodded. He opened a website and spun the laptop for Vincent. "Your account details."

Vincent input them, then phoned his bank on his cell.

Decker hit more keys. "Okay."

Vincent keyed his password into his phone. An automated teller confirmed a transfer of $350,000 into his account. "Okay."

Throwing down five bucks for his untouched coffee, Decker left.

Vincent blew out a heavy breath. That was the easy part. Now all he had to do was vanish so completely he left not one single track for anyone to follow.

He'd been wowed there for a moment by John's grand ideas and magical touch. Pity it hadn't panned out. But John had committed a cardinal sin. Like the Marines, you never left a man behind. Respect and watching each other's backs — nothing could function without that, be it a crime syndicate, corporation, or group of people out to change the world. Cale wasn't just a fat old cop, he was one of them. So everything was John's fault. If only he'd stuck to healing. Changing the world? That was for assholes.

***

A bead of sweat ran from Rashid brow. He stared at the clock on the gray wall. With no second hand, the minute hand seemed all but glued in place. Had they altered the gearing so it moved slower, so time in there dragged even more? A good psychological game to break people. He tried to swallow, but his mouth was too dry. 87 minutes ago, he'd banged on Interrogation Room Four's paint-chipped door and asked for water. Well, 87 minutes by this clock was probably nearer two hours. He wouldn't give them the satisfaction of knowing his discomfort by asking again. He stared at the mirror. Other than his own, how many faces stared back? It didn't matter. They could play all the games they liked; they already knew what to expect from him — nothing.

Just wait 'til Abrahams arrived, his $650-an-hour attorney. Pulling a stunt like this, these imbeciles wouldn't know what day it was, let alone what time.

But why today? Whenever they'd hauled him from his cell over the last four days, they'd been aggressive, yes, but civil, allowed him water, his lawyer present. What was different about today?

Agents Lumiere and Carmody strolled in.

"Morning, Rashid. And how are you today?" said Lumiere, like a waiter feigning interest in a small-tipping diner.

Rashid glared.

Carmody stood at the door, arms folded, his off-the-rack suit straining over his biceps. His necktie askew, Lumiere sat at the table and opened his file.

Rashid stared at the agents. An ill-fitting suit and a tie mauled into a laughable half-Windsor. How could people who couldn't even dress themselves hope to outwit John and him? Yes, these imbeciles had somehow procured some information pertaining to the accounts he'd used, but it was pitifully short of providing enough to convict anyone of any illegality. His and John's plan was faultless. It was only a matter of time before they'd be released. He could wait. Lumiere could go hang.

Lumiere smiled. "So, how's the lovely Sana? I understand she visited yesterday."

Why wasn't Lumiere recording this session? What was going on?

"And how's little Aisha? Bet she misses her daddy." He smiled again.

Rashid wished he was a man of violence, like Ben, or even Vincent. Wished he could forsake the Qur'an and slam that grin right into the table. Let Lumiere pick bits of tooth out of that ridiculous mustache he sported to make his chubby baby face look like puberty wasn't just a dream. What a magnificent figure of authority. But what was Lumiere playing at? Surely he wasn't threatening Sana and Aisha? Abrahams would crucify him. Crucify the entire FBI.

Lumiere stared into space. "You know, it's funny how—"

"Where's Mr. Abrahams?"

Lumiere tutted. "Rashid, please. It's so rude to interrupt someone. As I was sa—"

"I want my attorney!"

Lumiere sniggered. "Yes, well, what we want, we don't always get." He slid a photograph from his file. A photograph that hadn't been there yesterday. Not of Sana and Aisha. But a clear threat against loved ones all the same.

Rashid stared at it. Gulped. No, no, no! Not now. Not when they were so close to their goal. With a trembling hand, he wiped the sweat from his brow. Had Allah abandoned him? How had they got this? "I... Where..." He slowly looked up at Lumiere. "What do you want?"

"Oh, Rashid. You know what we want. And you know we're going to get it. The only question is what sacrifices you're prepared to make by delaying it."

Rashid hung his head. He was out of time. Someone had changed the rules. Someone desperate. Someone who wanted John buried. Buried quickly.

Lumiere slid another photo over. "Like I was saying, before being so rudely interrupted, it's funny how events in one part of the world can have a domino effect and," he chopped his hand on the table, "affect events around the other side." He smiled, then noisily blew out a breath. "Is it hot in here? Tell you what, Agent Carmody and I will pop out for a nice glass of lemonade, give you a chance to think things through. How's that?"

Rashid said nothing.

"Good." At the door, Lumiere turned. "Sorry, Rashid," he slapped his forehead, "where are my manners? Can I get you anything? Lemonade? Iced tea maybe?"

Rashid glowered. They had him. There was no escape.

***

"Yes, sir," said Bob, "based on the information we supplied the FBI, Al-Alawi's probably squealing like a stuck pig as we speak."

"Excellent." If they could crack Al-Alawi, they'd nailed Connolly. Forever. Rising from his desk, Tom gestured to the Oval Office's couches. "And do I need to know the details?"

"It's probably best you don't, sir."

Tom glanced up while sitting. "Oh?" He didn't want to hear that. He wanted to hear that the details were too mundane to be worth recounting. "Bob, this all has to be whiter than white. We can't risk Connolly having even the tiniest cause for appeal, let alone a decent defense."

"Not a problem."

"So, whatever it is, it is legal."

"I prefer the word 'ethical'."

"Ethical?"

"You get to save the world, Mr. President. What could be more important than that?"

"Just so long as we don't give Connolly any ammunition. He finds a loophole and walks, we're all screwed. No telling what he'd pull next."

"Sir, there, er, is another option."

Any solution that saw Connolly buried was welcome. "There is?"

"As prison statistics show, sir, countless inmates fall victim to stabbings, suicide, even—"

Tom held up his hand. "I thought we'd covered this, Bob?" He wanted to end the threat Connolly posed, but he would *not* sanction murder.

"We did, sir. But that was before we knew just how dangerous Connolly is. And after Manchester, it'd be easy to make it look like the work of some religious whacko."

"He's not dangerous banged up."

"Ain't he? If he starts healing again? Spreading his philosophical poison again? He's a captive audience in the slam, sir. Who's to say he won't become more dangerous than ever?"

Tom drew a long slow breath. It was possible. But...

Bob saw his hesitation. "Mr. President, you don't feed a tumor and hope it goes away. You cut it out. Kill it."

What if Connolly did poison the minds of his fellow inmates? What would happen when they were released? Or what if he never even made it to prison but got off on a technicality? "Bob..."

"Sir?" Bob looked eager to please.

"... Connolly will be punished for his crime. But if we murder him, why don't we just burn the Constitution, too? I'll proclaim myself king, we'll institute martial law to control the masses, and, before we know it, we won't bat an eye at shooting someone for jaywalking."

Bob nodded. "You understand I wouldn't be doing my job and protecting the country if I didn't avail you of all the options, sir?"

"Duly noted."

Bob stood. "Thank you, sir."

Tom bowed his head.

Bob headed for the door, but paused. "Sir?"

Tom looked.

Bob placed a cell phone on Tom's desk, next to a photo of Tom, Beth, and Courtney. "If ever we need to, er, resume this conversation, this is a secure, untraceable line. I can have a team in place inside an hour."

This conversation had ended. "Goodbye, Bob."

38

The Turning of the Screw

Lumiere retook his seat. "So, Rashid, any thoughts?" He plucked the photo of Rashid's parents leaving the Al Falaj Hotel in Nizwa, Oman, from Rashid's grasp. He sucked through his teeth. "You know, the less enlightened hate one of their own fraternizing with the enemy. Take it out on anyone they can — that person's friends, parents, siblings. Still, hide your loved ones in a different town, under different names, open a false bank account — how's anyone ever going to find them? Course, it only takes one moron to open his big mouth and..." He ripped up the photo of Rashid's parents and tossed the bits away. "Come on, Rashid, only a fool thinks he doesn't have a price."

Rashid swallowed hard. He'd organized everything after his mother had been beaten in the street because some imbecile believed his association with John brought shame on Allah. But he couldn't protect his family if he was in prison. So did he have a price? "A man's worth isn't measured by what he has that glitters, but by what he does that matters."

Lumiere glanced to Carmody. "This from a guy who's just stolen a billion bucks. You gotta love him." He turned back, smiled, then tore up the second photo of Rashid's parents.

They had him! His chin quivering, Rashid prayed to Allah for the strength of 1,000 angels to enable him to do what must be done. For, no matter the consequences, some things *must* be done. His reflection in the mirror caught his eye, the reflection of someone so drawn, so weary, beaten by everyone and everything. But he was Rashid Al-Alawi. He'd come to this country penniless and built an empire with nothing but his intellect and the will of Allah. Allah would not abandon him now. He stopped slouching on his chair and straightened the twisted collar of his orange jumpsuit. He looked Lumiere squarely in the eye. The plan had seemed foolproof. Alas, it wasn't. He had to abandon it. Recast his priorities. Formulate a new plan. And use the negotiating skills he'd spent a lifetime perfecting — how to cajole and twist, barter and feint — to broker a deal that ensured he got what he needed. "I want American citizenship for my parents, my sisters and their—"

Lumiere slung papers across the table.

Rashid's heart pounded as he tentatively reached for them. They seemed to grant citizenship to everyone he wanted. How had Lumiere guessed? "How do I know they're genuine?"

Lumiere beckoned over this shoulder. Carmody opened the door.

A gray-haired man bustled in, his weak jaw set in quiet rage. "I'm sorry, Mr. Al-Alawi." He turned to Lumiere. "You never heard of Miranda, gentlemen? Believe me, I hope you like the smell of burger grease, 'cause once I've—"

"Mr. Abrahams." Rashid offered the documents.

"Mr. Al-Alawi, please, don't sign anything, don't say anything. After this treatment, I'll—"

"Please." Rashid ruffled the papers.

Abrahams scanned them.

"Are they genuine?" asked Rashid.

"Yes. But I'd counsel against—"

Rashid nodded. "Your advice is noted. Now if you'll simply sit and bear witness, please."

Lumiere didn't smile. "We're not interested in you, Rashid. Only Connolly."

Abrahams bent down to Rashid. "Mr. Al-Alawi—"

"Please!"

Abrahams conceded and sat in silence.

Rashid sighed. "Once they're safely out of Oman, you've got a deal."

Lumiere skidded his cell across the table. Then *USA Today*, its cover story a train derailment in Milwaukee. Rashid cautiously picked up the phone. What in the name— He squinted at the screen: a picture of his parents and relatives, on a plane, holding a copy of the same newspaper.

"Ten minutes ago," said Lumiere. He tossed a final document to Rashid. "A gesture of goodwill."

Rashid examined the document. It gave him immunity from prosecution. He could return to his life with Sana. His whole family would not only be safe, but here with him. He'd have his life back. No, a better life.

"One-time deal, Rashid," said Lumiere.

Rashid drew a deep breath. Him imprisoned; his family endangered? Or freedom? "It..." Staring down at the table, he rubbed his forehead. Did he have a price? "... wasn't insider trading."

Lumiere sniggered. "Come on. You telling me you had a damn crystal ball?"

"You could say." Rashid looked up. "Oh, it was brilliant. John was brilliant."

"So everything *was* Connolly's idea?"

"Oh, yes. Everything." Once he'd started talking, it was surprisingly simple. Even cathartic. "Using the presidency as misdirection was pure genius. The whole country was watching New Hampshire while the real action was on Wall Street. And the healing? Ha, who wouldn't believe he could change the world?"

"So how did he pull that off?"

"The healing?" Rashid shrugged. "That was the one secret he wouldn't share."

"So Wall Street, then?"

"There's an old movie set, maybe, 80–90 years ago, starring, er, Robert Redford and Paul Newman, if memory—"

Lumiere waved his cell with the photo of Rashid's family. "You want this plane to develop engine trouble and turn back?"

"No, no. This is the beauty of it. You see, he stole the idea. In *The Sting*, two hustlers develop a con using the telegraph system."

"Telegraph?"

"You know — Dot, dot, dot. Dash, dash, dash."

"Yeah, yeah, yeah."

"So," said Rashid, "by holding up the relaying of the results of a horse race, they influence a mobster into betting on the wrong horse and clean him out."

"So you influenced people to bet on the wrong stocks?"

"No. We delayed the changing of the prices so *we* could bet on the *right* stocks."

"And you have evidence to support this?"

"Oh, yes."

"So when can we see—"

"Oh, no." Rashid sniggered. "No, no. Everything's secure and that's how it's staying. You don't understand how dangerous John is now."

"That's for us to worry about. You give—"

Hammering the table, Rashid jerked up. Leaned across. Glowered Lumiere right in the face. "Don't you get it? No one knows where the money is except John. He's richer than God. You think he couldn't buy any agent here? The only thing keeping me and my family alive is he doesn't know where I've stashed the records."

Lumiere rocked back on his chair. He hit a button on his cell, staring into Rashid's wide, frightened eyes. "Yeah, hi. This is FBI Agent Lumiere calling for the Director of the Central Intelligence Agency, Bob Schecter... What's it concerning?"

Rashid paced away from the table, clutching his head. "No, no, no..."

"A problem with Gulf Air flight 427, from Muscat, Oman, to—"

Rashid spun back. Shouted, "Okay! Okay!"

"Thanks. I'll get back to you." Lumiere hung up.

Rashid stabbed a finger at Lumiere. "I want it in writing that if anything, *anything*, happens that means I can't testify, you'll still honor the citizenships for my family."

"And what do you think's going to happen?"

"Hey, a simple yes or no?"

"I'll have to run it by Legal, but it shouldn't be a problem."

"I want it with my lawyer within the hour."

Lumiere nodded to Carmody, who left. "But you don't deliver, I guarantee they're on the next plane home. And don't try yanking my chain. We've another source. Everything'll be cross-checked."

They already had some information, but nothing comparable to his, or they wouldn't have offered a deal so eagerly. But Rashid had gotten everything he needed; now he had to give enough to keep it. So ... he gave. And John's story came flooding out. A childhood memory of *The Sting* had set John's scheme in motion, after he'd read of the stock exchange's computer upgrade. By day, he gorged on the public libraries' programming and encryption books and made abundant use of their free internet service to network with every hacker possible in online chat rooms. In the evenings, he begged for just enough money to eat and buy clothing at Goodwill, so the libraries wouldn't bar him as a bum looking for a flop-house. Then, while perfecting his computing skills, he researched offshore banking and extradition treaties. It took him years. Literally.

Then, even with the technological expertise, he still had no means of initiating his plan without high-tech hardware and specialist software. Plus, because of the intricacies, it had to be a one-time hit, so he needed a massive pot: the bigger the pot, the greater the returns in the shortest time, so the lower the chance of getting caught.

Next came a distraction: something had to keep the nation a-buzz so that, even on the slowest news days, attention was focused well away from the financial markets.

John spent years researching hypnosis, motivational techniques, Eastern healing, religious doctrine... Rashid had no idea how John pulled all the pieces together to achieve what he appeared to achieve. But Rashid didn't need to know how it worked — no matter how incredible the 'healing' was, he was only interested in the money.

Finally, after years and years of dedication, John found himself in the right place at the right time and snatched his destiny.

"Come on. Even my math says you can't turn 64 million into 1.2 billion in just a week," said Lumiere.

"Try 2.3 billion."

Lumiere jabbed at him. "Hey, I pick up that phone again, I'm not putting it down 'til that plane's back in Omani airspace."

"I used to think I knew computers, but watching John," Rashid smiled, "it was like watching Monet turn a blank canvas into an exquisite landscape... The things he could do."

"Wanna name one?"

"No networked computer can ever be 100% secure. Why d'you think your PC always needs virus and firewall updates, software patches? Because there's always a way around every security system. And there's always someone who finds it."

Lumiere beckoned for more.

"I don't know how, but John hacked the credit card companies. Charged every account he could something small, maybe $50, small enough not to attract immediate attention, then doubled it all on the stock exchange."

Lumiere heaved a sigh and picked up his cell. "Don't say I didn't give you a chance, Rashid." He dialed.

"What?"

"Hacking credit cards? The stock exchange? Two billion bucks? All while he was off saving the world?"

"TJ Maxx had the details of 45 million credit cards stolen. Do you honestly think the hackers did that with a pen and paper or sophisticated, automated software? And 45,000,000 at $50 a time is over $2 billion. Surely even your math can figure that?"

Lumiere frowned at Rashid, then hung up. "He stole a billion bucks, then doubled it scamming the markets?"

Rashid nodded. "I provided the high-spec computer gear, and the contacts and respectability to be dealing in such amounts. For that, he doubled my fortune."

"But why be so greedy? Why not just cut and run with the credit card money before anyone even knew they'd been hit?"

"If you could walk away with $2 billion for just seven days' work, would you? You see, John's stock program is so automated, it texts your cell the moment something falls within its parameters. All you do is phone your broker. So, when it's so easy, who could resist?"

Lumiere scratched his head, flabbergasted.

Rashid smiled. "It's like watching a bird fly — there's an incredible amount of aerodynamics involved, but all you see is something beautiful in its simplicity."

"And you can we prove all this?"

"Not the credit card scam. You want to go after him on that, I can't help. But the stocks? All the broker accounts, trading history, the complete paper trail?" He nodded.

"And the program?"

Rashid smirked. "Why? Thinking of retiring, Agent Lumiere?"

Lumiere glared.

"Stashed in cyberspace."

"Okay," Lumiere nodded, "Just tell us where and—"

"Sorry. Poison pill."

"What?"

"It's booby-trapped. Once activated, John has to enter his password within 60 seconds, or it self-deletes."

Lumiere sighed. "So how in hell we gonna prove it works?"

"60 seconds is ample time for me to show a jury how it delays stock prices."

Nodding, Lumiere toyed with his pen. "But why crash the market? I mean, you did all you could to avoid detection."

"We needed to get out before we were caught." Rashid smiled. "And this exemplifies the exquisiteness of John's plan. If someone unloads two billion dollars' worth of stocks in just minutes, the market panics, thinking he knows something, so everyone sells, causing a crash. Then people demand answers. An investigation. But if everyone believes it's the result of the Son of God bringing down a heavenly wrath on Man's greed... Well..."

"And if we hadn't had the Morrison and Pitt lead already, we couldn't have held you and you'd have disappeared."

"Precisely. As I said, John's work was brilliant. Utter genius." Utterly drained, Rashid heaved a sigh. It was over. He couldn't do more to protect those he loved. But at such a price?

**

Collar turned up against the wind, an FBI agent strolled past the conservatory. Sana muttered in Hindi. She snatched her cookie dough ice cream and marched into the kitchen. "For my own protection, my ass."

It was unlike Sana to curse. But then, these were exceptional times. Mary followed her to the stools at the island.

Rashid had been transferred to a 'secure' location getting on for two weeks ago and had been denied all contact with the outside world. John, however, still languished in prison. It wasn't hard to do the math. Especially since Rashid's family had arrived, all bearing green cards. But

314

why were they in a hotel under FBI 'protection', not here? Was retaining their new citizenship conditional upon Rashid testifying and putting John away? Rashid knew everything. Everything. And now so did the Prosecution, as had been disclosed to John's lawyer during discovery. Boy, was John in deep trouble. Not that Rashid was the main problem: that was John.

Mary had taken a cash advance on her plastic and hired the best lawyer she could – Nathan Sisco. But despite her pleading, John refused to mount a defense. A case of this magnitude would normally take months of preparation, but the authorities were so desperate to bury John, they'd moved heaven and earth to fast-track it. What had John done? Instructed Sisco not to waive time, which sped up the process, just as the Prosecution wanted. It was as if John had a death wish.

Yet conversely, he hadn't given up. He was defiant, almost arrogant, as if daring the establishment to do its worst. Fine... If he had nothing to hide. But the FBI had obviously gotten something in exchange for Rashid's deal. Yet, still John wouldn't defend himself.

Endlessly pacing, Mutt whined, unable to understand why his master had abandoned his faithful companion. Mary knew just how Mutt felt. She wanted to whine, too.

"Do you think it really was all about the money?" asked Sana.

"You've been married 26 years. You tell me."

Sana put her ice cream down. "Sometimes ... I catch Rashid staring into space, and he swears he isn't, but I know he's dreaming about all the things he could be achieving if he wasn't devoting so much time to us, these days."

"Hell," Mary laughed. "A hundred million isn't an achievement?"

"But is it, for a man like Rashid? Like John? Look at ... Look at an Olympic sprinter. He doesn't just want to run faster than you or me, he wants to run faster than everyone on earth. Faster than anyone ever has. And once he's done that, he wants to run faster than he did last week, then faster still. He doesn't just challenge the world, he challenges himself. So when does he stop? How can he possibly win?"

Mary nodded. Can you take the drive out of a driven man without destroying the man? Had John and Rashid reached so far, so fast, they'd become overwhelmed by their own power and, like junkies, been unable to refuse one more fix? John had sworn to bring the world to its knees if he had to. And diplomacy was a poor stable mate to tyranny when it came to bringing change. Had John's Godlike powers turned him from an altruistic benefactor into a malevolent dictator?

Mary shook her head. "No. It wasn't the money."

"So why couldn't they just let it go?"

"Because it was the right thing to do." Every step of their journey, John had asked her to trust him. And with every step, Mary had fought against doing that. But the fight was over. John had done the right thing, for reasons she didn't yet know. She had faith in him. And only through faith would they survive. Only through faith would the whole world survive.

39

The Tyrant's Will

An egg splattered across Mary's face. She cowered. Pawed at her eyes.

Two police officers bolted over and scurried her up the snow-mottled courthouse steps to the stone-columned portico. Behind the metal barriers, the crowd screamed abuse. Muslim and Christián, Hindu and Jew brandished banners of hatred for the false prophet who'd promised them the world, but then only plundered their dreams. John had achieved the impossible with such a show of solidarity: he'd taken a world torn apart by bigotry, war, and greed, and created one in which all men stood together, as equals, as brothers. Was this why he remained silent? Sacrificing himself to show people that by forsaking their differences and working toward a common goal against a common enemy, the world could become one?

***

Resting on the jury box's walnut balustrade, Edward Leichmann sighed. "Less than a month ago, my grandchildren visited for the holidays — Holly, seven; Matty, nine; and," he smiled, "little Belle, just four. They're at that wonderful age when Christmas is truly magical. Santa. Flying reindeer. Elves. And this year *was* truly magical. Not because of Santa, or reindeer, or elves, but because of one man," he pointed at John, who sat with a bespectacled man mopping his brow, Sisco. "John

Connolly showed us the true meaning of Christmas: how love for our fellow man really can change the world. I told Holly, Matty, and little Belle of Mr. Connolly's deeds. They're so young, so impressionable, so ... fragile, I wanted them to see that while the world can be a dangerous, scary place, it can also be filled with hope and unabound love. And I'm sure I wasn't alone. I'm sure many of you good people looked to John Connolly with that magical Christmas wish we all have: that the world will become a better place."

He strolled in front of the jury. "But then we learned differently, didn't we? So, boy, did I feel stupid." He smoothed a hand over his bald scalp. "And mad, too. Because I'd sworn to protect my grandkids from the evils of the world and I'd failed them. And I'm sure many of you good people felt just as cheated, just as angry."

He hung his head a moment, then looked at them. "But I want you to forget all those feelings of anger — feelings like that have no place in a court of law. See, if I'm to protect Holly, Matty, and Belle, and help you protect your loved ones, the only things of relevance are the facts. And believe me, the facts are all you'll need. You see, in my 34 years of practicing law, I have never, I repeat, *never* come across a case so clear-cut. I will present to you documents of stock transactions and bank statements. I will present software able to access the stock exchange systems. I will present witnesses, not only to proffer expert testimony as to John Connolly's motive, opportunity, and means, but personal friends who'll testify his only goal was not the betterment of Mankind, but to live like a king by, and I use John Connolly's own words here, toppling our government and crippling our economy.

"Ladies and gentlemen of the jury, I love America, I love the American people — the greatest people in the greatest nation on Earth. Together, I'm confident we'll do the right thing and ensure America stays that way. Thank you."

Mary clasped her mouth as Leichmann strolled to his desk. If Leichmann delivered only half of what he'd promised, he'd crucify John. Crucify him.

She looked at Leichmann and his army of colleagues, then at John sitting just with Sisco — a man so weedy he barely looked capable of carrying his briefcase by himself, let alone a court case. Despite John having millions stashed somewhere and refusing to help himself, she couldn't help but beat herself up for failing him. John needed her and she wasn't there for him. And to think today was the New Hampshire primary — the day John had intended to usher in a new age of prosperity and hope to the entire world!

Judge Stanton looked at Sisco, his voice as gravelly and dark as his complexion. "Mr. Sisco?"

Sisco had warned that the Prosecution might wheel Rashid straight in to give as damning a testimony as possible to bury John, then bring on all manner of investigators and experts to confirm that evidence and 'pat the earth down'. If John did nothing, the case could be over in just days and he'd spend the next 20-plus years regretting his stubborn stupidity. But John had remained silent.

Praying John had relented, she stared at Sisco, wondering what he'd say to sway the jury in John's favor. But he didn't move, just stared down at a document.

"Mr. Sisco," said Stanton, "do you have an opening statement?"

Sisco's wooden chair screeched on the marble floor as he stood. "Your Honor, the, er..." he glanced to John. John nodded once. "The Defense waives an opening statement."

What? This was when Sisco was supposed to refute the Prosecution's statement and paint John as a philanthropic hero. This was as good as telling the jury John had no defense because he was guilty. "Oh, God, no." John was going to be crucified.

"So noted," said Stanton. "In that case, Mr. Leichmann, are the People ready to proceed?"

"We are, your Honor."

"Very well. You may call your first witness."

"I call Rashid Al-Alawi," said Leichmann, pouring a glass of water.

***

Breath ragged from adrenaline-fueled fear, Rashid gazed deep into his own eyes in the courthouse's restroom mirror. "*And even if We opened for them a gateway to Heaven and they ascended into it, they would yet say,* 'Our eyes are deceiving us. We are bewitched.'." He stared, searching for the strength to do what must be done. It had to be there. For the sake of all those he loved, it had to be. He leaned forward. Searched deeper.

His and John's plan had seemed foolproof ... until some fool had interfered and given the FBI details of his trading accounts. That information had been leverage. But the threat to his family had been the deal clincher. That moment he'd had to abandon their plan. Hurriedly cobble together another. Then improvise. The result? A plan of such dire consequences, he'd barely slept for four days. But he had nothing else. If he didn't follow his plan, everyone would be lost. His parents and sisters had been flown back to Muscat, Oman, yesterday, to reside under the protection of the American Embassy. Protection! If he testified, they'd be allowed back into the U.S. Safe. Free. If he didn't, they'd be cast out like dogs and left to the mercy of the mob, who saw violence as the highest form of praise to Allah. His plan was his only hope.

The restroom door squealed. Lumiere poked his head in. "Rashid! You're up!"

Rashid closed his eyes. Out of time. If his strength deserted him now, all was lost. He hung his head. "Just 10 seconds. Please."

"No longer. Or I'll drag you to the stand by your balls." Lumiere left.

Did everyone have their price, as he'd always believed? No. Not every *one*. Every *thing*. Some things such a high price. Like the price of freedom. Rashid looked back at his reflection. He straightened his pastel blue silk tie. His hands trembled. He looked at them. Willed them still. They refused. His father's silver cufflinks glinted in the mirror. His father.

It'd taken 27 years for Rashid to redeem himself — he wasn't going to shame Allah or his family again.

He looked into his eyes again. His hands steadied. His breathing eased. He smiled.

There was only the last stage of his plan to execute now. Thanks to the deal he'd brokered with the FBI, this stage would guarantee those he loved were safe and free. All of them. There'd be nothing anyone could do about it. He'd left it so late they'd be powerless. Despite his despair, he smiled. Such a meticulous plan.

He had one chance. He grabbed it. Rashid clambered up to stand on the creamy marble basin. His deal guaranteed his family's safety should he be unable to give evidence. And he had no evidence to give. "Forgive me, Sana, my love."

He dove off, headfirst.

The last thing Rashid ever felt was the crunch of his head hitting the marble floor and his neck snapping.

320

Lumiere burst into court. Raced to Leichmann. Whispered. Leichmann's glass dropped. Shattered.

"Do you have a first witness, Mr. Leichmann?" asked Stanton.

"Your Honor, I, er," Leichmann held his forehead. "I... Your Honor, could I beg the court's indulgence and ask for a sidebar?"

Stanton scowled. "The case has barely begun and you're already stalling, Counselor? Both counsels, approach the bench."

Leichmann trudged over. Sisco ambled over, too, glancing around curiously.

Mary looked back. Where was Rashid? Had he thought better of betraying John?

At the back of the packed court, Abrahams found Sana, whispered, then handed her an envelope. Sana opened it. She gasped. "No." People turned. "No!" She dashed from the courtroom.

"The court will adjourn for one hour," said Stanton. "At which time this case *will* proceed." He pounded his gavel.

Wandering along the marbled corridors and between fluted columns, Mary searched, but Sana had disappeared. What had happened? An anxious knot twisted in her stomach. She looked for the restrooms: the final bastion for every upset woman. She found them easily, the men's having a makeshift cordon of chairs with two policeman standing guard. Had someone attempted a daring escape?

In the women's restroom, sobbing came from the third stall. Mary knocked on the door. "Sana?"

No answer.

"Sana, it's Mary. What's happened?"

After a moment, the latch clicked.

Mary eased the door open.

Collapsed over the toilet, Sana sobbed as if the world was ending. Mary hugged her. "Oh, Sana, what is it?"

No response. But Sana still clutched the note — obviously the key. "May I see?" Mary eased it away.

Sana,

Please forgive me for what I've done, my love, but should I not have done it, I'd either have to betray John and damn the entire world, or betray my family and see their lives endangered. This was my only option. Please understand that what I do, I do for you and for Aisha, so she may grow in a world blessed with peace and prosperity, and not ripped apart by poverty and greed. I'm sorry, my love. Forgive me.

Mary gawked. The men's room. The police. Rashid's disappearance. "Oh, no." She hugged Sana. "Oh, Sana, I'm so sorry."

***

Elbows on his desk, head in his hands, Tom muttered. "Oh, for the love of God."

"I'm sorry, sir," said Simon. "Al-Alawi had never displayed any suicidal tendencies. The agents had no reason to suspect he was planning this."

"Damn it." Tom dragged his hands down his face. "He's timed it perfectly."

"There's still the paper trail, sir. And Leichmann wrote the text on jury selection and winning cases."

Tom blew out a big breath. "And the Defense still hasn't listed any evidence or witnesses?"

"No, sir. I guess it's possible Connolly's just given up."

"You think?" Tom shot him a sideways glance. The paper trail did indeed lead to Connolly, but not the money. God only knew where he'd stashed that. With Al-Alawi's testimony, Connolly had been as good as imprisoned already, but without it? Still, Leichmann was the best the country had, and even if Connolly got only four or five years on a lesser charge, he'd be discredited once and for all.

"What about New Hampshire?" asked Simon.

The primary was today. Tom had intended visiting to ensure the forecast landslide vote of approval materialized and proclaimed to the nation that he was the country's only real choice.

Simon shrugged. "If we leave—"

Tom held up a hand. "We're going nowhere 'til we know where this case is heading. We'll ... we'll announce the First Lady had a bad night. Stomach bug or something. We'll get there late afternoon."

"Okay. I'll make the arrangements."

Tom sighed. Once news leaked that Connolly might escape conviction, the world would be on Tom's case again. And not without justification. Connolly's run for the presidency and the stock crash had proven he *could* topple governments, *could* cripple economies. And he'd proven it with a psychopathic coldness, not caring whom he hurt or how. Terrifying. Such power untempered by compassion and mercy was utterly terrifying. The world did right to quake at the threat of John Connolly. No nation on the planet was safe. And therein lay the problem. If Connolly wasn't stopped, the world wouldn't only attack Connolly, but attack those sheltering him: America and the American people. What measures would China, the Middle East, even the European powers take to safeguard their own national security?

Tom had to stop Connolly. Save America. Save the world.

But first things first. With a great sigh, he yanked open his right top drawer for some paper to toy with writing a speech that would apologize for his tardiness in New Hampshire. A phone stared up at him. A cell phone. A cell phone with a secure, untraceable line. Tom stared back at it.

He slammed the drawer shut. Connolly was the most dangerous man on the planet. But the only way to defeat evil wasn't with greater evil, but with good.

Wasn't it?

40

The Crucible

Court reconvened, Leichmann said, "Your Honor, I'd like to move for a—"

"Hold it right there, Counselor," said Stanton, with a stern glare. "I'm not going to rearrange this court's entire docket because of today's unfortunate turn of events when everyone who can be present is available to proceed. Now, the Prosecution has pushed for this trial from day one — don't tell me you're requesting a continuance because you're ill-prepared without just one witness?"

"Er, no, your Honor," said Leichmann. "On the contrary ... I, er, just thought maybe Mr. Connolly should be allowed a little time to grieve for his friend. But if the court is happy to proceed, the Prosecution is more than able."

"I'm pleased to hear it. Proceed."

So proceed Leichmann did. Big-time. His onslaught began with a clerk reading Rashid's statement detailing the mechanics of the $2 billion crime spree with which John had shaken the very world.

Still reeling from Rashid's suicide, Mary gazed at Leichmann. She'd assumed that without Rashid to testify, John was all but home free... However, with Rashid's statement and a succession of expert testimonies, it quickly became apparent that the trail of devastation John had plowed through the financial world was as wide as an eight-lane freeway. There was nowhere John could hide from what he'd done. If Rashid had sacrificed himself to save John, it had been in vain.

And through all the testimonies, John sat with barely a flicker of emotion, as if he weren't on trial, as if Rashid weren't dead, as if the world were spinning on just fine.

"At the most rudimentary level," MIT's Doctor Trent Shay smoothed down his blond locks, "trading stocks is a simple game of chance, a case of predicting whether a stock's price will go up or down, giving you a 50/50 chance of success."

"The same odds as tossing a coin?" said Leichmann.

"Yes." He smiled.

Mary sighed. If all statistics professors were so charismatic, colleges would be bursting with female math majors. The jury would go for this guy big-time.

"Sounds so easy?" Leichmann shrugged. "I always thought playing the market was so difficult it was only for fools and rocket scientists. But it's easy money, if the odds are so in your favor?"

Shay smiled. "I'm sorry, no. You see, that's only the probability of getting one trade right. If we go back to your coin-toss analogy, you've got a one in two chance of correctly predicting it's heads. But if you want to predict the next toss, too, the probability of each toss is multiplied, doubling the difficulty. So for example, to predict three tosses would mean multiplying the first toss, at a one in two chance, by the second at one in two, which would give you one in four. Then that's multiplied by the third toss, again at one in two. So the likelihood of successfully predicting three heads has plummeted to only a one in eight chance."

Leichmann looked at the jury. "Every toss doubles the difficulty? So the more tosses you make, the greater your chances of being wrong?"

"Exactly."

"So how does that affect Mr. Connolly's stock trading history?"

Shay laughed. "Mr. Connolly made 213 trades and never lost on one. The probability of that's one in two to the power of 213."

Leichmann smiled. "Sorry, Dr. Shay, math wasn't my strong point. Two to the what?"

"It's a number with 65 digits."

"65 digits!" Leichmann shook his head. "That doesn't even sound like a real number. And even though you were good enough to print it out, it still sounds like fantasy." He collected an 11-inch roll of paper on a spindle from his desk. "With the court's indulgence." He gave the loose end of the paper to Shay, then shuffled backward, unreeling a string of 9-inch numbers, each printed on a sheet of letter-size paper and taped together into a banner. "Is this the number, Dr. Shay?"

"It looks like it."

Leichmann backed into the defense counsel's desk. "Oops. Sorry, it's bigger than I thought. I'll take it this way." He pointed to the main aisle to the courtroom door.

"Objection, your Honor. Prosecution is showboating!"

"Overruled. I'm interested in seeing this number myself."

Mesmerizing the crowd, Leichmann smiled, still unreeling. "Are we there yet?"

Mary cringed. This was unbelievable. John was as good as dead.

Shuffling farther and farther from the bench, Leichmann finally reached the end. "Ah, there you go."

Mary shook her head. The banner had to be going on 50 feet long if it were one. She looked at the jury. They just gawked at the numbers.

Leichmann raised his voice to emphasize how far away he was. "Can you hear me clearly right over there, Dr. Shay?"

"Yes. Yes, I can."

"Is this the number?"

"It is."

"Thank you. Now, Dr. Shay, to the nearest million, what are the odds of winning the lottery jackpot?"

"45 million to one."

Leichmann nodded to his colleague, who stood and unwound another roll, one so much shorter he could hold the complete banner at arm's length — 45 million to one.

Leichmann puzzled at the banners which read:

'45000000 to 1'

'131640364585696483372397534604588040398618869250686389 06788872192 to 1'

"I always thought the odds of winning the lottery were astronomical, but next to this..." Leichmann blew hard. "So, odds this big must be like those of winning the lottery, being struck by lightning, *and* attacked by a Great White shark all on the same day?"

Sisco leapt up. "Objection, your Honor. Leading the witness."

"Let me rephrase, your Honor. Dr. Shay, in your expert opinion, could Mr. Connolly legally make 213 successful trades?"

"Absolutely impossible."

Mary buried her head in her hands. Leichmann sure knew the law. But he was a master of psychology, too. Who wouldn't trust attractive, charismatic witnesses, presenting evidence in such an entertaining way?

"Your witness, counselor," said Leichmann.

Sisco glanced at John, then sighed. "No questions, your Honor."

Even the simplest of cases could drag on for weeks — witness testimonies would be delayed by objections; there'd be direct examination, cross-examination, then redirect, and, finally, re-cross of *every* witness; there'd be recesses, motions, maybe surprise witnesses, newly uncovered evidence... Mary bit her lip. Hour upon hour, Leichmann had paraded in witnesses — FBI agents, stock analysts, ex-hackers, fraud investigators — who'd all sworn John couldn't have made so much money legally, so he must have hacked the computer systems. Leichmann had even wheeled out Harvard's leading psychology expert to testify that John had a God complex and therefore had no understanding of right and wrong since, to God, everything was not only possible, but beyond question. And hour upon hour, Sisco hadn't asked a single question in John's defense. John didn't need Leichmann to bury him; he was burying himself.

John whispered to Sisco. Sisco hung his head. John leant closer, whispered again.

Oh, please, no... What was John advocating now?

Sisco heaved himself from his seat. "Your Honor, sidebar, please?"

Stanton beckoned to both counselors.

Sisco said, "The Defence asks if it concedes to Mr. Connolly having made the money trading stocks, will the Prosecution forgo calling further expert testimony?"

"Mr. Sisco," Stanton sighed, glaring at Sisco, "now, I don't know what's going on here, but if you're vying for a mistrial, Counselor—"

"Your Honor, I'm only following my client's instruction."

"Your Honor," said Leichmann, "if the Defence concedes to stealing the money, the—"

"No," said Sisco. "*Making* the money. We still plead not guilty."

Leichmann snorted. "Your Honor, this is ridiculous. With Connolly's background, there's obviously some catch. Hell, why don't we just dismiss the witnesses, throw out the evidence, and stick him on the stand now to proclaim his innocence?"

"Okay," said Sisco.

"Excuse me?" said Leichmann.

"Mr. Connolly's agreeable to that."

Stanton glowered from his high position. "Mr. Sisco, according to your pretrial disclosure, you're introducing no evidence and calling no witnesses. If it wasn't for, let's call it, the 'eccentricity' of your client, I'd be making serious inquiries into having you disbarred. Now you're telling me your client wants to roll over, without any plea-bargaining, and admit to the crime?"

"On the contrary, your Honor. The Prosecution may have proven it's impossible to trade stocks so successfully legally, but Mr. Connolly believes that without further evidence to support Al-Alawi's limited testimony, the Prosecution only has circumstantial evidence linking him to the crime. For all we know, Al-Alawi could've been the real brains behind things and invented my clients involvement. Without further evidence, there's a strong case for reasonable doubt as to my clients role in these events. Now, if the Prosecution forgoes calling further witnesses, Mr. Connolly will give the Prosecution that vital link: he'll admit to planning the operation himself."

Stanton said, "Mr. Sisco, I seriously—"

"One second, your Honor." Leichmann turned to Sisco. "You're telling me, if the Prosecution rests now, you won't mount any defense and Connolly will admit, to the jury, to masterminding the entire operation, and take the stand for full cross-examination?"

"Yes."

***

Leichmann brandished papers. The impossibility of legally trading so profitably established beyond doubt, but with his star witness gone, he obviously saw only one way to skin a cat: first you grab a cat... "I have here statements of the sale of stocks to Rashid Al-Alawi." He handed them to John on the stand. "Let the records show I've handed the defendant prosecution exhibits 10 through 16. Now, Mr. Connolly, is it a fact that Mr. Al-Alawi bought these stocks purely on your instruction?"

"Yes."

Mary covered her eyes. This was a defense? Where were those John had healed to testify as to his philanthropic character? Where were the experts proffering alternative theories on how he could have made so much money legally? And what the hell was John doing? Looking at a possible 25-year sentence, he'd taken the stand, only to condemn himself with the carefree abandon of a man scattering bread for ducks gliding across a peaceful pond. Mary could barely watch.

Leichmann nodded. "So can we assume that all of Mr. Al-Alawi's investments over the period in question were for the same reason? Your advice and yours alone?"

"Yes."

"And is it safe to say he sold them for the same reason?"

"Yes."

"Because you told him to?"

"Yes."

Holy mother of God. Was John the defendant, or the primary witness for the Prosecution? John couldn't have dug himself a deeper hole if he tried.

Leichmann took the documents back. "Thank you, Mr. Connolly." He picked up more papers. "Your Honor, prosecution exhibits 29 through 38." He handed these to John, then ambled over to the jury. "And what are these, Mr. Connolly?"

"Records of balance transfers from one bank to another."

"From whose account to whose account, if you please, Mr. Connolly? The real owners, not the dummy corporations."

"From Rashid's account to mine."

"And the amounts, please?"

"Seventeen million, nine hun—"

"Round up, Mr. Connolly. We won't argue over the dollars and dimes at this level."

"$18 million, 22 million, 41 million, 36 million—"

Leichmann shook his head to the jury. "36 million dollars? Tell me, do many vagrants have multi-million-dollar offshore accounts?"

"Objection—"

Stanton smirked. "I hardly think so, Counselor. Overruled."

"Thank you, your Honor," said Leichmann.

Leichmann was so easy, so smooth, like a seasoned actor returning to a cherished role. But why was John being so cooperative? When would he strike back? Mary's heart pounded. Could he fight back? Maybe he didn't have anything to fight back with.

"So you admit, Mr. Connolly, that all the proceeds from the sales of Mr. Al-Alawi's stocks on January 8 went directly into accounts in your name?"

"Apart from those the FBI froze in the Morrison and Pitt account, yes."

"So you must also admit the stock crash of January 8 was entirely of your creation?"

"Yes."

Some jurors shook their heads; others glared as if John had just torched their homes. They'd already reached their verdict. Mary wiped her teary eyes. Even Leichmann couldn't prevent the tiniest of smirks from sneaking out. Why wouldn't he? John had hung himself.

"And Mr. Al-Alawi didn't mind giving you all this money?"

"No."

"No?" Leichmann shrugged to the jury. "He didn't mind you risking the 64-million-dollar fortune it'd taken him a lifetime to amass?"

"No."

"He didn't mind risking his family's well-being?"

"No."

"Because he knew there was no risk?"

"Because he trusted me. He was my friend."

Leichmann laughed. "Mr. Connolly, I've got friends, but there's no way I'd let any one of them risk 64 bucks of mine on a one-horse race, let alone 64 million on the stock market. You honestly expect us to believe he trusted you with his entire fortune out of friendship?"

"Yes."

"Mr. Connolly, I put it to you that the only reason Mr. Al-Alawi trusted you was because he knew there was no risk, because you had illegal access to restricted information from the stock exchange and because you'd proven to him such information was sound?"

For the first time, John hesitated. "Yes... No... Yes."

Leichmann smiled. "If you'd care to pick just the one answer, Mr. Connolly."

"I did."

"No, you picked three."

"One."

"Objection, your Honor," said Leichmann. "The witness is non-responsive."

Stanton nodded. "Mr. Connolly, failure to answer will see you held in contempt."

"With respect," said John, "there are 590,077 words in the English language. I select mine with the greatest care. If Mr. Leichmann believes I didn't answer his question, maybe he should look to how he selects his."

Stanton glowered. "Mr. Connolly, the one thing more likely to see you held in contempt than refusing to answer counsel's questions is smart-mouthing the judge. Now, if you please?"

Mary cringed. No one was more likely to lose his case than a smartass. Even someone as wise and knowledgeable as John.

John sighed, as if weary of dealing with a troublesome child. "Yes, Rashid knew there was no risk. No, I didn't illegally access restricted information. Yes, I proved my information was sound — yes, no, yes."

The judge studied John, then turned to Leichmann. "Mr. Leichmann, to avoid confusion in the future, kindly refrain from asking compound questions."

Leichmann bowed his head. "I stand corrected, your Honor."

Mary bit her lip so hard it bled. Antagonizing the court, the Prosecution, *and* the judge could only spell disaster. She barely muttered, "Oh, John. What are you doing?"

Leichmann turned to John, smirking like a boy about to rip the wings off an insect. "Mr. Connolly, I put it to you that you hacked the stock exchange's computer system and installed software which delayed the updating of prices, thereby providing profitable inside information on the movements of stocks. Isn't that right?"

"No."

"No?" Leichmann threw his arms up at the jury in disbelief. "So you didn't illegally hack the system, didn't illegally install software, and didn't illegally obtain knowledge of prices... Okay, so could you remind us how many of your trades lost value?"

"None of them."

"A 100% strike rate?"

"Yes."

"You expect this court to believe you gambled on 213 different trades and never lost a single penny *legally*?"

"Yes."

This nightmare just got worse and worse. Mary cupped her hands to her face. By sacrificing himself, thereby reneging on his deal to testify, Rashid had tried to save John. But he'd already given the Prosecution too much. John had crashed the world's stock markets. Crippled the nation's economy. Made billions in the process. He was guilty and they'd crucify him. Rashid's sacrifice was in vain. Unless it wasn't a sacrifice, but rather the act of someone racked with remorse.

Leichmann chuckled, shaking his head. "Okay, Mr. Connolly, if you achieved such an incredible track record legally, which any expert your counsel cares to call will substantiate as impossible, what methodology did you use? GARP, CANSLIM, strong fundamentals, chart analysis? A pin in the *Wall Street Journal?* Or is it something we can buy as a 'secret' e-book on your website for just $19.99?"

"Objection," said Sisco. "Badgering the witness, your Honor."

"If you could keep your comments to the case, Counselor," said Stanton.

"My apologies, your Honor," said Leichmann. "Just so hard to believe." He knew just how far he could push to show how preposterous John's story was — no matter how many statements he withdrew, once heard, they couldn't be unheard. "So, Mr. Connolly, how do you pick a winner?"

"You wouldn't believe me."

"Oh, I think you'll find I'm a man of surprising faith, Mr. Connolly. But if the simple truth's too much, why not give us an example?" Leichmann gestured to the jury. "With Christmas credit card statements arriving, I'm sure these good people wouldn't object to a tip from the country's hottest financial guru."

"You'd like a demonstration?"

Leichmann grinned. "Why not?"

John turned to Stanton. "Could I have copies of the *New York Post* for today, one week ago, and two weeks ago, please?"

"The *Post?*" asked Stanton.

"We're interested in the financial markets, not sex scandals, Mr. Connolly," said Leichmann.

John answered Stanton. "Please."

Stanton instructed a clerk to check the papers left for recycling in the break rooms or to go to the library a block away, which kept back copies.

"Okay," said Leichmann, "in the meantime, let's get back to the money. You've already admitted it was all transferred to your accounts, but it's not there now, so where is it?"

"I've spent it."

"Excuse me?"

"I've spent it."

"You've spent $2.3 billion?"

"Yes."

"Spent it?"

"Yes."

"Not hidden it under your mattress, 'cause we can check?"

"Objection. The question is asked and answered, your Honor."

"Sustained."

Leichmann chuckled. "Spent it? Two point three billion dollars. Jeez, must've been some day at the mall. Would you care to tell us on what?"

"I could show you, if you'd like?"

"Show us?" Leichmann scoffed. "Must be some pair of shoes."

"Objection—"

"Withdrawn," said Leichmann, without hesitation.

"Would you like to see or not?" said John.

"Oh, please." Leichmann folded his arms. "Please, I'm intrigued."

John took a DVD from his pocket. "Your Honor, could I—"

"Whoa!" Leichmann thrust his hand up. "Your Honor, this should've been listed for discovery. It's obviously been available for some time."

Stanton looked down to a woman in front of his bench who seemed to be permanently squinting. "Would the court reporter please read back the last exchange between Mr. Leichmann and Mr. Connolly."

The reporter read, "*Mr. Connolly:* 'Would you like to see or not?' *Mr. Leichmann:* 'Oh, please. Please, I'm int—'"

"Yes, thank you." Leichmann waved. "I know what I said."

The judge fingered his gavel. "Mr. Leichmann, the defense didn't introduce this, you did. Mr. Connolly?"

"Yes?"

"I'm allowing you a little latitude here. Ensure you don't abuse it."

"Thank you."

A TV and a DVD player were wheeled in. Mary shuffled to the edge of her seat. Finally, John was making a play. But was it too little, too late? He'd admitted his guilt in taking the money and causing the crash. What could he possibly show to redeem himself?

The screen revealed an African shanty town, stick-thin people, and pot-bellied children crawling with flies...

"Objection, your Honor—"

Stanton held up a hand and turned to John. "This is a courtroom, Mr. Connolly, no place for political posturing. This better be going somewhere."

"It is." John pointed. "This is Chad, a country devastated by poverty and war." The camera took the viewer into a long wooden shack, roofed with solar panels. It was a schoolhouse filled with smiling kids and computers. "Through education, we hope to show how development can unite a country and bring prosperity to its people. We're financing programs like this across Angola, Somalia, Rwanda."

Mary grinned. So during all those hours John had pored over Rashid's laptop while they traveled, he wasn't just researching stock prices, but making preparations for what to do with the proceeds. Finally, the world would see John wasn't a common thief, but a great humanitarian.

The scene changed to the Thar Desert region of Western India. A woman rocked a scrawny child who wouldn't stop screaming. "Dysentery's a major killer in many parts of the world because of poor sanitation." Bulldozers tore up the ground. "This will be our first water-treatment plant. We've similar projects in Bangladesh and Cambodia."

An Oriental man limped along a rutted track toward a small construction site. "In the Guangxi province of China, we're building a—"

"Your Honor, goes to relevance," interrupted Leichmann. "Even if Mr. Connolly has accounts to back up all this—"

Sisco slammed a file on his desk. "Right here, your Honor."

Leichmann waved it away. "— while worthy causes, the issue is not how Mr. Connolly spent the money, but how he obtained it."

"Sustained," said Stanton. "This is irrelevant, Mr. Connolly." The playback was stopped and Stanton instructed the jury to dismiss this evidence.

"What!?" Mary glared at Leichmann. Yeah, and the Nazis were only doing their jobs, too.

"Thank you, your Honor," said Leichmann. "Now, Mr. Connolly, I'm sure my esteemed colleague," he gestured to Sisco, "will later be highlighting the similarities between yourself and that well-loved folk hero Robin Hood; however, robbing the rich, even to give to the poor, is still a crime."

"Which is why I robbed no one, Mr. Leichmann."

"That's for the good ladies and gentlemen of the jury to decide. Now—"

"No. For you to prove. Beyond a reasonable doubt."

Leichmann held his hands out to the judge. "Your Honor?"

Stanton frowned. "Mr. Connolly, this is not a debate. You'll speak only when asked a direct question. Understood?"

"Yes."

"Thank you, your Honor," said Leichmann. "And for your information, Mr. Connolly, your guilt over taking the money and being responsible for the crash has already been established. All we're really doing is arguing over the length of your sentence."

"Objection!" cried Sisco.

"Sustained."

"Sorry, your Honor." Leichmann smiled.

Again, once heard, it couldn't be unheard. Hell, he was fiendishly clever. But he was right. Instead of defending himself, John had admitted his guilt to the world. He'd go to prison. This truly was the end.

The clerk scuttled back in, carrying a bundle of *New York Posts*. John had them passed to Stanton.

Stanton glowered. "If this is some elaborate hoax, I swear—"

"No hoax."

Leichmann laughed. "How much longer are we going to allow this charade to continue, your Honor?"

"About one more minute."

"If you could turn to page two of today's paper, please," said John.

Stanton did so.

John took a small, thin envelope from his pocket. He offered it. "Mr. Leichmann?"

Leichmann checked his watch, then trudged over and snatched the envelope. "And?"

"Open it."

Stanton looked up. "What am I looking for, Mr. Connolly? And make it quick — you've got about 30 seconds."

John gestured to Leichmann.

Leichmann slumped, looking at the jury as if he knew this was just a desperate man stalling for time, praying for a miracle.

"Mr. Connolly," Stanton glared, "if you're wasting the court's time, I'll find you in contempt so fast—"

"Please," said John to Leichmann, "open it."

Leichmann waved it. "How's one tiny scrap of paper going to prove anything?"

"Open it and find out," said John.

Leichmann heaved a great sigh to the judge.

Stanton shook his head. "Think you're in trouble now, Mr. Connolly? Believe me, you got 10 seconds before things get a whole lot worse."

John stared at Leichmann.

Leichmann smirked. "This just another of your clever, little games, John?"

Mary's heart pounded. Her breath broke in rasps. She couldn't take anymore. She jerked up. "Open the damn envelope!"

Stanton's gavel smashed. "Silence in court."

Mary shouted. "So open it!"

Stanton pointed his gavel. "Want to find yourself in contempt, young lady?"

A male juror shouted, "Open it!"

"Open it!" bellowed a middle-aged woman from the back of the court.

"Open it!" All over the court, people shouted, "Open it!"

Stanton hammered his gavel. "Silence! Silence in court!" As the dissent died, he glowered at Leichmann. "Open the damn envelope, Counselor."

Leichmann heaved another breath. Finally, he ripped it open. He laughed. "What in hell's name...?" He plucked out some small papers. "Lottery tickets?... Your Honor?"

Stanton peered at John, as if judging him that very moment.

"Your Honor?" repeated Leichmann

Stanton read the most recent jackpot numbers, "5, 17, 28, 29, 33, 52." He looked at Leichmann.

Leichmann shrugged.

"I said, 5..."

Leichmann sighed, but checked the first ticket.

"... 17, 28, 29 ..."

Leichmann sniggered. "Oh, come on."

"... 33, 52."

Dumbfounded, Leichmann rubbed his head.

Mary gasped. She remembered the card trick John had performed for Rashid and Aisha, so, so long ago. Just a little card trick. She'd marveled, but instantly dismissed it. But that was why John had mounted no defense: he didn't need one. He was innocent and could prove it with just a handful of lottery tickets and some old newspapers — he could see the future.

The whole case against John was garbage. Utter garbage. Oh, it was undeniable logic when applied to an ordinary guy trading stocks the way John had. But just like the doctors had tried to find 'real world' solutions for John's healing miracles to protect their beloved science, so all the expert witnesses had tried to rationalize John's trading according to the world they knew. Unfortunately for them, they'd all forgotten that one overriding factor: John wasn't bound by the laws of 'their' world — his specialty was making the impossible possible. And that was how Rashid had conned them — people's lack of faith to believe the evidence before their very eyes. Rashid had concocted the stock market scam. Concocted the computer hacking. Concocted the illegal software. Concocted it all to protect John and everything he'd planned. It was all a con playing upon people's need for logical answers to explain away miracles, to be able to pigeonhole every tiny little thing in the world — label it, classify it, understand it, dismiss it. A simple con. Rashid had given the FBI exactly what they wanted, so they'd give him what he wanted — his family's safety. The consummate dealmaker, Rashid must've honed an airtight contract guaranteeing his family's citizenship should it be impossible for him to testify. Unable to uphold his side of the deal and give evidence to convict John, he'd taken his only option to see his family safe and John free. But what a price! Thank God it wasn't in vain.

She smiled, excited.

Arrogant and awkward, John had lulled Leichmann into false security. Lulled the whole establishment. Like a street hustler, he'd played Leichmann for a cheap mark and there wasn't a thing Leichmann could do.

She laughed. The whole world had changed because of one little card trick.

John looked at Stanton. "And last week's, please."

Stanton thumbed to the results, while Leichmann held the ticket to the light, checking for joints or printing irregularities.

Stanton read: "7, 9, 13, 14, 31, 38."

Leichmann rubbed his forehead. "Could I see that, please, your Honor?"

Stanton brandished the last paper, then flicked to the results. "1, 8, 21—"

Holding the last ticket, Leichmann's hand flopped down. "22, 29, 33. Your Honor, this, this is … is just another scam. I mean, the chances of hitting the jackpot just once are … well, who knows."

"45,057,474 to one," said John.

"45,000,000 to one, your Honor." Leichmann whined. "So three times? Someone knocked these together on a PC using Photoshop. Come on, the guy's playing us."

"Er... Excuse me?"

The whole court turned.

At the back of the courtroom, a man peeked out from beneath a greasy comb-over. "Sorry to, er, interrupt, your Honor, but, er, my name's Larry Addle. I head the Fraud Investigation Unit for the State Lottery Commission."

Leichmann threw up his hands and gasped a great breath. "Oh, you gotta be kidding me."

"And what are you doing here today, sir?" asked Stanton.

Addle gulped. "I, er... Mr. Sisco asked—"

"No, no, no." Leichmann dashed to Stanton. "Your Honor, you can't build an entire defense on surprise witnesses and surprise evidence. None of this was listed in pretrial disclosures."

"He's not my witness, your Honor," said Sisco. "I had no idea why Mr. Connolly wanted him here to be able to call him."

Stanton beckoned Addle. "Sir, if you please?"

Leichmann snickered. "Your Honor, this trial's turning into a damned circus."

"You'll watch your mouth, Counselor, or you'll find yourself in contempt."

"Sorry, your Honor." Leichmann skulked to his desk.

Once Addle's credentials were verified, he authenticated the three winning tickets.

Head in his hands, Leichmann groaned.

"And how often do you play the lottery, Mr. Connolly?" asked Stanton.

"Usually, only once or twice a year."

"And?"

"And I win. But until now, I've never known what to do with the money for the best, so I just invested it."

"So why use it to attack the stock exchange?"

"Those with the power to change things for the better don't understand responsibility and compassion, only profit and loss. How better to guarantee their cooperation than by threatening what they hold most dear?"

Stanton gazed at his gavel, twirling it in his mighty hands. Finally, he said, "Ladies and gentlemen of the jury, our penal code is most explicit in stating what constitutes a crime. In this instance, the Prosecution has to prove, to the extent there is *no reasonable doubt in the mind of a reasonable person* that Mr. Connolly took property not belonging to him. Yes, Mr. Connolly was entirely responsible for the sale of those stocks which ultimately led to the stock market crash, but he cannot be held accountable for the panic selling of others. And while expert testimony states it's impossible to make so many successful trades, as we've witnessed, Mr. Connolly's precognitive abilities do," he sniggered, "no matter how implausibly, plainly exist. The Prosecution has, therefore, failed to show, beyond a reasonable doubt, any evidence of illegal activity. I hereby direct you to return a verdict of not guilty."

Whispers snaked around the jury. The foreperson, a chubby woman with frizzy hair, stood. "We find John Connolly not guilty, your Honor."

The court erupted in applause and cheers.

Stanton banged his gavel. "Silence. Silence, please." He turned to John. "Mr. Connolly, when you could prove your innocence so emphatically, why didn't you end this charade long before you arrived here?"

"Can I speak freely?"

Stanton nodded.

"Nothing would've given me greater pleasure, your Honor, not for myself, but for those who supported me and felt betrayed, and, not least, for Rashid. Especially for Rashid. But people have conspired to assassinate me; conspired to incarcerate me; conspired to discredit me. I needed my day in court. I needed the whole world to see my name cleared. That said, if I'd volunteered this information earlier, the authorities would've frozen every cent they could, as they did with the Morrison and Pitt account, and tied it up in court proceedings for months, even years, while the people whom the money has now saved would have gone on suffering, gone on dying. I couldn't allow that. I'm sorry, but I had to do the right thing."

Stanton nodded. "I'm sorry you've been put through this ordeal, Mr. Connolly. Now, I'd like to do the right thing — you're free to go."

Instantly everyone in the courtroom leapt up, and applauded and cheered.

Grinning, Mary clapped, too, crying so much that the world was just a blurry haze. She dragged her fingers over her eyes. She needed to see John, needed to see his moment of triumph, needed to see his people once more take him to their hearts.

Modestly nodding his appreciation of the support, John approached her. He smiled. Reached for her.

Jubilant people blocked her way. She struggled. Pushed. Wriggled. And finally...

She grabbed his hand.

They pulled.

Finally, she felt his arms about her again. Safe. Warm. Wanted.

His warm breath caressed her ear. "Thank you."

Her fingers clawed his back. She never wanted to let go. "Promise you'll never leave me again."

"I promise."

She leaned up, closing her eyes. Her mouth found the moist warmth of his. All around people celebrated their love, their freedom.

41

In God We Trust

Arm in arm, John and Mary stepped into the sunshine, the courthouse steps glistening with melted snow.

The metal barriers clattered to the ground as reporters and well-wishers surged forward. Cameras flashed. Microphones jabbed. Gone were the placards, the hate, the fury. But the brotherliness remained. Jubilant shouts thundered as people fought to be close to one so blessed, now risen again to save them.

John stopped atop the steps and gazed down into the people. His people.

The crush was scary, the attention crazy, but Mary smiled. She clutched John tighter. Who said you couldn't hope to change the world, only survive it?

John grinned at the CBB6 reporter. "Now I'm a free man, what's the first thing I'm going to do?" He turned to Mary. "Will you marry me?"

Mary gasped. She laughed, flung her arms round him, and kissed him.

The reporter asked, "Is that a 'yes'?"

"Yes!" said Mary.

The crowd cheered.

A reporter with a Russian accent shouted, "Have you any regrets about what you did?"

"Regrets? About saving millions of lives? Nuclear weapons have only ever been used once in aggression, but today their threat's enough to hold most of the world in peace. Now the world has seen what I can do, I hope it will be deterrent enough for governments to finally accept their responsibilities to their people."

Another question buffeted through the melee. "And have you a message for the American people?"

"Yes — I'm sorry. Sorry for deceiving you. You're good people and you deserved better. But I hope, now you know the reasons for what I did, you can forgive me."

Mary quickly added, "And, if it's not too late, go to the polls in New Hampshire. Make your voices heard. Free the world."

"You're still intending to run?" asked the reporter with a smile.

John looked at Mary. She smiled up at him. He held her gaze, then turned back. "And intending to meet with the U.N."

John the savior? John the president? The crowd cheered, again. John had promised to save them, to give them better lives, give them purpose. Now he'd shown the power he could wield, who'd ever be able to stop him? They waved and cheered, whistled and clapped for the wonders he'd bestow, the dreams he'd fulfill.

Mary gazed into the sea of jubilant faces. John had them. Had them all. The country was his again. The world would soon be his, too. His new age would come and Man would finally live the life—

Something splattered across Mary's face. "Damn it." She shrank away, pawing her eyes to see. Some damn asshole with another egg.

Someone screamed.

Another scream.

What the hell was happening?

The jubilation transformed into shrieks of horror.

Blinking away the albumen, Mary looked at her hands. What!? Egg wasn't red.

In the grip of terror, people elbowed, clawed, and battered each other to get away from Mary and John, leaving them floundering in oceans of space. John? She turned. The steely jawed reporter from the *L.A. Times* shrieked and fought away from John, who lolled against him.

"John?" Mary grabbed his arm.

John crumpled to the ground, blood and mangled tissue burst from the side of his head. Too heavy for Mary, he dragged her to the cold stone, too. She clutched him. Shrieked, "John!" She begged the crowd, the running, screaming crowd. "Help! Help me!"

Something grabbed Mary's wrist. She jumped. But it was John. "Mary, r— run."

"John, don't leave me. You promised me. You promised."

Two bullets ripped into John's chest.

Mary screamed, "No!"

Her gaze whirled around the crowd, the myriad of buildings. Who was it? Where? How could they escape?

The sanctuary of the courthouse was only feet away. She scrambled up. Hauled on John's arm. She had to save him. Had to. John kicked feebly, blood staining his dark blue suit black.

Gun drawn, a cop dashed toward them from the court's entrance.

Oh, thank God. They were saved. He'd protect them. Carry John to safety. Thank God. She reached for him. "Please. Help me!"

The cop spun as a bullet tore into his chest. Collapsed. Still.

Mary cried out, "Nooo!" Face twisted in frantic despair, she searched for a scrap of humanity in the goggle-eyed spectators now surrounding them at a safe distance. Surely someone would help? Surely someone would save John after all he'd done?

The mesmerized horde shrank even farther back, as if her pleading gaze burned.

No, it wouldn't end like this. No! She grabbed John's wrist in both hands. Hauled. He didn't budge. She prayed for the strength to move him, to save him. She bent her knees. Leaned back. Heaved with all her might. And John slid over the stone. Yes! She could save him. She could save him!

She bent. Strained again. Inched John toward the courthouse.

She reached for those cowering inside. "Help me. Please!"

No one helped. Most slunk further in, terrified of being drawn into such horror. A news crew gazed on, camera still rolling, an award for newsreel of the year more important than a life.

Dragging John one-handed, Mary clawed her other hand at the cowering hordes. "Please!" She sobbed. "For God's sa—"

Two bullets tore into Mary's back, another into her right side. Blood sputtered as they ripped straight through her and into the stone flags.

Mary staggered.

Still holding John's hand, she tried to pull him to safety, but swayed. Fell. Crashed down the stone steps.

Shimmering like a Christmas bauble caught in a crackling log fire's glow, Mary's pooling blood glistened in the crisp sunlight. Her breath shuddered as her life ebbed away. Where... where was John? He'd promised never to leave her. To love her. Always. Surely he'd do something. Race to her. Save her. Save them all.

***

On his back, blood flowing down the steps into the city, John gazed to the heavens. He panted. "Please ... for— forgive them." Blood streamed from his mouth, his nose. His gaze scoured the sky, as if searching for an answer. He gave the barest shake of his head. "Please..." He reached a trembling hand to the heavens. "No... No!" He shrieked, "Nooooo!"

Another bullet.

Darkness.

42

A World Without Color

Tom smiled at the familiar, friendly faces of the White House press corps in the briefing room. "— so we aim to be arriving in just a couple of hours, to thank the good people of New Hampshire for their tireless support."

Simon strolled on stage.

Tom continued, "The White House physician has given the First Lady a clean bill of health and says the fresh air up there is just—"

Simon whispered, handing Tom a document.

"Excuse me, ladies and gentlemen." He talked quietly with Simon. Simon left.

Tom adopted his most devastated expression — the one he'd practiced in the mirror earlier. "Er, I have some, er, most disturbing news." Tom blew out a heavy breath. "After being cleared of all charges in court just moments ago, John Connolly was assassinated—"

The entire press corps gasped.

"— while entertaining questions from reporters on the courthouse steps—"

The immediate shock over, questions bombarded Tom.

"Do we know who was responsible, Mr. President?"

"Have there been any arrests, Mr. President?"

"Mr. President, was it a religious shooting or—"

346

Tom froze. Let the world witness a president so shaken. He gazed at the clamoring hordes, who were too eager for a story to worry about what the world had just lost. It was going to work. It'd been a horrendous decision to have to make, the hardest of his career, but the welfare of six billion people had to take precedence over one single life. History would never know it, but he'd saved the entire world today. But he hadn't done it for recognition; he'd done it because it was the right thing to do.

Finally, he thrust his hands up. "Please. I've nothing further. But I'm sure I speak for all of us when I say my heart goes out to his family, his friends, and all those whose lives he touched. I can't say I agreed with John's politics, or ever witnessed any of the events so many have come to call miracles, but the American people — indeed, the entire world — have lost a remarkable man of vision. With the correct guidance, John could've become one of the most—"

Simon raced back. Whispered.

Tom squinted. "Missiles!?" Simon tugged Tom's arm for him to leave. Tom clutched his mouth, looking as if he'd just witnessed the horror of the assassination himself. He looked at the expectant faces of the world staring at him. "I— I'm sorry, ladies and gentlemen, I—" He bolted off stage, leaving the press still clamoring.

Tom shot along the hallway. It was only 60 feet, 20 paces, to the Oval Office, but it took a lifetime to cover the distance. Finally at his desk, he snatched the phone. "General, this is the President. Now what in the name of Go—" No, this was impossible. Utterly impossible. "Self-activated? What do you mean, our missiles have self-activated? ... No. No. How in hell—"

His other phone rang. He ignored it. Simon answered, then gestured to Tom. "Sir?"

Tom paced, holding his head. "At U.S. targets? Our own missiles?... Hell, I don't care what you have to do. End this. Now! ... I don't want to hear that, General, I—"

Simon tried again. "Sir?"

"You find a damn way. You stop this before—"

Simon shouted, "Tom!"

Tom glared. "For God's sake, Simon, what could be more important than this?"

Ashen-faced, Simon stared deep into Tom's eyes. "This."

Tom stared at the phone that trembled in Simon's hand. He looked back at Simon's face.

Simon shook his head, mouth agape, tears in his eyes.

Tom reached for the phone as if it were electrified. Slowly. Unwillingly. Knowing only pain lurked at the end of the line.

"This is President Stevens. ... President Jiang? Oh, please, please believe me, this is not an act of aggression. Our missiles are *not* launching at China. A technical mal—" Tom frowned. "Your missiles?! At your own cities? ... And you can't override them? But—"

Mrs. Shepherd stood in the doorway. "I'm sorry to interrupt, sir, but the President of Russia and the Prime Minister of Great Britain are on hold."

Tom tried to swallow, but his mouth was too dry. His trembling hand rubbed his forehead. "I'm sorry, Chengying ... And God be with you and your people, too."

Tom let the receiver clatter to the floor. He stared at Simon. The most powerful man in the world and his greatest ally ... helpless ... speechless ... so lost.

The First Lady bustled in. "Tom, I saw the press conference on TV — what's happened?"

Face drawn, Tom stared.

"Tom, you're frightening me."

His mouth moved, but words eluded him. This couldn't be happening. He'd served his country. Served his people. He'd done the right thing!

"Tom, please?" She scurried toward him.

Tom ached to run to Beth. Hold her. Comfort her. Be comforted. But... He hung his head. He couldn't bear to look at her. At what he'd done. Done to everything and everyone she loved.

Tom turned his back and looked out of the window. His voice croaked. "Simon." He cleared his throat. "Simon, would you take Beth to the residence, then get Courtney on the line for her, please?"

She looked at Simon.

Simon wiped away a tear.

Beth shook her head. "I'm going nowhere 'til someone tells me what the hell's going on." She grabbed Tom's arm. "Tom?"

"Simon. Please!" said Tom. "We haven't much time."

Simon shook his head and snatched a deep breath, as if waking from a dream "Yeah. Of course." He gestured to the door. "Mrs. Stevens."

"Tom!" Beth tugged his arm. He ignored her. "Tom!"

Simon yanked her arm. "Please, Beth."

"Oh, it's 'Beth' now?" She looked back to Tom. "Tom, what—"

Simon hauled her away. "I'm sorry, Beth, but move it. Now."

Muttering frightened dissent, she stumbled, trying to keep up with his pace.

Tom stared across the South Lawn into the bare trees. "I only tried to do the right thing." He shook his head. "God forgive me. God forgive us all."

Slick with melted snow, the Jefferson Memorial and the Washington Monument gleamed in the sunshine. Thomas Jefferson, founding father and co-author of the Constitution. George Washington, the nation's first president and instrumental to the Declaration of Independence. And Tom Stevens? For what would he be remembered? Nothing. Who'd be left to remember?

Tom cowered from the flash of the first thermonuclear blast. It was the last thing he ever saw, his retinas burned away.

The shockwave daggered slivers of glass into him and snatched him off his feet. His legs slamming into his desk, he cartwheeled. Hurtled across the Oval Office. Smashed into the fireplace below the Monet he loved so.

He crumpled to the floor.

Tom didn't have time to think of what his life had been. Didn't have time to think of what his life could be. Didn't have time to think of the pain, the loss, the horror...

Roaring like an erupting volcano, the fireball tore across the city, incinerating everything in its path. Tom buried his head in his hands. This really was it. This was—

The End.